D0333926

Amelia Carr grew up in Somerset, where she lives today, and is married with two daughters and four grandchildren. She has written numerous short stories for magazines as well as a number of novels under another name. She is involved in amateur dramatics and enjoys tap dancing. A SONG AT SUNSET is Amelia Carr's second novel with Headline Review.

By *Amelia Carr* and *available from Headline Review*

DANCE WITH WINGS
A SONG AT SUNSET

A SONG AT SUNSET

Amelia Carr

headline
review

Copyright © 2010 Amelia Carr

The right of Amelia Carr to be identified as the Author of
the Work has been asserted by her in accordance with the
Copyright, Designs and Patents Act 1988.

First published in 2010 by HEADLINE REVIEW
An imprint of HEADLINE PUBLISHING GROUP

First published in paperback in 2010 by HEADLINE REVIEW

1

Apart from any use permitted under UK copyright law, this
publication may only be reproduced, stored, or transmitted, in
any form, or by any means, with prior permission in writing of
the publishers or, in the case of reprographic production, in
accordance with the terms of licences issued by the
Copyright Licensing Agency.

All characters in this publication are fictitious
and any resemblance to real persons, living or dead,
is purely coincidental.

ISBN 978 0 7553 5998 1

Typeset in Joanna MT by Palimpsest Book Production Limited,
Falkirk, Stirlingshire

Printed and bound in Great Britain by
Clays Ltd, St Ives plc

Headline's policy is to use papers that are natural, renewable and
recyclable products and made from wood grown in
sustainable forests. The logging and manufacturing processes
are expected to conform to the environmental
regulations of the country of origin.

HEADLINE PUBLISHING GROUP
An Hachette UK Company
338 Euston Road
London NW1 3BH

www.headline.co.uk
www.hachette.co.uk

For my grandchildren, Tabitha, Barnaby,
Daniel and Amelia Rose, with all my love.

ACKNOWLEDGEMENTS

There are so many people who help to make a book what it is that it would take forever to name them all. The team at Headline, for instance – you're all brilliant. But I would like to say a special thank you to Marion Donaldson, my wonderful editor, who gives me inspiration and encouragement, and knows exactly how things should be. The sales team light up the sky with their enthusiasm, Sarah Douglas is never more than an email away, and my copy editor mops up any mistakes in the manuscript.

My agent, Sheila Crowley at Curtis Brown, is an unfailing support. Thank you, Sheila, for smoothing my path and cheering me on!

Another big thank you to my husband, Terry, for putting up with me living in another world for months on end. And to my daughters, Terri and Suzanne, their husbands, Andy and Dom, and my beloved grandchildren – to whom I have dedicated this book – just for being them!

Then I must belatedly thank my lovely nephew, Richard Spence, who built my website and keeps it current. The minute I pass him information, it's there in cyber space. Trouble is, sometimes I'm so busy writing I don't get around to updating him, so when it doesn't change for a while, it's my fault, not Richard's.

And last but not least, a thank you to my readers and everyone who has bought this book. I do hope you enjoy it!

Part One

ONE

CARRIE

October 1998 – Timberley, Gloucestershire

This afternoon I had the strangest experience. I saw Dev again. He was here, right beside me in my living room, his hair as thick and dark as it had ever been, his face unlined by the years. He was wearing a white medical coat, just as he had been the first time I ever saw him, in the early years of the war, when he was a doctor and I was a humble orderly, and he was smiling at me, that crooked smile that used to make my heart tip and the blood sing in my veins.

I could feel his presence in every nerve ending, and I spoke his name, held out my hands to him, wondering, yet eager. But I couldn't reach him. Close as he was, no matter how I moved towards him, the distance between us remained unbridgeable. A sob of frustration rose in my throat, the wonder beginning to take on the dark edge of hopelessness.

It *cannot be.* The words were a voice inside me, yet ringingly clear, and the despair ratcheted up a notch or two, dragging me closer to the darkness that was waiting for me.

Though every instinct was warning me not to, I looked down at my hands, hands as yet unveined and blemished with the spots that come with age, hands still reaching out imploringly to my beloved Dev, though I knew there was nothing he could do to help me.

They were covered with blood.

I'd dozed off, of course; I must have done. I sometimes do after lunch, and, I confess, a glass of sherry, and very enjoyable it is too. There's a certain luxury in being able to treat oneself to a drink and a nap in the certain knowledge that no one expects anything of you, that there is nothing to be done that can't wait. And sometimes, yes, I do dream, muddled, fuzzy dreams that might or might not contain echoes of the past. But not vivid, as this one was. Not so real that I feel it actually happened in that hinterland between full wakefulness and sleep. Not so clear that the aura remains with me for the rest of the day, taking me back not just to the events of half a century ago, but to the girl I was then, her emotions as well as her physicality, preserved like a rose frozen within a block of ice.

They do say, of course, that as you grow older the past becomes more real than the present. That whilst you may forget what it is you've gone into a certain room to fetch, though the purpose was clear in your mind a moment before, or where you've left your keys or your spectacles, you can remember with perfect clarity things that happened years ago.

4

I haven't reached that stage yet, I hope. It smacks of senility, if not of the dreaded Alzheimer's, of opting out of living because everything worthwhile has been left behind, that the here and now is a pale echo of glories past, and the future a barren wasteland from which the only escape is death. I may be seventy-eight, with stiff joints and aches and pains in places I never knew I had, and I certainly get tired a great deal more easily than I used to. But I don't feel old inside. Inside still lives the madcap girl I used to be, so it comes as quite a shock when I look in the mirror and see a face I barely recognise looking back at me, or when a stranger treats me with the sort of respect reserved for venerable age.

Seventy-eight is nothing these days, I tell myself when my knees feel a bit creaky or my fingers fumble with the lid of the jam jar. Central heating and labour-saving devices and the wonders of modern medicine have rolled back the clock, and there are plenty of people older than I am who are still active, taking holidays on cruise liners, trotting along to the WI each week, even playing a gentle game of bowls on the indoor green at the country club. Things have changed over the last fifty years.

When I was a girl it would have been considered a great age. My grandmother, for instance, was ten years younger than I am now when she died, and I remember people saying she'd had a good innings. 'A good innings', as if she'd scored a century in the village cricket match before being stumped or run out.

She was always old to me, a grand old lady in a black straw hat trimmed with fabric flowers, a black silk coat with another spray of flowers pinned to the lapel, black button shoes and thick grey stockings wrinkling around swollen ankles. Until she took to her bed, that is, warned by Dr Fosset against exertion following what he termed a heart condition and my mother called 'a funny turn'. She remained there for almost ten years, propped in state against the pillows as if she were Queen Victoria, rapping with her cane on the wall whenever she needed anything – which was often – whether it was a drink, or a snack of bread and cheese, or to be hoisted out onto the night commode that sat beside the bed. That entailed the efforts of two people; if my grandfather was pottering in the garden out of earshot, my mother would enlist my help, a duty I dreaded. But there was nothing for it. Granny must do nothing to exert herself. So I would have to climb onto the bed, brace myself against the cast-iron headboard with its bars and swirls and funny little screw-on knobs that had always fascinated me when I was a child, grasp her beneath her arms and heave whilst Mother manoeuvred Granny's lower half to the edge of the feather mattress. She was no lightweight, Granny. Years of inactivity, added to her love of food and a half-pint of bitter every morning at eleven on the dot, had bloated her so that to me she resembled nothing so much as a beached whale in a nightgown and pink hand-crocheted bed jacket.

You see? There I go again, wandering into the past. Perhaps I *am* heading for senility – heaven forbid! I hope that if that ever happens Andrea will take me to Bristol Suspension Bridge and heave me over the railing; I certainly don't want to end up in one of those care homes, sitting in front of a television set all day surrounded by a lot of old people who can't even remember what day it is, let alone have a sensible conversation. I've told her so often enough. 'If I get to that stage, just help me put an end to it,' I tell her. And: 'For heaven's sake, Mother, don't talk like that!' she says. And I smile wryly; I rather enjoy shocking her. I get that from my grandmother. She enjoyed saying things to shock people too, for all her grandeur.

I know what's triggered this revisiting of things that happened years in the past though. It was the letter that Andrea received a couple of days ago.

I was in the garden, trimming the untidy streamers that were hanging off the honeysuckle when she came out to find me. 'Mum, I've had a letter,' she said, and I knew at once that it was something important, both from the expression on her face – excited, yet nervous – and from the mere fact that it was a letter. I mean, nobody writes letters any more, do they? Even I have a computer; went to special classes for the elderly run by the College of Further Education, and learned how to use e-mail.

She got it out of her bag; I saw it was an airmail envelope.

'Gillian,' I said. 'It's from Gillian.' And my heart was racing and pounding so hard Dr Flowers would have had a fit if she'd been listening to it. I'd long since given up hope of ever hearing from Gillian again; now, resurrected, it pulsed in my veins.

'Not Gillian,' Andrea said.

'Ah.'

'It's from her daughter, Kathryn.'

My heart leaped again. Gillian has a daughter. I have a grand-daughter and I never knew it.

'But how . . . ? How does she know about us?'

'Long story.' Andrea smiled, held the letter out to me. 'You'd better read it. She wants to come over to England and meet us.'

I haven't been able to think of anything else, of course, these last few days. There's a constant bubble of excitement, not unlike a bad case of indigestion, and I don't know whether to laugh or cry. I've been singing to myself, the wartime songs of Vera Lynn, as I go about my everyday chores. And every so often I say her name, 'Kathryn', rolling it on my tongue and loving the sound of it. The emotion I'm feeling is not dissimilar to the emotions I experienced more than fifty years ago – trembling anticipation tempered with apprehension. And I find myself wondering, what will she think of me, the grandmother she has never met? If she's expecting a comfortable, motherly figure she's going to be disappointed.

Even more importantly – how much does she know? How much has Gillian told her? The letter gives nothing away.

Andrea and I talked it over and Andrea phoned to tell Kathryn we'd be delighted for her to come to England to visit, and that we would very much like to see Gillian again, too. But I don't think there's much hope of that. The rift between us is too deep and has gone on for too long.

I remember the dream, and the blood on my hands. Like Pontius Pilate, I've learned that no amount of washing will take that away.

I just hope and pray that Kathryn will accept that it all happened a very long time ago and not question me too much. I shall stand firm, of course, just as I always have, and refuse to discuss it. If it matters to her, it won't be easy; I don't want to destroy the chance of forming a relationship with my only granddaughter. But there are some things that have to be. I decided that long ago and I'm not about to change my mind now. She'll have to take me as I am, or leave me, just as her mother did before her.

But however prosaic that may sound it doesn't keep me from hoping that her choice will be different from Gillian's; that somehow Kathryn will find it in her heart to forgive me.

TWO

A month earlier, Ontario, Canada

If Gillian Dupont hadn't taken a bad fall and fractured her pelvis the letter from England might well have been left unanswered as others, in the past, had been. It had arrived during that horrendous week she'd spent in agony, believing what the doctors had told her: that the X-rays had not shown up any broken bones, and the awful pain she was suffering was as a result of severe bruising. She should try to keep mobile, to keep the joint from stiffening up, they'd said. So, after the first couple of days when she could barely move without having to stifle a scream, she'd dragged herself around the ground floor of her home, using the swivel chair from the study as a walking frame and trying, when she could find the courage, to take a step on her left leg, the one on the side that had taken the full force of the fall. With no success whatsoever. The moment she put the slightest weight on the leg, the pain was excruciating.

'You have to try. That's what they told you,' Don, her husband, said.

'I can't, Don. I just can't!' she said, tears gathering behind her eyes, tears that came partly from the constant agony that was wearing her down and partly from frustration. It wasn't in Gillian's nature to accept defeat. But putting weight on her left leg was absolutely beyond her.

The stairs were another problem. She could manage them only by sitting and hoisting herself up or down one step at a time. She made it to her bedroom each night by sheer effort of will and, having scaled the mountain that the staircase had become, she had to shuffle to the en suite on her bottom and lever herself up on the toilet seat, taking the full weight on her arms. If Don was at home he'd follow her, step by slow step, and haul her to her feet, but he wasn't always there, and in any case she hated being reliant on anyone, even her husband of forty years.

She had still been upstairs on the morning the letter arrived, brought with her breakfast tray by Angelica Savorini, who came to clean through twice a week, and she felt her stomach clench the moment she saw the handwriting on the airmail envelope.

Andrea, her sister. Andrea had written once or twice before, and though she could have passed Andrea in the street and not known her, given that she had never met her, she recognised the bold black scrawl instantly.

She delayed opening the letter until she'd fortified herself with a cup of tea – not as strong as she made it herself; Angelica never had the patience to let it brew long enough – but a lifesaver none the less. She wondered if perhaps Andrea was writing to inform her that their mother had died – she was, after all, heading towards eighty now – and was almost surprised by the lurch of her heart, the momentary edge of fear that any opportunity to set things right between them would have gone for ever. But when she tore the envelope open and began to read, it quickly became clear that this was just another attempt by Andrea to elicit some contact before such an eventuality.

It would mean so much to Mum. She'd love to see you, I know, but if that is impossible, couldn't you at least write to her, and perhaps send some photographs of yourself and any family you might have? She keeps pretty well, on the whole, but there's no denying she's getting older, and one of these days it's going to be too late. Besides, it was all so long ago, and I honestly don't believe she ever meant to hurt anybody. It's just not in her nature. Couldn't you find it in yourself to make some contact with her? She is your mother, after all's said and done. Nothing can change that.

'Oh!' Gillian tossed the letter aside, angry, now, that Andrea should once again be putting her into this impossible position, and guilty too, though after what had happened she didn't know why she should be the one to feel guilt. For a moment she almost wished that the letter had been to inform her that Carrie had passed on; at least when that happened there would be no more letters like this one, no more unwelcome strings jerking her back to a past she had spent her life trying to escape. Then once again the guilt kicked in. Perhaps she *should* at least write to her mother; if she didn't, when it was too late she might regret it. But she couldn't deal with it right now. The physical pain she was enduring had brought her low. She couldn't cope with emotional turmoil on top of it. It was all just too much.

She struggled out of bed, retrieved the letter, and put it out of sight in one of the drawers in her fitted wardrobe. She'd think about it when she felt better, but to be perfectly honest, she didn't think it was going to change anything. Not now. Her position was too entrenched.

The two or three steps back to the edge of the bed seemed like a marathon; by the time she'd settled herself again and the screaming pain had receded to a dull, insistent ache she'd almost forgotten about Andrea. All she could think of was her stupid hip, and how ill she felt.

It really had been such an idiotic accident, and she had no one to blame but herself. Well, maybe Connie, her three-year-old Labrador retriever. But Connie had simply been doing what young dogs do – being boisterous and excitable. If Gillian hadn't thought that she heard the telephone ringing inside the house and set off along the drive like a sprinter in the Olympics – *sprinting? At her age? When was she going to begin to behave in the dignified manner that should come naturally to a woman in her middle fifties?* – Connie wouldn't have joined in the fun and run right in front of her. Somehow Gillian had managed to catapult over her and land on the hard surface of the drive, hip first. When she tried to get up a sharp cold pain had knifed through her pelvis, fierce and fiery, yet oddly ice-cold at the same time, and she collapsed onto her back. Tried again with the same result. She called for help and luckily her neighbour, Paula Matthews, heard her. She came to see what was wrong, enlisted the help of her husband, Ed, who fetched one of the pine dining chairs from the kitchen, and together they got her indoors. Ed drove her to the hospital, she was X-rayed, told nothing was broken, and sent home.

But when, a week later, she was still in dreadful pain, Don took her back to the hospital, a second X-ray was taken, and this time a 'significant fracture of the pelvis' was revealed.

'It's very easy to miss when it's only just happened,' she was told by an earnest — and rather red-faced — doctor, to whom she had replied tartly that if it was so easy to miss, why hadn't she been told to come back for a follow-up examination, not sent home to walk on it. Don was furious; he hadn't finished with the hospital, he'd told Gillian, but she was inclined to let it go. Confrontation always upset her.

She was admitted to hospital then, forbidden so much as to set a foot to the ground, and plastered into skin traction, with a weight hanging over the end of the bed to pull the ball joint of the hip from the socket to allow it — with luck! — to heal. Gillian thought she now knew what it must have felt like to be put on the rack by a medieval torturer.

It was hot in the hospital room. Gillian, sticky with perspiration, was desperate for a cotton nightdress. She'd brought pretty, silky ones with her; she'd wanted to look good. Now she realised comfort was more important. She phoned Kathryn, her daughter, and asked if she could call in to Gillian's house on her way to visit and collect some.

'I'd ask your father, but he's bound to bring the wrong ones. They must be cotton, and he never seems to be able to tell one fabric from another.'

Kathryn chuckled wryly. 'That's men for you! Yes, of course I'll do that for you, Mom.'

'You're an angel, Kathryn. They're in the drawer of the fitted wardrobe in my room.'

'OK, Mom. I'll find them.'

'Bless you,' Gillian said.

And gave not a thought to the letter that she had hastily concealed there.

It was, of course, virtually the first thing that Kathryn saw when she opened the drawer.

Kathryn was not the sort of person to pry; she would have been outraged at any suggestion that she was. But as she pulled out one of her mother's Victorian-style nightgowns a thin sheet of lined paper, caught in its folds, fluttered to the floor. As she bent to pick it up she could hardly fail to notice the signature; with only a few lines of writing above it, it stood out boldly in the centre of the page.

'Your sister, Andrea.'

Kathryn frowned, puzzled. 'Your sister, Andrea.' Gillian didn't have a sister. She'd been orphaned as a child, and brought up by an aunt and uncle, Lizzie and Walter, in a small mining town in Somerset, England. This letter couldn't possibly belong to her. But what was it doing in a drawer in her bedroom?

She read the couple of lines above the signature.

'Couldn't you find it in yourself to make some contact with

her? She is your mother, after all's said and done. Nothing can change that.'

Kathryn stared at the page. She had begun to tremble, a nervous flutter in the pit of her stomach. Though she had not yet even begun to comprehend, she had the feeling that she was standing on the brink of some dark, fathomless chasm, and her instinct was flight. Once, not so long ago, Kathryn had embraced the unknown as an adventure to be savoured. No more. The tragedy of a year ago had left her vulnerable and raw. She'd improved enormously since the time when simply getting through each day was a major achievement, but still, it took very little to set her nerves jangling in a way that felt alien to her, but which was totally beyond her control. As long as everything ran on normal lines she could cope – just about. Anything out of the ordinary upset her out of all proportion. And this was certainly out of the ordinary.

The instinctive apprehension was attacking her now, stirring the familiar threads of panic, but even stronger was an over-whelming need to know what on earth it was she'd stumbled upon. There was something here that was odd beyond compre-hension; she absolutely had to know what it was.

The first page of the letter was still in the drawer, along with an airmail envelope. She picked it up, scented with the lavender bag on which it had lain, glanced at the address at the top: Timberley, Gloucestershire, England. It meant nothing whatever to her. Then she began to read, the trembling growing ever stronger as she took in the meaning, though now she was completely unaware of it. She could think of nothing but that Gillian had a sister, Andrea, in England, and a mother too. Or had. Perhaps the letter had lain in this drawer for years . . . Kathryn fished the envelope out of the drawer, checked the date of the postmark and felt her stomach clench again. It had been posted just a couple of weeks ago. This wasn't past history, it was the here and now. The enormity of it hit her with almost physical force, and Kathryn sank down onto the edge of the bed, staring into space, staring at the letter, staring into space again.

It was beyond belief that there were family in England – close family – that she had no idea existed. Why on earth had Gillian kept it secret all these years? Why had she cut herself off from them? Pretended her mother was dead? Did the estrangement have something to do with the fact that she'd emigrated to Canada, or was it the other way round – she'd emigrated because there had been a terrible falling out? But that couldn't be right; something must have happened long before that if she'd been brought up by Lizzie and Walter. Or had she? Was that a lie too? Kathryn felt the foundations of her world rocking beneath her. She simply didn't know what to think, what to believe.

For a long while she simply sat, her thoughts racing. Then she replaced the letter in the drawer on top of the lavender bag. The scent rose, cloying, a scent that she had always, in the past, associated with her mother. Kathryn thought she would never again smell dried lavender without remembering the moment she discovered that, contrary to everything she had been led to believe, she had a grandmother and an aunt alive and living in England.

Gillian was asleep.

Kathryn stood in the doorway of the private hospital room juggling the plastic store bag containing the two nightgowns and another concealing a miniature bottle of Scotch whisky she'd brought because she knew her mother enjoyed a nightcap, and felt her stomach churn all over again.

With the covers concealing the contraption attached to her leg, Gillian looked exactly as she always did. A little paler, perhaps, the lines between nose and mouth etched more deeply by two weeks of constant pain. But she had persuaded a nurse to find the time to wash her hair – a complicated operation involving a bowl of water propped behind her head – and it had settled back into its natural waves, framing and softening her face, with only a quarter-inch regrowth of dark roots and a small silvery patch at one temple to betray the fact that she was overdue for her regular six-weekly touch-up. She'd put on some make-up, too, a slick of rosy lipstick and eyeliner in the soft brown she favoured. Gillian never fell into the trap of wearing too much make-up, but she didn't like to be without it either. Her hands lay splayed on the bed cover, the brown age spots that had appeared over the last few years picked out by the harsh overhead lighting, the diamond cluster of her engagement ring slipped to one side of her finger above her wedding ring as it always did because it was a little too large for her and she'd never got round to having it made smaller.

'If I put on weight it'll be a perfect fit,' she'd always said. Except that she never had. She might be fifty-six years old now, but she was still trim and fit, and even lying in a hospital bed she looked a good ten years younger.

Physically, she was still unmistakably Kathryn's mother. And yet, as she hesitated in the doorway, Kathryn felt she was in the presence of a stranger. Gillian might look the same; Kathryn was aware now that she really didn't know her at all.

Why, Mom, why? Whatever happened to make you lie all these years?

The clatter of a trolley in the corridor behind her. Guilty as a naughty child, Kathryn pushed the bag containing the whisky deep into the folds of her skirt as a nurse powered in.

'Wake up, Mrs Dupont! Time for your medication! And your daughter's here to see you.'

Gillian's eyes flew wide open. 'I'm not asleep!' Her tone was indignant.

'Well, I don't know what else you'd call it.' The nurse winked at Kathryn and counted tablets into tiny plastic beakers. 'Now, let me see you take them.'

Gillian looked at Kathryn, raised her eyes heavenward. This is like being a child again, that look said. But she swallowed the tablets anyway with a glug of water from the carafe on the bedside locker.

'Right. You take care now, Mrs Dupont.' And she was gone, clattering away down the corridor in search of her next victim.

'As if I could do anything else, chained to this bed,' Gillian said drily.

Another glimpse of normality – Gillian's familiar dry humour – briefly lighting a pathway through the thicket of confusion, yet somehow making Kathryn's newly acquired knowledge seem all the more bizarre.

'I brought you . . .' Glancing furtively over her shoulder to make sure the nurse wasn't hovering, Kathryn opened the plastic bag containing the whisky just enough to allow her mother to see what was inside. 'But for goodness' sake don't start tippling

19

until after the nurses have done their night rounds. They'll smell it on your breath and that'll be the end of that.'

'Oh, Kathryn, you're a life-saver!' More normality – absolutely Mom, ever the rebel. 'And did you find my nightdresses?'

The nerve was back, jumping in her throat. 'Yes . . .'

'Oh, thank goodness. I'm going to put one on right now.'

Gillian was wriggling herself upright, pulling off the man-made silk shift she was wearing with not so much as a hint of false modesty. Kathryn helped her into one of the cotton nightgowns, marvelling that a woman who was always so naturally uninhibited could have kept such an enormous secret for the whole of her life. But then, perhaps the fact that she was capable of hiding things so successfully that you never for one moment guessed that there was anything hidden was the biggest secret of all.

'I'll take this home and wash it.' Kathryn bundled the silky shift into the bag she'd brought the cotton nightgowns in.

Gillian's hand reached out, covered hers.

'Are you all right, darling?'

Kathryn snatched her hand away.

'Fine.'

'You seem a bit . . . edgy.'

'I'm fine.'

'How are you and Rob?'

'We're OK.' It wasn't the truth, and Gillian knew it.

'Honey, you really should try to sort things out. Don't push him away . . .'

'Mom, I don't want to talk about it.'

'Oh, Kathryn, you never do. You really should open up. Bottling things up only makes them worse.'

You're a fine one to talk! Kathryn only just stopped herself from saying it aloud. But she was glad she'd snatched the words back. Anxious as she was to ask her mother some pertinent questions, this was neither the time nor the place.

'You know what I think?' Gillian was saying. 'I think you should take a holiday. Get right away, somewhere you've never been before. You and Rob together. You could start over . . .'

'Mom, I do not want to talk about it.'

'Oh, Kathryn.' Gillian sighed, shook her head. 'So what do you want to talk about?'

You. You and my grandmother and my aunt, Andrea. But she couldn't. Not with her mother chained to her hospital bed with a weight dangling from her ankle and a nurse who might come bustling in at any moment.

'Connie seems fine,' she said instead. 'She was bounding about all over the place when I called in for your things.'

'I hope your father is exercising her properly. She has so much energy, and I don't want her chewing the furniture out of boredom . . . Oh, one good thing. They did a bone-density test, and I definitely do not have osteoporosis. The fracture was entirely due to the force I landed with. They're hopeful that means it'll heal pretty well and I won't have to have a hip replacement.'

'Good.'

But it was mostly going over Kathryn's head. Reminded by her mother of the tragedy that had torn her world apart, all Kathryn could think was: Oh Ben, you had a great-grandmother in England, and a great-aunt too. And none of you knew.

21

THREE

The dark hours of the night.

In the past year and a bit Kathryn had witnessed too many of them. In the beginning, the sleeping tablets prescribed by the doctor had taken care of them, but she had hated the way they made her feel next day, as if she were drowning in thick pea soup, uncoordinated in both body and mind. They hadn't stopped the pain, either. It lay waiting to ambush her the moment the drugs began to wear off, and the dull misery was, in its own way, every bit as unbearable. Sometime, somehow, she had to come to terms with reality. Putting off the moment was both cowardly and foolish. So she'd stopped taking the pills. And established an intimate relationship with the wee small hours, when every creak of a settling timber sounded loud as a gunshot in the enveloping silence, and the rain against the window whispered Ben's name.

She could feel his presence then, as real as if he were still there. She could smell the baby scent of him, sweet from his bath, with the faintest overtones of milk. She could feel the tug of his mouth on her breast; the peachy softness of his skin and the firm grasp of his tiny fingers around hers. But already it was hard to conjure up an image of his face, though she could still see the individual features: wide blue eyes framed with impossibly thick dark lashes, button nose, perfectly defined pink mouth.

Her baby. Benjamin James. Who had died from meningitis aged fifteen months one week. And whose loss had left her adrift in a meaningless world. To all intents and purposes she had begun functioning normally again. But inside she was hollow, and the hollow was filled with grief.

Tonight, however, when Kathryn woke at 3 a.m. it was not Ben who was there, picking at the corners of her consciousness, but her enigmatic mother and her long-hidden secrets. The questions were all there, racing around her mind like a string of galloping horses, and the shock of her discovery hit her all over again, swamping her with its enormity.

Kathryn slid out from under the duvet and went downstairs to make herself a cup of warm milk, as she invariably did when sleep was evading her. Soft snuffling snores were emanating from the spare room where Rob now slept. Generally when she heard them they fired slow-burning resentment that he could sleep easily, undisturbed as she was by the little ghost who never left her, waking or sleeping. Tonight, however, she found herself longing to return to the days when they had shared everything.

Rob had been her first love. They'd begun dating in high school, and the closeness between them had grown from that first, almost magical, time, and had roots that had seemed rock solid as the old oak tree where Rob had once carved their initials and surrounded them with a slightly lopsided heart. He was more than a lover and a husband, he was her rock, her confidant, her best friend. When anything was troubling her, he had always been the one to whom she turned. He wasn't always overly sympathetic: if he thought she was making much of very little he'd tell her so, and his down-to-earth common-sense attitude somehow put things into perspective. Such as the time when she'd scraped her new car. 'For heaven's sake, it's only a chunk of metal,' Rob had said. 'You're in one piece, that's all that matters.' But when something was really wrong he was always there for her. She'd used to share everything with him, the good and the bad, and there had been no need to hide her secret self, her vulnerability. Rob had been her other half, the mirror to her soul.

No more. The barriers between them felt insurmountable and their communication was reduced to the barest exchanges necessary to underpin the minutiae of daily life. Useless to wish she could talk to Rob, a real heart-to-heart, sharing all her shock and confusion at what she'd learned. Her fault, probably. Certainly Gillian seemed to think so. She didn't know about the separate rooms, of course – no one did. But she did know things were very wrong between her daughter and son-in-law; though they put up a public front, you'd have had to be blind not to see it, and Gillian was, by nature, very perceptive, especi-ally where Kathryn was concerned. She knew too that often people expressed their grief in different ways so that it tore them apart. That they looked for a reason for what had happened

24

and for someone to blame, and took out their suffering on those closest to them.

'You shouldn't be so hard on Rob,' she said. 'Ben was his son too. He's hurting just as you are.'

And Kathryn wanted to retort that he wasn't, he wasn't! Or at least, he didn't seem to be. He was getting on with his life as if nothing had happened. Which was unbelievable, given that he was the one who was supposed to have been looking after Ben that night. The one who'd given him his bottle – which he'd promptly thrown up – and changed his diaper and not noticed how unnaturally white and unblemished the skin on his little bottom was, and put him to bed where he'd fallen asleep without a whimper although he should have been hungry, assuming he'd be better in the morning after a good night's sleep.

'I honestly didn't think there was much wrong with him,' Rob had said afterwards. 'He didn't seem really ill, just a bit off colour. I've seen him much worse – when he had that chest infection, coughing and crying. There didn't seem any need to bother a doctor . . .'

'Rob, he had meningitis!' she'd screamed at him.

'I didn't know that,' he'd protested, aggressive as he always became when he felt he was in the wrong. 'He didn't seem that ill. And there were none of the signs you hear about, no rash or anything . . . You'd have said the same if you'd been here.'

But Kathryn hadn't been there. She'd been at a friend's shower party, and the weather had turned bad – a late blizzard – and she'd stayed over, something she never normally did. And for which she would never forgive herself. Because by next morning, when Rob couldn't wake Ben, it was too late. The disease had taken hold overnight; he was beyond saving.

The trouble was, she didn't only blame herself, she blamed Rob too.

She hadn't, in the beginning. She'd been too numb, too needy for a comfort it was impossible to find. In her black despair she'd clung to him, the only one who might possibly understand the utter desolation that had left her hollow, a chasm filled only with pain. But, as the weeks turned to months, instead of bringing them closer their grief, manifesting itself in different ways, had driven them apart. Kathryn wanted to talk constantly about the little son she had lost; Rob said that going over and over it was helping no one and they had to move on. Kathryn mooched about the house, weeping; Rob went back to work, strove to carry on as normal. He said she needed to start trying to pick up the pieces; she thought he was displaying a total lack of feeling, for her, as well as an indifference to their loss. An indifference that was a betrayal of Ben.

That was when she had begun to blame him, though she had sworn she never would. And the seed took root and sprouted and flourished in the dark empty places inside her, and sent out tendrils that invaded every part of her being. She didn't want him near her any more; she who had once curled in his arms recoiled from his touch. When he was not there she castigated herself for it, for what she was doing to him, to them, but the moment they were together again he would say or do something that fired her up once more and the pain and the resentment of his acceptance of the situation made her say things she didn't mean, things she was ashamed of. Which drove him ever further into his protective shell of defensive indignation and pretended indifference. They were like angry strangers now, had been for the past six months. Miraculously they were still living together, but with a divide between them that could not be crossed.

'There's no point going on like this,' Rob had said after one horrible row.

'No, there's not,' she'd shot back.

'You want to split up, then? You want me to move out?'

The truth was she didn't know what she wanted, beyond wanting Ben back, whole and well, and growing up. In her arms. In her life. But she only said: 'Oh, do what you like.'

'All right, I will.'

The enormity of it hit her then, that she had lost not only her child but her husband too, and all her anger dissolved in a great wash of desolation. But still she couldn't bring herself to turn to him. She ran from the room, the tears coursing hot rivers down her cheeks, and wept, bent double from the pain, arms wrapped around her cringing, empty body, wept until her eyes were swollen and her throat sore, wept until the sobs were dry husks that racked her still. Rob had not come looking for her, proof, she thought, that he really didn't care about her. But he hadn't moved out, either – well, only as far as the spare room – and she was glad about that. She really didn't think she could have coped with the emotional upheaval and upsetting practicalities of a separation and divorce on top of everything else.

Gillian seemed to think getting away was the answer. Today wasn't the first time she'd suggested it.

'You need a holiday,' she would say. 'Go somewhere where you've never been before. Somewhere that isn't full of memories.'

'They come with me, Mom. I can't leave them behind.'

'Kathryn, I think you have to try. You don't want to lose Rob too, and that is what is going to happen unless—'

'You think I don't know that, Mom?'

'At least you're back at work now,' Gillian said, still striving to reach her daughter. 'That should help take your mind off things.'

'Well, it doesn't,' Kathryn said. But that wasn't quite true.

She'd gone back to work as a realtor for the same company she'd been with before she'd given it up to become a full-time mother; they'd been great, taking her back though she was fairly sure they'd created the vacancy especially for her when she'd enquired about the possibility. She was good at her job, she knew, and when she was looking round houses, valuing them, preparing brochures, talking them up to prospective buyers, she did actually manage to forget for a little while. For a little while she could become again the businesswoman she had once been, thinking of nothing but the job in hand.

But it had its drawbacks too. The houses where one of the rooms had a cot with fluffy blankets and a mobile twirling over it. The paddling pool or climbing frame in the back yard – not that Ben had been old enough for either when he'd died, but he would have been by now. Kathryn had to block them out, remain objective. But it wasn't easy. And always, when she got home, the purposeless darkness was waiting. Just her and Rob, who seemed to be moving on without her, and the photographs and the soft toys she couldn't bring herself to dispose of, and the empty room that used to be a nursery.

She went there sometimes in the dark hours when she couldn't sleep, curled down into the elephant beanbag with her mug of warm milk, imagining she could hear his even breathing in the stillness, see the mound under the cot blankets in the shadows. Not tonight, however. Tonight she sat at the pine table in the kitchen and thought about the secrets her mother had kept, and the family in England who desperately wanted her to get in touch with them.

By the time Gillian was discharged from hospital a week later, Kathryn had done plenty more thinking.

She'd wondered whether she should talk to her father, ask him some of the questions that were running circles in her brain, but decided against it. It could be that he was as much in the dark as she was, and raising the subject of what she'd discovered could be a catastrophe. She really had to talk to Gillian first.

She was frustrated, too, that she hadn't taken note of the address at the top of the letter. All she remembered of it was that it was in Gloucestershire; if only she had more she could go on line and look the place up. But she'd been too startled to take in any details, and now, burning with curiosity though she was, she couldn't bring herself to sneak into her mother's house and go back for another look. That really would be prying.

Now that the first shock had worn off, Kathryn was beginning to feel oddly excited. Roots she hadn't known she had were pulling at her; she acknowledged she not only wanted to find out about her unknown family, she wanted to meet them. Their very existence was somehow creeping into the gaping hole left by the loss of Ben and her estrangement from Rob. But for the moment there was nothing she could do but contain her impatience and wait for an opportunity to talk to Gillian.

FOUR

'Mom, there is something I have to talk to you about.' There was no mistaking the seriousness of Kathryn's tone, nor the nervousness underlying it. Gillian's heart sank.

'Oh, no, Kathryn. You're not going to tell me that you and Rob—'

'No, no. Nothing like that.'

They were in the kitchen of Gillian's home, high in the hills overlooking the lake on which the town of Edmondsville had grown up. Why is it that the kitchen is invariably the venue for important family discussions, Kathryn wondered. But in this case there was a good reason for that. The chairs there were high and firm, and Gillian, home now from the hospital and getting about on crutches, found them a good deal easier on her hip than the soft leather sofas in the living room, less of an effort to get into and out of. It was handy for the coffee-maker, too; both of them had a steaming fragrant brew within easy reach. And Don had absented himself to watch a television programme; the low purr of the presenter's voice crept through the dividing door, otherwise there was nothing to impinge on their privacy.

'What, then?'

Kathryn pulled her coffee towards her, but merely curled her fingers round the mug, twisting it back and forth on the coaster.

'Mom, you remember you asked me to collect some cotton nightdresses for you when you were in hospital? Well, there was something else in the drawer. Something I couldn't help seeing. A letter.' She paused, waiting.

'Oh.' Just that. But Gillian's face was speaking volumes. Guilt. Shock at being found out. A confusion that was totally uncharacteristic.

'Well?' Kathryn paused again. 'I was hoping you might explain it to me.'

'You shouldn't have looked at it,' Gillian accused.

'I know, and I'm sorry. But I did. And I really want to know what it means.'

'Well, if you read it I should have thought that was obvious,' Gillian snapped. She was becoming aggressive, as she often did when caught on the wrong foot. This wasn't going to be easy. Time to go on the offensive herself, Kathryn decided.

'I've always been given to understand you were brought up in Somerset by Lizzie and Walter,' she said.

'From the age of eight, I was.'

'But you always said it was because you were orphaned. That your mother was dead. Why would you say that, Mom, if it wasn't true?'

'To me she was. Kathryn, I really don't want to discuss this.'

'And you have a sister too,' Kathryn persisted.

'Whom I don't know. She's eight years younger than me, and we had totally separate upbringings. Kathryn, please, drop the subject. They are nothing to me, and nothing to you.'

'How can you say that?' Kathryn exploded, exasperated. 'They're your family – mine! You can't just sweep this under the carpet.'

'It's the way I want it,' Gillian returned stubbornly. 'Lizzie and Walter are my family. They're the ones who were there for me. That woman . . .' her lips tightened '. . . that woman means nothing to me at all. I barely know her. And I really don't want to.'

Kathryn shook her head, totally bemused. 'But . . . what happened, Mom? Why were you with Lizzie and Walter?'

She was doing sums in her head. Gillian had been eight when she had been taken in by her aunt and uncle; Andrea was eight years younger than Gillian. There was a link, but for the moment she was struggling to see what it was. The words of Andrea's letter came back to her. *I honestly don't believe she ever meant to hurt anybody . . .*

'Couldn't your mother cope?' she asked. 'With a new baby and you too? Is that why she sent you to live with Lizzie?'

Gillian laughed bitterly. 'You could put it like that, I suppose.'

'She abandoned you. In favour of Andrea. Is that what's behind all this?'

Gillian was becoming visibly agitated.

'Kathryn, will you drop this, please!'

'No, Mom. If you've been feeling hurt all these years because your mother kept her new baby and farmed you out . . . I can

33

understand how you must feel. But it doesn't mean she loved you any less, just that—'

Gillian snorted. 'Love had nothing to do with it.'

Kathryn's eyes narrowed. 'What do you mean?'

'OK. If you really want to know.' Her voice was hard now, and so was her face; she steepled her fingers in front of her mouth momentarily as if even now she wasn't sure she should let the words escape. 'OK. My mother did not actually abandon me, as you put it. When I was eight years old she was sent to prison. That is the reason I went to Somerset, to Lizzie and Walter. My sister, Andrea, was born while she was in custody. Are you satisfied now?'

'She was in prison?' Kathryn repeated, stunned. 'But what for? What did she do?'

Gillian was silent, her lips pressed tightly together, the muscles of her cheeks taut.

'But didn't she take you back when she was released?' Kathryn asked. 'Surely—'

Gillian snorted again. 'She wanted me to go home, yes. But I was thirteen years old by then. I didn't want to go back there . . . where it happened. And my mother and sister . . . they were strangers to me.'

'Lizzie didn't take your sister in too, then?'

'No. They couldn't have coped with a baby as well as me, and besides—' She broke off, her eyes cutting away as if to blot out whatever it was she was seeing.

'Andrea was fostered out to a family in Timberley,' she went on after a moment.

'Timberley is in Gloucestershire.'

'That's right. It's the village where I was born. It's quite a long way from where I was in Somerset – or at least, it was in those days. And in any case, there were . . . issues. I never saw Andrea.'

'But your mother – didn't you want to be with her?' Kathryn pressed, trying to understand. 'If you were eight years old when she went to prison, then *she* wouldn't have been a stranger to you, surely?'

Gillian stared down at her hands, twisting her loose engagement ring around and around.

'I didn't remember my mother at all,' she said quietly.

'What do you mean, you didn't remember her?' Kathryn asked, puzzled.

'Just that. I suffered what I think they termed "traumatic amnesia". I didn't remember anything from . . . before, and I still don't. My life began when I went to Hillsbridge, to Lizzie and Walter. They became my parents. And now, I really don't want to talk about this any more.' She struggled to her feet, reaching for her elbow crutches. 'Do you want more coffee?'

'Mom, for goodness' sake, sit down! You've only told me half a story.'

'More than I wanted to.'

'Mom, please. I can see this is difficult for you. When I raised the subject I had no idea, honestly, but . . . don't you think it might help, talking about it? Not having to keep it from me any more?'

'Not really, no . . .' Gillian was trying to pour more coffee into her mug, but her hand was shaking, and some splashed onto the stripped pine worktop. 'Oh, now look what you've made me do! This will stain . . .'

Kathryn leaped up. 'It's OK, I'll see to it.'

She grabbed a cloth, mopped up the spill. When they were seated again, their coffee mugs refilled, there was an awkward silence. Then, to her surprise, Gillian said: 'I suppose you want to know what my mother did to end up in prison?'

'Well . . . yes.' Of course she wanted to know, but for some reason she had been avoiding asking the direct question again.

'And why I don't want anything to do with her.'

'Yes.'

'Very well. I suppose you might as well know the truth.' Her eyes, defiant now, met Kathryn's directly. 'What did my mother do? She murdered my father.'

Kathryn pulled her VW into the side of the road. Her head was all over the place – not the best state to be driving in; she'd only just avoided jumping a red light, and traffic seemed to be leaping at her from unexpected directions. From here, the town of Edmondsville spread out beneath her, but the familiar collage of parks and tower blocks, street grids and waterfront might have been the landscape of the moon, so alien did it appear to her tonight. And the constant shifting of the lights reflected on the dark surface of the lake seemed to mirror the turbulence of her thoughts.

Kathryn had thought she'd been prepared for anything. But the revelation of her grandmother's crime had absolutely taken the ground from under her feet.

When she'd got her breath back she'd wanted to know more,

of course. But Gillian had volunteered very little and, given that Kathryn could now understand just why the subject was so distressing to her, she didn't like to press her. In any case, Gillian maintained that she knew only what she'd been told by Lizzie and Walter. Her own memory of what had happened had been wiped clean.

The bare facts: they were all Kathryn had so far.

She turned off the engine of her car and twisted her hair, shoulder length and dark, away from her face and into a knot at the nape of her neck. Then she tilted her head back into the collar of her hands and ran over the information she'd gleaned.

One evening in the summer of 1950, Caroletta Louise Chapman – her grandmother – had shot dead Frank Chapman – her grandfather – in the home they shared with Caroletta's parents in the village of Timberley, Gloucestershire. Caroletta, or Carrie, as she was known, claimed it had been in self-defence. She had been found not guilty of murder, but guilty of manslaughter and she had been sentenced to eight years' imprisonment. When she had been released, with time off for good behaviour, she had, incredibly, gone back to live in Timberley. Andrea had been returned to her mother, but Gillian had refused to have anything to do with her.

At eighteen, she had married Don Dupont, and they had emigrated to Canada, where Don had got a job with a pharmaceutical company. That, as far as she was concerned, was the end of it.

'Does Dad know?' Kathryn had asked.

'Of course he does!' Gillian had retorted. 'You don't think

I could have been married to him for nearly forty years and not told him?'

'You didn't tell me.'

'That was quite different. There was no need for you to know. And you wouldn't, if you hadn't . . .'

Gone prying.

Or, to take it a stage further, if Andrea hadn't written. Kathryn hadn't asked Gillian if she intended to reply. Given her extreme reaction it was fairly obvious that she did not.

Kathryn stared down on the panorama that was Edmondsville and drowned in the tumultuous swell of Gillian's secret. How had she lived with it all these years? Learning that her grandmother had been convicted of killing her grandfather had shocked Kathryn to the core, and she was at one remove. Gillian had had to deal with it at first-hand. The trauma of losing both her parents in such terrible circumstances must have been devastating for a little girl; small wonder that she had tried to erase it from her life. But even so, Caroletta was her mother, and she was still alive. Was she really a monster, as Gillian implied? Or had she been driven to the limits of extremity by unimaginable circumstances?

Gillian's only take on what had happened came, it seemed, from what Lizzie had told her. But it was perfectly understandable that Lizzie had been biased. Frank had been her brother, after all. And it was easy to see how her opinions had been imposed on the blank canvas of a confused young mind. The tragedy of it was that Gillian had cut herself off so completely from her mother, never given her the chance to put her side of the story. And it was eating her up inside, however she might try to deny it.

A great wash of sadness engulfed Kathryn, not only for Gillian but also for Caroletta. Kathryn knew from bitter experience what it was to lose a child. But at least she had closure. How much worse it must be to have a daughter who was still alive but had disowned you. Whatever Caroletta had done, it was the cruellest punishment Kathryn could imagine. She found herself wishing desperately that she could do something to put things right between the two of them before it was too late. There was no way now, of course, to undo the past and reclaim the lost years. But if she could engineer some sort of reconciliation it could only be a good thing for both mother and daughter. Gillian shouldn't be carrying all this bitterness inside; one day, when it was too late, it would come back to haunt her, Kathryn felt. And Caroletta . . .

The urge to contact her English family and find out the truth of what had happened was suddenly strong. And, bizarrely, Gillian's suggestion that she should 'get away, somewhere you've never been before' in order to get her own life back on the rails was there too, an insistent little voice in her head.

Kathryn sat quite still for a moment, scarcely breathing as the idea grew and took shape. And as it did, she felt herself infused with a sense of purpose.

She'd get Andrea's address from her mother – surely she wouldn't refuse to give it to her? – and she would reply to the letter herself. Then, if they wanted her to, she would go to England, meet the family she had never known she had. If she could get to the bottom of what had happened all those years ago and find some explanation, perhaps she could banish the demons that Gillian refused to confront for herself.

Buoyed up with barely suppressed excitement she started the engine and set out for home.

Kathryn had expected opposition from her mother when she told her what she intended to do, and asked her for Andrea's address, but Gillian was oddly resigned.

'It's no more than I expected,' she said. And: 'You know where I stand. I think I've made my feelings perfectly clear. But you're a grown woman, Kathryn. What you decide to do is up to you.'

It occurred to Kathryn to wonder if perhaps, after the initial shock of discovery, Gillian was actually relieved that the truth had finally come out, and if perhaps she was even glad to be able to relinquish responsibility for deciding whether or not to reply to her sister's letter. Maybe she even harboured some secret regrets with regard to the estrangement, but was too entrenched in the position she had taken to backtrack now. But she knew better than to say so.

With the letter in her possession, Kathryn now had an address. Bush Villa, Timberley was, Gillian told her, the family home, where she had been born and lived for the first eight years of her life. Presumably Andrea lived there with her mother. But the signature gave no indication as to whether or not she was married, and Kathryn had no option but to address her reply to 'Andrea Chapman'. She wrote a carefully worded letter, saying she would very much like to come to England to meet them, and included her telephone number. Three days later Andrea called.

Understandably, the conversation was a little stilted and

40

awkward, but the message was clear. Both she and her mother were delighted to hear from Kathryn; of course they would love to meet her. When was she thinking of coming?

'Well, as soon as possible really . . .' Kathryn had already floated the possibility that she might like to take some vacation to her boss at Select Properties and he had raised no objection.

'You'll stay with us, of course,' Andrea said.

'Oh . . . I don't want to impose . . .'

'You wouldn't be.'

Kathryn hesitated. She wasn't sure that was a good idea. Andrea and Carrie might be family, but they were also strangers. Kathryn thought she would really rather have her own space, a bolt hole she could retreat to if things were awkward, rather than be in Andrea and her grandmother's pockets the entire time.

'I'd really prefer to be in a hotel,' she said, hoping Andrea would not take offence.

She didn't. In fact, Kathryn rather gathered that Andrea was relieved. She probably felt the same way about too much proximity too soon, but had been obliged to offer accommodation.

'OK, if you let me know when to expect you, I'll make a booking.' There was something in her matter-of-fact assumption of responsibility that reminded Kathryn of her mother. But there the similarity ended. 'Thanks so much for getting in touch, Kathryn. I can't tell you how much it means to Mum. She's writing to you, I know, but I wanted to call you straight away; let you know how pleased we were to hear from you.'

That had been it, more or less. No questions, no answers.

They would keep for another day. And no mention of Gillian, either. Presumably, Andrea was taking it as read that the situation there was as it always had been.

Next day, Kathryn firmed up her request for a few weeks' vacation, went on line and booked flights. All that was left to do now was to tell Rob.

'I'm going to England to visit my mother's family,' she said.

She was microwaving a frozen chicken pasta dish for her tea; Rob – a self-employed accountant – had had a long lunch with a client and he'd said he'd grab a takeaway later if he felt like it. Right now he was sitting at the dining table, a load of paperwork spread out in front of him. There was more space here, he claimed, than in the recess under the stairs that had become his office when the spare room had been turned into a nursery, but his invasion meant that Kathryn had to eat on the counter.

'Lizzie and . . . what's his name?' Rob said, without looking up. 'I didn't think you liked them much.'

'Walter.' She didn't contradict him; it was true, she wasn't overly fond of Lizzie and Walter. Not that she knew them very well; they'd come to Canada once or twice for a holiday, and she had visited them in England with Gillian and Don before, or after, going on to spend time with Don's family. But she'd never really taken to them. Walter was OK, she supposed – a quiet man who had barely registered on her radar – but Lizzie she found daunting, rather sour and opinionated, too quick to complain and criticise. 'No, not Lizzie and Walter,' she said. 'Mom's real family.'

He frowned. 'I didn't know your mother had any other family.'

'Well, she has. A mother and a sister. No, don't look at me

like that, Rob. I didn't know either until recently. She's had nothing to do with them since she was a girl.'

She had his full attention now – quite a novelty these days – but she really didn't want to go into it all just now. As always, the resentment was niggling beneath the surface, not exactly articulated, but intrinsic. *You didn't want to talk to me about your own son. Why would you care about my mother's family?*

'Anyway,' she said, 'I'm going to England to meet them.'

'You've just gone ahead and fixed all this up?' He sounded put out.

'Yes. It doesn't make any difference to you, does it?'

'I could have come with you.'

'I didn't think you'd want to.'

'Why not?'

'Oh – Rob!' The microwave pinged off; Kathryn removed the plastic carton, gave the contents a stir, put it back in for another three minutes.

'What about your job?' he asked. 'Surely they aren't happy for you to take off at a moment's notice?'

'They're perfectly fine with me taking a break. Anyway, you know as well as I do they can manage very well without me. They only took me back because they felt sorry for me. Were concerned about me. It was nice that *someone* was,' she couldn't resist adding, though the minute she'd said it, she regretted it.

The barb went home.

'Oh, for goodness' sake, Kathryn, give it a rest,' Rob snarled. 'You really do know how to stick the knife in, don't you?'

'I would have thought,' she retorted acidly, 'that you'd be glad to be rid of me and my miseries for a couple of weeks.'

43

They were back to battle stations.

'Oh, do as you like, Kathryn,' Rob snapped. And returned to his work.

'Don't worry, I will.'

And she had. Two weeks later, with all the arrangements finalised, Kathryn was on the plane, bound for London Heathrow.

FIVE

Late October 1998, Heathrow to Timberley, Gloucestershire

The placard, looking as if it had once been one side of a packaging carton, is inscribed in black felt-tip pen, the letters at least four inches high: 'KATHRYN SAWYER'.

Though she was bemused at first by the sea of faces in the Heathrow arrivals hall, searching in vain for one that bears some resemblance to her mother, Kathryn can scarcely avoid seeing it. The woman holding it aloft is tall, short dark hair streaked with grey, wearing a dark green quilted jacket. She wears no make-up, or at least, none that is visible, and her face looks a little leathery, as though she spends a lot of time outdoors.

Andrea. It must be, but rather than the similarity she was looking out for, Kathryn is surprised by the difference between her and the always immaculate Gillian. Kathryn weaves her way through the crowd, towing her suitcase behind her. She feels terribly shy suddenly.

'Hi. I'm Kathryn.'

'Kathryn! Thank goodness!'

'Sorry you've had such a long wait. My flight was delayed.'

'Aren't they always? Never mind, you're here now. Let's go and find my car. Can I carry something for you?'

'It's all right.'

'Let me take your bag. It's quite a trek to the car park.'

'If you're sure . . .' Kathryn relinquishes the squashy holdall that is hitched, along with her purse, on her shoulder. 'Thanks.'

They set out in the direction of the lifts, Andrea striding out purposefully in thick-soled flat shoes, Kathryn, in heeled boots and with her case to manoeuvre, struggling to keep up.

'I hope I can find the car again,' Andrea says. 'These places are a nightmare. I hope I can find my way out of the airport, come to that! I don't often have to come here, thank the Lord.'

'You shouldn't have come today,' Kathryn says. 'I could have taken a taxi.'

'All the way to Gloucestershire? It would have cost you a fortune! And you wouldn't want to be bothered with the train after a long flight like you've had. Ah . . . here we are. That looks like my jalopy. Still there. Well, I don't suppose anybody would want to steal *that*, but you never know.'

The 'jalopy', as she calls it, is an ancient Saab, the dark blue chassis streaked with splashes of mud. Andrea unlocks the boot and clears a space amongst an assortment of paraphernalia.

'There we go, there's room for your suitcase. We'll put your bag on the back seat.'

The interior of the car is almost as cluttered as the boot. There's what looks like a riding hat and crop, and Kathryn has to shuffle a water bottle, apple core and empty crisp packet in the well of the front passenger seat in order to settle her feet comfortably.

'Sorry about the mess,' Andrea says cheerfully. 'I meant to give it a good clean before I picked you up, but I didn't have time. I had to get the vet out to one of my horses, and by the time we'd sorted her out, the morning was gone. I reckoned a dirty car waiting for you was better than a clean one arriving late.'

'Absolutely,' Kathryn agrees. 'You've got horses, then?'

'Yes.' Andrea pauses for a moment, concentrating on manoeuvring the large, heavy car out of its bay and Kathryn holds her breath as she comes perilously close to hitting a smart new BMW parked alongside. Then, completely unfazed, she continues: 'I run a riding stables in the village.'

'Oh, I didn't know.'

'Why should you? There's a lot we don't know about one another, isn't there?'

'A stable, though. I never imagined . . .'

'You don't ride?'

'No.'

'Your mother used to, when she was a little girl.'

Kathryn is startled. 'She's never said.' And then she remembers: Gillian has no recollection of her life in Timberley. Strange, though. You'd think a love of horses would have surfaced, even if people and events were a blank page. But to her knowledge, Gillian has never been on a horse, or expressed a desire to ride.

'Your stable is in the village, you say . . . ?'

She winces again as Andrea blockbusts her way over a roundabout adorned with a mock-up Concorde.

47

'Yes. At Timberley Hall. Where you're staying, actually.'

This is unreal.

'I'm staying at a riding stable!'

Andrea laughs.

'Not exactly. Timberley Hall was a grand country residence. Then, during the war, it was used as a hospital and convalescent home by the US Air Force. By modern standards it's much too big for a family home, though. Nowadays it's a hotel. Nice rooms for visitors, banqueting suites where people who can afford it can have their wedding reception, or even get married – you know the sort of thing. Registrar in a room filled with flowers instead of the traditional church service. They applied for a licence to hold weddings as soon as the law permitting it went through.'

'And the stables . . . ?'

'Were once part of the estate. I rent them from the owners of the hotel.'

'It sounds nice.'

'I'm very much at home there. But then, I would be. I lived for the first six years of my life on the farm next door.'

'Right.' Kathryn is impressed by Andrea's openness, the casual way she talks about her past – so totally different from Gillian's secrecy.

'And what about you?' Andrea asks.

Miraculously, she has manoeuvred her way onto the M4 without incident; they are now trundling along in the centre lane, Andrea totally oblivious to the drivers tailgating her and giving her angry glances as they are forced into the outside lane in order to overtake her.

'What do I do for a living, you mean?'

'Yes. Tell me all about yourself. That's probably better than me trying to talk and drive at the same time.'

Yes, Kathryn thinks, it probably is! So she embarks on a résumé of her job and her life.

She doesn't mention Ben, though. And she certainly does not say that her marriage is all but on the rocks. There are some things that will keep until she knows Andrea better.

But from what she's seen of her so far, she likes her. There's no pretence about Andrea, none whatsoever. It makes a welcome change.

The motorway sign says 'Services ½ Mile'. Andrea moves into the inside lane.

'We'll stop for a cup of tea. I need petrol, anyway.'

They find a parking space and go into the service concourse, heading for the cafeteria. It's quite busy, lorry drivers tucking into all-day breakfasts, a couple of harassed-looking men in suits, mobile phone in one hand, sandwich in the other, a group of people who look as though they've been attending a funeral, the men in black ties and white shirts, the women buttoned up into smart dark jackets, a family with small, over-excited children. Kathryn averts her eyes from the toddler chasing his older siblings around the tables, teddy bear trailing behind him. Some things are just too painful.

Kathryn and Andrea join the queue at the hot drinks station – Andrea has a pot of tea, Kathryn a large American coffee – and push their plastic trays along the counter to the till.

'This is on me,' Andrea says, searching in a battered leather shoulder bag for her purse. Kathryn doesn't argue; the only English money she has is in large denomination notes, tucked into the back of her travel wallet. They find a table that is not cluttered with used crockery and sit down.

'Actually,' Andrea says, 'I thought this might be a good opportunity to have a chat before we get home.' She pours her tea, stirs in three heaped spoonfuls of sugar, raises her eyes to meet Kathryn's. 'I don't know how much your mother has told you about the reason things are . . . as they are . . . between her and us. And it might be better to clear the air before you meet Mum.'

Kathryn's skin prickles a little with nervous anticipation.

'The truth is,' she says, 'I didn't even know you existed until I came across your letter.' She explains how it came about. 'If I hadn't found it, I doubt I'd know even now. I was always led to believe Lizzie and Walter were Mom's only family.'

'Lizzie and Walter.' Andrea's tone is hard; she speaks their names with distaste, and the lines around her mouth, like cracks in old leather, deepen. 'They have a lot to answer for. I know they took your mother in and gave her a home when she needed one, but they destroyed any chance of us being a family. They turned Gillian against Mum, so she didn't want anything to do with her. It broke Mum's heart. She's never got over it. When she came out of prison—' She breaks off, looking questioningly at Kathryn. 'You do know Mum was in prison, don't you?'

Kathryn nods, uncomfortable. 'Yes.'

'And you know why?'

'Yes.'

Andrea sighs. 'I suppose I should be more charitable to Lizzie

50

and Walter. After all, Frank — your grandfather — was Lizzie's brother. But to drip-feed a child with hatred for her mother, poison her mind to that extent . . . it's wicked.'

'They were the only family Mom knew,' Kathryn says, feeling oddly almost responsible for the fact that Gillian has not acknowledged her mother for almost fifty years, needing somehow to try to excuse her. 'She didn't remember anything of her life before . . . what happened. Still doesn't. She says they called it "traumatic amnesia". I suppose today you'd have therapy for something like that, but fifty years ago things were different. And to be honest, I don't think she wants to remember. After all this time she's more comfortable just blotting it out.'

'Certainly Lizzie didn't want her to remember,' Andrea says flatly. 'They had no children of their own — Gillian filled the gap. Lizzie would have been afraid that if Gillian remembered her mother, she'd lose her. So she made damned sure that didn't happen.'

'Understandable, I suppose.' Kathryn sips her coffee, cool enough now to drink. 'If they'd grown to love her as their own—'

'Wicked,' Andrea says, uncompromisingly. 'Whatever she did — or didn't do — Mum didn't deserve that.'

Kathryn frowns, puzzled by Andrea's turn of phrase.

'I didn't think there was any doubt about it. According to Mom, she confessed.'

'She did.' Andrea pushes her teacup to one side, leans quilted-jacket elbows on the table so that her head juts towards Kathryn. 'Personally, I think there's room for doubt.'

'In what way?'

Andrea leans back again. There's a thoughtful expression on her face as if she is weighing up what to say.

'Mum said she did it and she's stuck to that story ever since. Even to me. I just don't believe her, that's all. I think she was covering up for someone. Someone she thought would get a much tougher sentence than she did with her plea of self-defence – been hanged even.'

Kathryn's heart leaps. If Carrie is innocent it would put a whole new slant on things. But perhaps it's just what Andrea *wants* to believe. Even without the conditioning that coloured her own mother's view of what happened, it must be very hard to accept that your mother is responsible for your father's death. And loyalty is bound to play its part.

'Have you told her you don't believe she did it?' Kathryn asks.

'Of course. But it's like batting my head against a brick wall. She refuses to talk about it. I don't know why, after so long, she insists on sticking to her story, but I suppose she has her reasons.'

Kathryn is thinking furiously. 'But surely the police investigated at the time?'

Andrea pulls a wry face. 'The police, as you call them, was our village bobby. The detectives were based miles away, with more important things on their minds. They had a so-called accidental shooting and a confession that seemed feasible. They took the easy way out and chose to believe her. Why make work for themselves?'

'I suppose . . .'

'Anyway, I know Mum, and I don't believe she's capable of

shooting anyone, even if she didn't mean to kill them. She's just not the type to be waving guns about.' She pauses, pouring herself another cup of tea. 'I'm not the only one with doubts, either. Mary Hutchins—'

'Mary Hutchins?'

'At the farm. Mary who looked after me while Mum was in prison. She took a very different attitude to the one Lizzie took with your mother. She always said Mum wasn't to be blamed, that I shouldn't believe all I was told. Since I've been old enough to think about it, I wonder if she knows something. But she won't be drawn. She's as much of a closed book on the subject as Mum is.' She glances at her watch, changes tack.

'If you've finished your coffee we really ought to get going – we're still some way from home. I just wanted to make sure you were aware of what happened before you meet Mum. We'll talk again when we've got more time.'

She gathers up her bag, dumped carelessly beside her chair, and gets up. Kathryn does the same. As she follows Andrea out to the car, it strikes her as ironic that the daughter who was born whilst Carrie was in prison, and who had scant contact with her mother for the first five years of her life, should be the one who is close to her now, whilst Gillian, who enjoyed eight years of her mother's care in her formative years, should be the one who has disowned her. It could be, of course, that Lizzie and Walter brainwashed her, as Andrea said, drip-feeding venom into Gillian's impressionable young mind. She wouldn't put such a thing past Lizzie. But all the same . . .

She wonders if Andrea will continue the conversation when they're back on the motorway, but she doesn't. Instead she makes the sort of small talk that is the bedrock of communication between two strangers who are feeling their way towards familiarity. Two strangers who are related by blood, but who did not know, until a few weeks ago, of one another's existence.

The village of Timberley lies in a fold of the Cotswolds, seven or eight miles off the motorway, and practically the entire distance is covered by way of narrow roads winding between swathes of open farmland.

It is late afternoon now, and the light is fading to a dull grey haze. The trees are shedding their leaves in earnest, and have been for a couple of weeks, judging by the thick carpeting on the verges, and the red and gold that still remains on the half-bare branches is muted in comparison with the glorious hues of the Canadian fall, where the sun sets the trees on fire against an impossibly blue sky.

In spite of the twists and turns, Andrea drives at what seems to Kathryn to be a reckless pace; more than once she has to brake sharply and run the nearside wheels into the rutted gulley at the edge of the road. The only time she exhibits caution is when they come upon two horseback riders, a woman on a handsome chestnut and a child on a grey pony. Then she slows to a crawl, the engine barely ticking over as she passes them, and accelerates only gently even when they are some distance away. The woman raises her hand in acknowledgement of the consideration; Andrea raises her own hand in reply.

'Don't want to spook the horses,' she says to Kathryn.

The road dips down a lane where the trees meet overhead to form a canopy, twists sharply once or twice, and then straightens out. There are a couple of cottages, grey Cotswold stone, built into the hill to one side of the road; a tractor bearing a hedge trimmer is moving slowly along, slicing the tops off the hedges on the other. Andrea overtakes it.

'Well, this is Timberley,' she says.

Kathryn sits forward, peering into the gathering gloom.

There are more houses to her right, bigger and better maintained than the ones further out of the village, with lawns sloping down to the edge of the road, and what appears to be a cemetery to her left. Directly ahead, sitting on a triangular fork in the highway, is a pub – the King's Head. It has tables and chairs set out on a paved forecourt and a cross of St George flag fluttering from a pole that projects at an angle above the door.

Andrea nods in the direction of the lane that forks off to the right.

'Bush Villa is down there.'

But she's branching off to the left.

'I thought I'd take you straight to Timberley Hall. I'm sure you want to get unpacked and settled in. I'll come back for you about half-six, say? That should give you time to freshen up, shouldn't it? Mum doesn't like to eat too late. She says it gives her indigestion, and she can't sleep.' She slows. 'Here we are, then.'

'Oh my goodness! It's very *grand!*'

Timberley Hall is set well back from the road behind an expanse of parkland; an elegant Georgian house, perfectly proportioned, with a flight of stone steps leading up to a central front door and a raised portico giving a focal point to the grey slate roof.

Kathryn saw it on the Timberley website when she was surfing for background information about the place, but she never imagined it was where she would be staying. She thought Andrea would book her into a local pub or B & B, at a farm perhaps. She blanches momentarily, wondering how much this is going to set her back. As if she had read her mind, Andrea grins.

'Don't worry, I've arranged a discounted rate for you. Perks of being part of the furniture.'

She bombs up the drive that bisects the parkland, and lurches to a halt outside the main entrance.

'I'll come in with you. Make sure everything's OK.'

She opens the boot, swings Kathryn's bag onto her shoulder, starts towards the stone steps.

'So where are your stables?' Kathryn asks.

'Round the back. Well out of the way of the house. I don't suppose the lord of the manor was any keener to have his home smelling of horses than people would be today.'

She opens the impressive front door, white painted and adorned with a gleaming brass knocker. The room inside is every bit as imposing as the exterior of the building. Once, presumably, it had been the grand entrance hall; now a reception desk in dark mahogany has been installed. A couple of wing chairs, upholstered in a tapestry design, flank a huge open fireplace where a log fire glows; an enormous Oriental rug covers a good area of the stained-wood flooring; jugs of chrysanthemums sit on occasional tables.

A girl appears as if by magic from a doorway behind the reception desk. She's smartly dressed in a navy-blue jacket over a pink and white striped shirt, and Kathryn can smell the freshly washed scent of her hair.

'Kayleigh. This is my niece, Kathryn. She's booked in for two weeks.'

'Oh yes, of course. Mrs Sawyer, isn't it?' She's scanning the computer screen; Timberley Hall might be an old building, but the management is bang up to date. She produces a registration form and a pen, all chirpy efficiency. 'I've put you in Room Six, Mrs Sawyer. It has lovely views over the Cotswolds. I think you'll like it there.'

Andrea gives Kathryn a sideways grin.

'I knew they'd look after you. Right, now that's all sorted I'll get along. Let Mum know you've arrived. And I'll be back about half-past six. OK?'

'Yes . . . fine . . .'

'See you later, then.'

And she's gone.

The view from Kathryn's room might well be superb in daylight; now it's too dark to see much, just the silhouette of the rolling hills on the skyline. She pulls the drapes, chintz heavy with overblown roses. The room has a double bed with a cover of the same fabric, a chair upholstered in cerise pink, and there is a tray with kettle, cup and saucer, small cartons of milk and assorted bags of tea, coffee and sugar on a glass-topped side table. Kathryn switches on the kettle and while she waits for it to boil she hoists her case up onto the bed, shaking out some of her clothes and hanging them in the fitted wardrobe. Then she makes herself a coffee, finds her toiletries bag, and carries both into the en suite bathroom. The bathroom is pink, which makes her wince, but at least there's a shower. She strips off her travel-weary clothes and gets under it, letting the water cascade over her from head to toe. The water could be hotter, but it's bliss all the same.

When she's finished, she wraps herself in a towel – no complimentary bathrobe here – and looks for a hair dryer, afraid that might not be supplied either. But she finds one in a dressing-table drawer. As she's drying her hair, she is suddenly assailed by a wave of homesickness.

She finds her mobile phone and texts Gillian to let her know she's arrived safely, then, after a moment's hesitation, she texts Rob too, which somehow only seems to make the feeling of homesickness keener. She's tired, she supposes, after the long flight, and she wishes she wasn't going to her grandmother's for supper tonight. She had been looking forward to meeting her, even if her excitement had been tinged with trepidation. Right now, however, she feels she's facing something of an ordeal. But she can't cry off. They'd be dreadfully hurt. And besides, she hasn't eaten today except for the plasticky scrambled egg and warmed-over Frankfurter sausage that had passed for breakfast on the flight, and she doesn't know if Timberley Hall serves evening meals. Her booking is for bed and breakfast only.

Kathryn finishes drying her hair, selects a pair of trousers that seem to have survived the flight without looking as if they've come out of the rag bag, and a red cashmere sweater, and starts getting dressed.

*   *   *

Gillian's mobile rings to tell her of an incoming text. It's from Kathryn. Gillian is relieved to know she's arrived safely, but the realisation that she is actually there, in the place where it all happened, starts her stomach churning.

She's a little puzzled as to why it should elicit such a violent reaction; it's not as if she can remember any of it. She has no recollection of that terrible night, nor of anything that went before. But she supposes that the memories are still there, locked in her subconscious, and some part of her remembers her distress – the uncomprehending terror of an eight-year-old child – and shrinks from it.

Should she have faced it long ago? Had therapy or even hypnosis to unlock the hidden demons that have shadowed her down the years? Certainly Don thinks so. From time to time over the years he's urged her to seek help, but she's never wanted to. The prospect of being forced to relive the past, confront the trauma head on, had been just too daunting; she couldn't bring herself to do it. Better simply to try to put it all behind her, pretend it had never happened. And she did, quite successfully, most of the time.

Now, though, with Kathryn learning the truth and actually going to England to meet her lost family, all kinds of long-buried questions are floating to the surface like litter in a pond, and Gillian finds herself wondering if perhaps she was too hard on Carrie, too ready to go along with Lizzie's assertion that she was a wicked woman. There's no doubt that Carrie is guilty of shooting Gillian's father, but why did she do it? Lizzie said that Carrie had cold-bloodedly murdered Frank because she wanted her freedom. As a child, Gillian didn't understand what

Lizzie meant by that – though of course when she was older she was able to hazard a pretty good guess – but she took Lizzie's word for it with the implicit faith a child has in the person to whom they look for guidance along with their every need. Now, though, she wonders, should she at least have tried to understand? Was there more to it than Lizzie led her to believe?

She thinks of Kathryn in Gloucestershire with Carrie and Andrea, her mother and sister, who are strangers to her, and feels the tug of some invisible cord around her heart.

Her finger hovers over the options button on her mobile, on the point of sending some message that Kathryn can relay to Carrie. But she really doesn't know what to say, and she's not sure she wants to say anything at all. The gulf between her and her mother is too deep, the years of estrangement a barren no man's land she cannot begin to cross.

She saves Kathryn's message, flips the cover down over her mobile, and puts it away in her purse.

SIX

Five minutes before Andrea is due to collect her, Kathryn is down in the hotel lobby clutching a carrier bag containing two bottles of wine, which she bought at the airport, and feeling decidedly nervous. She tries to distract herself by picking up a few glossy pamphlets from a display rack on the reception desk, but glancing at the pictures of local attractions stretches her to the limit of her concentration. There's no way she could interest herself in reading about the Tyndale Monument at North Nibley or the Wildfowl Trust at Slimbridge. The only flier that holds her for more than a moment is one advertising Andrea's riding stables. She does pony trekking, apparently – there's a picture of a string of ponies making their way sedately along a tree-lined bridle path – and gives lessons, as well as hiring out horses to experienced riders.

Kathryn checks her watch, looks out to see if Andrea has arrived, but there are no cars on the forecourt and no sign of lights heading up the driveway. She wanders some more, checks her watch again, wondering if she reset it accurately when she arrived in London. But the clock over the reception desk shows exactly the same time.

The girl who checked her in an hour ago looks up from some paperwork.

'I wouldn't worry if I were you. Andrea's not known for punctuality.'

Kathryn smiles, but says nothing. She doesn't want to be drawn into a conversation; she guesses the receptionist is curious about her and her relationship with Andrea. Fortunately, rescue is at hand. The broad beam of headlights shears in through the stained-glass panel above the door; Kathryn looks out again and sees the bulky shape of the Saab. A nerve jumps in her throat. This is it, then. No turning back now. She's going to meet the grandmother she never knew she had. The grandmother who went to prison for the murder of her husband.

They drive back into the village; make a left turn at the pub that sits on the junction.

'It's well within walking distance,' Andrea says. 'I often don't bother using the car. But tonight . . .'

There are houses all along the lane on both sides, old, well-established dwellings on the right, newish bungalows on the left. At one time the houses probably had an uninterrupted view over open countryside, Kathryn guesses. Andrea pulls up a few hundred yards into the lane, and backs onto a drive that slopes up to a double garage.

'This used to be a stable,' Andrea says. 'We had the loft down and made it into a garage when I got my first car.'

'You've always lived here then?' Kathryn asks.

'Apart from the first five years of my life, yes. Originally it was a rank of three cottages, two-up, two-down. My great-grandparents took one of them when they were married. Later, when the other two fell vacant, my great-grandfather bought them too. He was a local craftsman, and doing quite well. He knocked two into one to make a decent-sized family home, but never got around to incorporating the third. It's only used as a glory hole nowadays.' She hesitates; Kathryn has the impression there's something she's not saying. Then she goes on conversationally: 'I'm sure if we put the whole lot on the market some enterprising buyer could knock through and make a really big family house, but we've never had the need, the money, nor the inclination to do anything with it.'

'Right.' Kathryn's a bit confused, but no doubt it will all make sense when she sees the place in daylight.

Andrea closes the garage doors and bolts them, leads the way out through a smaller door on the side onto a paved path that runs along the back of the building. There are lights showing in an extension set at right angles to the main house, but the small windows they are passing are all in darkness. This is, presumably, the undeveloped and unoccupied cottage. Bright moonlight illuminates a large garden and what looks like a greenhouse on the other side of the paved area.

There's a small porch at the point where the L-shaped extension juts back from the main house. Andrea opens the door, which had been left on the latch, and the green-painted back door beyond.

'Mum – we're here!'

The kitchen is large, square, functional, and, to Kathryn's eye, old-fashioned. A table, laid with a blue checked gingham cloth, sits in the centre, the worktops, covered with what appears to be oilcloth, are resting on cupboards that flank a free-standing cooker. Several saucepans bubble on the hob. The rather harsh lighting emanates from a single 100 watt bulb with a white plastic bowl-shaped shade situated more or less centrally over the table. The room is filled with the mouth-watering smell of roasting meat, and a bottle of red wine, opened to breathe, stands on the table.

Kathryn feels claustrophobic suddenly. She wishes she could make her excuses and run. She hears footsteps on bare wood and glances to her right, where two or three steps lead down to an unseen room beyond.

'Kathryn!'

Kathryn smiles; her lips feel stiff.

'Hello.'

'Oh, Kathryn!'

Carrie Chapman is small and neat. Snow-white hair is swept away from a heart-shaped face and fastened in a pleat, her eyes are bright, clear blue. Her skin is smooth, with fewer lines and wrinkles than her daughter, or so it appears to Kathryn, perhaps because she's spent less time outside in all weathers than Andrea, perhaps because the ballerina-type hairstyle is pulling it taut. She's wearing a loose shirt in jade green over navy-blue trousers, and looks much younger than her age.

Kathryn has wondered and worried about the etiquette of meeting her grandmother for the first time; whether she would be expected to hug her, for instance. But Carrie doesn't seem about to sweep her into her arms, she just stands there, looking Kathryn up and down, smiling and shaking her head as if she simply can't believe she is real.

'Let me take your coat, Kathryn,' Andrea says.

Kathryn slips out of her jacket and Andrea disappears down the steps with it.

'Well, Kathryn, this is such a treat!' Carrie says. 'I don't know what you'll make of us, I'm sure. We're in a bit of a backwater here compared to what you're used to, I expect. But I can't tell you how glad I am you've come to see us.'

'I wanted to,' Kathryn says. 'As soon as I found out, I knew I wanted to meet you. You are my family, after all. I just wish I'd known about you years ago, but Mom—' She breaks off, not quite knowing how to finish the sentence.

'Your mother has her reasons, I know.' The sadness is a shadow in Carrie's eyes. 'How is she?'

'She's fine . . . well, not *fine* actually. She had a bad fall a month or so back and fractured her pelvis, but she's on the mend now.'

'She fractured her *pelvis*?' Carrie repeats, sounding shocked and concerned. 'How did she come to do that?'

Kathryn explains, feeling a little more at ease. Recounting the details of Gillian's accident is safe ground, much easier to discuss than an estrangement of almost fifty years.

'Poor Gillian!' Carrie sounds so distressed that Kathryn is left in no doubt that she still cares deeply for her elder daughter.

Andrea has returned to the kitchen and been listening to the saga. She is less sympathetic.

'Oh, well, these things happen,' she says lightly. 'Can I get

65

you a drink, Kathryn? Gin and tonic? Wine? There's red opened, and a white chilling in the fridge.'

'Red wine would be lovely . . . oh, and by the way, I brought these . . .' She retrieves the carrier bag containing the wine, which she rested against the leg of the kitchen table while taking off her coat.

'Oh, my dear, you shouldn't have! There was no need . . .'

'I wasn't going to arrive empty-handed.' Kathryn would like to have brought flowers too, but there has been no opportunity to buy them.

Andrea pours a glass of red wine for Kathryn and another for herself, and a white for Carrie. Carrie raises her glass in Kathryn's direction before she takes a sip.

'Just make yourself at home, my dear. I need to see to the dinner.'

She goes to the cooker, sets her glass down on the worktop within easy reach, and strains vegetables into colanders. When she opens the oven door to take out the joint, already resting on a serving dish, the delicious smell in the kitchen intensifies – not just the aroma of roasted lamb, but rosemary and garlic too.

'That smells wonderful,' Kathryn says, sipping her wine.

'Just good plain cooking.' Carrie now seems to be doing half a dozen things at once, but she's ready to delegate. 'Will you carve, Andrea?'

'I usually do, don't I?' Andrea grumbles.

They clearly have a routine, mother and daughter, and it seems to work.

'Right,' says Carrie, 'that's it then. Shall we eat?'

*   *   *

The meal is as delicious as it smells: crisp roasted potatoes, vegetables as perfectly cooked as Kathryn has ever eaten, and fresh mint sauce to accompany the lamb.

'It's mostly gone to seed now, but I managed to find enough to make some sauce,' Carrie says.

'You grow your own mint?' Kathryn asks, impressed.

'Grow it?' Carrie laughs. 'It grows itself! Stopping it spreading is the biggest problem. It's lucky we've got such a big garden.'

'Mum's a great gardener.' Andrea piles extra roast potatoes onto her plate. 'The cabbage and the parsnips are home-grown too.'

'I like my garden,' Carrie agrees. 'It's a lot to keep up together, though. I have a lad from the village to dig it over for me in the spring – that's too much for me now. But I do everything else myself.'

'You should taste her tomatoes!' Andrea says. 'They're nothing like the rubbish you buy in the supermarket. And the smell of them . . . oh, going into Mum's greenhouse when the tomatoes are growing is like going to heaven.'

'They've all finished now,' Carrie says regretfully. 'I made some chutney, though, with the green ones. You must take a bottle home with you if you've got room in your suitcase.'

For a moment Kathryn thinks she might raise the subject of Gillian again, but she doesn't. For tonight, at least, they're all staying on safe territory, feeling their way, getting to know one another.

The roasted lamb is followed by apple pie and custard, the pastry feather-light, the apple just tart enough to give it an edge. Carrie is clearly a wonderful cook as well as a keen gardener. But the lack of sleep last night and two or three glasses of wine are taking their toll on Kathryn. Her eyelids are drooping, and she's beginning to feel very distant. Carrie notices that she's gone quiet.

'You're tired out, my dear,' she says. 'I think you need to get to bed.'

'I'm fine . . .'

'No, you're not. You're falling asleep where you sit. I think you should take Kathryn back to the Hall, Andrea. There's another day tomorrow.'

'Mum's right.' Andrea gets up. 'I'll get your coat.'

'What do you think of Timberley Hall?' Carrie asks while she's gone.

'Very impressive, what I've seen of it.'

'It is, isn't it? I used to work there, you know. In the war, when it was a hospital.'

'Really?'

'Oh, yes, it holds a lot of memories for me . . .'

Andrea is back, wearing her quilted jacket and carrying Kathryn's coat.

'I'll tell you all about it one day,' Carrie says. 'But for tonight you need your bed.'

'I guess.' Kathryn slips into her jacket. 'Thank you so much . . .' She hesitates. 'I don't actually know what to call you.'

'Grandma . . . Carrie, if you'd rather . . . I don't mind. What matters is that you're here.'

'Grandma,' Kathryn says. She likes the sound of it.

'We'll see you soon then. Good night, Kathryn.'

'Good night, Grandma. And thanks again.'

'My pleasure.' And Carrie's face shows she means it.

'That wasn't so bad now, was it?' Andrea says as they drive back up the lane.

'It was wonderful. And Grandma is . . .'

'Quite a character.'

'A really nice lady.' What Kathryn is actually thinking is that it's hard to believe that the sweet-faced elderly woman who loves gardening and is an excellent cook could ever have murdered anyone, least of all her husband.

But of course, she doesn't say so.

'See you tomorrow then,' Andrea says when she pulls into the driveway of the Hall.

'Yes.' Kathryn is so sleepy now anything more than a monosyllable is beyond her.

She goes into the hotel, up to her room where she falls into bed. As she curls under the covers she sees Carrie's sweet face, and wonders again what on earth happened all those years ago to have such a terrible and far-reaching outcome. But it's all becoming muddled, slipping away from her.

Within minutes, Kathryn is deeply asleep.

Part Two

Carrie

SEVEN

Timberley, Gloucestershire

I can hardly believe Kathryn is here. I feel as if I'm living in a bubble of unreality. It's hard to believe, too, that this self-possessed young woman is my granddaughter, my little girl's child. She's taller than I expected – Gillian was quite small for her age, but then of course the last time I saw her she still had a few years' growing to do. She's darker than Gillian too, and her eyes are golden brown. But when I look into her face I can see myself at her age – same shaped nose, a definite tip-tilt, same wide mouth, and I know she's no imposter. Strange to think she must be a good fifteen years older than I was when I had Gillian; that by the time I reached the age she is now I had served a prison sentence and lost my first-born.

I don't want to think of that, though. Not yet. I shall have to, I suppose, sooner or later. So far she's tactfully avoided the subject, but the questions are bound to begin when she feels she knows me well enough.

'How is your mother?' I asked that first day, and she told me Gillian had fractured her pelvis, and made it sound as if that was the reason she was not here too, though both of us knew different. She admitted she hadn't even known I existed until a couple of weeks ago, but when I asked her how much her mother had told her, she simply said: 'Not much.' Neither of us mentioned the reason for our estrangement, but then, we have to feel our way before getting round to all that.

She was fairly evasive about her own circumstances too, though it seems she has suffered a tragedy of her own. When I asked if she had any family her face went shut in, a sort of carefully constructed mask.

'I had a little boy,' she said. 'But we lost him last year to meningitis.'

'Oh, I am so sorry,' I said, knowing it was a quite inadequate response, and she went on telling me about her job and her husband – something not quite right there either, I suspect – and the town in Ontario where they live. Safe ground for the moment. The rest will, I hope, come later.

Later might be sooner, of course, if she were staying with us. We did offer, but I expect she thought it was too soon to be trapped in such intimate contact, and to tell the truth, it really wouldn't have been very convenient.

Although Bush Villa is quite a big house, it has only three bedrooms, and two of those don't have separate entrances. The master bedroom – mine – is to the right of a central landing, but you actually have to go through the smallest bedroom to reach Andrea's room, on the front of the house. I suppose it was the only option open to my grandfather when he knocked two of the old rank of three cottages into one, and I dare say the lack of privacy didn't matter back then. Nowadays, however, it's a different matter. Kathryn wouldn't have wanted to have Andrea traipsing through her room, and I don't suppose Andrea would have been very enthusiastic about it either.

There would be no problem with space for visitors, of course, if I'd done something about incorporating the third dwelling, the one we call 'the cottage', or even had it made habitable. But it would have cost a lot of money at the prices builders charge today, and in any case, it holds too many memories for me. I wouldn't feel comfortable with the cottage as part of the main house. So it remains a sort of glory hole. One of the two minuscule downstairs rooms I use as a potting shed, the two tiny bedrooms, reached by way of a curving stone staircase, are stacked with boxes of things that belonged to Mother and Father, things I packed up to dispose of and never did. The front downstairs room, I never go into at all.

No, the cottage will never be converted in my lifetime. Sometimes I wonder if it is destined to remain empty and unloved for ever. Certainly my fate was sealed by the fact that my grandfather never got around to knocking the original rank of three into one, as he'd planned.

There was a great deal of talk of it, I remember, when I was small. But my grandfather died when I was five – of appendicitis and peritonitis, I've always thought, though at the time no one seemed to know what was wrong with him – and that was the end of that. Soon afterwards my grandmother became ill with her 'dicky heart', as she called it, and her bed was moved downstairs into the parlour. My parents moved into her room, and

I took over theirs. I shall never forget how excited I was with the extra space and the privacy. Knowing that Mother and Father were no longer just the other side of the connecting door, but a whole world away across the vast expanse of the landing, made me feel incredibly grown up. I could shut my door and be quite alone with my imaginary friends and my precious doll, Vera. Vera had a beautiful porcelain face and blue glass eyes that actually closed, and a white flounced dress and long-legged bloomers, all made of silk . . .

Oh my goodness, there I go again, wandering! And so far back! Seventy years, at least! Though it seems to me they've passed in the blinking of an eye . . .

Anyway, I grew up in that room. And when I married Frank, at the tender age of just sixteen, he moved into it with me. Later, when Gillian was born, she had the little adjoining room that had once been mine.

It wasn't ideal, of course. Nothing about our marriage was. But we had no choice. 'Making the best of a bad job,' Mother called it. Because I'd committed the unforgivable sin of falling pregnant before I had a ring on my finger.

My first big mistake. The one that was to trap me into marriage with a man I didn't love, a recipe for later meeting someone who would come to mean the whole world to me. Which, in turn, would set in motion the chain of events that has brought us to where we are today.

It couldn't happen today, of course. There are single mothers everywhere. There's no shame any more in having a child out of wedlock, and certainly none in having sexual intercourse with a man you're not married to. But things were very different then. Everyone pretended to be virtuous, even if they were not; girls who gave away their favours were considered less than respectable, and to fall pregnant was to have 'let yourself down'. It was then up to the young man in question to 'do the honourable thing' and more often than not, he did. Which was fine if the couple were in love. Plenty of unions that began as shotgun marriages settled into relationships that grew and matured into happy lifelong commitment.

The trouble with Frank and me was that we were not in love. Oh, I thought I was, for a little while, in the beginning. But in reality I had not the first idea of what love meant. What I felt for Frank was nothing more than the infatuation of a young girl with a good-looking lad. Real love, I learned later, is so very different. The frisson of electric attraction might, initially, appear much the same, but to feel it with the soul as well as the body is quite a different experience, deep and complete. When you truly love, no sacrifice is too great; I would have laid down my life for Dev, still would. Nothing can change that; nothing ever will.

Frank − well, I knew, even before I married Frank that it wasn't what I wanted. But, as I said before, it was what was expected, and I was too young to fly in the face of convention, especially when I could see no alternative.

I was fifteen years old, and in the second year of my apprenticeship at Hortons, the drapers, in Marlow, when I met him. He was eight years older than me, very good-looking in a dark, swarthy way, and a stranger in the area, which only added to his attraction. He hailed from Hillsbridge, a mining village in

Somerset, which seemed like the other side of the world in those days. He had escaped from the coal mines where he had worked as a carting boy, and got a job on the railways in Gloucestershire.

Very possibly our paths would never have crossed if I had not got a puncture in my bicycle tyre riding home from work one Saturday evening that spring.

I rode my bicycle the three miles from Timberley to Marlow every day, come rain or shine. It was more convenient, since the bus service was an hourly one, and I could never be sure of leaving work on time. Mrs Horton, the draper, had a strict policy that we could not shut the shop if there was a customer so much as looking in the window, and if I just missed one bus I would have had to wait an hour for the next.

That evening it was after nine before we were able to turn the sign on the door to 'Closed'; Saturday was market day in Marlow, and as usual the town had been busy until dark. Tired, hungry and anxious to get home, I set out, but when I had gone about a mile and a half I realised I had a tyre so flat the wheel rim was grinding on the road. I stopped in a gateway, hard churned mud from the twice-daily egress of a herd of cows on their way to be milked, and unclipped my pump. But no matter how much air I pumped into the tyre, more seemed to escape. I must have unwittingly ridden over something sharp enough to make a really bad gash. Utterly fed up, I unscrewed the pump and was just fixing it back into its bracket when I heard a motorcycle approaching along the lane.

I straightened up, waiting for it to pass, and as it did I saw two lads on a Douglas – I was rather interested in motorcycles, strange, for a girl, I suppose, but there you are. As it rounded a bend in the lane I heard it slowing. Then, to my dismay, it was coming back, stopping beside me.

I really wasn't happy about this. Lads out on a Saturday night with a week's wages in their pocket could be rowdy and silly; if they started running rings round me I had no way of escape. And I didn't know either of them.

'Having trouble?' one of them called over the roar of the motorcycle engine.

'I'm fine, thank you.'

I rescued my bicycle, propped against the gate, and began pushing it along the lane. The lads rode alongside me, zigzagging to keep balance. 'Want a lift?'

'No, thank you.'

'Where are you going?'

I didn't answer, just kept walking, eyes fixed straight ahead of me.

'You've got a flat tyre.' That was the boy on the pillion.

'Oh, go to the top of the class!'

'I could mend it for you.'

'No, thank you.'

'Oh, leave her to it.' The rider revved the engine.

'No, hang on. Drop me off, eh?'

The pillion rider dismounted, began walking alongside me. By the light of the moon I could see that he was dark, good-looking. 'I'll catch up with you later, mate!' he called to the rider, who, after a few moments' hesitation, roared away. My heart was in my mouth, but for some reason I felt more excited than nervous.

'You shouldn't be on your own at night,' he said.

'I'm perfectly fine,' I said. 'I do this every day.'

He gave me a sideways grin.

'I shall have to go this way more often.'

I said nothing.

'Do you want me to try and pump up your tyre?' he asked.

'It's no good. Unless you've got a repair kit. And I don't suppose you carry one of those in your pocket.'

''Fraid not,' he said ruefully. 'Oh, well, I'll see you home anyway.'

'There's no need.'

He shrugged. 'My mate's gone now. I might as well. And you'll have to come out with me tomorrow to say thank you.'

So, that was how it all began.

Except that it almost did not begin at all. Mother and Father were not in the least happy that I had agreed to meet a man so much older than I was, whom I did not know at all. I begged and pleaded, pointing out that he had seen me safely home, in vain. The next evening, when I was supposed to be meeting him outside the King's Head, I was forbidden to leave the house and Mother went instead. She came back, puffed up with righteous determination, saying that she had told him in no uncertain terms that I was much too young to be going out with a man of his age, and that if he had an ounce of common decency he would realise that.

'I don't think he'll be bothering you again,' she said smugly.

I went to my room and cried, tears of disappointment and humiliation. Father came in and sat down on the edge of the bed beside me. He was always softer with me than Mother was.

'Come on now, my love, don't upset yourself,' he said. 'There are plenty of nice boys in the village. We wouldn't mind you seeing one of them. Someone your own age. What about Jack Thomas? He's a nice lad.'

I snorted. Jack Thomas was a farmer's boy with a red face and raw-boned hands. There was no way I'd go out with him.

'How could Mother do that?' I wailed. 'How could she make me look such a fool?'

'She's only got your best interests at heart,' Father said. 'Now just try and forget all about it, there's a good girl.'

I was quite sure that I'd never see Frank again. What lad would want to court a girl whose mother turned up instead of her and gave him a lambasting? But Frank wasn't one to give up so easily. The following week he turned up outside Hortons when I was at work.

I was just one of Mrs Horton's three assistants. Mary Saunders was a couple of years older than me, and fully qualified, and Renee Targett was a year younger than me, and a first-year apprentice. It was Mary's job to dress the windows, but Renee and I were expected to dust the display every day when the shop was quiet. On the Tuesday we'd been exceptionally busy, and it was late in the afternoon when we got to the task.

I went to fetch the feather dusters whilst Renee opened up the shutters that separated the window from the shop; when I came back she was jiggling with excitement – not an unusual occurrence. Renee was what my mother called a 'flibbertigibbet'.

'There's a man out there, just staring in. He winked at me!' She rounded her eyes at me. 'He's ever so handsome.'

I peeked round the shutters. It was Frank! I withdrew hastily, my face flaming.

'You'll have to do the window, Renee. I'm not going in there.'

Renee's jaw dropped. 'You know him?'

I nodded, hushing her, for fear Mrs Horton would overhear, and busied myself tidying the cotton reel drawer.

'Has he gone?' I asked when Renee emerged from the window.

'Yes, worse luck. Who is he, Carrie? Is he after you?'

'Oh, don't be silly.' But my heart was beating furiously and I could still feel the flush in my cheeks. 'Anyway, he's gone now, you say.'

But he hadn't. When I pushed my bicycle through the little alley at the side of the shop half an hour or so later, he was waiting. And he had a bicycle too, leaned up against the wall.

'I'm not allowed to see you,' I said.

'So your mother said. She's a tartar, isn't she?'

'Not really!' I said, stung to her defence. 'She just thinks . . .' I hesitated. I didn't want to draw attention to the difference in our ages. 'She says I don't know you well enough.'

He grinned. 'That's easily put right. I see your bicycle's mended. There's no law against me riding home with you, is there?'

I couldn't argue. I didn't want to. He rode alongside me all the way to Timberley.

'You'd better not come any further,' I said when we reached

82

the King's Head. 'I'll be in real trouble if they see me with you.'

'OK,' he said. And cycled off, back the way we'd come. I was all of a dither, nervous and excited. I couldn't believe he'd defied my mother; I couldn't believe I had. And I still didn't expect to see him again. But the next evening when I left work, there he was, waiting.

Very soon it became a habit. Frank met me from work, cycled home with me, cycled off again. I felt as though I was living the dream; this exciting boy – man – wanted to see me so much he was prepared to ride all the way to Timberley and back, doing nothing more than chatting. Surely he'd get fed up before long? The thought of him disappearing from my life was so dreadful that when he suggested I should find some way of getting out of the house to meet him during the evening I was easily persuaded.

I am not by nature deceitful, but feeling as I did about Frank, I soon learned to be. It was summer now, the evenings were long and light, and I made the excuse that I was going to Renee's house. Renee was primed to cover for me, should anyone ask, and she was a willing accomplice. I would walk down the lane where Frank would be waiting for me, out of sight of the house, and we would go for a walk across the fields, or into the woods.

It couldn't last, of course. Whether someone saw us and told Mother, or whether she was just too astute I never knew, but one evening when I got home she was ready for me, simmering with fury.

'Where do you think you've been?'

'To Renee's . . . I told you . . .'

'Don't lie to me, madam. You've been with that boy.'

On the point of denying it, I made up my mind. I'd had a birthday, I was sixteen now. And I was tired of sneaking out to meet Frank.

'Yes, I have,' I said defiantly. 'And I shall do it again – you can't stop me seeing him. I love him!'

There was a dreadful scene, of course. But in the end Mother realised, I suppose, that there was nothing she could do, short of locking me in my room. So I began meeting Frank openly, and, grudgingly, Mother and Father came to accept him, though they never liked him. And though I hate to admit it, they were right. I was seeing Frank through the proverbial rose-tinted spectacles; they, I suppose, were looking at him through the eyes of experience, and they could see that it was only a matter of time before I came to regret my bid for freedom and to realise that what I called love was, in reality, nothing more than infatuation.

They were sweet halcyon days. Looking back now, it's hard to believe that that naïve girl was really me. Though I can recall every detail as clearly as if it happened yesterday, it is as if I am watching one of those old films that they show on afternoon TV, with myself as the central character. But that aura of heady romance couldn't last and my childhood – for all that I thought I was so grown up, I really was still a child – was soon to come to an abrupt end. Because I became pregnant.

For weeks I kept it to myself, hoping desperately that it would all go away and things would return to normal. I wondered how I could have been so stupid as to let him do what he did, but I knew the reason. It hadn't been that I'd been carried away on a wave of passion – in fact, I hadn't enjoyed it at all – but that I was afraid he would finish with me if I went on refusing to let him so much as touch me. He had become very truculent about my resistance, and there was no denying the underlying threat that was really nothing more than emotional blackmail. Frank did have a dark side and could 'turn funny' if he didn't get his way, I had discovered. But I was still too besotted with him to want to lose him. Anyway, one thing had led to another, and now I'd missed a period and was on the point of missing another, and I was in a total panic, frightened, ashamed, not knowing what to do. I was dreading my parents finding out because I knew they would be furious as well as disappointed in me, and I was afraid to tell Frank in case I never saw him again.

But of course, I had to.

'No – you can't be!' Frank said, shocked. 'We only did it the once.'

'Twice.'

We'd gone for a walk down Watery Lane, and I'd taken my courage in both hands and told him that I thought I was pregnant.

'You can't be.' The hand that had been around my waist as we walked, inching up to try to touch my breast, was now stuffed into his pocket, and it wasn't just the shadow of the overhanging trees that was making his face dark.

'I think I am. I feel sick all the time and I've got this niggly pain in my stomach and . . . What are we going to do, Frank?'

'God knows,' he snorted, shaking his head. Then he turned and started walking away from me up the lane.

I ran after him. 'Where are you going?'

'Leave me alone. Just leave me, all right? I can't get my head round this, Carrie. Why didn't you say something before?'

'I wasn't sure . . . Frank, you can't just walk off and leave me. We've got to talk. I'm going to have your baby!'

'So you just bloody said.' He stopped and turned on me. 'How do I know it's mine, anyway?'

'Of course it's yours!' I felt as if I'd been slapped in the face.

'Well, it had bloody better be. Don't think you can make a fool out of me, Carrie.'

'I wouldn't . . . I couldn't! What do you think I am?'

For a few moments Frank was silent. He stood there, blowing breath out through his teeth in sharp, audible sighs. Then he said: 'I suppose you want me to marry you.'

It was what I'd hoped for. But I hadn't expected it to be like this. I'd wanted him to gentle me, reassure me that everything was going to be all right, that he loved me, even. Instead he had become a frightening stranger, and suddenly I wasn't at all sure I wanted to marry him.

But I couldn't see that I could do otherwise. I knew of an unmarried mother in Marlow who'd kept her baby; she lived in poverty, looked down upon by everyone, and the little boy had names called after him in the street. And the story went that a girl who'd disappeared from Timberley a few years back had been locked up in an institution for being an unmarried mother. I was sixteen years old, with no means of supporting a child, and I wasn't even sure I could count on my parents for support. I had to swallow my pride and my misgivings and be grateful that Frank was willing to give my child a name.

'I don't know what else to do,' I said wretchedly.

'Well, I've made my bed, I suppose I shall have to lie on it.' Frank sighed through his teeth again. Then he grinned suddenly, an unexpected return to the man who had beguiled me. 'At least if you're married to me I'll know no other bugger will have you,' he said.

I thought there would be hell to pay when we told Mother and Father, and the worst of the recriminations would come from Mother. She was a matriarch like her mother before her, but without Granny's sense of humour, and very daunting. She ran the household with a rod of iron, and when she was displeased she was capable of meting out days of cold, silent treatment. Father, on the other hand, was a quiet, gentle man, though he did have quite a temper when he was finally roused.

To my surprise, however, when Frank and I told them our news, Mother took it with a certain resignation. She said that she'd always known something like this would happen, though she'd hoped she'd brought me up to know better. It was Father who really took it hard. He went white, then red, then white again.

'You bugger!' His voice was low and shaking. 'Our Carrie was a decent girl until she met you. I should have put my foot down and sent you packing. Her mother tried to, and I stood up for her because I trusted you to take good care of her. I never thought it would come to this. If I had—'

'These things happen, Mr Williams,' Frank said, trying to sound jaunty.

For an awful moment, I thought Father was going to hit him. He wasn't a big man, my father – Frank was a good head taller than he, and much broader – but he was beside himself with a fury I'd rarely seen in him. His hands were balled to fists, clenching and unclenching, and his teeth bared.

'Don't give me that, you cheeky little sod!' he grated. 'Haven't you got an ounce of common decency in you?'

'At least I'm standing by her, Mr Williams,' Frank said. 'At least I'm going to marry her.'

'Oh, you think so? Well, let me tell you, our Carrie can't get married without our permission – she's a long way off twenty-one. And I don't want her marrying the likes of you. I'd rather take the shame and look after her myself, thank you very much.'

'Father . . .' I was horrified.

'I mean it, our Carrie. He might have ruined your life once, I'll see to it he doesn't ruin it again. We know nothing about you, nothing,' he snarled at Frank, 'and our Carrie is too young to know her own mind. I won't see her tied to the likes of you.'

'Oh, Jack . . .' Mother was shaking her head. 'He's that upset he doesn't know what he's saying,' she said to Frank. 'We've had a shock, both of us. But at least you're trying to do the right thing now. He'll come round. He'll have to. We can't have our Carrie's name dragged through the mud. You'll come round, won't you, Jack?'

All the fire seemed to go out of Father suddenly. He looked old and beaten, as he was, of course. Squaring up to Frank was one thing; going against what Mother had decided was for the best was something entirely different. She'd win in the end, and he knew it.

'Well, you'd better treat her right, or you'll have me to answer to.' Father waggled his finger right under Frank's nose. 'And I tell you this, Frank, I shall never forgive you. Just keep out of my sight, all right?'

He turned away and I saw that his eyes were full of tears. In all my life I had never seen Father cry. That, I think, was the very worst thing for me, knowing I'd reduced my lovely father to tears. I bit hard on my lip, wishing with all my heart that I could turn back the clock. But of course it was too late for that. The die was cast. Father would never forgive Frank, and I would never forgive myself.

Frank and I were married a month later, very quietly, in the village church – the special licence had taken three weeks to come through. I wore a blue silky dress that Mother made for me, and carried a bunch of lilies of the valley picked from our garden. Afterwards we went home and ate iced fruitcake and sipped sherry from the best glasses, which had belonged to my grandmother. And Frank moved into my room, my bed. It was a single bed, so we were very cramped, and I hardly slept. As a new bride, I should have enjoyed lying close; instead I shrank from Frank's hot body, was irritated by his gentle snores, and felt guilty and wretched.

There was talk in the village, of course, conversations that ended abruptly when I passed by, eyes that followed me with curiosity and righteous condemnation. I held my head high and tried not to mind. And worse by far was the way my life was totally changed. I had to give up my apprenticeship at the shop as soon as I started to show, and I missed the company of the other girls dreadfully. Helping Mother with the household chores was tedious, after the variety of the shop, and she was often in a bad humour, snapping at me for not doing things the way she wanted. Sometimes it seemed I could get nothing right, and I was blamed even for things that were not my fault, such as when the wind blew down the prop supporting the washing line and the clean sheets ended up dragging across the muddy garden. 'You didn't push it in far enough,' Mother raged as we washed them again in the big stone sink in the scullery, wrung them out, and put them through the mangle.

She was every bit as snappy with Frank as she was with me, and Father avoided speaking to him at all unless he had to. The atmosphere was thoroughly miserable, and Frank took to spending a good deal of time in 'the cottage'. He got an old wing chair that someone had thrown out, by the look of it – the upholstery was stained with blotches of goodness knows what, and smelled of stale tobacco smoke that had been absorbed by the fibres – and parked it in the front room of the cottage. A couple of days later he came home with an octagonal occasional table with a wonky leg and half the beading missing, and that went into the cottage too.

'Whatever are you doing, bringing that rubbish here?' Mother asked bad-temperedly, and Frank replied that he would like to have somewhere to go in the evenings where he would be out of their way.

'I thought you'd be glad to have me out from under your feet,' he said.

'You can't go in that cottage this weather!' Mother snapped. 'You'll catch your death of cold.'

But Frank had thought of that, too. He bought an Aladdin heater, new, this time, from the hardware shop in Marlow, a black tin chimney-shaped thing with tripod legs, and a can of paraffin. It didn't give out a great deal of heat, but it was enough to take the chill off the air, and each evening when he'd finished his tea – which Mother would plonk down in front of him on the kitchen table so hard that you'd think she would have broken the plate – he'd put on his cap and muffler and depart to the cottage, taking the *Daily Mirror* with him.

Sometimes, if I didn't have any darning to do, I'd go with him – the light in the cottage wasn't good enough to see to sew by. But it was fine for knitting, as long as I wasn't working on a fiddly bit. I had bought several skeins of baby wool and was busy making little matinée jackets and bootees. Some of the best times I had with Frank were in the cottage. I can see us now, him sitting in that old wing chair, hands stretched out at right angles to his body at shoulder height with the skein of wool spread between them while I rolled it into a ball. Away from the bad atmosphere in the house, we were able to talk and laugh like any normal couple. We even made love a few times, there on the old rag rug I'd brought in to add to Frank's furnishings and I quite enjoyed it. Lovemaking wasn't something I'd ever taken to really, and certainly not in our bedroom, where I was always terrified Mother and Father would be able to hear us through the wall. But there in the cottage it was quite fun, a bit of an adventure.

Sometimes, looking back, I wonder if perhaps, under different circumstances, we could have been happy. If we'd been able to get a house of our own, if the war hadn't happened, if I hadn't lost the baby . . . perhaps we could have found some measure of contentment. But it wasn't to be. At that time there was no way we could afford our own home, and the war was coming, whether we believed it or not. And I lost the baby, the whole reason for us being trapped in this unsatisfactory life.

I was six months gone when I miscarried. Six months! The baby was a little boy, so they told me, but they never let me see him. I was left empty and heartbroken and guilty, as if it were all my fault. Frank, however, really didn't seem to care. If anything, I think he was relieved. I couldn't bear it that he could be so unfeeling about his own flesh and blood, and so unresponsive to my distress, and I hated him for it.

I grieved alone, and though it was to be years before the final crunch time came, I honestly believe that it was then that our marriage ended for me. If it had ever begun.

EIGHT

I didn't sleep well last night. I had no trouble at all dropping off – because of the wine, I suppose. I very rarely drink wine, though I do like my glass of sherry or a little tipple of whisky and water sometimes. Wine invariably makes me sleepy, and it certainly did last night. But a couple of hours later I was wide awake, my mind and all my senses buzzing, and after that I only managed to doze. I heard Andrea's alarm go off at five thirty; heard her creeping down the stairs.

She's a good girl, Andrea. I don't know what I'd do without her. She's always been there for me, even when she was a little girl. She could always lift my heart. In those dark days when I first came out of prison, when Gillian refused to have anything to do with me, I was often down. I tried to hide it from her – she was only five years old, after all – but she always seemed to know. She'd stroke my face and pat my hand, perhaps bring me a posy of wild flowers – primroses or campion or what-ever was in season – and she'd say: 'I'm here, Mum. I'm not going to leave you,' with a wisdom far beyond her years. It was a miracle really; I should by rights have been a stranger to her. But somehow we had this bond; we understood one another and the love between us, though never stifling, was as natural as breathing.

It's still that way. We can communicate without words, support one another unconditionally without invading one another's privacy. She never asks me about the past these days; she knows I don't want to talk about it and is content to let things be. I think that she suspects that the version of events that was made public at the court hearing had only a nodding acquaintance with the truth, but I think, too, that she is a little afraid of finding out what actually happened. Well, that's fine by me. There are some secrets I shall take to my grave. The last thing I want is for all that to be raked over again.

To get back to Andrea. I do wish she'd found a nice man and married; she'd make a wonderful wife and mother. But it's never happened. There was a time when I hoped she and Tom, Mary and Geoff's eldest son, would end up together. She was very sweet on him. And there was a young man called Roger, but he was going off to London to join the Metropolitan Police, and Andrea said she couldn't live in London, she couldn't bear to leave her horses, and that was the end of that. I hope it was the truth; I hope she didn't have to give him up because of my prison record. And I hope too that I wasn't the reason she stayed. Glad though I am that she's still here, I'd hate to think I was the cause of her letting that chance pass her by. But there's no doubt about it, her horses are her life, and I can't help thinking that if she'd really loved him she wouldn't have let anything stand in her way. She certainly seems happy, though at the moment she's got her worries. There's talk that the Hall is up for sale, and she's afraid the new owners will want her out of the stables. And she does work incredibly hard. She's up every morning and out of the house by six, winter and summer, seven days a week. I don't remember when she ever had a holiday – well, I do, though it was a good few years ago now. Geoff Hutchins at the farm said he'd look after the horses, with the help of the local girls who come in to muck out and the like for the love of it, and Andrea was supposed to be going to Devon for a week. Two days, she lasted. Went on the Monday and was back on the Wednesday. She couldn't enjoy it, she said, kept worrying and wondering, so she might as well be home.

That's Andrea for you. Doesn't give two hoots about her appearance, ploughs every penny she earns back into the stables; has no other real interests, as far as I know. But she's the best daughter any mother could wish for, and I thank God for her.

I stayed very quiet this morning when I heard her up and about. If she'd known I was awake she'd have brought me up a cup of tea and that would have made her late. As a rule, Andrea's not much of a timekeeper, but she's got a strict routine as far as her horses are concerned, especially on a day when she's got riding lessons booked, and she's got one this morning at ten.

Anyway, I lay low until everything went quiet downstairs, then I got up, put on my dressing gown and went down. The kettle was still warm – Andrea always puts in far more water than she needs. I boiled it up again, made myself a cup of tea and sat down at the kitchen table to drink it. I'd have been more comfortable in the easy chair in the living room, but it's so dark in there. The privet hedge between the house and the road is only a few feet from the front of the house, and it's grown too tall. I used to keep it down, but these days the best I can do is run over it with the clippers to keep it tidy; Andrea gets cross with me if I get up the stepladder to have a really good go at it, and she's probably right to be concerned. One of these days I'll get in a gardener to chop it back, but I wouldn't want too much taken off. If it wasn't there, people walking up and down the road, and going to the shop across the way would be able to look right into the living room.

The kitchen gets the sun in the morning, though; it shines in at the window above the sink, and sends a path of yellow light right across the table. I love sunlight, always have, though I came to value it even more after being shut up in prison for five years.

I'm glad it's a nice day, for Kathryn's sake, if nothing else. After coming all this way it would have been miserable for her if it had been pouring with rain. I wonder if she's up yet; probably not. She'll have a good lie-in, I should think. She looked dead beat when she left last night, hardly able to keep her eyes open. What a nice girl she is, though, doing her best to hide it. And bringing wine too – Gillian's certainly brought her up right.

Thinking of Gillian puts a cloud over the sun for a moment. You'd think after all this time I'd have got used to it, but how do you get used to losing a child? She's a weight round my heart; she haunts me still, and I never stop hoping that maybe one day I'll see her again. But I'm not going to dwell on it, especially today. Kathryn's here, and I'm going to make the most of that.

I'm not sure what her plans are today but I'm going to get some lunch up together just in case. I thought I'd pop some potatoes in the oven to bake and get a half-pound of ham from the shop across the road. She might not come, of course. She might have decided to have a quiet day, exploring. I should think she will come; surely getting to know us is the whole purpose of being here. But she might think coming back this morning would be overdoing it.

I finish my tea and swill out the cup under the tap. I'll make a pot later on, when I have my breakfast, but for first thing I made do with a teabag. They don't taste the same as a good brew left on the hob to keep warm, but I'm getting used to them, and as Andrea says, they are convenient. Then I walk out onto what we call 'the bricks' – the paved area outside the back door – to have a look round the garden. There's not a lot to see now, but my chrysanths are still doing well. I picked a nice vase yesterday to put in the living room – long stems, big yellow blooms – but when Kathryn was here we never got beyond the kitchen. Perhaps today . . .

I love my garden. I never tire of planting things and watching them grow. Funny really. When I was a girl I never thought of gardening myself; that was Father's job. It was when I was in prison that I found out I had green fingers. A gang of half a dozen of us were assigned to help the gardener in the vegetable plot and the nursery, and I loved it. Out there I could forget that my liberty had been taken away, forget Frank and Dev and Gillian and Andrea, think of nothing but nurturing the ground, weeding, hoeing, pricking out seedlings, watching tender green shoots grow and flourish. The sense of achievement, the wonder of it all, has never left me. The peace, undisturbed by anything other than the languid buzzing of a dumbledore, is balm for my soul. I have a pair of robins who come down to watch me work, one of them so tame he'll sit on the handle of my spade, feathers puffed out, beady eyes following me, and I think of the sparrows and starlings and wood pigeons in the prison garden whom I used to envy because they were free to fly away when they chose, soaring up over the old stone walls, not incarcerated as I was.

But long before that I'd learned how much living close to nature meant to me. As a girl, at home in Timberley, I'd taken it for granted. It was only when Frank and I moved to Bristol, a year or so after we were married, that I realised how much I missed it. That was in 1938.

Ever since I'd known him, Frank had worked in the railway sheds as a cleaner, washing soot and coal dust from footplates, polishing brasses bearing the name of the railway company until they gleamed. But that autumn he got the chance of a good lift up, working as a fireman. He was to be working out of the main depot in Bristol, which of course meant that we would have to move there.

When I got over the first shock I was excited and nervous too, and I think Mother and Father had similar mixed feelings. They were glad to be rid of Frank, but they didn't want to lose me, and I think they were genuinely worried about me going off to live in a city with a man they'd never really liked, let alone thought of as a son. Mother, in particular, became very emotional, crying and making me promise to write and come back to see them whenever I could, as if I were going to the other side of the world, not fifteen miles down the road. She even bought me a writing pad, blue lined paper, and matching envelopes, and cried again as she presented me with them.

To make things worse, of course, there was a lot of talk that there might be another war. To be honest, most of what was going on went over my head. Czechoslovakia, which seemed to be the root of the trouble, was a very long way away, and Mother was more likely than not to turn off the wireless when the news came on. 'We don't want to listen to stuff like that,' she would say impatiently, burying her head in the sand, of course, but mostly, I think, because she was frightened. Now, the thought that something awful might be going to happen and I would be far from the nest brought her close to panic.

'You take care,' she said, tears in her eyes yet again as we got ready to leave with our few bits and pieces in Chalky White's taxi for the rooms we'd rented in Bristol. 'If this war comes, I shall be worried to death, you all the way down there.'

'I shall be fine, Mother,' I said. 'And there isn't going to be a war. Mr Chamberlain has sorted all that out.'

Mother sighed. 'I hope so. After the last time . . . we don't want another do like that.'

'And there won't be.'

I was buoyed up with anticipation for the adventure ahead, hoping that in fresh surroundings I would at last be able to come to terms with the loss of my baby – a loss that haunted me still – and that I might be able to forgive Frank for seeming not to share my grief. I even dared hope I'd be able to rekindle some of the excitement of being in love that I'd felt in the early days, before everything had gone wrong. Away from the restrictions of Bush Villa, with a home of our own, anything seemed possible.

As for the threat of war . . .

To my shame, I experienced a *frisson* of excitement when I wondered if the doommongers might be right. Young and naïve and hungry for life as I was, there was a dark romance in the idea of the country facing the dangers of war together, of valour and sacrifice and young men in uniforms marching and fighting and perhaps dying. I had no real conception of the sordid reality, of the deprivation and fear and grief. And anyway, there wasn't going to be a war. 'Peace for our time,' that was what Mr Chamberlain had said, and if you couldn't trust your own Prime Minister, who could you trust?

NINE

It's about a quarter past ten, and I'm dusting round the living room, when there's a knock at the front door. Hardly anyone comes to the front door except for the postman and the milkman; everyone else comes through the garage and across the bricks. I peek round the curtains, but I can't see who's there; they're hidden behind the forsythia bush. I go to the door, pull back the curtain that's there to keep out the draught, and draw the bolts.

It's Kathryn, smiling a little uncertainly.

'Goodness me!' I say, pleased. 'But why ever didn't you come around to the back?'

'I didn't really like to . . .'

'Silly girl! Well, come on in; don't stand out there.'

'Are you sure it's convenient?' But she's following me into the living room.

'Of course it is! It's lovely to see you.' I snatch up the duster from where I left it on the chiffonier, anxious to make everything look nice and tidy.

'I wasn't sure. I went round to the stables, but there wasn't anybody there.'

'No, Andrea's got a riding lesson. I've got a pot of tea on the go. Would you like a cup?'

Kathryn hesitates. 'I'm not a great tea drinker.'

'Coffee, then.'

'That would be nice.'

'It's only instant, I'm afraid. I expect you like the proper stuff.'

'Instant's fine.' Kathryn's looking around, thinking what an old-fashioned room, I shouldn't wonder, with the carved wooden fire surround and the leather-topped boxes each side of the hearth, one for coal, one for wood, and Mother's china shepherd and shepherdess on the mantelpiece. But she's looking at the vase of chrysanths.

'What beautiful flowers!'

'Out of my garden.'

'You grew them? Grandma, you're amazing!'

'Oh . . . anybody could do it if they've got the time.' But I'm pleased, all the same.

We go into the kitchen and I make Kathryn a cup of coffee, aware that we're still very much feeling our way with one another. I wish – I really wish – that I'd been there when she was growing up. That I'd been able to hold her when she was a baby and get to know her through all the stages of her growing up. But regrets are a waste of time. She's here now, that's what matters.

'Are you comfortable up at the Hall?' I ask.

'Absolutely. It's a splendid place.'

I pour myself a cup of tea and sit down opposite Kathryn. The sense of wonder is invading my senses again, that after all these years I am sitting across the table from the granddaughter I never knew I had.

'You said you used to work there,' Kathryn says. 'At the Hall.'

'Yes. When your mother was a baby. I remember gentry living there when I was a young girl, but in the war it was given over to the military to be used as a convalescent home for wounded soldiers.'

'You were a nurse?'

'Not back then. I did train later, and worked my way up to be a sister. But in those days I was what was called a VAD. We did all the menial jobs, polishing floors, emptying bedpans, washing and shaving those that weren't up to doing it themselves, that sort of thing.' I smile. 'And before that, I was an ambulance attendant in Bristol.'

'In Bristol? I thought you'd lived here all your life.'

'I have mostly. It was only a couple of years.' But the catalystic ones. If we hadn't gone to Bristol none of what happened would have happened. Frank and I would have grown old together, I shouldn't wonder, unfulfilled, yet bruggling along as many folk do. I would never have known Dev, known what it is like to be loved, and to love so much. And that I cannot regret. For all the terrible consequences, I would not trade that, even if I could.

'So you went to Bristol to work as a VAD in the war?'

'No, no, we were already there. We went in 1938, with Frank's job.'

Her eyes narrow, almost imperceptibly, at the mention of his name, but she presses on.

'And what was that? Oh, sorry, I don't mean to sound like an inquisition, but I don't know a thing about my family history, and I'd really like to fill in some of the blanks.'

'He worked on the railway . . .' I say, and tell her the story. She's listening avidly, her eyes never leaving my face.

'So where did you live?' she asks. 'Did you have your own house?'

I laugh. 'Not likely! We couldn't have afforded a place of our own. No, we rented some rooms in a house in St Paul's.'

'An apartment.'

'That's much too grand a word for it. It wasn't self-contained, like you'd expect nowadays. Like I say, it was just rooms, off the upstairs landing. And we considered ourselves lucky to have more than one, I can tell you, though we had to share washing facilities and all that sort of thing with the landlady.'

'How awful!' Kathryn looks shocked, as well she might. It must seem like another world to her, and in some ways that's how it seems to me now. It's hard to believe how we managed back then. I certainly wouldn't want to go back to it. But I suppose at the time we really didn't expect anything different.

I can see it all now, though, in my mind's eye, and I remember that, expectations or not, I was pretty soon disenchanted with life in Bristol. With Frank out at work for long hours I was very lonely, and I came to hate seeing him get dressed in his new uniform – a heavy black donkey jacket, khaki-coloured serge shirt, and a cap with a shiny peak. It might not have been so bad if Mrs Hibbert, our landlady, had been friendly, but she wasn't. Or if the house had not been so claustrophobic, but it was. For the first time I realised just how horrible it must have been for Frank in Timberley, having to come home each evening to a house where he was, and always would be, an outsider. No wonder he'd been so keen to take the job in Bristol. It had as much to do with him wanting to get away from my mother and father as it did with his prospects of promotion.

Our flat, as we called it, was in the inner city area, surrounded by other houses and a parade of shops. The front door opened more or less directly onto the street, and what was laughingly called 'the back garden' was no more than a small square of patchy grass, a couple of peony bushes and a misshapen apple tree that no longer bore fruit worth eating. Not that we had the use of it, anyway; it was out of bounds except for Tuesdays and Thursdays, the days I was allowed to hang out my washing on the line that ran from a hook on the corner of the house to a branch of the apple tree. Even then, Mrs Hibbert would watch me like a hawk from the kitchen window, making sure I was keeping to her rules. And once, to my fury, she moved all my carefully pegged-out washing, squashing it onto just a short length of the line, right under the branches of the tree, to make room for some of her own. I was afraid to complain, though. I had the same respect for her as I'd had for Mrs Horton, my old employer, the sort of respect young people had in those days for their elders. But it didn't mean I liked her.

She was a dragon of a woman, stout, with jet-black hair (dyed, I'm sure), Marcel-waved into what looked like a sheet of corrugated iron, and a collection of floral wraparound pinnies that she wore over her skirt and jumper in the house. And she liked nothing better than reminding me in subtle ways that she owned the house and I was merely a tenant. She would come upstairs at any time she chose, stalking along the corridor between our bedroom and living room to attend to an aspidistra that sat in a china pot in the landing window. She kept the key to the bathroom (which we shared with her) in a cup in her kitchen, so we had to ask for it whenever we wanted a bath and return the key to her afterwards. (It was a horrible bath, freestanding on the bare boards of what had once been a bedroom, the enamel chipped and green stains under the cold tap, and the water for it was heated in a gas boiler that stood alongside and then dipped out with a saucepan.) And once, when he got home from a late turn, Frank found the front door bolted. In bed and asleep at the top of the house I didn't hear him knocking, and if Mrs Hibbert heard, she ignored him. Frank had to sleep on a park bench. That was the only time Frank really fired off at Mrs Hibbert. Mostly he was dismissive of my complaints about her and said he couldn't understand why I let her upset me so. Perhaps he found sharing a house with a stranger he paid rent to was easier than sharing on sufferance with his wife's parents who resented him and held him responsible for their daughter's disgrace.

All this, and the change of location hadn't done anything to change the way I felt about Frank as I'd hoped it might, either. I still couldn't shake the awful conviction that I'd made a terrible mistake in marrying him. But I couldn't see what I could do about it. I was trapped in a miserable life with a man I didn't really love.

Then, just when I could see no light whatever at the end of the tunnel, everything changed And the person responsible for all of that was Grace Moxey.

Grace worked in the chemist's shop just along the road from our flat. I used to go in for tins of Gibbs Dentifrice and bottles of aspirin, and I liked to linger, looking at the lipsticks and perfume that I couldn't afford to buy.

Grace and I got friendly, though our circumstances could hardly have been more different. She was single, city born and bred, and lived with her parents in one of the posher parts of town. She was always immaculately made up, and owned a whole wardrobe of fashionable clothes. She could even drive a car – her father had an Austin. I thought she was the most glamorous person I'd ever met; I don't know what she saw in me. Perhaps she was as fascinated by my life as I was by hers. But, whatever, we got on like a house on fire, and soon I was going into the shop for a chat, not just when I wanted something.

We took to going into town together when she had her afternoon off. Because half-day closing was pretty general, most of the shops were shut, but we would look in the windows, and stop in a café for a cup of afternoon tea or an ice cream.

One afternoon in the spring of 1939 when we were enjoying knickerbocker glories in Verrechia's Ice Cream Parlour in Castle Street, our conversation turned, unsurprisingly, to the threatening war.

'You know they're talking about bringing in conscription?' Grace said. 'Does that mean your Frank will have to go in the army?'

'I don't think so. He works on the railway and that's a reserved occupation. I'm not sure he could join up even if he wanted to.'

'Well, we're all going to have to do our bit,' Grace said, unbuttoning her jacket. 'I've already volunteered.'

'You're going to join the Forces?' I was immediately, selfishly, dismayed at the thought of Grace going away.

'Not the Forces, no. They want women to help out in the hospitals. I'm going to go to classes at the Red Cross to learn first aid and home nursing. Mr Barlow is giving me time off work to do it. He says it's his contribution to the war effort.'

Was there no end to the adventure and variety in my friend's life?

'You're so lucky, Grace!' I said enviously.

'You could do it too.'

'I couldn't be a nurse! I don't know the first thing about it.'

'Neither do I. Just because I work in a chemist's shop . . . That's what the classes are for. To teach you the basics. I don't suppose I'll be actually nursing, anyway. Just doing the menial stuff. Though there might be other jobs – driving an ambulance, for instance. There aren't that many women who can drive.'

I was quiet for a few moments, digging ice cream out of the tall glass with a long-handled spoon. Then: 'Where are these first-aid classes being held?' I asked.

'You *are* thinking about it!' Grace sounded triumphant.

'Just wondering, that's all . . .'

'They're at the Red Cross place in Page Park.'

That really meant nothing to me. I was still a stranger in Bristol.

'And when you've trained, where will you go?'

'One of the hospitals. Brenton Stoke, I shouldn't wonder. They're going to build extra wards in the grounds – they've got plenty of space there – to cater for the casualties if there are air raids. Which there probably will be, what with all the aircraft factories here, and the docks . . .'

Grace had finished her ice cream. She got an embossed leather cigarette case and box of Swan Vesta matches out of her bag, extracted a du Maurier and lit it. I sometimes wished I smoked – there was something so sophisticated about a cigarette balanced between scarlet-tipped fingers. But I never had, and I certainly couldn't have afforded to buy cigarettes out of my housekeeping allowance.

'Anyway,' Grace went on, 'I should think it's very likely we'd be sent to Brenton Stoke, which would be quite convenient really since it's on our side of town.'

She looked at me speculatively, wondering perhaps if I had noticed her use of the word 'we'. I had, of course, and excitement was fluttering in the pit of my stomach.

The thought of doing something so different, so challenging, was irresistible, especially since I could justify it as being my contribution to the war effort.

'I'll talk to Frank about it,' I said.

Frank was not enthusiastic, but he didn't veto the idea entirely either.

'What will it cost?' was his first question.

'I don't know.'

'Well, you'd better find out, hadn't you? You can't go spending what we haven't got.'

'I won't. But anyway, this is about more than money. It's about doing my bit.'

I didn't add that I secretly hoped I might earn a small wage if I got a job at a hospital. Frank had his pride; a husband should bring in enough to provide for his family. A wife who had to work was a matter for shame.

'Try to send you off somewhere, will they?' he asked.

'I shouldn't think so . . .'

'Well, I don't suppose there's any harm in you doing the classes,' Frank said doubtfully. 'If you're set on it.'

It was all I needed. I went with Grace to the Red Cross HQ and signed up to take my first-aid and home-nursing certificates. I got a uniform: a blue dress and a starched apron with a large red cross on it, collars, cuffs, and stout black shoes, which, to Frank's disgust, I had to pay for, though I could claim back some of the outlay when I actually started working for the Civil Nursing Reserve. I hardly dared tell him that I was supposed to have a greatcoat, hat and gloves too! But I was very proud of myself when I put it on, and I think Frank was proud of me too.

'You look a treat, Carrie,' he said, pulling me towards him.

'Don't! You'll make it dirty!' I squealed. However thoroughly he washed when he came home from work, there was always coal dust encrusted round his fingernails.

'If you're going to be looking after people who've been

blown up by a bomb you'll have a lot worse than a bit of coal dust on your apron,' he said, and kissed me.

Again I wriggled away, recoiling inwardly. I really didn't like kissing Frank any more, and I couldn't understand why I'd enjoyed it so much in the beginning. It had been a novelty, I supposed, strong arms round me, the scent of a man and the feel of his body pressed against mine exciting my senses. No more. Now Frank's attentions were a duty to be endured, and I was glad that mostly he came to bed too tired to do anything but fall asleep.

Pleased as I was with my new uniform, I was less pleased that seeing me in it made him feel skittish.

'Don't you dare,' I said as he reached for me again. And closed the door firmly after me as I went into the bedroom to change into my well-worn skirt and jumper.

I started work at Brenton Stoke Hospital soon after that, and wondered why I'd bothered to learn the rudiments of nursing and why I was still attending classes and reading every nursing manual I could lay hands on. All that was required of me was fetching, carrying and charring, as the new wards were set up in readiness for the expected air-raid casualties.

The building work was nearing completion, prefabricated wards that were only expected to last about ten years, but there was a thick layer of dust everywhere, and the floors were filthy with mud from the workmen's boots. No matter how often I scrubbed and polished, there were still patches I'd missed, and the matron, on one of her tours of inspection, would tell me they must be done again. There were beds to be pushed into place, lockers to be lined up beside them, curtains to be hung. There were endless boxes of equipment and medical supplies, all of which had to be ticked off on an inventory, and there were blackout blinds to be tacked to the windows.

I was already familiar with the difficulty of blacking out effectively; I'd helped Frank nail lino over the windows of Mrs Hibbert's rooms as well as our own, and as she had bay windows in her front room we'd had our work cut out. I hated how dark it made the rooms too. At least at the hospital it was proper blackout material, which could be taken down in daytime to let some sunlight in. As I stood on a chair, however, my arms aching from the weight of the material that I'd seemed to be holding in place since the beginning of time, I wondered just what I'd let myself in for.

Grace, of course, was spared all this. She was still working at the chemist's and only coming out to the hospital in her spare time. And she'd managed to get on to the list of ambulance drivers too. She'd already been tested and passed as competent, and was looking forward to the new challenge.

Like the beds, the ambulances were all ready, large saloon cars that had been converted by cutting off the back of the bodywork and fitting a canvas cover that would roll up from the back to allow casualties to be loaded in. They were housed in corrugated iron shelters in the hospital grounds; each day as I passed them, I would eye them longingly. If only I could drive an ambulance! But I couldn't, and there it was. And at least if the war came, I'd be doing my bit. I wouldn't be a glorified charwoman and builder's labourer indefinitely.

In my stupid naïvety, I began to wish that something would

actually happen. It seemed we'd been going on in this state of expectation and uncertainty for ever, making preparations, circling round Hitler like small boys in a playground threatening to fight, yet reluctant to strike the first blow.

And then, almost taking me by surprise, it began. Hitler had invaded Poland, the British and French ultimatum to suspend the attack ignored. At 11 a.m. on 3 September the Prime Minister made the formal declaration.

England was at war.

TEN

When I look back on the autumn and winter of 1939 and the spring of 1940, the thing I remember most is the feeling of anticlimax. We had expected the air raids to begin as soon as war was declared. Sandbags were piled up around the city hall and sticky tape crisscrossed over windows. We took our gas masks everywhere we went, slung over our shoulders in little carrying bags, and practised putting them on and trying to breathe normally — not easy, when the face mask felt so claustrophobic and the strange rubbery smell turned your stomach. Children had been evacuated from the cities, food and petrol rationing had begun. But nothing happened.

At the hospital, instead of being full of purpose and excitement as I'd expected, the days stretched endlessly. I was tired of washing floors in empty wards, and when I was occasionally sent over to help out in the two wards of the main hospital that were still in use for cases of pneumonia, minor operations or the casualties of street accidents, I was not made welcome.

The ward maids there were very jealous of what they considered their territory and looked down their noses at the civil nursing auxiliaries. 'Neither use nor ornament,' was how they described us, and any chance they had they'd go running to Sister, or even Matron, with drummed-up complaints about our shortcomings.

It was through these secondments that I first encountered Dev – or Dr Devlin, to give him his proper title. And it was far from being an auspicious meeting.

One of the regular ward maids was off sick with a heavy cold and I was assigned to help her partner, Lily, with the morning routine, which meant pulling out all the beds from one side of the ward into the centre, cleaning the walls and floors thoroughly, and then pushing them back again.

We were about halfway down the ward when an entourage swept in through the double doors: Matron, portly and imposing in pin-tucked grey poplin and a starched white cap, a white-coated doctor and a couple of fresh-faced students.

'Oh my Lord, they're doing their rounds and we haven't finished!' Lily exclaimed. 'Look sharp and help me get these beds back where they belong.'

In my haste, I didn't notice that my bucket was behind me. I stepped back, caught the handle of the mop with my hip, and water went everywhere. It could have been a scene from a hospital comedy film, but to me it felt like a nightmare.

'What do you think you're doing?' Matron had turned an unbecoming shade of puce.

'I'm sorry, Matron . . .' I was vainly trying to stem the flow, which was swirling in a soapy lake around my feet.

115

'She looks like King Canute, only without his throne!' The accent was unmistakably Irish, the tone amused. I raised my eyes from Matron's highly polished shoes, now just inches from the flood, to an angular face and dark hair. The eyes, sparkling with humour, were startlingly blue.

He was laughing at me, making the two students at his heels snigger. It was more humiliating even than Matron's cold fury. I wished the ground would open up and swallow me.

Christmas came, and as yet, no bombs, no fire and brimstone. But when Frank and I went to Timberley for Christmas Day, Mother did her best to get me to move out of Bristol. She resorted to her usual tactics of trying to steamroller me with a combination of bossiness and concern for my welfare that amounted to emotional blackmail – 'I can't sleep for worrying about you, Carrie. If you won't think of yourself, think of me, making myself ill. Do the sensible thing and come home.' But the new life I was leading was giving me the confidence to stand up to her.

'I'm sorry, but I'm staying, Mother,' I said firmly, and hoped I would be as assertive with Lizzie, Frank's sister. We were going to visit her next day, and I had always found her intimidating.

We travelled to Somerset by train – working on the railways, Frank could get concessionary tickets. As we disembarked in Hillsbridge the engine was taking on water from a tank at the far end of the platform, steam escaping in noisy bursts, and I felt inordinately proud. 'My Frank does that,' I wanted to say, and for the first time in ages I took his arm.

It was a long, uphill walk to the miner's cottage where Lizzie and Walter lived. Frank tapped on the door and opened it. A small scullery led into a tiny living room. Saucepans bubbled on trivets over the open fire, and steam that smelled of boiling cabbage wafted up amongst the Christmas cards, which had been hung like washing on a line across the room.

Lizzie greeted Frank warmly, and gave me a curt nod. She no more approved of me than my parents did of Frank. She thought I'd trapped him into marriage and had even once intimated that she doubted there had ever been a baby at all. Walter, on the other hand, was always nice to me, but then Walter was nice to everyone. He was a gentle little man with hands veined black with coal dust and mild blue eyes. He kept homing pigeons and sang with the male-voice choir when he wasn't underground. But at home he was very much under Lizzie's thumb.

'Nice to see you, m'dear,' he said. 'Are you going to have a glass of port?'

'I don't know how much there is left,' Lizzie said, throwing him a cross look. She hadn't intended to share her bottle of port with me, I guessed.

'I'm sure there's enough for Carrie to have one. And what about you, Frank? A nice drop of Teacher's?'

'If you can spare it.'

'Course I can! If you can't have a drop of Teacher's at Christmas it's a poor show. And when it's gone, it's gone.'

He poured whisky for himself and Frank and port for Lizzie and me, and raised his glass. 'Cheers! Happy Christmas.'

Lizzie was pointedly ignoring her drink, fiddling with saucepans, and I took only a couple of sips, then set my glass down. I wondered if Lizzie would pour it back into the bottle when she cleared away.

We exchanged presents. We'd got soap for Walter and a miniature bottle of perfume for Lizzie, luxuries we could ill afford. Frank always made do with the cake of Lifebuoy, and I never bought perfume for myself, though I did have a tiny bottle of Evening in Paris that Mother and Father had given me one birthday, and which I eked out by saving it for special occasions. To Frank's delight, his present from Lizzie and Walter was a packet of cheroots, a rare treat, but when I tore the paper from my present I discovered a voluminous cotton pinafore.

'Thank you,' I said, feigning gratitude.

'I got it at the church bazaar,' Lizzie said smugly. 'Mrs Higgins makes them. The minute I saw it, I thought, that's just the thing for Carrie.'

'She's got starched aprons now,' Frank said proudly. 'She's joined the Red Cross and she's working as a nurse.'

Something of an exaggeration, but at least it took the wind out of Lizzie's sails for a minute.

'Good for you, Carrie!' Walter said, but Lizzie, recovering herself, threw me a black look.

'I hope you're not neglecting your husband.'

'Course she's not,' Frank said, beaming. He always seemed totally unaware of his sister's antagonism towards me.

'Nor nursing soldiers. All sorts goes on between nurses and patients, I've heard,' she continued, unabashed.

'What are you on about, Lizzie?' Walter asked, turning a little pink.

Lizzie jerked her chin in my direction.

'She knows.'

'I've yet to nurse anyone,' I said with as much dignity as I could muster.

'I'm going to have one of these cigars,' Frank said. 'Would you like one, Walter?'

'Don't mind if I do . . .'

Things became a little easier, but I could tell from the expression on Frank's face that Lizzie had put something in his mind that he hadn't thought of before. And he didn't like it one little bit. Frank always did have a very jealous streak.

New Year, and still no patients for our wards. We were being found all kinds of odd jobs to keep us occupied. I remember washing down the paintwork of the window frames and doors, outside as well as in, and a messy job it was too as the hospital was surrounded by trees and the white paint was thick with a winter's green slime as well as bird droppings. Dr Devlin came by whilst I was doing it, with Mr Hobson, one of the surgeons who came to Brenton Stoke twice a week to operate, and pointed to my bucket of water.

'Better watch out. She's a devil at causing a flood,' he joked to Mr Hobson.

I coloured and bristled, hating him for making fun of me. But at the same time, he fascinated me. There was something about that lilting accent that was irresistible, something behind those very blue eyes that suggested he was a bit of a rogue.

It was the same whenever our paths crossed. He would make some cheeky remark, I would flush with embarrassment and resentment. But afterwards I couldn't stop thinking about him.

And then another disaster occurred, one that was to change everything.

One of the ambulances had been used overnight to collect the victim of a street accident – a man who had been knocked down crossing the road. With vehicle headlamps half blacked out it was an all-too-common occurrence. But for some reason the crew had not got round to cleaning it last night, and since I had nothing better to do, I was sent to do it.

I wasn't best pleased. I'd been using the time to read some of the manuals that Kath Devonish, a second-year probationer, had loaned me, and practising my bandaging skills on a life-size doll that I'd found in one of the lumber rooms.

A big grey Buick had been left outside one of the shelters. It had been raining last night; the bodywork and windscreen were mud-splattered and there were muddy footprints as well as blood in the interior. I cleaned it inside and out, refolded and stowed the blankets, checked over the equipment, gratified to realise how familiar I was becoming with paraphernalia that had been a mystery to me just a few months ago. Finally I climbed into the cab to dust the dashboard – and noticed the keys had been left in the ignition.

I don't know what got into me then. I certainly never intended to try and drive the thing, but for some reason I was tempted to turn on the engine. It throbbed to life, and the chassis pulsated around me, and for a mad moment I pretended I was Grace. I depressed the clutch, fiddled with the gear stick, and, I suppose, bore down on the accelerator pedal without realising it. Before I knew what was happening, the ambulance shot back with a jolt, there was a horrible crunching noise and the engine cut out.

I went cold; my stomach spasmed. I sat for a moment, anchored by pure fright, then climbed out to inspect the damage. Miraculously the ambulance had jolted straight back and the wings were untouched. But the roof had run into the shelter, bringing down a section of guttering. I went cold all over again, icy shudders that made me feel sick.

And from behind me a voice with an unmistakable Irish accent said: 'And what in the world have you done now?'

'I don't know what happened! All I did was . . .' My voice tailed away. There was no way I could excuse myself or explain.

'You're not working for the Jerries, by any chance, are you? You certainly seem to be doing a fine job sabotaging our war effort all by yourself.'

He was laughing at me again.

'You're a fine one to talk!' I snapped furiously. 'The Irish aren't even on our side!'

Ireland had chosen to remain neutral. It was something of a sore point with a lot of English people. His eyes levelled with mine.

'So what do you think I'm doing here?'

'Spying, for all I know.' It was a stupid thing to say, but I was beyond caring. I was cornered, and my instinctive reaction was to hit out.

He threw back his head and laughed.

'What's so funny?' I snapped. 'I suppose you'll report me now for that, too . . .' My eyes lighted again on the damaged canvas cover and the piece of guttering hanging drunkenly from its rivets, and my chin wobbled as the shock and shame surged through me in a hot tide.

'I'll have to think about that.' He leaned in at the driver's door and retrieved the keys. 'Come on, Nurse. Come with me.'

He was going to haul me straight to Matron.

'I was only trying to clean the cab,' I said desperately.

'Ah, you'll have to think of a better excuse than that.' But the twinkle was back in his eyes. 'And it seems to me you'd do that better after a nice cup of tea.'

I stared at him.

'Hot sweet tea for shock. Have they not taught you that yet in your first-aid classes?'

'But . . .' I gesticulated helplessly at the damaged ambulance and shelter.

'We'll sort that out later. That shelter is too small for the Buick — whoever left it to go inside is clearly to blame. And keys in the ignition . . .' He sucked breath between his teeth. 'Now, do you want that cup of tea or not?'

I hesitated. Drinking tea when I was supposed to be working was probably further grounds for disciplinary action. But I did feel very shaky, and he was a doctor, only one rung down the ladder from God in the hospital hierarchy. I went with him.

At this time of day the canteen was all but deserted. We collected mugs of tea and Dr Devlin carried them to a corner table. 'I'll take them. We don't want any more accidents, do we?' he said. I followed him, feeling an utter fool.

'So, Nurse Chapman, what made you volunteer to flood wards and crash ambulances?' he asked, his eyes teasing me over the rim of his cup.

I pulled a face. 'Why do you have to keep going on about it?'

'Because you've made my day more than once. But I can see it's a bit of a sore point, so I promise not to mention it again. Provided . . .' that wicked twinkle '. . . you tell me what I can call you besides Nurse Chapman.'

A sharp twist of surprise; a voice warning me of danger ahead. And an unexpected thrill of excitement, the thrill of the forbidden, and all the more potent for that. Suddenly I felt ridiculously skittish.

'Well, you could call me Mrs Chapman.'

'Sure, don't I know that? What I'm asking is, what goes between the "Mrs" and the "Chapman"?'

'Caroletta,' I said. No one ever called me that – I was Carrie to everyone – but I wished they would. Carrie was a plain name for a plain little country girl. Caroletta was someone entirely different, brave and free, glamorous and romantic.

He looked surprised. 'That's not a name you hear often.'

'No. My mother's Aunt Edith was in Italy – she was lady's maid to the daughter of a countess. Edie suggested it when I was born, and my mother liked it.'

'Ah,' he said, 'that explains it. You're something of a dark horse, Caroletta. Now, if I'm going to call you Caroletta, you can stop calling me Dr Devlin. My name is Patrick, but my friends know me as Dev. Though it might be wise to stick to the "Doctor" when Matron's around.'

The twist of excitement spiralled again, and with it a twinge of unease. Though Dr Devlin was clearly a practised flirt, it wasn't something I was at all used to.

'I think it might be,' I said faintly. 'I'm in enough trouble as it is.'

He sipped his tea, holding the cup between his hands. Nice hands, I could not help but notice. Broad, strong fingers, nails cut short and straight. Very clean, not ingrained with coal dust as Frank's were.

'What were you doing anyway, trying to move the ambulance?' he asked.

'I wasn't . . . I just wanted to see how it felt . . .'

'Do you drive?'

'No, but I wish I could. I can't think of anything I'd rather do than drive an ambulance.'

He considered. 'You could always put your name down to be an attendant, though. At least that way you'd be riding beside the driver.'

'Could I do that?'

'Why not? If you've done your first aid.'

'Oh, I have. And I'm still studying every chance I get.'

'Apply, then. I think they're fully staffed at the moment but you never know when a vacancy may crop up. Set your sights on what you want, Caroletta.'

For a blissful moment the dream seemed almost within my reach. Then reality hit me, depositing me unceremoniously back on earth. 'They're not likely to look kindly on someone who damages an ambulance and demolishes the roof of a shelter when all she's supposed to be doing is cleaning the blooming thing.'

'Oh, I shouldn't worry about that.'

'That's easy for you to say. It's not you in the firing line.'

He grinned, looked at his watch. 'Time to get back to work, Caroletta.'

'Time for me to go and own up, you mean.'

'Not a good idea.' He got up, picked up his cup and saucer. 'Just leave it to me. I'll sort this one out for you. Get off with you now. And try to behave yourself, for today at least.'

I went. I hadn't the first idea how he was going to explain the damage I'd caused, but I thought that with his charm, and in his position, he could probably get away with almost anything. I could well imagine he had Matron eating out of his hand and if I was lucky I might just escape a wigging.

Considering my narrow escape, I was feeling decidedly upbeat. Dr Devlin's suggestion that I should become an ambulance attendant had given me a goal, the prospect of something to aspire to and work for, which filled me with optimism. And it wasn't only that. Having him flirt with me had made me feel young and attractive, something I hadn't felt in a very long time. I guessed it was his way to talk to all the women as he'd talked to me, but that really didn't matter, any more than it mattered that I was married and shouldn't be flirting at all. What harm could there possibly be in sharing a cup of tea if it made me feel this good? It wouldn't happen again, I'd make sure of that, but for the moment I was enjoying the way my world had opened up, if only for a brief moment in time.

ELEVEN

I put in my application to become an ambulance attendant the very next day. But for all my good intentions it wasn't so easy to forget the way Dev had made me feel when he'd flirted with me. Or, indeed, to stop thinking about him at all. He crept into my thoughts at the unlikeliest moments like a compelling tune that plays repeatedly on a turntable inside your head, and a prickle of excitement would shiver over my skin and a dark excitement surge deep inside me. When our paths crossed, he might give me a sly wink, or make some outrageous remark, and I would feel as if I were blushing from head to toe, though I'm sure I was not. Fortunately I didn't have the sort of fair skin that reddens so easily. But although I did feel dreadfully guilty about my secret 'crush', as I thought of it, I still never imagined for a moment that things would go any further. Dev was an impossible flirt, his banter nothing but harmless fun, and I was enjoying it for what it was. That was all there was to it. But I think I knew, all the same, that I was enjoying it all too much. I was playing with fire, and it scared me a little even as it thrilled me.

Much later, Dev told me he'd had similar misgivings, and been taken by surprise when he'd realised just how much I'd come to mean to him. 'I always liked a bit of fun with the girls, married or single, but I'd never let it go any further than that with the married ones. Why would I? I'd no wish to wreck anyone's marriage – or get meself beaten to a pulp by some angry husband. In fact, I'd no plans to get involved with *anyone*. I was too fond of my freedom to fall in love. Or so I thought. But you . . . I couldn't get you out of my head, Caroletta. Nothing mattered but you. And when it came to that, it frightened the life out of me, I can tell you.'

And that, I suppose, is the way it was for both of us. The fun became serious slyly, like a thief in the night. And by the time we were aware of it, it was much too late to walk away.

When did the warning bells begin to ring for me? When I looked at Frank and really, truly regretted marrying him; not just the nagging dissatisfaction but a fully formed thought? That if I were single, maybe I could be with someone who made me feel the way Dev made me feel?

When Peggy Denham, one of the VADs, mentioned that it was obvious Dev fancied me? Though I told her not to be silly, I couldn't deny the warm glow of elation that coursed through me, wondering for a moment if it might be true, before the familiar guilt kicked in.

When Frank told me he wanted me to give up my job, because he was fed up with me not being there when he got home from work, and the violence of my reaction took me by surprise?

The desolation that swept through me at the prospect of having to quit nursing made me feel the bottom was dropping out of my world, and it was only later that I realised: it wasn't giving up nursing that would be such a devastating loss, it was the thought of not seeing Dev again.

But the moment when I truly realised that I was on the cusp of something far more than an innocent flirtation came when Dev caught up with me one day in the sluice and asked me if I had heard the news.

I dumped the bedpan I was cleaning, and swivelled round. 'What news?'

He was leaning against the counter, hands in the pockets of his white coat, grinning enigmatically.

'Ah, no doubt I should leave it to your boss to tell you.'

'Tell me *what*? Oh, come on, you can't keep me dangling.'

'Well, Caroletta, I think you're going to be an ambulance attendant. If you still want to, that is . . .'

'Oh my goodness!' I clapped my hands over my mouth, tasted soap and disinfectant, and hurriedly removed them again. 'You're teasing me!'

'Would I do that? No, one of the girls is a mobile VAD. She's off to a military hospital on the east coast, and I've recommended you as her replacement.'

I was hopping up and down and squealing with delight.

'I take it you won't be turning it down, then?'

'As if!'

He pushed himself away from the counter, laid a finger on my lips.

'Don't get too excited now, or you'll have Sister in here

128

wanting to know what's going on.' His finger traced a path to the corner of my mouth, lingered in the dimple there. 'And no more trying to drive the damned thing either,' he said, turned, grinned at me from the doorway, and was gone.

I was shaking with tumultuous joy that my dream was about to come true, and something else, something that had leaped in me at his touch. In a daze I put my own finger to my mouth, gingerly, as if I were touching hot coals, and ran it down the same path that he had traced.

I think I knew then, if I had not known it before, that for me at least, this was far more than the flirtation I had pretended it was. I wanted more, much more. Somewhere along the way, a line had been crossed, and it was time for me to draw back. I was set on a very dangerous path; this foolishness had to end here and now. But oh, I didn't want it to! I didn't want it to end at all!

May 1940. Suddenly the war that had seemed so distant and unreal took on a new and frightening immediacy. Denmark and Norway had been invaded, Holland and Belgium surrendered. The British Expeditionary Force were encircled on the French coast. At the beginning of June a huge fleet of vessels comprised of anything that could sail took part in Operation Dynamo, and crowds waving Union Jacks were waiting on the south coast to cheer home the thousands of soldiers who had endured days of bombing and machine-gun bullets as they huddled on the beaches of Dunkirk. Within days, the Nazi swastika was flying from the Eiffel Tower and the Arc de Triomphe, a week or so later the French had signed an armistice, putting half of their country under occupation.

We knew what that meant for us, of course. If the bombers could use French airfields, they would be well within flying distance of targets that had been out of their range before. And Bristol, not only a major port, but also the home of several aircraft factories, was certain to be within their sights. It was rumoured that even before war had broken out, German reconnaissance planes had been over, taking aerial photographs of the sites at Filton and Yate, both of which were practically on our doorstep.

Mother wrote frantically, telling me I must come home to Timberley, and even Frank urged me to go whilst I still could. But of course I defied them both. Nothing on earth would have persuaded me to leave Bristol. For the first time in my life I was independent, doing a job I loved. I felt fulfilled and purposeful; I even enjoyed the aura of danger to be faced, the frisson of sharp fear and the adrenalin pumping through my veins when the siren wailed like a banshee. I felt alive; nothing would have induced me to go home to the tedium of rural Gloucestershire, even though it would have taken me away from the temptation that was Dev.

But harsh reality was about to kick in. The strange hiatus in which we had been living was about to explode into death and destruction.

Our war was about to begin.

I had been transferred to the role of ambulance attendant at around the time our ill-equipped troops were landing in Norway. We worked in three shifts, eight hours on duty, eight hours on standby – which meant reporting in if the siren went off, which it sometimes did, even though in those early days it was always a false alarm – and eight hours off. Sometimes at weekends we worked an extra shift, so that every so often we had a whole weekend free.

Later, when the bombing started in earnest, there were also four men on each shift whose job it was to pull victims from the rubble, and a 'sitting case' car to carry those with minor injuries. But in the early days it was often just Grace and me in the Ford V8 she had been assigned to drive.

With the escalation of the war she had given up her job at the chemist's, and she managed to persuade the superintendent to let us team up. It was lovely to be able to resume our friendship, even if our long girlie chats were over a bare Formica-topped table in the canteen instead of in cafés and restaurants.

My new status also meant I saw a great deal more of Dev. It was perfectly acceptable for doctors to socialise with ambulance crew, and quite often he would drop into the rest room or canteen when we were there and sit chatting whilst he drank tea and chomped his way through a sandwich containing whatever sparse and tasteless filling the staff had been able to lay their hands on. It was all perfectly innocent – in fact he no longer seemed to flirt with me as he once had – but given my new awareness of my feelings for him I found it disconcerting, though I couldn't help but be fascinated to learn more about him.

His home, it seemed, was County Leitrim – a place I'd never heard of. He'd graduated from medical school in 1936 and decided to try his luck in England because it was nigh on impossible to find an appointment in Ireland.

'Ah, they had it all sewn up,' he said, grinning ruefully. 'In Ireland, medicine runs in families. Practices pass from father to son, and I was an outsider. There'd never been a doctor in our family before me. My father was a schoolmaster and not nearly grand enough to have any friends in the medical fraternity. They can be very full of their importance, don't you know, doctors. You're either one of them or you aren't, and I didn't help myself either. I couldn't be sucking up to the great and good to get my foot on the ladder. So I crossed the Irish Sea, and I've been here ever since.'

'In Bristol?' Grace asked.

'Sure.'

'So I might have filled one of your prescriptions!' Grace dimpled at him. She'd taken quite a fancy to him herself, and often flirted outrageously. 'I worked in a chemist's shop until I took up ambulance driving.'

'And what about you, Caroletta?' he asked, including me in a conversation that could well have left me even more of an outsider than Dev had been in the tight-knit Irish medical community. But it was not a question to which there was much of an answer.

'Carrie was a housewife,' Grace said.

'Ah, I'm sure she was more than just that. My mother is a housewife. But she does all manner of things besides. She has hidden depths, my mother.' Dev was giving me one of those narrow, secret looks that made a nerve twist in my stomach.

'Oh, Carrie is an open book,' Grace said, and for the first time since we'd become friends, I was annoyed with her breezy self-confidence and ready answer for everything.

'And why did you call her Caroletta?' she asked archly.

My irritation spilled over.

'Because it's my name,' I said.

The first raids on Bristol and the surrounding area were more of a nuisance than anything else. The sirens would sound and we would go into full operational mode. In the hospital, baths would be filled to the brim in case the water supply was lost, and nurses scurried about the wards making sure the bedridden had their gas masks to hand, and grey ARP blankets to cover their heads and shoulders if the windows should shatter. At home, people had to leave their beds or half-eaten meals to seek shelter, and production of vital equipment in the factories ceased as workers evacuated the premises that might well be chosen for bombardment. Everything was disrupted day after day, night after night, but the planes that came could have been counted on the fingers of two hands, sometimes just one, and more often than not they missed their target. Two people were killed by a bomb that landed on Lower Maudlin Street, in the city, but that was outside our area, and we were not called to attend. Truth to tell, I was a bit fed up about that. All the action seemed to be passing me by.

Throughout July and August it was the same. Sometimes the aircraft that flew over were reconnaissance planes, and though they dropped the odd bomb when the opportunity arose, they were mostly wide of the mark. The docks at Portishead were attacked a few times, but again, that was well outside our area; the Bristol Aeroplane Company at Filton was obviously high on the list of installations the Luftwaffe were anxious to put out of action, but apart from a hit from a lone bomber that damaged the roof of the Rodney Works they didn't achieve much, and there were no casualties, apart from the He III itself, which was shot down over Dorset on its way home, we later heard.

And then on a perfect day towards the end of September came the raid we'd expected, but begun to believe would never happen.

It was approaching midday, and Grace and I had taken a couple of grey ARP blankets and spread them out on the grass out of sight of the hospital to make the most of what was left of summer. I was lying flat on my back, staring up at the ivory castles of cloud in the deep blue of the sky and enjoying the warmth of the sun on my face when the siren began to wail, and moments later the air was reverberating with the low drone of aircraft engines, instantly recognisable as German bombers. They emerged from the biggest cloud, an arrow formation, sparkling like a jewelled brooch in the sunshine.

We were already on our feet when we heard the whistle of bombs and, moments later, the boom of the first explosion, no more than a couple of miles away. The aeroplane works was being attacked again, and this time the Luftwaffe meant business. The blue sky was now mottled black, as if a cloud of gnats had swarmed in, and even at this distance the noise of the falling bombs and the crack of the anti-aircraft guns at the post that had been set up to protect Filton was deafening.

Adrenalin pumping, we went into the hospital to await instructions.

'This is going to be bad,' Grace said over the jangle of the ambulance bell.

There was a haze over the sun now, thick, acrid smoke that stung my eyes and burned in my throat. A gas main had been hit and the flames from it leaped up into the sky, an awesome inferno. The streets were scattered with broken glass and chunks of debris, and the roofs had been blown off some of the houses. But the aircraft works had taken the brunt of it – this time the enemy bombers had been right on target – and that was where we were headed.

The planes had gone now, skedaddling for home before our boys could arrive on the scene. After the first breathless hush it was the fire engine and ambulance bells that created a crazy cacophony of sound, along with the occasional explosion as a delayed bomb went off. Nearing the perimeter fence of the aircraft works, we passed a green open space known locally as 'the polo field'. Tramping stoically across it in the direction of the road were two small boys. Grace screeched to a halt and wound down the window.

'Where the hell do you think you're going?'

'Home, miss.' The older boy, maybe seven or eight, brushed his hand across a solemn freckled face, leaving a track of fresh dirt where his fingers touched.

Both boys, I could see now, were filthy, their shorts and pullovers mud-splattered, wet tidemarks extending from their sodden socks and sandals almost to their knees. The younger boy's arms were covered with what looked like nettle rash, and he was close to tears.

'You shouldn't be out in the open!' Grace scolded them. 'There's a raid on – they could come back. Where have you been?'

'Just playing down the polo, miss. When the planes came we scarpered and Joe fell in the nettles. And then we hid in the tunnel, but it's a bit of a mess down there.' He looked anxiously down at his mud-caked legs and feet. 'Our mam's going to kill us.'

'Go straight home, do you hear?'

She pulled away again but we had gone hardly any distance when the world caved in. A huge explosion rocked the ambulance. Clods of turf and mud-brown earth flew through the air like enormous hailstones, thudding into the chassis and splattering on the windows. Grace jammed on the brakes, jolting to a sudden halt and for a moment we sat rigid with shock, our ears ringing with the reverberations of the exploding bomb. Then the same thought occurred to both of us.

'Those kids . . . !'

We leaped out of the ambulance and ran back along the road. The smaller of the two boys was lying face down close to the wire fence but at first I could not see his brother. Then I spotted him. The force of the explosion had tossed him through the air like a broken toy; he was crumpled and unmoving against the trunk of a tree. Somehow we scrambled over the fence. Grace went to the small boy and I ran across the open ground to the older one, my heart in my mouth.

He was still breathing, but I could see, even before I checked him over, that he was very badly injured indeed. I glanced back at Grace; the smaller boy was sitting up now, looking miraculously unharmed.

'We're going to need a stretcher here,' I called.

'OK,' she called back.

I kneeled beside my patient, clearing mud from his airways, checking him over again. His breathing was shallow and ragged, and I didn't like the look of him at all. Then his eyes fluttered open.

'Joe? Where's our Joe?' he managed.

'It's all right. He's fine. Lie still now. Don't try to move. We're going to take you for a ride in an ambulance. Can you tell me your name?'

'Ted,' he whispered. Then his entire body tremored in a series of spasms, his jaw clenched and unclenched, and his eyes rolled back so that only the whites were visible.

Grace was back, heaving the stretcher over the fence and scrambling over herself after it. Together we rolled Ted onto the stretcher. Against the six-foot-long canvas he looked very small, and his freckles were an angry brown rash against the parchment of his face. Joe was still sitting beside the fence, too shocked to cry, but gazing in horror towards his brother. We took a moment to check him again, and try to reassure him, then addressed the problem of how we were going to get the stretcher to the ambulance, given that the fence was an insurmountable barrier.

'Is there a gate in this damned thing?' Grace asked.

'Has to be somewhere.' But we couldn't see one.

Bells jangled, loud, fainter, louder again as the sound carried up the main road. It sounded like a fire engine. We laid the stretcher down on the grass and I scrambled over the fence and ran into the road, waving furiously.

For a moment I thought the fire engine would mow me down; it lurched to a stop just feet from me.

137

A fireman I recognised as Reg White, who in another life delivered mail to our house, leaned out. 'What's up?'

'We need help.'

'So does half Filton.'

'It's a child. He's badly hurt. We can't get the stretcher over the fence on our own.'

The word 'child' had the desired effect. Men of assorted ages and sizes piled out to help. Two firemen climbed the fence and between them passed the stretcher to two more on the roadside. Then they hoisted Joe over, and Grace and I lifted the canvas cover to allow them to slide the stretcher inside.

'That's a couple of Harry Broadribb's kids,' one of the firemen said. 'We'd better try to let their mother know what's happened.'

Grace had the engine running, and I climbed into the back of the ambulance.

The couple of miles back to the hospital seemed endless, then we were pulling up at the main entrance, the canvas was rolled back and willing hands unloaded the stretcher. A porter swung Joe up into his arms; I watched as they disappeared inside, and only then realised I was shaking, not just my limbs, but a deep-seated tremble that came from deep inside me.

'Come on, Carrie, we'd better go.' Grace sounded calm and purposeful, cheerful almost, and I marvelled at her composure. Perhaps because I was the one who had tended Ted, I somehow felt totally responsible for him, and I was very worried that though I had done my best it would not be good enough.

Overhead the sky was clear blue, broken by nothing more ominous than fragments of lacy cloud. No enemy planes, not even any of our own, the locally based fighters, which had scrambled too late to save us.

Death and destruction had come on a perfect September day, and for those of us involved in the rescue operation it was not over yet. Beware of getting what you wish for, they say. I'd yearned for excitement, and it was turning sour in my stomach. I'd wanted to be an ambulance attendant, and I'd got my wish. Now, shaken and sick at heart though I was, there was work to do.

I have no idea how many times Grace and I drove back and forth to the Filton aeroplane works that afternoon; truth to tell I never even began to count. A hundred and thirty-two people had died in the raid, I heard later, ninety-one of them workers at the aircraft factory, where the air-raid shelter received a direct hit. They were not our responsibility – bodies had to be collected by the mortuary van, if there was enough left of them to be taken to a mortuary. But there were more than three hundred injured and they had to be taken to the hospital or one of the first-aid posts for treatment. Grace and I worked non-stop, just one of a fleet of ambulances that had been deployed from all over the city, ferrying casualties with injuries more horrible than I had imagined in my worst dreams.

It was late afternoon before things slowed up a little and we waited as the tons of rubble were cleared in case someone was, by some miracle, still alive beneath it. Then, weary, sick at heart, our uniforms filthy with dust and stinking of smoke, blood and vomit, we headed back to the hospital.

TWELVE

The woman was gaunt, round-shouldered, wearing a floral patterned dress and shapeless cardigan, with a scarf tied turban-fashion to cover her head. A bang of dark hair escaped to swirl over her forehead. She was weeping.

I had seen dozens of people weeping today, milling around the perimeter of the stricken factory, and smoking much-needed cigarettes as they waited for news outside the hospital. But this one was pushing a little boy in a broken-down pushchair that he had clearly outgrown years ago, a little boy in mud-splattered grey shorts and a pullover, whom I recognised instantly.

Joe Broadribb. My heart contracted. Clearly he was all right, though not up to walking far, but Mrs Broadribb's obvious distress did not bode well for Ted.

As we cleaned out the ambulance – no mean task – I kept wondering how young Ted was, picturing him and his brother tramping stoically across the field, filthy but unhurt, hearing his rueful: 'Our mam's going to kill us!' And in grim contrast, the same little boy lying badly injured in my ambulance. A boy who had gone out to play on a sunny September morning and been caught up in a nightmare.

I shouldn't let it get to me, I knew. But I couldn't help it. I'd been prepared to deal with whatever came my way, but in my imagination the casualties had been grown men and women, not a child with a cheeky grin whom I'd spoken to minutes before the unthinkable happened.

The hospital, which only yesterday had been quiet and ordered, resembled a battleground. Every bed in the new wards was now occupied and more patients lay on trolleys in the corridors. Nurses scurried back and forth tending to them, porters trundled beds, orderlies squeezed through the mayhem with stacks of fresh linen.

'I'm going for a cup of tea,' Grace said. 'My throat is like sandpaper.'

Mine was burning too, raw from dust and smoke, and the stench of burned flesh, a little like roasting pork, had lodged in it so it was not just a smell but also a taste. But I couldn't even begin to wind down until I had found out what had become of Ted.

I went in search of Rose Dixon, the nurse who had greeted us when we brought him in. I found her in the room that had been designated for treating less serious injuries and waited while she dressed a deep gash on a man's hand. When she turned, thrusting the receptacle of blood-soaked gauze and wadding at me as if I were still an orderly, I took it without a word. She had more important things to do than dispose of spent dressings, and I wanted a moment of her precious time.

'The little boy we brought in this morning,' I said as the patient swung down from the treatment couch and went on his way. 'How is he doing?'

For a moment her face was blank; she'd treated so many people today they had all blurred into one, I supposed.

'Ted Broadribb,' I said. 'Nine or ten years old. Internal injuries, I think.'

'Ah, yes.' Her face cleared. 'He didn't make it.'

It was what I'd expected from the moment I'd seen the weeping woman who I guessed was his mother, but the confirmation hit me all the same like a hammer blow.

'Oh, no!' I wailed.

Her jaw tightened, the impatience of the experienced – and overworked – nurse with a raw amateur.

'You'll see a lot more like him before this is over. Put it behind you and get on with the job.'

She was right, I suppose, but I couldn't see it like that and I hoped I never would. I didn't want ever to be so dismissive of the death of a child, even if it made me a better nurse. Hot tears were burning behind my eyes; my head was bursting with them. Tears of fatigue and anger, tears for a little boy lost in a war that had nothing to do with him. I turned away before she noticed them, blindly picking my way back along the cluttered corridor to the 'dirty room' where I dumped the soiled dressings in the waste-disposal bin. Then I leaned against the big stone sink, bowed my head, and let the tears come, hot rivers running furrows down my dirt-encrusted cheeks.

'Caroletta?' Dev's voice. I gulped, trying to regain control of myself. 'Are you all right?'

'Yes, fine, I'm just . . .' I didn't dare turn to face him, didn't want him to see my tear-streaked face and swollen eyes. But my voice, thick as black treacle, would have given me away and before I tensed my shoulders rigid he must have seen them shaking.

'What's the matter?'

I didn't want to tell him. Dev was a professional, like Rose Dixon. He would have as little patience with my inability to remain detached as she had been.

'Come on, Caroletta, tell me about it.'

His voice was kind, concerned, and it was my undoing. I swivelled round, covering my face with my hands, and before I could stop myself it was all pouring out.

'He was just a little boy, full of mischief,' I finished miserably. 'Oh, I know I'll be no use to anyone if I fall apart like this, and you must think me a complete fool, but—'

'I don't think anything of the sort,' Dev said. 'We none of us forget the first patient we lose, and we never get used to it, whatever the hard nuts might have you believe. You just have to learn to deal with it.'

'I can't,' I said passionately. 'I never will. Not a child . . .'

He put his arm around me in a way that was more brotherly than flirtatious.

'What you need right now is a good strong drink,' he said.

I tried to smile. 'Chance would be a fine thing. A cup of tea is all I'll get.'

'With a drop of the hard stuff in it.'

There was something strangely comforting about the return to the old, irreverent Dev, with his teasing Irish eyes.

'I don't drink,' I said.

'You haven't lived then. Come on now, come with me.'

'I can't go anywhere like this . . .' I was scrubbing at my face with the heels of my hands, certain that the tracks of my tears were still there in the grime for all to see.

'And can you tell me who's going to be looking at you?' He shook his head. 'Women! We're only going next door, anyway.'

Next door. His office. I'd never been inside it before, never had cause to, though through the open door I'd glimpsed a big old desk piled high with patients' files and shelves of what I assumed were medical books. As I followed him in I realised just how small it was, scarcely bigger than a cupboard. Besides the desk there were just two chairs, a metal filing cabinet and a hand basin protruding from the wall beneath the window. Dev pushed the door shut; behind it his jacket, brown and fawn tweed, hung on a hook. In all the time I'd known him I'd never seen him wearing anything but his white medical coat.

'Sit yourself down, now.'

He crossed to the filing cabinet, opened a drawer and pulled out a bottle of whiskey that was hidden there. 'This'll do you the power of good. There's nothing like a drop of Jameson to pick you up when you need it.'

I was shocked. 'You drink on duty?'

'Only a nip now and then when things get rough. Do you really think I'd breathe whiskey fumes all over my patients, and Matron too? Not a drop will pass my lips before I've finished for the day. But you're off duty now, and this is what

I prescribe as a pick-me-up. Well, that and a cigarette. But I don't suppose you smoke either.'

There was a mug on the desk amidst the tangle of files and paperwork, a white mug decorated with a frieze of dancing leprechauns. He took it to the sink, rinsing it clear of coffee dregs. 'See, I'll even let you use my own special cup.'

'I don't want it. Really.'

'No arguments.' He poured some whiskey into the mug and passed it to me. 'Come on now. But you'd be wise to just take a sip if you're not used to it.'

The smell of it wasn't too bad. I'd expected my stomach to turn the way it always did at the smell of brandy. But then, Mother had always given me brandy for the very purpose of making me sick if, as a child, I needed to be, and I suppose I associated the smell of it with that. I sipped, felt the whiskey burn my throat, and spluttered. But I rather liked the river of warmth that followed its path to my stomach. I took another sip, and another.

'Better now?'

I nodded, and without asking me first, Dev leaned over and replenished my mug.

'I don't want any more!' I protested.

'Doctor's orders. You've had a baptism of fire, Caroletta.'

'But I shouldn't fall apart like this.' Tears filled my eyes again. 'I just don't know if I'm cut out for this, Dev.'

'Sure you are. Don't be putting yourself down. You've the makings of a fine nurse, Caroletta, and you wouldn't be worth your salt if you weren't upset by what you've seen today. But you're not going to fall at the first hurdle. You've more in you than that.'

'I certainly hope so.' I bit my lip, and for a little while we sat without talking whilst I sipped my whiskey and slowly pulled myself together. The images of the day were still clear in my mind, the sadness at the tragedy of a little boy lost no less moving, but there was a certain calm now in the silence that had fallen between us, and a comfort in the sense of experience shared. I could feel, too, the stirrings of a determination to overcome my desire to run away and hide, and instead to do whatever I could for all the other men, women and children who would need my help before this war was over.

After a while, Dev reached over and touched my hand. 'OK now?'

His fingers were resting on mine. I nodded, looked up, and as our eyes met something sharp and sweet twisted within me. Suddenly I was as aware of his touch as if he had been conducting hundreds of volts of electricity into me. Breath caught in my throat; all I wanted was to have his arms around me, to feel his lips, warm and alive, on mine, to burrow into him and forget the horror of the day in the closeness of him. And for an insane moment I thought I saw my own longing reflected in his eyes.

I got up, too quickly, and my head spun.

'I must go. Frank will be wondering what on earth has happened to me.'

Mentioning Frank's name was the best way I knew to break the spell, and something unreadable flickered in Dev's face before he said, sounding concerned: 'Are you all right to get yourself home? I'd take you, but . . .'

'You've got work to do. I'll be fine.'

I had to get out of there. Another minute and I'd make a complete fool of myself, betray the feelings I was beginning to realise were spiralling out of control.

'Try to get a good night's sleep,' Dev said.

'I will,' I said — though I doubted it. 'Thanks for the drink. And for listening to me.'

A corner of his mouth lifted. 'My pleasure.'

He opened the door for me. I did not look back as I walked away down the corridor, but somehow I knew that Dev was standing in the doorway, watching me go, and the knowing was a warm place inside me that nothing — not the traumas of the day nor my guilt at my own dangerous yearning for a man who was not my husband — could touch.

'Where the hell have you been?'

I'd let myself into the house and managed to get upstairs without encountering Mrs Hibbert; very often when she heard my key in the lock she appeared like a vengeful wraith from her own living room, as if I had no more business in her house than an intruder. But I couldn't escape Frank.

'We've had a terrible day. There was a bad raid . . .'

'It's gone eight o'clock. You were due off at two.'

'I couldn't leave. There were dozens of casualties . . .'

'I've had no tea. There was nothing in the cupboard.'

'Oh, for goodness' sake, Frank! I had a job to do.'

'You're my wife. That's your job. And look at the state of you! Carrie, I don't want you doing this.'

'Maybe I don't want to do it any more. Not after today. But I'm going to.'

'Even if you worry me to death?'

A pang of guilt that I'd resented his belligerence.

'Well, I'm here now.'

I went to put my bag down on the table, misjudged it. It toppled onto the floor, spilling everything out onto the rag rug. I groaned and dropped to my knees to pick it all up and Frank got down to help me. Then he rocked back onto his heels, glaring at me accusingly.

'You've been out drinking!'

'No, I—'

'Don't lie to me! You stink of it!'

'Dev gave me a little nip of whiskey, that's all.'

'Dev? Who's Dev?'

'Dr Devlin. I've told you about him.'

'Not that you go out drinking with him.'

'I haven't been out drinking with him. I was upset and he—'

'Shut up, Carrie. I don't want to hear any more of your lies.'

I could have done without this just then.

'And I don't want to talk to you. How can you be so horrible, Frank? I've had a dreadful day and I'm tired and—'

'Drunk.'

We were still on our knees, shouting at one another. Mrs Hibbert would be rapping on the ceiling of her living room any minute. She did that if we made too much noise. I tried to get up, too quickly, and went dizzy. I staggered, felt the sofa behind me, and sank into it, bumping against the arm.

'I think you'd better go to bed, Carrie,' Frank said grimly.

'I can't go to bed. I've got to get you something to eat.'

'You're in no fit state. I'll have some bread and cheese. Go to bed, for goodness' sake. I'm sick of looking at you in this state.'

He yanked me up, propelled me across the landing into the bedroom and left me there. I got out of my filthy clothes, piling them in a heap in the corner, pulled on my nightdress and got into bed. It was almost completely dark except for a tiny pearl of fading daylight on the ceiling above the window. The blackout curtain had come loose from one of its tacks; we'd have to fix that tomorrow or we'd have the air-raid warden knocking at the door and giving us a roasting.

The events of the day were all around me, a thick, miasmic cloud of snapshots and emotions. Torn and mangled bodies. Heaps of rubble. Clods of flying earth. A little boy lost. Grief. Fear. Exhaustion. The selfless bravery of the rescue squads. A woman in a headscarf weeping. Frank yelling at me. Dev.

I tried to catch the feeling of safety in the eye of the storm that I'd felt in his office, wanting to hold on to it as a drowning man might cling to a piece of driftwood. But it was all spinning away from me in the suffocating darkness.

I must have slept because the next thing I knew the bed was dipping and I felt the heat of Frank's body next to mine.

'Carrie?' he said softly. 'Are you asleep?'

He was reaching for me, wanting, perhaps, to build bridges across the chasm between us. I lay perfectly still, keeping my breathing deep and even. I didn't want him to touch me. I didn't want him to make love to me. If you could call what he had in mind 'making love'. I didn't want him. I wanted . . .

Frank retreated to his side of the bed and it was all I could do not to sigh with relief. We might not be yelling at one another any more, but the gulf between us had never been deeper.

THIRTEEN

When the first night raid on Bristol happened on the evening of 24 November, I was on duty.

The preceding weeks had been reasonably quiet, and although the siren frequently had us on high alert, the raids had been limited to pirate attacks with nothing like the devastating results of that first attack on Filton. But heavy losses were causing the Luftwaffe High Command to rethink their tactics. And so they came under cover of darkness, targeting the docks and the railways, and destroying much of the historic old city in the process.

That night is etched in my memory in shades that resemble Dante's Inferno, orange and scarlet and vermilion, the most violent of electric storms against the pitch-black of the sky, night turned to hellish day. And through the flames, all haloed with clouds of smoke, the crumbling skeletons of church spires and rooftops, tottering, collapsing like a pack of cards. The incendiaries came first, whining and squealing, then the heavy bombs, each explosion reverberating in the still air like the roar of a hungry beast. And all the while the drone of dozens of enemy aircraft, that low, menacing hum that was instantly distinguishable from the sound of our own aircraft engines.

I remember the smell, high explosives and burning rubber, the choking dust, the grit that thickened our eyelashes to a heavy fringe and snagged in our hair.

I remember the way my heart raced, the tightness of fear in my chest, the adrenalin that surged through my veins, prickling like nettle rash on my skin. And tiny snapshots locked in time. A woman's leg, wearing a sensible shoe, protruding from the rubble – when it was dug out, there was no body attached to it. A volunteer fireman having to be forcibly restrained outside his house, because he believed his family were still inside. A gas main exploding, sending flames shooting skyward as if it were an erupting volcano. It was the stuff of nightmares, yet somehow none of it touched me in the way that the death of little Ted Broadribb had done. It was as if what I'd felt that day had somehow immunised me to the worst of what was to come. Nothing would ever have quite the same impact on me again.

And I remember Dev, working like a Trojan amongst the battered and bloodied casualties we brought back to the hospital.

Since the evening of the Filton raid, when little Ted had died, and I had finally acknowledged the depth of my feelings for Dev, I had done my best to avoid him wherever possible, and I suspected he might be doing the same. He no longer stopped by to chat with Grace and me, there were no more sly winks or saucy banter, and whenever our paths crossed he was quick to hurry away on some pressing business. He was very busy, of course, even though extra doctors had been drafted in, but

I couldn't help feeling there was more to it than that, and it made me cringe to think that I might have laid bare the way I felt about him and made him wary. Though nothing had really happened at all, I couldn't help feeling I had made an utter fool of myself, and I castigated myself for being careless enough to stray beyond the boundaries of the harmless diversion into much more dangerous territory. But still he was constantly in my thoughts and whenever I clapped eyes on him something happened to my heart. Telling myself it was wrong and had to stop made not the slightest difference.

It didn't help, either, that Frank was being nicer to me. Perhaps he felt guilty about yelling at me that night when I'd had such a dreadfully upsetting day; perhaps the fact that I'd admitted to having a drink with a doctor had given him pause for thought. Whatever, he had seemed to be making an effort, snapping at me less and even giving me a kiss and a cuddle before he left for work and when he came home, if I was there. For a long time he had reserved gestures of affection for the times when he wanted it to go further; now he might even come up behind me when I was cooking, or washing up, put his arms round my waist, and nuzzle me. Whenever he did it I cringed inwardly, but tried very hard not to show it. I wished he would leave me alone and that made me feel guiltier than ever and very depressed, because I realised now that I'd made a dreadful mistake in committing myself to a lifetime of regret, trapped in a marriage with a man I did not love.

I'd discovered feelings I'd never dreamed I could have, a magic that could sing silently in my soul, however wrong I knew it to be.

But I never thought for a moment that Dev might feel the same way. And even if I had, I would have told myself nothing would ever come of it.

And then March 1941 happened and everything changed. Act One was over, Act Two about to begin.

February had been a reasonably quiet month. Bad weather had put a stop temporarily to night raids, though the pirates still came by day, but as the weather improved, so the night attacks intensified again. We had been very busy, as Parnall Aircraft at Yate was being targeted, and Yate fell within our area of responsibility. But on the evening of 16 March, I had a much-needed night off duty.

Frank was away, I wasn't sure where. He was very secretive about certain trips, which probably meant they were carrying some sort of defence supplies from the local factories to the south coast. I made myself supper, sausages that I'd queued for ages for at the butcher's, and powdered potato, Pom. I listened to the wireless for a bit, and decided to have an early night. The long shifts had been taking their toll on me, and you never knew whether what sleep you could get would be disturbed by an air raid.

I was dead to the world when the siren sounded. The bloodcurdling wail crept into a pleasant dream, then, as I surfaced through thinning layers of unconsciousness, I recognised that it was real. I threw back the blankets, shivering as the chill air shocked my warm skin, and reached for the warm jumper and slacks that I'd left within easy reach on a chair beside the bed. I'd never got into the habit of sleeping fully clothed, and generally, if the siren hadn't sounded by about nine o'clock one could expect a quiet night.

There was a cellar beneath Mrs Hibbert's house, accessed by way of the forbidden garden. Mrs Hibbert always sheltered there when the Luftwaffe came, taking her budgie, Joey, in his cage with her, and if Frank and I were at home we did the same. Uncomfortable as I was in her company, it was a better option than going to a crowded public air-raid shelter, and closer to our bed when the planes went away. I never went to the cellar via her kitchen, though, and she had never suggested I should. Though it was by far the shortest route, the kitchen was her private domain and she didn't like me so much as setting foot in it – peculiar, really, since all over town people left their front doors wide open so that perfect strangers could take shelter if they were caught out in a raid. But that was Mrs Hibbert for you. So I always let myself out of the front door and went along the passageway at the side of the house.

As I emerged from the front door that night the sky was already alive with flares and the first incendiaries were falling, their piercing whine rising in a crescendo before they landed randomly. I ducked back into the hallway as one came whistling down and landed in a sunburst of flame on the roof of a house on the opposite side of the road.

Close! Much too close for comfort! I watched for a few moments, mesmerised by the speed with which the fire took hold. The ARP warden, Bill Higgins, must have been in the vicinity; he came running, his tin hat bobbing along the top of the hedge that bordered our front garden like a boat on the ocean, yelling instructions.

'Get that fire out! It's a bloody beacon! Call the brigade! Who's got the stirrup pump?'

For an officious bully who liked to play the hard man he sounded in a blue funk. I couldn't imagine he'd have much luck with getting the fire brigade, either. Given the number of incendiaries that were falling they were going to be stretched to the limit and it would be first come, first served.

More incendiaries fell, some hitting targets, some landing harmlessly in allotments or on patches of waste ground, excavating craters and burning out. But enough buildings were ablaze to turn night to day, not grey or golden daylight, but the strange vermilion illumination of a world gone mad.

The air was throbbing now with the heavy engines of approaching bombers; time to make for the cellar. I pulled the door shut behind me and dived round the side of the house. The cellar door was open; I ducked through and inched gingerly down the stone steps into inky blackness, surprised Mrs Hibbert hadn't lit the storm lantern as she usually did.

'Are you there?' I called.

I could hear Joey, the budgerigar, tweeting furiously, but from Mrs Hibbert there was no reply.

I descended the last step, steadying myself against the rough stone wall of the cellar, and my foot encountered something that yielded beneath it. I shrank back as if I'd trodden on a hot coal, tested it again with my toe, and heard a low groan.

Carefully I edged down the last step until I was standing on solid concrete. My eyes were beginning to adjust to the dark now, and when I turned my head the flickering light from the flares and the fires allowed me to see that it had indeed been

Mrs Hibbert I'd almost trodden on. She was spread-eagled at the foot of the steps, Joey in his upturned cage a few feet away from her.

I felt my way between the garden implements to the shelf where the storm lantern and a box of Swan Vesta matches were kept, and got the lantern going. I righted the bird cage, and Joey, seemingly none the worse for his precipitate descent into the cellar, scrabbled up the bars to his perch where he fluffed his feathers and twittered indignantly. But Mrs Hibbert lay still and unmoving.

By the light of the storm lantern I examined her as best I could, doing all the things I'd been taught. I had a problem finding her pulse at first and thought she might be dead, then, relieved, I felt a faint thready tick beneath my fingers. Her other arm was twisted beneath her and I was pretty sure it was broken at the wrist, but most seriously she was still unconscious. Either she'd struck her head when she fell, or something had happened to cause her to fall, a stroke, maybe, or a heart attack – I had no way of knowing. Either way, she was as much in need of medical attention as the victims of the bombing.

I swore to myself, a word I'd heard Frank use, but not one that was usually part of my vocabulary. It wasn't going to be easy getting an ambulance to her with a heavy raid like this going on, but I had to try. The fact that I was an attendant myself might help me to swing it.

I could hear bombs falling as I climbed the steps, loud thuds, but not that close. The nearest telephone box was two streets away; I rarely used it since, apart from Grace, nobody I knew had a telephone. If I walked it would probably take me six or seven minutes, but I had no intention of walking in the middle of an air raid. I was going to run! I scooted along, keeping as close to the garden walls and hedges as I could.

The house on the opposite side of the road that had been hit by the incendiary was well alight now; it didn't look as if Bill Higgins had been successful in getting a fire engine to attend, and his stirrup pump had been of little use either. The family who lived there, a little man with a false leg, his wife, and their three daughters, all spinsters in their thirties or forties, were out on the pavement surrounded by what possessions they'd managed to drag out. They, too, had a bird in a cage, and what looked like a goldfish bowl rested on top of an occasional table.

I made it to the telephone kiosk, but no matter how I jiggled the receiver, I couldn't get a dialling tone. Perhaps the lines were down. As I was weighing up which first-aid post would be the nearest to run to, I heard a wave of bombers coming over again. I didn't fancy being out in the open, but staying in the telephone box wasn't a good option either: if the panes shattered there'd be glass flying everywhere. I pushed open the door and rolled under a bush in a neighbouring garden just as the first bomb came whistling down, again far too close for comfort. I squeezed my eyes tight shut and pressed my hands over my singing ears, waiting for the inevitable explosion that would follow, wondering if my last moment had come.

The boom, when it came, was ear-splitting and the ground trembled beneath me, reminding me, bizarrely, of the cake-walk at the travelling funfair that used to visit Marlow twice a year. Once, as a child, I'd worn holes in the palms of my gloves because I'd stayed so long on that shuddering, shivering bridge. As the reverberations became echoes I thought I could hear the rumble and slither of falling masonry, low thunder amid the cacophony of more bombs falling. They were further off now, though still too close for my liking, but definitely going away over the city, and the crackle of anti-aircraft fire started up, lacing the dark, smoke-filled sky with tracers of lightning.

I scrambled out from beneath the bush, wondering what had been hit. I had a horrible feeling that the closest explosion had come from the direction of our street. Well, at least the emergency services would be here in force in a few minutes; no need now for me to race off to a first-aid post to get assistance for Mrs Hibbert. I started back the way I had come, a wary eye on the sky; there could yet be another wave of bombers.

The closer to home I got, the stronger the nauseating smell of the bomb became, and the air was thick with dust and grit, stinging my eyes and catching in my nostrils and throat. Then, as I rounded the corner and our street came into view, I stopped short, at first disbelieving the evidence of my own eyes.

The front of our house – an end of terrace – was more or less intact, but there was a peculiar hollowness about it. Light shone through shattered windows and torn blackout curtains like ghostly will-o'-the-wisps skittering behind the dead eyes of a corpse. It might have been a cardboard stage set, realistic but insubstantial.

Shock seemed to stall my heartbeat and turn my stomach to molten jelly. I had seen plenty of bombed-out houses before, but nothing had prepared me for this. I stood in my own street, gaping at the ruin of my own home, breathing in the pulverised minutiae of my own life, numb and robbed of coherent thought. Then reason returned with a rush and all I could think of was Mrs Hibbert, unconscious in the cellar when the bombers had come.

People were milling about on the pavement, blocking the gateway. I tried to force my way through them and was intercepted by Bill Higgins.

'Clear the way now!' He spread his arms wide like a signpost. 'Everything's under control here. There's nothing to see.'

'I live here!'

'You can't go in there. It's all going to come down in a minute. Clear the way now!'

'Mrs Hibbert—'

'She'll have gone to the shelter.'

'She has not gone to the shelter! She's in the cellar.'

He opened his mouth to argue, then his piggy features registered alarm, the same panic under pressure I'd been almost amused by earlier. Now it made me furious. The man was just not up to the job. Parading around in a uniform was all he was good for.

'Mrs Hibbert is in the cellar,' I repeated. 'Oh, for goodness' sake!' I tried to push past him again but he was having none of it. His authority had been questioned and the ignominy of it returned him to his officious self.

'Just leave this to us, miss. Help needed here, men!' he called.

Three or four burly chaps in battledress separated from the crowd and Bill Higgins stood aside to let them through. Before he could stop me, I slipped past, following them.

In the passageway along the side of the house it was almost possible to believe nothing had happened; the moment I turned the corner into the back garden the full scale of the disaster became evident and shocked me all over again. The rear of the house had come down like a pack of cards: roof tiles, beams, masonry, all piled together in a tightly compressed heap from which clouds of dust rose like smoke. Within the shell of what remained, bits of floors jutted out at crazy angles, pieces of furniture clinging precariously, sliding and crashing down at irregular intervals along with showers of plaster and grit. When I moved, glass crunched under my feet, and I was treading on goodness knows what else – fragments of linoleum, soot from the chimney, which had been filleted open from top to bottom, feathers, fabric, smashed china. The entrance to the cellar was buried beneath it all and though the men set to work at once, tearing at it with picks, shovels and their bare hands, it was clear the Rescue and Demolition team with their heavy lifting gear would be needed before we could reach Mrs Hibbert.

In retrospect I'm sure it was not long before they arrived; then, waiting, with beams shifting and debris falling in showers like April rain, it seemed like a lifetime. Each new collapse ran shock waves through me, but the silences between were almost worse, the tension of waiting for the next rumble almost unbearable. The front wall and the section of the side of the house that was still standing was clearly unstable; as Bill Higgins had said, it could collapse at any moment. And there was always the risk that a gas main had ruptured and gas could be escaping into the cellar.

I retreated to the end of the garden, perching against the

low stone wall with my arms wrapped around myself, shivering from shock and the bitter cold of the night. I didn't want to get in the way of the rescue operation, and I didn't want Bill Higgins to evict me. I felt I owed it to Mrs Hibbert to be here, and in any case, where would I go? Some community centre where they would give me weak tea and a blanket, I supposed. It was not an appealing prospect.

The R & D people arrived with their hoists and, a little later, a lorry with a search lamp and small generator. I could see little now of what they were doing; they had erected a tarpaulin over the lamp to keep it from showing to any more bombers that might come over. But I stayed where I was, only walking the breadth of the garden and back again every so often to keep the blood moving in my cold limbs. Two girls in tin hats and the uniform of the Red Cross arrived – the designated ambulance crew – but I didn't recognise them and guessed they must be from one of the city stations. They didn't notice me in the dark at the end of the garden, and after a few minutes they left again, presumably having been told it would be some time before the casualty was brought out. And still I waited. From time to time I checked my watch, though time had ceased to have meaning, and counted off the slow minutes to one hour, one and a half. The two girls returned, and this time one of them saw me. She came down the path, her little torch picking out the cracks and crumbling holes in the paving stones.

'Hello. What are you doing here?' Her cut-glass delivery reminded me of Grace, or rather, a parody of Grace, who, although well-spoken, had not, as far as I knew, attended a finishing school or ladies' academy.

'I'm waiting for them to get into the cellar.' My jaw was set with the cold, so my voice sounded tight as a ventriloquist's dummy.

'Is the person who's trapped a relative of yours?'

'No, my landlady. I live – used to live! – up there.' I jerked my head in the direction of what had been the upper floor of the house.

'Oh dear. Poor you. But at least you're in one piece. And I'm really not sure it's a good idea for you to be here if it's not your mother or something who's in there. Things could get nasty again, you know.'

'Yes, I do know. When I'm on duty I do the same job as you. Well, I'm an ambulance attendant, anyway.'

'Oh, right. Goodness me.' Her tone was warmer, friendlier, one colleague to another.

'I think I should be here, someone Mrs Hibbert knows, if she's still alive when they bring her out.'

'Yes. Right. There's nothing like a familiar face . . . You're frozen, though. How long have you been out here in the cold? I'll see what I can find for you . . .'

She marched off, stoically picking her way through the debris, and returned with an ambulance blanket and a flask of tea.

'This might help.' I threw the blanket around my shoulders, shrinking into the scratchy warmth, and she poured tea into the plastic beaker and passed it to me. 'So how come you weren't in the cellar too?'

Between sips of tea I told her what had happened, and realised just how lucky I had been. If Mrs Hibbert hadn't fallen, if I hadn't gone for assistance, I, too, would be under tons of rubble, and no one any the wiser.

Time was passing more quickly now; I was no longer checking the minutes off on my watch. And the danger of another attack seemed to be passing too. For a long while there had been no more enemy aircraft overhead, and apart from the occasional boom of a delayed-action bomb exploding and the shrill tinkle of an emergency vehicle bell, the city seemed to have fallen quiet.

It was after two when the R & D men finally managed to free Mrs Hibbert. Unbelievably, apart from the thick layer of dust that blackened her face and clotted in her hair, she looked almost exactly as she had when I'd shone the storm lamp onto her earlier. And, even more miraculously, she had regained consciousness, though she was rambling and incoherent.

They had hoped to have a doctor in attendance, Ginny, the Red Cross driver, had told me, but it seemed he had been delayed somewhere and it was decided to transport Mrs Hibbert to hospital as a matter of urgency.

The ambulance was larger than the one Grace and I manned, a converted van. As we loaded Mrs Hibbert in, she suddenly became lucid, gripping my wrist feverishly.

'Joey . . . Joey's down there . . . You must get him out, Mrs Chapman! I can't go without Joey . . .'

'Who's Joey?' Ginny asked, obviously worried someone else was trapped.

'Her budgie.'

'A budgerigar! We can't take a budgerigar in the ambulance.'

'I can't go without Joey!' Mrs Hibbert was becoming very distressed.

'Can you hang on a minute?' I asked Ginny.

164

I ran back round the passage; to my amazement the rescue men had already found Joey, still tweeting furiously and fluttering about in his cage. He seemed totally unharmed by his experience.

'It's all right, we'll look after him,' one of the neighbours promised, and I was able to go back and reassure Mrs Hibbert that her bird would be taken care of until she was in a position to reclaim him.

I went with her in the ambulance to the city hospital, waited whilst she was examined and admitted. By the time I came down the flight of stone steps again, the sky was beginning to lighten, pale pink streaks of dawn in a deep grey sky. A flight of pigeons swooped low over the battle-scarred city, a single cloud that was in reality a pall of black smoke hung low on the horizon. I was utterly exhausted; beyond wondering how I was going to let Frank know what had happened, where I was going to go, what I was going to do. And I was due back on duty in a couple of hours' time.

I'd recently taken up smoking; most of the girls did, and it helped pass the time whilst we were waiting for the siren, as well as going some way to calming frayed nerves. Now I felt in my bag for my cigarettes and book of matches, leaned against the wall, once protected by iron railings, now bare but for the piles of sandbags, and lit one, drawing the smoke deep into my lungs. It made my head spin, and my mouth tasted vile. I dropped the cigarette and ground it out with the toe of my shoe.

The feeling of aimlessness was like a drug, making my limbs heavy and clouding my every thought in a thick woolly haze, and the prospect of walking the several miles to Brenton Stoke was a dreadful one. But I doubted there would be any taxis or buses at this hour, and in any case, I had no money for one. Everything I owned was buried in a pile of rubble. I wondered vaguely whether I would be in hot water for losing my uniform, stupid in retrospect, but I had become used to having to account for every bit of kit and was still very much in awe of the powers that be.

There was a telephone box on the corner; without much hope, I felt in my coat pockets. And, glory be! My fingers curled around a handful of loose change. I heaved open the door of the telephone box, praying that I would be able to remember Grace's number. When I tried to think of them, the digits kept muddling themselves up in my head, but − another miracle − when I inserted my fingers into the little hollowed-out circles of the dial they somehow seemed to know what my brain had forgotten. The phone was ringing, ringing interminably. Then a man's voice answered, sounding anxious. 'Hello. Moxey residence. Mr Moxey speaking.'

I pressed Button A, my precious coins fell.

'I'm really sorry to bother you so early,' I said. 'But please could I speak to Grace?'

I lit another cigarette as I waited. Grace had said she would come and pick me up, that I shouldn't even try to start walking. The tobacco still tasted strong and bitter, but I persevered this time, smoking it down to the cork tip so that my fingers trembled uncontrollably against my lip.

When a Humber pulled up at the kerb I took no notice; I

was looking out for Grace's father's Austin. Then I heard someone calling my name.

'Caroletta!'

It sounded like Dev, I thought; I must have fallen asleep right there, leaning up against the wall. And then, unbelievably, there he was, leaping out of the car, leaving the door swinging open, crossing the pavement towards me with long loping strides.

'Don't you know how to worry a man half to death!'

'Dev! What are you doing here?'

'Well, come to look after you, o' course! Grace gave me a call the minute she heard from you. Oh, Caroletta, Caroletta, I can't let you out of my sight for a minute, can I, without you get yourself into a pickle.' Reassuringly, it was his old, jovial banter. He steered me to the car, installed me in the front passenger seat.

'By Jesus, look at the state of you! You could be one of those little lads they used to send up the chimneys in days gone by.'

I looked down at my trousers, filthy and scagged at the knees, at my mired shoes that were depositing pulverised plaster, mud and leaves from the garden on the carpet in the well of his car. 'What a mess! I'm sorry . . .'

'And so you should be! I'll set you to work with a dustpan and brush, just see if I don't.'

'Oh, Dev . . .' I was perilously close to tears.

'Ah, get on with you!' And suddenly he wasn't joking any more, but deadly serious. 'You're in one piece, my darling, and that's all that matters. Now I'm to take you to Grace's home, so you can get a hot bath and a rest.'

It dawned on me suddenly that Frank didn't yet know what

had happened, and might return to find the house in ruins and me missing. 'I must let Frank know,' I said, in some agitation. 'He's been away since yesterday . . .'

'I'm sure you can make a phone call to his place of work from Grace's home.' There was an edge to Dev's tone, and I felt suddenly, inexplicably, that I'd offended him in some way.

'Thank you so much for coming to get me,' I said, as if to make up for it.

'Old Nick himself couldn't have stopped me.' Dev was silent for a moment, then he gave me a sideways glance. 'When I heard your house had taken a direct hit I thought I'd lost you, do you know that? I pity the poor souls I've been treating tonight with you on my mind.'

We were driving through the city, bumping over craters in the road and a flood like a river that bubbled from a burst water main, past landmarks reduced to rubble and sections of terrace left standing like a single canine left jutting from an old man's toothless gums. It was an alien landscape, a world gone mad.

But there was a warm place inside me that nothing could touch. Though I had lost everything, in that moment I felt truly blessed.

FOURTEEN

The bombing of our house was a catalyst that changed everything, and in particular, it changed me.

When the first shock-induced daze began to lift, I actually felt a new confidence. In the past, though I'd always done what I had to do to the best of my ability, I'd wondered how I would cope in a really dire situation, and feared I might crumble, as I had when I heard of young Ted's death. Now, I had been put to the test and found an inner strength I'd doubted I possessed. That, in itself, was a satisfying feeling.

I realised too what a fragile thing life is, and how uncertain is the future – any future. Stupid, really – I'd seen death and destruction many times since the war had begun, and yet I still felt I was somehow invincible. Death and destruction was something that happened to other people. Now I knew that was not true, and it was sobering, and yet at the same time liberating. I didn't want my life to end before it had really begun. I didn't want to die without ever knowing what it was to live, to love, and to be loved in return. I had to seize the moment.

It was not just my possessions that disappeared that night, pulverised by a German bomb, but the girl I had been, my past, and the future that would almost certainly have been mine, as a dutiful wife and mother. And the repercussions would echo down the years, shaping everything that would follow.

Later that day, when Frank returned from his south coast assignment, he telephoned me at Grace's and we arranged to meet at the ruins of our home to see if anything could be salvaged.

In daylight, the devastation shocked me all over again, but realising how lucky I was to be alive, I tried to be stoical as we foraged the rubble, and was grateful when we found a few things – my favourite shoes, high-heeled, peep-toed, Frank's Brownie Box camera, a few pots and pans, one of my pair of irons and the ring to rest it on when it was hot, our wedding photograph, which had stood on the dressing table. The glass was crazed, but the wooden frame and the picture itself were undamaged. The dressing table was more or less intact too, the mirror shattered and the legs splintered, but we were able to salvage what had been in the drawers – underwear, Frank's socks and suspenders, my precious stockings, some warm jumpers and cardigans. They were all filthy, of course, coated with powdery grey dust, but when they'd been laundered they would be wearable again. The things that had been in the wardrobe, though, were damaged beyond repair. We were left with virtually nothing but the clothes we stood up in and, heaven knows, they weren't up to much, and we had no home. It was a pretty bleak prospect.

There were agencies, of course, that were supposed to help out in this sort of situation, but it was a frustratingly long-drawn-out process, and even after we'd queued for hours at the city hall, reported what had happened and been given the necessary chitty, we were pushed from pillar to post like so much lost luggage, and all without getting much further. There was a waiting list for the houses that had been requisitioned from people who had evacuated, and we were pointed in the direction of the WVS for the replacement of our clothing and personal effects. I didn't care for that at all; it made me feel like a second-class citizen, trying on a selection of someone else's cast-offs. They might be far better quality than the things I had lost, donated, as they had been, by the well-to-dos of Clifton and Redland, but at least the ruined skirts and slacks had been my own.

The one thing we were not short of was goodwill and the kindness of good friends. But in the event this was the cause of serious disagreement between Frank and me.

As soon as he heard what had happened, Jim Norris, the driver Frank fired for, offered to take us in. We could have his front room, he said, until the council came up with alternative accommodation. I should have been grateful, I knew, but I had severe reservations. I really wasn't keen on sleeping on the floor, on a bed made up of pillows, or having to live with a family I didn't know and had been foisted upon. The idea of having to use a stranger's kitchen and lavatory was daunting, and I didn't suppose Mrs Norris, however kind-hearted, would be overly keen on the arrangement either. It wouldn't be long before she started to resent us being there, and the tensions would mount. In any case, it really wasn't practical for me to live so far from the hospital. And Grace's parents had said that I was welcome to stay with them as long as I needed to.

When I suggested that this would be the best solution, however, Frank became very sour.

'If you think I'm going to offend Jim, you've got another think coming. He's offered us his front room out of the kindness of his heart, and I'm not going to hurt his feelings telling him it's not good enough for you.'

'It's not that it's not good enough,' I argued. 'I wouldn't be able to get to work from the other side of town.'

'So, you won't be able to get to work. They'll have to understand your circumstances have changed.'

'If I was to stay with Grace, I would be able to get to work.'

'What, stay there on your own?' Frank sounded scandalised. 'Me in Totterdown and you in St Andrews? What are you thinking of?'

'Perhaps it's you that ought to understand circumstances have changed, Frank,' I snapped. 'My job is every bit as important as yours.'

'I'm the one that brings in the money, and that's as it should be.'

I knew better than to mention that my small wage had proved very useful.

'It's not just about money, though, is it?' I said instead. 'It's for the war effort. They need me.'

'I expect they need people at other Red Cross posts too. Ones you could get to from Totterdown.'

My heart sank at the very suggestion.

'Brenton Stoke is where I work. I'm not going to leave my friends in the lurch. You can go to Jim's and I can go to Grace's. Just for now. We can have another think when we see what the council offers us.'

'I don't want to offend Jim.'

This isn't about offending Jim, I thought. This is about you keeping me under your thumb . . .

'If he's got any sense he'll see it's the best way. And I bet his wife will be glad. Having you sleeping on the front-room floor is one thing, but having me as well . . . that's something else entirely.'

We argued some more, but in the end I had my way. For the first time I'd defied Frank, and it was exhilarating. Frank went to Jim's and I moved into the spare bedroom Grace had offered.

I felt like a bird released from a cage.

I loved everything about living in Grace's home. It was like moving into another world.

Her father, a bank manager, still went to work each day in a bowler hat and three-piece suit comprising a black jacket, waistcoat and striped trousers, and in the evenings he donned an ARP uniform and went out to patrol the streets. Her mother, the epitome of gentility, worked tirelessly for the WVS. She was a bird-boned lady with a core of steel; I never saw her without rouge and lipstick, her iron-grey hair combed into immaculate waves, and she smelled deliciously of lavender. A daily woman came in to conjure up meals that were incredibly good, in spite of the shortages, and to keep the house sparklingly clean.

There was a separate dining room and lounge, an indoor lavatory downstairs and a bathroom upstairs that actually had hot running water. There was a huge kitchen with an Aga cooker and an Anderson shelter at the end of the garden.

Best of all was my bedroom. It was decorated in yellow – walls painted the palest primrose, candlewick bedcover and curtains in deeper daffodil – so that in spite of the blackout blind the room seemed always to be bathed in sunshine. The tiny dressing table had triptych mirrors that I could adjust to catch angles of myself I'd never seen before, and the narrow wardrobe had panels carved with oak apples and berries. There was a picture on the wall that looked like an original – a watercolour of a flowering geranium in a clay pot. When I examined the signature in the bottom right-hand corner I saw it was 'E. Moxey'. Grace's mother was called Elizabeth; it was she who had painted it, I supposed. I could well imagine her in more peaceful times sitting for hours with her palette and brushes, creating delicate detailed works of art. Everything about Grace's home and family was ordered and genteel, even now, in a city under siege.

I loved that bedroom and I loved the privacy it offered me. I loved the fact that I could keep it neat and tidy, that I could arrange my lipstick and face powder on the dressing table with no fear of it being swept aside to make way for Brylcreem, keys and a used handkerchief, that the floor, with its sunshine-yellow rug, was free of heaps of dirty clothes Frank had shrugged out of and dropped where he stood, and there were no coal-caked boots kicked off in a corner. I loved the soft feather mattress and pillows, and not having to share them with Frank.

I was a single girl again, living in undreamed-of luxury, and it was a little corner of heaven.

The rebellion that had been simmering in me ever since Frank had tried to force me to move with him to Jim's home, and which had been stoked by the bad-tempered, bullying way he often treated me, grew stronger. Whereas before I'd reluctantly accepted that as Frank's wife I had few rights of my own, now everything in me kicked against it. Why should that one mistake, made when I was just sixteen, define the whole of my life?

I gave up on fighting my feelings for Dev – a hopeless task, in any case – and instead luxuriated in exploring them. But that didn't mean an end to my inner turmoil. I was on a roller coaster, sometimes riding high on the sheer exhilaration that came from seeing him, hearing his voice, thinking about him even; sometimes I was dipping down to the depths, doubting that I was anything more to him than any of the other nurses, a colleague, a girl to flirt with, a challenge, perhaps. Then I would recall how he'd come to the hospital for me on the day after the bombing, and the things he'd said: 'Don't you know how to worry a man half to death . . .' 'I pity the poor souls I've been treating tonight with you on my mind . . .' 'I thought I'd lost you . . .' – relishing them, yet wondering whether he had really meant what he said. I thought of the looks we'd exchanged, I thought of the little touches – his finger in the dimple of my chin, his hand on mine – and felt again the excitement bubbling inside me. The guilt would kick in then, for however much I might resent Frank's attitude towards me, no matter that I regretted marrying him, I *was* his wife, and my upbringing had programmed me to respect that.

But whereas before the sense of duty had been stronger than the attraction I felt for Dev, now the scales had tipped the other way. Though nothing further had happened, though we were never alone together, Dev was in my head and in my heart, and that was how I wanted it.

'You know the Royalty cinema's gone, don't you? Nothing but a heap of rubble,' Bonnie Parfitt said. Bonnie was another ambulance driver. With the intensification of the bombing raids our strength had been increased. We now had two and sometimes three crews on each shift, and we had been given quarters in a new, prefabricated block where we gathered to await the warning that was our call to action.

'Oh my God, no!' That was Phyl Devonish, her partner. She was knitting, as she always did, whilst we waited to be called out, sea-boot socks for sailors. The wool, navy blue and oiled, sat in a thick ball on the floor beside her. 'Oh, the nights I've had in the back row of the circle at the Royalty!'

'Though I don't suppose you could name a single film you've seen there.'

'Who goes to the pictures to watch the films?' Phyl laughed. 'Oh, look what you've made me do now! I've only gone and dropped a stitch.'

She bent over her knitting, brows furrowed as she tried to weave the dropped stitch back onto her needle.

'And I'll bet that's not all you've dropped for a sailor!'

They always bantered this way, Bonnie and Phyl. It eased the tension of waiting. But it made me vaguely uncomfortable, especially when Dev was in the room, as he was tonight. He had taken on a roving role, driving himself to call-outs when a doctor was needed, rather than waiting at the hospital for the patients to be brought in, and often joined us.

I put down the Ethel M. Dell novel I'd been pretending to read and eased myself out of the canvas chair.

'I'm going to put the water on for the flasks and get a cup of tea while I'm about it. Anyone else want one?'

'If you're offering. It's cold enough in here to freeze the balls off a brass monkey.' Bonnie shivered and slipped a little lower under the blanket she'd wrapped herself in. The rest room was heated only by an Aladdin stove, and though we clustered around it, it had little effect on the bitter cold of a winter night.

'Me too,' Phyl chimed up, and though Grace was dozing, chin resting on the upturned collar of her greatcoat, I didn't want to leave her out.

'Tea all round then.'

Dev levered himself out of the chair he'd been occupying. 'I'll give you a hand.' He followed me along the narrow corridor to the little kitchen.

'So, how are things going with you?' he asked as I filled the kettle.

Though the words were mundane enough there was something in his tone that made them intimate – or was that just my imagination?

'Oh – you know.' I tried to sound casual, but my heart had begun to beat fiercely.

'It must be difficult for you, not having a home of your own.'

Again, there was something in his tone that suggested more than he was actually articulating.

'It's not very nice, losing all your possessions.'

'And having to live apart from your husband.'

It wasn't my imagination. He was testing the water. Wasn't he? My heart contracted again, and I was overcome with a reckless impulse to discover once and for all if my feelings for him were reciprocated.

'To be honest, I'm not missing him at all,' I said.

Dev's eyes narrowed. 'Ah, but would he say the same thing?'

'I don't know, and I don't much care.' I couldn't believe I was daring to talk like this.

'Ah . . .' Dev said again.

He was leaning back against the sink, hands in pockets, just looking at me, and suddenly desire and uncertainty over-whelmed me, sweeping away the last bit of caution.

'Were you really worried about me the night we were bombed?' I asked.

'You know I was.'

'I know what you *said*. But . . .'

He smiled faintly. 'You think I talk that way to all the girls. Ah, maybe I do, Caroletta. I kissed the Blarney Stone, don't you know. But I was only telling the truth this time. If anything had happened to you . . . it would have broken my heart.'

'Really?' The warmth was rushing in, liquid and sweet.

'You mean the world to me, Caroletta.'

'Oh, Dev . . .'

I wanted to say that he meant the world to me too, but somehow I couldn't do it. My bravado had gone, and I was

178

shy again, basking in joy yet tongue-tied. He reached out his hand, I took it, and he pulled me towards him, gently but firmly, until our foreheads touched. For timeless moments we stood there, motionless, whilst the electricity crackled between us and I felt as if every muscle, every nerve ending was being drawn irresistibly towards him. Slowly I tipped my chin and then it was not our foreheads that were touching but our lips, still tentatively, but with the vibrant promise of harnessed power and energy.

When we drew apart, our hands were still linked, and I was trembling.

'So,' Dev said softly. 'What are we going to do? Am I to see you away from this place?'

'Oh, yes . . . yes . . .'

'Tomorrow? We're both off duty in the afternoon. We could go for a drive.'

'All right.'

'Shall I pick you up then? Say two o'clock?'

Footsteps in the corridor outside. We sprang apart and I grabbed the tin tray, holding it like a breastplate.

'Hasn't that kettle boiled yet? We're all gasping!' It was Bonnie, still wrapped in her blanket so that she looked like a Mexican hobo.

'It won't be long.' My voice sounded unsteady.

Dev went to the window, pulled back a corner of the blackout blind and peered round it. 'Better not be. The stars are shining – I wouldn't be surprised if the warning doesn't go off any time soon.' By contrast, he sounded his usual breezy self.

I put down the tray and began setting out mugs; Bonnie

poured milk into them and I was glad I didn't have to do it. My hands were shaking so much I felt sure she couldn't help but notice. The sugar, in its little glass bowl, was brown and crusted from spoons wet with tea or coffee, but it was too precious to waste.

Just as the kettle came to the boil, the alarm did indeed sound.

'Thank the Lord for that!' Bonnie said. 'It's the waiting that's the worst, isn't it?'

Normally I would have agreed with her; tonight I wanted the waiting to go on and on, so I could sit quietly and relish what had just occurred. But I couldn't. I had a job to do, and so did Dev.

Now, he picked up the tray and carried it into the rest room, and there was no opportunity for us to exchange another word. In fact, he barely glanced at me as we drank our tea and waited, with the others, for our first call of the night.

Once again the bombers came in force, and Grace and I were kept too busy for me even to think about Dev. We dealt with the usual crop of casualties – a man who had fallen trying to get up onto his roof with a stirrup pump to put out an incendiary fire; a messenger boy from a warden's post, blown off his bicycle; a policeman with nasty shrapnel wounds. We had to wait whilst a family were dug out of their Anderson shelter, watching searchlights carve bright beams into the dark sky and the darting shells soaring like a stream of fire-flies towards the gleaming underbellies of the bombers, and listening to the constant pounding of the guns interspersed with the occasional thud and explosion that we felt through the soles of our feet before it ran like a cataract in reverse up our legs and shivered in our guts. The family, thankfully, were not badly hurt, though very shocked, and a girl of ten or eleven was suffering a severe asthma attack.

Our most unpleasant job was a woman who had been caught in the blast whilst running to the shelter; she'd lost both legs and her face was a grisly mask of burned and bleeding flesh. There was nothing to be done for her, and we weren't actually supposed to carry the dead, but the mortuary van had apparently taken a hit, and was totally out of action, and we couldn't leave her lying there. I gritted my teeth as Grace and I loaded what was left of her onto one of our blankets and into the ambulance.

'We must make sure and ask for that blanket back,' Grace said as we drove, crunching over broken glass and lurching into potholes, to the mortuary. 'There'll be hell to pay if we go back without it.'

By the time the mortuary staff relieved us of our burden, however, the blanket was so soaked with blood and matted with bits of flesh that had glued themselves to it that we knew it was beyond saving. We'd just have to return without it and take the consequences.

The worst of it was over, though, by the early hours. Back at the hospital we washed the dirt from our ambulance with buckets of cold water that numbed my fingers, and went in to clean ourselves up with more cold water.

'My God, what a sight you are!' Grace laughed as I took off my tin helmet.

The mirror reflected my face – dusty grey, with pale streaks where rivers of perspiration had run, and a huge dark smudge on my chin, whilst my forehead, which had been covered by the helmet, was a white shelf under my tangled hair.

'You don't look so great yourself.' I ran cold water, reached for the soap. We scrubbed our hands, started on our faces, and as the icy water refreshed me a little Dev was there again in my thoughts.

I checked over my shoulder to make certain we were alone.

'Grace, I've got something to tell you. You'll never believe it, but Dev has asked me to go out with him. Tomorrow afternoon.'

'No!' Grace's startled eyes met mine in the mirror. 'Are you going? Hang on, stupid question, of course you are!'

Grace knew all about my 'pash', as she called it, on Dev, and that my marriage to Frank was far from rosy. In fact, she'd urged me to leave him and make a fresh start alone.

'Well, I suppose so . . .' I said. Though the excitement was still bubbling in me, my courage was beginning to fail me. 'I want to, of course, but . . .'

'But you're scared of stepping outside the fold.'

'I'm scared full stop!' I admitted. One thing to dream; quite another to make that dream reality. And besides, even if I hadn't been a married woman, I wasn't used to going on 'dates'. Frank had been my first and only boyfriend.

'Carrie, you can't chicken out now!' Grace reached for a thin grey towel, blotted her face and looked at me over the top of it. 'Look, this is what you've been wanting for weeks – months. Ever since you met Dev, as far as I can make out. For goodness' sake, girl!'

'You think I should go then?' I asked tentatively.

'Of course you should! Life is far too short and too precious to miss out on something you want so much. God, we mightn't be here next week, any of us. We could catch a bomb tomorrow night, for all we know. So could Dev. You've got to live life for the moment and the hell with worrying about the future. Because there might not be one.'

A nerve jumped in my throat and the excitement was back, bubbling deep inside me. Grace had voiced my own thoughts, and to hear them spoken out loud was like a benediction.

He wouldn't come. I was absolutely sure of it. But I got ready, all the same. I'd slept fitfully, waking every hour or so, compulsively checking the clock on the bedside table before drifting off again. I'd got up soon after noon and made myself breakfast, all alone in the comfortable kitchen. Breakfast that I was far too nervous to eat, and most of which I scraped, feeling guilty at the waste, into the kitchen bin.

Still unable to believe I was really doing this, I went upstairs to begin getting ready. Choosing what to wear was no great dilemma since I owned so little, but I settled on a blue wool skirt Grace had donated to me and a pale lemon blouse. My stockings were full of lacy cobwebs where I'd darned them and I had to take great care pulling them on. At the little dressing table I applied face powder, lipstick and a touch of rouge, and fastened my hair up into what I thought was a flattering bang over my forehead. The back, I left loose. Dev had only ever seen me with it pinned up to clear my uniform collar. Now it fell in natural waves almost to my shoulders. I surveyed my image critically in the triptych mirror and felt quite satisfied. But the rouge was too much – perhaps my cheeks were flushed anyway. I rubbed at them with my handkerchief. Better.

I got my coat from the wardrobe, a swingy little jigger that had also once belonged to Grace, and slipped on my shoes. They, at least, were my own, the ones I'd rescued from the debris of our home.

And saw, from the window, a Humber pulled up at the kerb outside.

Oh my God, he was here! And early, too! All of a dither, I grabbed up my bag and coat and ran downstairs, pulling it on as I went. Though there was no one in this street who really knew me, or anything about me, the car, parked there, was drawing attention in a way I was desperate to avoid.

The house was still quiet; Grace must still be in bed, I supposed. But as I opened the front door I heard her voice. 'You're going then?'

I looked up. She was leaning over the banister rail wearing a pair of silky pyjamas. 'He's here . . .'

'Good luck!' she called.

I couldn't answer. A knot of nervousness was constricting my throat. I simply smiled, a rictus grin of panic, and went out, pulling the door shut behind me.

When he saw me coming, Dev got out of the car and came round to open the passenger door for me.

'Well,' he said, 'you didn't oversleep then. And my, do you look grand!'

'Oh, thank you . . .' I wasn't sure if that was for the compliment or the fact that he was holding the car door open for me. Not that it mattered. And he looked pretty good himself. He was wearing a tweed overcoat over a pair of brown corduroys, and his hair, which usually flopped over his forehead, was neatly combed, with just a touch of Brylcreem.

'Are you ready for this then, Caroletta?' he asked, and his eyes were sparkling with that hint of wickedness that I always felt was truly Irish; the hint of wickedness that had always made me unsure whether this was all just a game to him, and I was no more to him than a diversion or even a challenge. I still wasn't absolutely convinced that was not the case. But last night in the kitchen had been different. Dev hadn't sounded as if he was joking or flirting. There had been something very special between us, and I had truly believed, for the first time, that my feelings for him were reciprocated.

But I was still dreadfully nervous, my tummy churning at the enormity of what I was doing, the excitement dark-rimmed with guilt, like a corona around the sun.

The edge of awkwardness lasted whilst we drove across the bomb-scarred city and out onto the Downs. There, Dev parked on a grassy area that looked across the Avon Gorge to Leigh Woods. They rose like a turreted city from the river mist and disappeared into the thick low cloud above, a bare brown vista that would soon turn green with the promise of spring.

'So, Caroletta, what are we going to do?' Dev asked, and I knew instinctively that he wasn't talking about our immediate plans for the afternoon, but the long-term future.

'I don't know.' I burrowed down into the collar of my coat so that it covered my chin.

'Well, let's not worry about it for now then. Let's take each day as it comes.' He reached across, covering my hand with his. Tentatively I turned it over and our fingers entwined. 'You're here with me now,' he said. 'That's all that matters.'

I nodded, and the warmth came flooding in, dispelling my nervousness and my doubts and most of the guilt.

'Shall we go for a walk?' he asked.

'Why not?'

A million reasons. My shoes were not the most suitable for the wet ground underfoot, we might see someone we knew – unlikely but possible – the rain might begin again at any moment. But really none of it mattered.

I was with Dev, and it felt so right. So right and natural as he tucked my hand into the crook of his arm, steadying me over the uneven ground. So right as we talked easily about anything and everything. So right as we lapsed into companionable silence. And so right when he kissed me, hidden from the road that bisected the Downs by a stand of trees.

When he drove me back to Grace's home, dropping me at the end of the road because I was afraid we might be seen, there was really no need for his question: 'Are you going to come out with me again, then, Caroletta?' and no need for me even to think about my reply.

This was what I wanted more than anything else in the world. For the moment I wasn't going to worry about the future. As I'd already acknowledged, we might not have one. The present was all we could be sure of, and for me that meant

Dev. The first man I'd loved, the only man I could imagine loving, ever.

I gave him a coquettish smile, lending a little levity to the frightening potency of my emotion.

'What do you think?' I said.

FIFTEEN

There was an unreality about those weeks as winter turned to spring and Dev and I continued to see one another whenever we could. An unreality and a dark magic. We didn't discuss the future, except obliquely; it was a far-off country. Instead we lived for the day, and the impermanence lent a *frisson* to each and every moment we spent together, keeping the romance fresh and adding the piquancy of what seemed like something very special, stolen out of time.

We walked on the Downs and in Leigh Woods; we drank bitter-tasting tea or chicory-flavoured coffee in smoke-filled cafés or at mobile canteens, set up to cater for those who had lost their homes; we even went to the zoo, laughing at the antics of the monkeys, watching the long-legged pink flamingos wading sedately across their pond, marvelling at Alfred, the great ape, who returned our gaze balefully from behind the bars of his cage.

'Wouldn't it be terrible if the zoo was hit?' I said, and

wondered why it should seem so unthinkable when hundreds of human beings had been killed or wounded. Because it wasn't the animals' war, I supposed. You couldn't explain to a polar bear or a chimpanzee that all this horror had a purpose – to prevent our world being overrun with Nazi ideals. A bear or a chimp would still be caged whoever was in power.

'You've a tender heart, Caroletta,' Dev said, and he tucked my hand into the crook of his arm in what had now become a habit with us, but was about the extent of our intimacy. Yes, we kissed when there was no one to see, and those kisses sent quivers running through me and left me aching for more. But opportunity was limited, and in any case to go further would be to cross into uncharted territory: the territory that occupied the same forbidden land as making plans for the future.

It couldn't go on that way, of course. Every relationship must move on or die. I could sense that Dev was becoming impatient with the limitations and the secrecy, and it made me anxious. Easy enough to counter his advances, given the lack of privacy, harder to ignore the remarks that I knew were leading towards him suggesting I should walk out on my sham of a marriage so that we could be together.

To begin with I could almost discount them. The first time he mentioned the future was when we were in a café in the city centre, a funny little place with steamed-up windows, thick with the fug of tobacco smoke. We were adding to that, Dev smoking his pipe, a briar, well-chewed on the stem, and me a cigarette, as we drank cups of evil-smelling tea at an oilcloth-covered table.

'When this is over, Caroletta, I'll take you to the Ritz,' Dev said. 'Or, better still, to Dublin. We'll have tea at the Shelbourne Hotel. Everything tastes better in Ireland, don't you know? The milk is fresh from the cows, the meat so sweet it melts in your mouth. And the bread . . . My mammy makes soda bread like you could only dream of. I could eat a slice now, hot from the oven, with the butter melting in and a spoonful of her home-made plum jam.'

'It sounds wonderful,' I said.

'You'll love it. I'd like to take you now, right this minute, away from the bombs and the shortages and that husband of yours, and have you waiting for me in a little house of our own, miles out in the country where the air is sweet and the children walk across the fields to school. Now what do you think of that?'

'I think you were telling the truth when you said you kissed the Blarney Stone,' I said.

It was a distant dream, but sharing it made me glow with warmth. He made it sound so easy, but it certainly wasn't going to be that. There was going to be a lot of upheaval before such a cosy scenario was possible, and I shrank from the thought of it. Telling Frank our marriage was over would be bad enough; picturing the way my parents would react, even worse.

Strange as it seems nowadays, there was an awful stigma about divorce. The accepted thing was to make the best of a bad job and simply get on with it. If I left Frank, I'd be branded a scarlet woman, and the shame would reflect on my family. Living as they did in a small village, it would be bound to cause them distress as tongues wagged, just as it had when I had 'got myself into trouble', but even more so. 'That Carrie was never any better than she should be,' people would say, and Mother would want to die of shame. Knowing how disappointed they would be in me, and how hurt, made me shrink inwardly.

And so I managed to remain evasive when Dev urged me to bring our affair into the open. I wanted it desperately, but I didn't feel ready to face all the trauma that moving forward would bring. Life was stressful enough without adding to it. Better to live for the day, and let tomorrow take care of itself – if tomorrow ever came.

I desperately wanted more on a physical level too, and that was cause for more inner turmoil. I was, remember, a girl who had been brought up with a certain set of standards, besides which, I had taken solemn vows before God to be faithful to Frank. I wasn't sure if I believed in God or not, but although it was more of a superstition than religion, I still felt, deep down, that to renege on those vows would be a heresy that would bring retribution crashing down about my ears, and possibly Dev's too.

I wondered about his religious conviction. He was, after all, Irish, and I'd always understood the Irish were steeped in religion.

'Are you a Catholic?' I asked him once.

'Now what makes you think that?'

'Well, most Irish people are, aren't they?'

'There's the Church of Ireland too.'

'Isn't it the same thing?'

'Don't let Father O'Donaghue hear you say that! No, the Church of Ireland is Protestant. We're the Church of Rome.'

'So you *are* a Catholic?'

'I suppose. But lapsed. I haven't been to confession in years. Which is just as well, you might say. My mammy thinks I'll burn in hell, of course. She says a few Hail Marys every night for the salvation of my soul, I wouldn't wonder. Much good will it do.'

'You don't believe in God, then?'

'Sure I do. And the piskies and the leprechauns and the faeries at the bottom of the garden.'

'And the Ten Commandments?'

'Depends which one you're thinking of. Honour thy father and thy mother – that's a good one. And I don't believe it's right to steal, though I did once help myself to all the ripe apples off Biddy Murphy's tree. And a couple of gobstoppers from the counter of the village shop when Paddy Connor had his back turned. But there's some I'm breaking every day. And some I'd like to.'

'Which ones?'

'Well, for starters, how about coveting thy neighbour's wife? I'd have to plead guilty to that. And where that leads, there are others that follow. You don't need me to spell them out, surely?'

Thou shalt not commit adultery.

My cheeks grew hot.

'And it's what you were thinking of too, with all this talk of conscience before God. Go on now, admit it.'

'I was not!'

'You're a bad liar, Caroletta. Now, let me think, there's a commandment about that too. Thou shalt not bear false witness. See how easy it is to break God's holy law? You'll answer to

192

St Peter on the Day of Judgement for that alone. So, as the old saying goes, you might as well be hanged for a sheep as a lamb.'

'That is ridiculous and you know it!'

He was laughing at me, pulling me close so that our hips fitted snugly together, and desire, sharp as honed steel, was twisting inside me when a man hove into view, a small Scottie dog on a tartan lead trotting ahead of him.

I wrenched free. 'Do you think he saw us?'

'Ah, who cares? Isn't it what we both want? You as much as me, Caroletta. Don't deny it, now.'

He was right, I couldn't deny it. Afraid as I might be of crossing the Rubicon, I longed to be as close to Dev as one human being can be to another. Just those few moments when my body had been pressed close to his had started fires within me that flamed so brightly they overwhelmed me, made me want to throw caution to the winds. But of course it wasn't so easy. Dev had lodgings with an elderly couple in Filton; I would never have dreamed of taking him back to my room at Grace's, and to book a room in a hotel for a few hours would have been far too contrived.

We were, in any case, much busier again. Bad weather in late March had cooled things off, figuratively as well as literally, but with the coming of April the skies had cleared and the raids began again. One, in particular, that people called 'the Good Friday Raid', had been especially bad. It had come in two phases, and the second, straddling a line between Bristol Bridge, in the centre of the city, to Horfield had been perilously close to our base. Another gasometer, this time at Canons Marsh, was hit, a huge explosion sending a rush of flame soaring up into the night sky. Almost two hundred people were killed and something approaching four hundred injured that night. Though much of the devastation was outside our area, the pressure on the crews there was so great that we were called out again and again to horrific incidents.

Had we but known it, however, that raid of 11 April marked the end of the main blitz on Bristol, and although the bombers still came there were not as many as before, and even that was more by bad luck than design, since they were headed for the Glasgow and Liverpool shipyards and factories, and we suffered only if they were frustrated in their objective. The airfields and the aircraft works were still targeted by day as well as by night, but the residential areas suffered far less than before.

Towards the end of May Frank and I were offered a little house in Bishopston, vacant because the husband was serving with the army overseas and his wife had taken their three children to relatives in Wiltshire to escape the bombing. It was one of a long rank that lined the street, with a tiny garden at the rear and a hydrangea beside the front gate; inside there was a front room, a dining room and minuscule kitchen, and the staircase led up to three bedrooms, the main one surprisingly large. All the owners' furniture was still in place – a green chenille three-piece suite, a drop-leaf dining table, matching chairs and sideboard, a gas cooker, and well-used but serviceable beds. There was crockery in the sideboard and cutlery in the drawers. The family had taken the bedding with them, apart from a pile of patched and darned sheets and an old pink eiderdown, the cover of which was so rotten that it went in holes wherever you touched it, spewing feathers, and though the council had at last come up with a grant to allow us to replace some of the things we had lost, the shops were so empty that buying new was a virtual impossibility. The WVS came to the rescue again, however, with sheets, blankets and a bolster, so we did not have to sleep on the bare ticking mattress.

Frank, of course, was delighted. He wanted us to be living together again as man and wife, and he was sick to death of having to sleep on Jim's front-room floor. I, on the other hand, would have been perfectly happy to continue as we were, seeing each other only occasionally. I didn't want to leave the sunshine-yellow room and the peace of Grace's house. I didn't want to have to share a home and a bed with Frank. I hadn't liked it before; now, having tasted freedom and privacy, I wanted it less than ever.

The only thing that cheered me was a wicked thought: when Frank was away at work, it would be somewhere where Dev and I could be alone. I pictured him parking the Humber some way off, so as not to attract attention, and walking back. I'd be watching for him, peeping round the front-room blackout curtain, so that I could open the front door and let him in quickly before he was spotted on the doorstep. I imagined how it would be to have a whole house to ourselves, how I would set out glasses for whisky — always provided I could get hold of some! — how I would prepare a meal for us in the little kitchen with him lounging against the sink watching me. Where I thought I was going to stash the whisky so Frank would not find it, and how I would explain the depletion of our precious rations, I don't know, but I didn't let details like that spoil my fantasy.

And then, of course, Dev would make love to me, perhaps on one of the two narrow beds in the second bedroom, with the collection of Dinky toys on the shelf above. Or even in the hallway, on the red and green runner that matched the stair carpet. To me, that felt deliciously decadent. I imagined Dev's mouth on mine, his hands caressing me, his body above mine. I imagined the way his bare back would feel under my fingers when I slid my hands inside his shirt, the long, hard muscles in his upper arms and thighs. I imagined every detail except the moment of union. Though I knew I wanted it, to actually anticipate that was to move into forbidden territory, and really I didn't want to think of such intimacy at all. It was, to me, the frenzied pumping of Frank's sweaty body after he had entered me with no preliminaries at all, just urgent hands pushing up my nightdress, the spreading of my legs and the thrust of him into me. And afterwards, when he was spent, the roll away and the annoying drone of his snore. I had never experienced the joy of abandonment, the delicious luxury of two people becoming one. I had never been teased to a screaming point of desire where I would beg for fulfilment. I had never climbed to the stars or lain sated and contented afterwards. Only my deepest instinct told me there was something wonderful that I was missing, and I wasn't ready to speculate what it might be.

But I wanted to be alone with Dev, oh, I wanted that, all right. And one day when we met up on the Gloucester road, just a few hundred yards from the street where Frank and I were living, I screwed up my courage to make a suggestion.

'Why don't you come and see my new house?'

'What's this, Caroletta?' His very blue eyes were narrowed.

'Don't you want to?'

'Do you want your neighbours to talk? I thought talk was something you wanted to avoid.'

A pang of guilt. I thrust it aside, intoxicated by my own daring.

'They hardly know us yet. A lot of the houses are empty, anyway. And the windows blacked up at the ones that aren't. If I go first, and then you follow in a few minutes, nobody will think anything of it.'

Again, Dev gave me that narrow look and I wondered what was going on behind it. Then: 'I can't be doing with creeping about like a thief in the night. We'll walk up the street together, or not at all,' he said.

My heart gave a nervous leap into my throat, my courage almost deserting me.

'If we go to the corner, we can see if there's anybody about.'

We walked to the corner: the street was deserted. One side was in sunshine, the other in shadow.

'Are you sure about this now?' Dev asked. 'Your husband's not going to come home and find me there, is he?'

'No, he won't be home till six or so.'

'Well, that's all right, then. I don't want some swarthy rail-wayman beating the living daylights out of me.'

If I hadn't been so nervous I might have laughed. Certainly Frank wouldn't be very pleased to come home and find a strange man in the house with his wife. But he came from a back-ground that had an old-fashioned respect for the professional classes. If I introduced Dev as a colleague, Frank might very well call him 'Dr Devlin' and offer him a cup of tea, though I would no doubt have to answer to him afterwards.

We met no one on the street but a couple of small boys, one marking out a hopscotch grid on the pavement with a chalky stone, the other dribbling a ball. Neither of them so much as glanced at us.

'This is the one.' I opened the gate, put my key in the lock of the front door and pushed it open. Dev followed me inside. My breath came more easily, though my pulse was racing.

'So, Caroletta, alone at last!' Dev put his arms round me. I wriggled free, panicked suddenly.

'Come on, you've got to see the house. That's what you're here for.'

'Is it indeed?' But he followed me dutifully from room to room.

'This is the dining room . . . and see, there's a cupboard under the stairs . . .'

'Useful if the Jerries come.'

'And the kitchen . . .'

'Ah, the kitchen . . .' He put his arms round me again, pushed me up against the sink.

'You haven't seen upstairs yet . . .'

'I've seen all I want to see.' His breath was hot on my neck. 'Sure, Caroletta, you know how to torture a man . . .'

'Behave!' But he was kissing my throat, my mouth, one hand on my breast, fumbling open the buttons of my dress, slipping his hand inside. Sparks ignited deep inside me, running a line of fire from my loins to the place where his fingers were stroking me, and the yearning between my legs compelled me to press myself against him. The sensation made me weak; I drowned in it.

His hand went to the hem of my skirt, bunching it up, sliding up my bare leg and pushing me harder against him whilst his finger probed into the moist heart of me, and I climbed on a heady cloud of delight to a place I had never been before. The dark thrill of stepping outside the pale was an added excitement, sharpening my awareness even as his touch sensitised my body.

A sharp rap on the door knocker, loud in the silent house.

I remember once, when I was a little girl, Mother taking a bucket of cold water to two dogs who were humping outside our front door. At the time I didn't know what they were doing, for though I was a country girl I had led a sheltered life. If ever I saw cows astraddle one another, Mother would say they were 'playing the fool'. It was years before I realised what that meant, but the bucket of cold water certainly put an end to the dogs' game. And that was how it was now, for me.

'There's someone at the door!' I whispered in panic.

'Let them go away again.'

'No, I'll have to answer it.' I was buttoning my bodice with shaking hands, checking my hair.

Heart pounding, I went along the hall. Was it a nosy neighbour? Or had something happened to Frank and they'd come to tell me? Given my swirling guilt, this seemed all too horribly likely: instant retribution for my infidelity. I opened the door a crack and peeped round.

'Please, miss, my ball's gone in your garden.' It was one of the small boys we'd passed earlier. 'Can I get it?'

I couldn't see a ball, but the lad knew exactly where it was. He dived into the hydrangea bush on hands and knees, grey-flannel-trousered bottom protruding from the lush greenery and the overblown pink puffs of flowers. A moment later he scrabbled back out, clutching his ball, and without a word of thanks, scooted out of the gate.

Dev was in the kitchen where I'd left him.

'It's all right,' I said. 'That boy had lost his ball, that's all.'

'And didn't I tell you to leave it?' He reached for me, pulling me towards him. But for me the moment for such things had come and gone. I could no longer enjoy his mouth on mine, his hand brushing my thigh as he bunched up my skirt again. Fear of discovery and overwhelming guilt were consuming me now.

I was back in the woods at Timberley with Frank. I was sixteen again, doing something I knew I shouldn't. The similarity stopped there, of course, for Frank had never awakened real feelings of desire in me. But the knowing I was about to do something irreparable was the same, and everything in me shrank from it. I couldn't cuckold Frank in his own house. However much I wanted to, I simply could not do it. I pushed Dev away.

'No! Dev, please, don't.'

He could have been angry with me, I know that now. And perhaps he was. He let my skirt fall back to my knees; he looked me straight in the eye.

'What's the matter?'

'I can't. Not here. I'm sorry.'

'I thought that was what you wanted. For just a moment there I thought . . .'

'I'm sorry,' I repeated miserably. 'I'm so sorry . . .'

'Oh, for goodness' sake stop saying you're sorry! You know what I should do? I should put you across my knee and spank you. And I should lay you down on that floor and shag you rotten.'

His words started the sparks again, but this time the feeling of panic was stronger. I wanted Dev out of the house, wanted it with the same urgency that a few minutes ago I'd wanted him.

'I think you'd better go,' I said.

'Are you not coming with me?'

I was curling up inside like a scrap of paper held over a flame.

'Better not. Someone might see us.'

His lip curled. He shrugged. He turned away abruptly and the distance stretched between us, a barren wasteland. Already in a state of high emotion, I felt his sudden coldness bring tears to my eyes.

'Dev – don't go!' I begged. His hand was on the knob of the door, turning it. 'Don't go! Not like this . . .'

'Will you make up your mind?' Same cold tone.

'Come back, please. I'll do whatever you want . . .'

The expression that crossed his face then frightened me.

'For God's sake, Caroletta, what do you take me for?'

Scarlet shame flooded my cheeks. 'But I thought you wanted . . .'

He released the door knob, turned back to face me.

'Well, of course I want you! What man doesn't want the woman he loves? But not like that!' His face was taut with what looked very like disgust.

'Yes, I'd have made love to you if you'd let me,' he went on. 'But I want a damn sight more than that. I want to have you in my bed and in my life. I want you on my arm and you not looking over your shoulder in case someone should see. And I think it's high time we sorted out where we're going with this, and you made up your mind whether we're going to go on sneaking around behind your husband's back, or whether you're going to tell him about us. So let's have the truth, Caroletta. What is it you want? Do you want to be with me? Or would you rather stay with that husband of yours?'

My stomach was tied in knots. 'I want to be with you,' I whispered.

'So you'll tell him, then? Tonight?'

Everything I wanted was there, almost within my reach. I only had to summon the courage to reach out and grasp it. But I was shaking with apprehension at the enormity of it. My sense of duty, both to Frank and my parents, was so deeply rooted it shackled me, and the moral code that had been instilled into me was a chasm I wasn't sure I could cross.

Dev's eyes were holding mine.

'Well? What is it to be?'

'I will tell him,' I said. 'But I've got to pick my moment.'

'And when will that be?'

'I don't know,' I said helplessly. 'Anyway, we need to make plans. I can't just walk out when I've nowhere to go.'

'Don't you trust me to look after you?'

'Yes . . . yes, of course I do, but—'

'If you love me, there's no "but".'

This was all moving too fast.

'I will tell him. I do love you and I want to be with you. More than anything. But—'

I broke off, unable to put into words the conflicting emotions that were tearing me apart.

'You know what I think, Caroletta?' Dev said, sounding more sad now than angry. 'I think that it's all well and good as long as we're going on the way we are. But I don't think you'll ever make the break. Look at you now – terrified someone is going to know I've been here and tell your husband. If you were serious about us, you wouldn't care.'

'I am serious! Of course I am!'

'Then let's do something about it. When did you say your husband will get back from work?

'About six.'

'OK.' Dev crossed his arms, took up a stance. 'Suppose I stay here until he comes home? We don't have to be on duty until eight. That gives us enough time. You can get some things together, and we'll tell him together. That way you won't have to face him alone.'

My heart was hammering and for a moment anything seemed possible. We could really do it! I could leave Frank and be with Dev! But then the fear was creeping back, the fear that made me a coward who hid behind excuses. Whatever Dev might say, I couldn't just walk out with no forward planning and preparation, and the thought of the confrontation between him and Frank was dauntingly dreadful. There was bound to be a terrible scene. They might even come to blows.

'I don't think that's a very good idea,' I said.

'So what do you suggest?'

'I will talk to him. Myself. But I've got to work it out first.'

'Oh, sure. You'll just put it off, Caroletta, that's what will happen. Let's get it over with.'

I was close to tears of panic and confusion.

'Dev, I really don't want to talk about this now.'

His face hardened. 'You see? Putting it off again.' His hand went back to the door knob. 'OK, have it your way.' He paused, then: 'But I think it would be best if we didn't see one another again until this is sorted out.'

I went cold. 'What do you mean?'

'I can't be doing with all this creeping around and deception. I know what I want – if you want the same, then tell Frank you're leaving him, and let me know when you have. After tonight I'll be on a different shift to you for a couple of weeks, but you know where to find me. From now on, we'll do this properly or not at all.'

'But, Dev—'

'I didn't think you wanted to talk about it any more just now,' he said. 'I'll see you later, no doubt.' And he opened the door and walked out.

I ran after him; he ignored me. It was the first time he'd ever spoken to me in that tone, the first time we'd parted without a kiss or a tender word, and it had shaken me rigid.

But at least he had left me in no doubt. Unless I summoned up the courage to leave Frank, it was over.

Tears streaming down my face, I watched him walk away down the street. He didn't so much as look round.

SIXTEEN

There was nothing for it; I had to screw up the courage to tell Frank I was leaving him. The alternative – that I would lose Dev – was unthinkable. He'd meant what he'd said, he'd made that clear by avoiding me that last night we had worked together, and now he was on a different shift he'd made no attempt to contact me. Already I was missing him dreadfully, and the huge hollow at the heart of me was as black as grief. But Frank had been working long shifts so our paths had barely crossed, and waiting for the opportunity to speak to him was a huge dark cloud hanging over my head.

It was the weekend before my chance came – on Sunday afternoon. Frank had been to bed for what he called an 'afternoon snooge' and I'd spent the time nervously rehearsing what I was going to say. At last he came back downstairs and settled himself in an easy chair with the *News of the World*. This was it, then. My stomach was tying itself in knots. I took a deep breath.

'Frank, do you ever wish you'd never married me?'

He looked up, startled. 'What?'

'Well, it wasn't the best of starts, was it?'

Frank shuffled the pages of the paper, turning to a fresh story.

'We're all right now, though, aren't we? Especially now I haven't got your mother and father breathing down my neck all the time.' He said it quite amiably, as if this was just a casual conversation.

I twisted my wedding ring round and round on my finger. 'But it's not enough, is it?'

He looked up again, his expression perplexed. 'What are you talking about?'

'Us. If you hadn't had to marry me, you could have had anyone you wanted.'

'I only ever wanted you. You were my girl, and now you're my wife. I'm happy with that. Aren't you?'

I took a deep breath. 'Not really, no.'

The shocked, disbelieving look that came into his eyes then wounded me, but I couldn't stop now.

'I'm not happy, Frank. I'm not happy at all. And it's not fair on either of us. I'm really sorry if you don't feel it too, but the truth is, I didn't know what love was when I married you, and now I do.'

There was a moment's stunned silence. I could almost hear Frank's thoughts whirring like a clock when it is preparing to strike. Then: 'Are you telling me there's somebody else? You've got another man? Is that what you're telling me?'

I swallowed at the knot of nerves that was constricting my throat.

'Well . . . yes . . . actually . . .'

Frank half rose, scattering pages of newsprint over the floor. His hands balled to fists. 'Who is he? I'll kill the bugger! Who is he?'

'He's a doctor . . .'

'A *doctor*! You've been carrying on with a bloody *doctor*! When you were supposed to be at work! Christ, I knew I should never have let you . . . Christ!' He slammed his hand down hard on the table, making the glass vase jump in its dish.

'I'm sorry,' I said lamely.

'You're sorry? I should think you are bloody sorry! If you think you're going to make a fool out of me with a bloody doctor—'

'I don't want to make a fool of you, Frank. That's the last thing I want.'

'But you have, though. I suppose everybody at the bloody hospital knows. How long has this been going on?'

'Not long.'

'Long e-bloody-'nough!' He hit the table again, again the vase jumped in its bowl. 'Christ, I should have known. I thought you'd been acting strange. You're in a dream half the time. And when's the last time I had you? You're always too fucking tired. And there was me, letting you be, thinking it was all because of this war. I should've known. In the old days you couldn't get enough of it.'

'That's not true! I never—' I broke off, unable to bring myself to say that I'd never wanted him, not really. That I'd only ever wanted to please him. Even now, when I'd told him I was in love with someone else, it was a step too far to deny him the past as well as the present and future.

In any case, Frank was not listening.

'So now I know the reason. You've been getting it some-where else!'

'No! Nothing's happened. But—'

'Oh, no, and I'm a Dutchman! What do you take me for, a bloody fool? There's only one reason a man starts carrying on with another man's wife. Only one thing he's after.'

That made me angry. 'Speak for yourself! Maybe it's all *you* were after. In fact, it was.'

'And I'm no different from any other man. But going at it with a married woman! I'd never do that. I'd draw the line at that. He's got you up the bloody spout, I suppose. That's why you're telling me now. You're in the bloody club, he's done a runner, and you know bloody well I'll know it's not mine—'

'I am not in the club. And he hasn't done a runner. But we do want to be together.'

'What? You think a *doctor* would want to be with the likes of *you*? Who the hell do you think you are? He's after what he can get, that's all, and you're fool enough to believe all the moonshine he's feeding you.'

'That's not true,' I said. I was shaking from head to foot. 'I love him, and he loves me.'

Frank blew all the air out of his lungs in an explosive expression of disgust and disbelief. 'For crying out loud, Carrie! Grow up!'

'Frank, you have to listen to me. I'm perfectly serious. This isn't just some silly fancy. We want to be together.'

He silenced me with a furious gesture. 'Just shut up, will

you? Shut up, you dirty little bitch!' He turned his back on me, heading for the door.

'Where are you going?'

'Anywhere to get away from you.'

'But we have to talk.'

'Talk to your bloody doctor.' He threw it over his shoulder; a moment later I heard the slam of the front door.

I ran to the window, pulling aside the blackout curtain, and saw him turn out of the gate, pulling on his railwayman's jacket as he went, so angry he was having trouble getting his arm into the sleeve.

When he was out of sight I realised I was shaking all over. I let the blackout curtain fall back into place and began to cry.

Thinking Frank might well throw me out when he came home, I went upstairs and packed a bag, though I wasn't sure where I was going to go. Dev would be on duty, and although Grace had said I was welcome to go to her house, I was reluctant to turn up on the doorstep. It had been one thing for her parents to offer me hospitality when we were bombed out, quite another for me to expect them to take me in because I had left my husband. In any case, Grace might well be out on her Sunday off – she had a new boyfriend, a design engineer at the aeroplane company, who had been refused permission to join the Forces because of the importance of his job. And besides, I still hoped that when Frank had calmed down we might be able to have a sensible discussion. I didn't like simply walking out and leaving so much unresolved. And so, in a turmoil of trepidation and elation, I waited for him to come home.

Darkness fell and Frank had still not returned. The siren sounded, its rising banshee wail making my stomach fall away as it always did, and the crack-crack of the anti-aircraft guns at Filton was sharp in the clear evening air. I went out to the gate, wondering where he was, and what I should do. The searchlight beams were slicing the darkness, throwing paths of light over the rooftops as they realigned. The street was deserted. No sign of Frank.

I went back into the house and put on the wireless to deaden the noise of the planes and the falling bombs, but the determinedly jaunty music was anathema to my jangling nerves, and I turned it off again. I made myself a cup of hot Bovril and drank it wandering around the house like a lost soul.

By the time the all clear sounded I knew it was too late for me to go out looking for alternative accommodation and Frank had still not come home. Perhaps he wasn't going to, I thought. Perhaps he had decided to walk out on me. Eventually I cleaned my teeth, washed my face, and got into bed. And, exhausted by the traumas of the day, I felt asleep.

I came back to consciousness with a jolt. There was someone in the room. I could hear them moving stealthily about and there was the faint sour smell of stale tobacco and whisky fumes. Then the bed dipped on Frank's side.

I lay perfectly still, not wanting him to know I was awake. Half asleep as I was, I didn't feel up to another row just now.

Then I felt his hand on my breast through the cotton of my nightdress. The smell of tobacco and whisky was very strong, wafting with his hot breath over my face. His hand went beneath the hem of my nightdress, up my bare thigh and he worked his thumb roughly inside me. My whole body jerked defensively and I pushed his hand away, drawing up my knee to form a barrier between us.

Frank muttered something under his breath, grabbed my knee and my shoulder, yanking roughly. Before I knew it, I was spread-eagled on my back, my arms piniored by my nightdress, which he had ripped open at the neck and pulled down, and he was on top of me. I tried to protest but my head had slipped between the two pillows that topped the bolster. I gasped aloud when he entered me; dry as I was, it might have been my first time. But Frank ignored me, pumping furiously into the burning pain, and I could do nothing but lie and let it happen.

It was over, I think, very quickly, though at the time it felt like for ever. Then Frank rolled away and I felt sticky wetness between my thighs.

'There,' Frank said, 'you can tell your doctor boyfriend your husband can still give you a good seeing-to.'

'You bastard.'

I freed my arms, pushed the sheet aside and got out of bed. More spunk ran out of me and trickled down my legs. I caught it with the hem of my nightdress.

I went downstairs, visited the outside lavatory, sat there, shivering, while the moonlight crept in through the gap at the top of the door. I was numb with shock and I shrank from going back into the house, let alone returning to the bed where my husband had raped me. But what choice did I have? I went back into the kitchen, drew a bowl of cold water at the sink and washed myself. Then I went upstairs for a clean nightdress – there was a patch of wetness cold against my legs on the one I was wearing and it was nauseating me.

Frank's breathing was slow and even; he was asleep. But there was no way on earth I was going to get into bed beside him. Stealthily, in case I should wake him, I found a blanket in the bottom of the wardrobe and taking my pillow, I went into the little spare room where the Dinky toys sat in a measured row on the shelf above the bed. Then I lay in the darkness, hugging my sore and abused body and comforting myself with the thought that now, at least, I was free to go to Dev.

Next morning, unbelievably, Frank seemed to want to behave as if nothing out of the ordinary had happened at all.

I'd slept only fitfully, and I was already downstairs when I heard him lumbering about, getting dressed. Instantly I was trembling again, but this time with grim resolve. He'd have been bound to see the bag I'd packed – I'd left it at the foot of the stairs where he'd practically trip over it – and I was ready for another fight. But when he came into the kitchen, already wearing his railway jacket and looking extremely hung over, he merely said: 'Have you made up my tea bottle yet? And my sandwiches?'

'You've got to be joking!'

'Well, I can't go to work without my snap, can I?' He still called his lunch refreshments 'snap', a leftover from his days as a miner.

'If you think I'm going to make your snap after what you did last night you've got another think coming!' I threw at him. 'You'll just have to make it yourself, Frank, today and every other day. I'm leaving you.'

'Oh, don't talk so silly!' But he looked genuinely shocked and upset. 'I'd had too much to drink, that's all. I don't know what you're making such a fuss about.'

'And have you forgotten why you had too much to drink? I told you, Frank. There's someone else. I'm sorry, but that's the way it is.'

His shoulders slumped; he rasped a hand over his chin.

'Let's not talk about it now, Carrie. I feel pretty rough.'

'I'm not surprised. And you've got nobody but yourself to blame for that.'

'I know. I felt like getting drunk. We'll talk tonight, when I get home. We'll work something out.'

'I won't be here when you get home tonight,' I said. 'I shall be on duty. And in any case—'

'Don't do anything rash, Carrie.' He was pleading now. I'd never seen Frank plead before. 'I don't know what I'd do if you left me. I know I must seem a pretty poor sort of a chap compared with a doctor, but you're my wife and I love you. I'll still be here for you, long after he's gone. Promise me you won't do anything rash. Promise me we can try and sort this out.'

'Oh, Frank . . .' Seeing him like this was just awful. He seemed like a broken man, and it was all my doing.

'Let's just forget all about it and make a fresh start.'

'I don't think I can do that.'

'Talk about it, at least. Promise me you won't walk out until we've at least talked about it.'

'All right,' I conceded. 'But it won't make any difference.'

To my horror, there were tears in his eyes.

'I do love you, Carrie. I know sometimes I've got a funny way of showing it, but—'

'All right, Frank, all right.' This was worse, by far, than his anger. I couldn't bear it. 'Get yourself some breakfast, and I'll make your sandwiches.'

I got a loaf from the bread bin and began to slice it. I supposed if I was walking out on him when he was begging me not to, the least I could do was make him a bottle of tea and a pack of fish-paste sandwiches. But if he thought I was going to give up my plans to be with Dev now then I was very much afraid that he was going to be disappointed.

SEVENTEEN

When Frank had left I was in a state of total flux. I began cleaning the house from top to bottom; leaving everything 'just so' seemed terribly important. But even that couldn't still my racing mind and tumultuous emotions. I was desperately anxious to talk to Dev but he would be on duty now, I knew. I thought of going up to the hospital but decided against it. If he was busy it wouldn't be the right time for a proper talk. Better to go on duty myself early and catch him when he finished his shift for the day. But I couldn't wait until then to speak to him – I simply couldn't.

I found some loose change, walked to the nearest telephone box and rang the hospital. As I'd half expected, Dev was on ward rounds, and I'd fed most of my money into the coin slot before he came on the line.

'Dr Devlin.'

Just hearing his voice made butterflies flutter inside me.

'Dev – it's me.'

216

'Caroletta!'

'I'm sorry to ring you at work, but I had to speak to you.'

'What's wrong?' For all that he had been so offhand with me the last time I'd seen him, he sounded anxious now.

'Nothing, but . . . I've told him, Dev. Yesterday. I told Frank about us. And that I was leaving him.'

For a moment there was total silence from the other end of the line. Then Dev said: 'You *have*?'

'Yes.'

'I can't believe you've done it. I thought—'

'I can't believe I've done it either! But it was just awful. Frank was—' I broke off. 'Can we talk – this afternoon, perhaps? If I come in early for my shift?'

'Yes, of course. We must. Come to my office. Say about four?'

'I'll be there.' The phone began beeping; I fed the last of my change into the box.

'Are you still at home at the moment?' he asked.

'Well, yes. I didn't have anywhere else to go.'

'OK, we'll sort something.' A brief pause. Then: 'You know, you've only just told me in time. A couple more days—'

'What do you mean?' I asked, puzzled and, for some reason, slightly alarmed.

'I'll explain this afternoon.' I could hear someone calling his name in the background. 'I'm going to have to go, Caroletta. But I am so very glad you called. And so very glad you've done it at last.'

'I know. So am I. Dev – are we really going to be together?'

'It certainly looks like it,' he said.

*　　*　　*

217

I walked back down the street in a bubble of happiness that still felt slightly unreal. We weren't into calm waters yet, there would still be storms ahead, but the worst was over. I'd told Frank I was leaving him, and I'd told Dev what I'd done. He'd be there for me now, supporting me, and I could face anything with him beside me. But the decision had been all mine, and I'd carried it through alone. There was a spring in my step now; I felt proud of myself, brave and free.

As I turned the corner I could see a car parked at the kerb and someone walking up the path of a house that could very well be ours and knocking at the door, but I thought I must be mistaken. Who would be calling on us? But as I got closer I could see that it was indeed our house. The man, smartly dressed, had given up knocking and was walking back down the path.

I quickened my step and called, 'Hello?'

He waited until I reached him, watching me intently.

'Mrs Chapman?'

'Yes. Can I help you?'

'I'm Mr Field. I work with Frank. Do you think we could go inside?'

I stared at him. He didn't look in the least like a railwayman, in his trilby hat and dark suit and little round-rimmed spectacles, and I had no intention of letting him into my house.

'I'm sorry, but I don't know you. What is it you want?'

Mr Field hesitated. He looked very ill at ease.

'I really do think it would be better . . .'

I was beginning to feel anxious myself.

'Mr Field, just tell me why you're here.'

'Very well.' He removed his spectacles, twiddling them between finger and thumb. Without them, his eyes looked pale and curiously naked.

'It's bad news, I'm afraid. Your husband . . .'

The strength seemed to drain out of my legs and suddenly I was shaking all over

'My husband? What about my husband?'

'He's had an accident. Rather a bad one.'

'Oh my God! He isn't . . . ?' I couldn't bring myself to say the word.

'No.' Mr Field put out a hand as if he was going to steady me, then thought better of it and went back to fiddling with his spectacles. 'But he is rather badly injured.'

'Oh my God!' I said again. And then: 'How? How is he injured? What happened? Where is he now?'

'He's at the BRI – the Bristol Royal Infirmary. Look . . .' he gesticulated towards the car that was parked at the kerb, 'why don't I take you there now, and I'll tell you what I can on the way?'

I was standing as if turned to a pillar of salt, shock robbing me of any coherent thought.

'Is there anyone else you'd like to inform?'

I shook my head.

'Anything you need to take with you? You may be there some time . . .'

Again I shook my head.

Mr Field opened the passenger door of the car, urged me towards it with a hand that never quite touched my waist.

'Then I suggest we get you there as quickly as possible. I really do think that would be best.'

219

I climbed into the front seat, still in a daze. Mr Field climbed in beside me. And as we drove into the city he filled me in with the details of what had happened.

Frank, it seemed, had somehow fallen from the footplate and slipped down between the engine and the platform. His legs – one in particular – had been badly crushed. He'd been rushed by ambulance to the BRI and Mr Field had been dispatched to break the news to me.

'We really can't understand it,' he said earnestly. 'Accidents will happen, of course, but Frank . . . He's one of our best firemen. Totally reliable and usually so careful. A lapse of concentration, I suppose, but all the same . . . no, we can't understand it at all.'

My stomach knotted. I could understand it, though of course I wasn't going to say so. Frank had been hung over and dreadfully upset, and he hadn't been thinking about what he was doing. And it was all my fault.

Oh, please let him be all right! I prayed silently. If he wasn't, I would never forgive myself.

By the time we arrived at the BRI Frank was in the operating theatre and there was nothing I could do but wait, drinking endless cups of bitter tea and torturing myself with guilt. I'd thought I was used to hospitals, but this was a wholly different experience. I got the receptionist to phone Brenton Stoke and tell them I was unlikely to be in for my shift today, but I didn't have any money to ring Dev again and could only hope he would get to hear what had happened on the grapevine, since I was in no position to ask specifically for a message to be passed on. And then there was nothing else to do but carry on waiting.

It was well into the afternoon when Frank was out of Recovery and back on the ward. A doctor, young, brash and obviously briefed by the surgeon, had explained to me that they had had to amputate one of his legs but it was still a horrible shock to see him lying there with a cradle supporting the bedclothes over the stump that was all that was left, hooked up to drains and drips. I felt sick to my stomach as I approached the bed. Frank was still groggy from the anaesthetic, but he recognised me all the same.

'What's happened to me, Carrie?' he muttered.

'You had an accident, Frank. You're in hospital.'

'My leg?' His breathing was ragged. 'Christ, it hurts like hell!'

Did he know they'd taken it off? If not, this wasn't the moment to tell him.

'It's all right, Frank. You're going to be all right.'

He nodded, still huffing over his top lip.

'You're here. That's all that matters. Carrie . . .'

'Yes?'

'Oh . . . I don't know what I was going to say. It's gone clean out of my head. But I'm so glad you're here . . . Don't leave me, Carrie. Don't go . . .'

His hand fumbled for mine; tears burning behind my eyes, I squeezed it. He was still holding on to my hand, but he was asleep.

Perversely, since such a short time ago I'd been impatient to walk out on him for ever, now the terrible guilt that was consuming me made me wish I could stay at his bedside. I couldn't, of course. Eventually, I was told politely but firmly that visiting time was over and I would have to leave.

I walked out into the cool of the evening feeling utterly drained, both physically and emotionally. I'd hardly slept last night, and the traumas of the last two days had exhausted every bit of my reserve of strength. Horror at what had happened to Frank was a weight around my heart. He'd survived the accident, but he'd never be the same again, and I couldn't help but feel that I had to take my share of the blame for that. He'd been in an awful state when he'd left for work, and that must have at least contributed to his moment of carelessness.

I wondered if I should go to work, albeit very late, but I couldn't face it. Things were much quieter now the air raids had abated; they'd just have to manage without me for one night.

I went home, back to my unusually clean house, which smelled of wax polish and soap, curled in a ball on the sofa, and fell asleep.

The sound of the doorbell crept into my dream. Muzzily I opened my eyes. The doorbell rang again and I realised it was no dream.

Instantly I was wide awake, cold with fear. Frank. Frank had taken a turn for the worse and someone had come to tell me. I jumped up, stumbling on a leg that had gone numb and a foot that felt like a pincushion, hurried to the door and opened it, expecting to see a policeman on the doorstep.

'Caroletta? What's going on?'

It was Dev.

'Dev! Oh, Dev! Come in.' He did, and I closed the door behind him. 'Oh, Dev, I've had the most awful day.'

'What's happened? You sounded fine when you spoke to me this morning. And then I heard this garbled story that there had been an accident and you were at the BRI. Are you all right?'

'Yes . . . it's not me.' My mouth was dry as parchment from the heavy sleep. 'Let's go into the kitchen. I need a cup of tea. Then I'll tell you.'

But I started the story anyway while the kettle boiled.

'What a thing!' Dev said when I'd finished. 'Poor old Frank.'

'It's just awful.' I poured boiling water into the teapot. 'And I feel terrible about it. He's lost his leg, and it's all my fault.'

'Ah, don't talk nonsense, Caroletta.' He reached for my hand, squeezing it. 'How can it be your fault?'

'Because he was so upset! Honestly, Dev, I've never seen him like that before. And he was hung over, too. He went out last night after I told him about us and got drunk—'

I broke off, unwilling to tell him the rest of the story, of how, when he had come home, Frank had raped me. I didn't even want to think about it. Yet in a funny sort of way I blamed myself for that too. It was just another manifestation of the terrible hurt I'd inflicted on him.

'It was an accident,' Dev said. 'It could have happened any time.'

I shook my head. 'I don't think so. If he hadn't been in such a state . . . he wasn't thinking what he was doing. He was thinking about us.'

Dev was silent for a moment while I poured the tea. I put his on the table in front of him and cupped my own between my hands, glad of the warmth and the comforting smell.

'So,' he said, 'what are you going to do?'

I knew what he meant, of course, but I wanted to avoid the question.

'What do you mean?'

'Well, this morning you were all set to come away with me. Does this mean you've changed your mind?'

'Of course not. But I can't walk out just now. He needs me, Dev.'

'I need you.'

But you're not lying in hospital with your leg amputated. Because of me . . .

'I have to be there for him while he's so ill. It would be just too cruel to . . . Oh, Dev, I really don't want to talk about this just now.'

He didn't argue, simply nodded. 'OK, my darling, it's your call.' But even in my dazed state, I could hear the resignation in his tone.

'You think I'm just putting it off again,' I said defensively.

'Aren't you?'

Tears welled in my eyes. This morning the future had seemed so bright. Now I felt trapped all over again.

'Oh, Caroletta, Caroletta.' Dev shook his head. 'Come here.'

He pulled me down onto his knee, arms encircling me, chin resting in my hair.

'At least you've told him. That's the biggest hurdle.'

He kissed me, and I clung to him, the tears running unchecked down my face.

224

'You want me to love you?' he asked softly after a moment.

Something inside me snapped shut. The memory of Frank raping me last night was still too fresh in my mind. I felt unclean, somehow, as well as sore. When Dev made love to me I didn't want it to be like this.

'Not tonight,' I whispered, feeling like a traitor.

'No.' His tone was gentle. 'You're tired out, I can see that. I think I should go and leave you to get some rest. Everything will look better in the morning, see if it doesn't.'

I didn't want him to go, but I thought it probably was for the best.

'Will I put you to bed then?'

He set me on my feet, supported me along the hall and up the stairs. I wondered if it was another ploy to try to make love to me, but he made no attempt to touch me beyond helping me out of my clothes and into bed. I thanked my stars that I'd changed the sheets this morning; I'd have hated him to see the evidence of what Frank had done. Then he pulled the covers over me, tucking me in as if I were a child, and leaning over to plant a kiss on my forehead.

'I'll let myself out, Caroletta. You try to get some sleep now.'

I listened to his footsteps going away down the stairs, heard the front door close after him, and the engine of his car start up. But I didn't sleep. The tears came again, tears that bled from my heart. This was what had so nearly been mine. This was what was slipping through my fingers.

Because I honestly didn't see how I could leave Frank now. And I didn't know how long Dev would be prepared to wait for me.

*   *   *

225

They say it never rains but it pours. Just when I so needed his support, Dev's father was taken seriously ill and he was given some of his long-overdue leave to go and see him.

I was back at work, but visiting Frank in hospital every day, and it was taking its toll on me. But I felt duty-bound to make the trip into town; Frank was still very ill and – as he began to recover physically – dreadfully depressed. It was only to be expected, I knew, but to see him so low made me feel guiltier than ever.

'Well, no one will blame you if you leave me now,' he said to me one day as I sat beside his bed on the hard, upright hospital chair, trying to think of things to say to fill the visiting hour.

A cradle still kept the bedclothes off the stump, hiding the fact that his leg was no longer there, though he swore he could still feel it, itching and paining him. He looked terrible, white and drawn and shrunken somehow, as if half his blood had been drained out of him, and his spirit too.

'Don't, Frank,' I said automatically.

'Well, they won't. I'm no good now to man nor beast.'

'That's nonsense. You've lost a leg, yes, but you're not the only one by a long chalk. And there are a lot worse off than you, too. Men who've lost both legs, been burned, blinded, had their faces shot away. And that's just the ones who haven't been killed. At least—'

'I'd have been better off if I had been killed. What am I going to do with only one leg? I can't go back on the railway. I'll never be a driver now. I couldn't even be a bloody porter.'

'I don't see why not. They'll fix you up with a false one.'

He laughed scornfully. 'Can you see me as a bloody porter? Dot and carry one all along the bloody platform? Is that how you see me, Carrie?'

'No, of course not. Oh, Frank, please try not to look on the black side.'

'Is there any other? I wish I *had* been killed. And so do you, I expect, truth to tell.'

'Of course I don't wish you'd been killed!' I said vehemently. 'How can you say such a thing?'

'You'd be free to go off with your doctor if I was out of the way.'

'Frank, stop it!' But my heart had contracted all the same.

He turned his head away, but I could see that he was crying, tears rolling silently down his cheeks. I leaned over and took his hand, blue-veined still from his coal-mining days, covering it with my own where it lay on the dark green hospital bedspread.

'Oh, Frank . . . I don't know . . .'

'Don't leave me, Carrie. If you do, I swear I can't go on. Not now. Not like this.' He said it softly, brokenly. 'If you go I might as well end it all.'

'Don't talk like that!' I said, frightened.

He wiped away the tears with the back of his hand but his eyes were still swimming. Then he snivelled loudly, snorted and his lips twisted in a grim parody of a grin.

'Oh, don't take any notice of me. It's just what I feel like, that's all.'

But I couldn't help feeling that he had meant what he said. It haunted me in the darkness of the night and kept a constant vigil just beneath the surface of my consciousness as I went about my days. Bad enough that my actions had precipitated Frank's accident and robbed him of his leg; how could I live with myself if he took his life? The state he was in it seemed entirely possible.

I simply couldn't take the risk. Not now. Not yet. I'd have to tell Dev that we must be patient for a little while longer. Wait until Frank had come to terms with the loss of his leg, and until he realised that there was no real happiness to be had with a wife who had stayed with him on sufferance and out of pity.

When Dev came back from Ireland I told him just that, hoping against hope that he would understand.

'Well, Caroletta, I suppose that makes the decision for me,' he said.

We were in his office. I'd be due off duty at 4 a.m.; Dev was due on at the same time. The hospital was quiet – ghostly, almost – lit only by the dim night-lights, and the office was a small oasis of brightness. When I'd opened the door and seen him there, reading through a sheaf of notes, my heart had contracted with love and I'd almost lost the will to say what I knew I must. I stood there silently for a moment, just looking at him. The lick of hair falling over his forehead, the pipe clamped between his teeth, his hands, square and capable, holding the clipboard, the smile when he looked up and saw me, everything about him made me melt inwardly. And broke my heart. But I knew I must not waver. There could be no future for us if I had Frank on my conscience. After I'd enquired after his father and he'd told me that miraculously he now seemed to be on the mend – something his mother attributed to countless novenae to St Theresa – he'd asked about Frank. And I'd had to steel myself to tell him that I couldn't leave him at the moment.

I'd expected disappointment and weary resignation, perhaps even a flash of anger. But I wasn't at all prepared for that response: 'I suppose that makes the decision for me.' What on earth did he mean by that?

'What decision?'

'To sign up. Serve with the Forces.' He tapped out his pipe into the ashtray.

I stared at him, speechless, and he grinned crookedly. 'Don't look so surprised.'

'But I am! You've never said anything about joining the Forces.'

'Truth to tell, I've been thinking about it for some time. The blitz is more or less over and I reckon I could be a lot more use serving with the army or the RAF. I'd have gone before now, more than likely, if it hadn't been for the fact that I didn't want to leave you. And going to Ireland concentrated my mind.'

'How?'

'The Republic is neutral, as you know, and I have to say I'm a bit ashamed of that. But a lot of my old friends have joined up to serve with the British Forces, and I have this urge to do the same – fly the flag for the Irish people, or something like that.'

'But you are flying the flag – here.'

'Any old codger could do what I'm doing. I should be where the fighting is, backing up our boys on the front line. It's what

I feel and, like I say, I'd have done something about it before now if it hadn't been for you. Now . . . well, if you're going to be staying with that husband of yours there's nothing to stop me, and it's likely for the best. I'll be doing what my conscience tells me I should, and it'll be easier for the both of us with me out of the way.'

'Oh, Dev, I don't want you to go.'

'I expect there's wives and girlfriends the length and breadth of the land saying much the same thing.'

'But suppose . . .' *Suppose something happens to you.* I couldn't bring myself to put it into words, but he seemed to know what I meant.

'Don't worry, darling, I'll be back. You know what they say about bad pennies. And by the time I am, perhaps you'll be a free woman.'

'I will be, I promise. When Frank is better I'll divorce him. I'll be waiting for you.'

A tap on the door. One of the oncoming shift poked her head round.

'Sorry to interrupt, but you're wanted, Dev.'

'The call of duty.' He gathered his things together. 'Look, Caroletta, we'll try to spend some time together before I go, if you want to.'

'Oh, yes . . . let's . . .'

'We'll talk about it tomorrow. I have to go now.'

'Yes, of course. I love you, Dev.'

He grinned at me crookedly. 'Ah, so you say.' And then he was gone.

* * *

Next day I was called to the hospital. Frank had taken a turn for the worse. An infection had set in and he was hovering at death's door. For what seemed like endless days and nights I stayed at his bedside, returning home only to grab a few hours' sleep and a change of clothes. Mostly he was delirious, but in lucid moments he grabbed my hand and held it so tightly the flesh was bruised, begging me not to leave him. I was racked by guilt for the part I'd played in bringing him to this, made worse by the fact that a couple of times I caught myself almost hoping he might die so that I would be free to go to Dev. That made me feel really wicked, and remembering what Dev had said about his mother praying to St Theresa I closed my eyes and begged forgiveness, begged St Theresa — whoever she was — to intervene and save Frank, knowing, even as I silently whispered the words, that I was a selfish hypocrite. I'd wanted Frank to die so that I would no longer be burdened with the decision to leave him; I didn't want him to die because I couldn't live with the heavy cross that would place on my shoulders for ever.

The crisis came on the fifth day. Frank tossed and turned, sweat pouring from his body, rambling incoherently. I sponged him down and trickled water into his mouth, grateful that I was at least able to do this for him in his extremity. It was, of course, before the days when relatives would be encouraged to spend time with their sick and dying loved ones, but the hard-pressed hospital staff, knowing I had nursing experience, were only too glad to delegate his care to me. I did what I could, hoping it would in some way exonerate me, and then, just when I felt sure that he had passed the point of no return, the fever broke.

He was still not out of danger, though, and I remained with him, afraid that if I left his distress would cause a relapse. It was another day before I felt able to go home and fall into bed. Exhausted, I slept the clock round.

It was Grace who broke the news to me; Grace who gave me the letter Dev had left for me. He had gone to sign up to serve with the RAF, and they had snapped him up. A key medical officer with one of their squadrons had died of a heart attack; a replacement was urgently needed as the squadron was due to be posted to North Africa within a few days. He apologised for not being able to say goodbye properly, but given the circumstances, he thought it was probably for the best. He would be in touch as soon as he was able.

I read the letter, too shocked even to cry.

My Dev, my love, had gone, with no chance for a proper goodbye.

I was on my own.

Except that I wasn't. I was pregnant.

Since the war had begun in earnest, Frank had never made love to me without wearing his 'overcoat' as he called it. 'This is no world to bring a kiddie into,' he'd say when the bombs were falling, and I knew he was right, even though, in the beginning, I'd longed for a baby I could carry to full term, who would be born healthy, alive, a baby I could suckle at my swollen, redundant breasts, a warm, sweet-smelling body to cradle against my heart. But the night he had raped me he had taken no such precautions.

Though that night it had occurred to me as a repellent,

fleeting possibility, in the days that followed I had been too preoccupied to worry about it. But nature takes its course, whether we are aware of it or not. At first, when my period didn't come, I tried to tell myself it was because of all the stress of the past couple of weeks. But I think I already knew it was more than that. And of course I was right.

Nine months later Gillian was born. Though to very different circumstances than Frank could ever have envisaged when he laid claim to me as his wife that balmy June night.

EIGHTEEN

'Eventually Frank was well enough to leave hospital,' I tell Kathryn. 'We stayed in Bristol while I was still able to work, but then we came home to Timberley. Frank was finished on the railway, we had no money coming in, and in any case we thought it would be safer for a baby out in the country.'

I've been talking for over an hour – the chime of the Westminster clock on the mantelpiece reminds me of that. I've talked about the raids, the devastation, the work I did, how we lost our home. But there's a great deal I've left out and I'm sure I don't have to tell you which parts. It must be as plain as the nose on your face what is far too private to tell anyone, much less a long-lost granddaughter. Now, though it's still all too clear in my memory, I skate over those last dreadful months in Bristol before we came back to Timberley. My utter desolation, Frank's neediness. 'He never was the same again,' I say, and that goes only the smallest way towards describing the way Frank had changed.

For a long time, physically, he was as weak as a kitten. Getting about on crutches was a tiring business and when he was eventually fitted with his artificial leg that was tiring and painful too. But much worse were the black moods that were never to leave him.

Once, in the early days, I found him rootling around in the little garden shed amongst bottles and packets left there by the previous occupants, and when I asked him what he was doing he said he was looking for rat poison, that he thought we had an infestation, and if he couldn't find any, I'd better buy some. But of course, I didn't. I had the most dreadful feeling that if he wanted rat poison, it wasn't for rats.

I became very scared after that, remembering the threat he'd made when he was in hospital. I hadn't left him; I was still there, little as I wanted to be. But in his depressed state anything was possible. When I got home from work – I was still working then – I would hurry in and call his name, and if he didn't answer straight away my stomach would lurch and I'd begin to feel sick. Not the sickness of pregnancy, though that was still plaguing me, but the sickness of dread, that I would find him unconscious from an overdose of painkillers that he'd managed to hoard, or hanging by his belt from the banister.

It was then that I decided it was only fair that I should write to Dev and tell him not to wait for me. With Frank the way he was, I could offer Dev nothing, not even hope. He should be free to meet someone else, and have a normal life with her. Some of Frank's depression had rubbed off on me, I suppose, and I could see no future for Dev and me.

Writing that letter was one of the hardest things I had ever done, and even then I clung on to a thread of hope that he might reply telling me he would wait for me for ever. But no letter came.

When I was six months gone I gave up my job. Truth to tell, I should have given it up earlier, but I was reluctant to lose the companionship and the few hours away from Frank. He still needed a good deal of care and attention; he was still given to dark moods that frightened me. And though my affair was never mentioned, I knew he was far from forgetting about it. I could see it in his face when he looked at me and knew that he was avoiding bringing it up because he was afraid that if he did I would tell him something he didn't want to hear. Unbelievably, he still wanted me and was trying to blank his deepest fears in the hope that it would all go away.

The last thing I wanted was to go home to Timberley, but there seemed to be no alternative. So home we went. Back to Mother and Father. Once again I was trapped in the life I'd thought I'd left behind for ever.

'So Mum was born here, in Timberley?' Kathryn asks.

I nod. But all this talking is making me thirsty.

'I could do with another cup of tea. How about you?'

'I'm fine.' But she follows me into the kitchen and perches on one of the kitchen chairs. I put the kettle on to boil, go to the fridge to get out the milk, and see the remains of last night's bottle of white wine there. Suddenly I fancy it more than a cup of tea. I get it out.

'We could always finish this up.'

'Grandma, you're a dark horse!' But she's smiling. 'Yes, go on then. But only if you're having one too.'

I fetch the glasses. 'Don't tell Andrea.'

'I won't if you don't.'

I'm struggling with the cork. Andrea had stuffed it back in so hard it almost needs a corkscrew all over again. Kathryn takes the bottle from me, wriggling the cork then giving it a sharp tug. It comes out with a soft 'pop', and I envy the strength in her young hands.

'There you go.' She goes to hand me the bottle but I push the glasses across the table to her. I'm not sure I trust myself to do it. All these memories are making me a bit shaky.

'You pour. Not too much for me, though.'

'So,' Kathryn says when we've each had a sip of wine, 'was Mum actually born in this house?'

'Yes, she was.' I curl my fingers round the fine stem of the wineglass. 'I was booked into a nursing home, but I went into labour in the middle of the night. I didn't want to disturb Mother and Father, and by the morning I'd left it too late. Father went for Mrs Weller – she lived just down the lane. She used to deliver babies and lay out the dead too, and she'd been coming in to change the dressings on Frank's leg. She was like the district nurse, I suppose, though we never called her anything but Mrs Weller. Anyway, by the time she got here, your mother was well on the way.'

I smile to myself, remembering, though there was nothing to smile about at the time. I was in quite a panic, desperate to push, and Mother telling me not to, not until Mrs Weller arrived. She was in a panic too, I suppose, thinking she might have to deliver the baby herself.

Mrs Weller came bustling in just as I was having another pain.

'Good Lord, Carrie,' she said, 'you aren't going to take up much of my morning, are you?' And over her shoulder to Mother: 'I hope you've got the water on to boil, Rose.'

'You want it now?' Mother was all a-fluster.

'I shall in just a minute. Go on now, off you go and leave her to me.' She was as brisk and cheerful as ever, in spite of the fact that under her gabardine coat she was still wearing a flowered overall rather than the big white apron she adopted when she took on the role of nurse.

'Can I push now?' I gasped.

'You push, my love,' she said, 'though Dr Flowers will have my guts for garters.'

Far gone as I was, I knew what she meant. If the baby arrived before Dr Flowers did, he'd miss out on his fee.

'He wasn't booked anyway,' I tried to say, but another contraction was starting, and I felt I was being ripped apart.

I don't remember much after that, just the pain and the panic and the sheer hard work, and then it was over and Mrs Weller was saying: 'Well, it's a little girl. A lovely little girl!' and I heard a hiccuping cry that became a series of thin wails.

I turned my head on the pillow that was damp with sweat, trying to see her, but she was in Mrs Weller's arms, and Mrs Weller had her back to me, going to the door.

'Rose!' she called. 'Come and take this baby, will you, while I see to Carrie?'

It was another half-hour or so before I saw her. Mrs Weller had washed her down and had her in one of the gowns I'd managed to get for her, wrapped her up tight as a chrysalis. Her face was red, her scalp covered by a feathering of dark hair. As I took her, afraid almost, she opened her eyes, blue as a September sky, and squinted up at me.

'Hello,' I said. 'Hello, Baby.' And felt such a rush of love and tenderness and pride it overwhelmed me.

'Have you got a name for her?' Mrs Weller asked.

'We've thought of a few, but we haven't quite decided.'

I could hear someone on the stairs. The slow, struggling gait told me it was Frank. Mrs Weller went to the door.

'Come on in, Mr Chapman. She's all ready for visitors. And so is your daughter.'

Frank came in cautiously, as if afraid of what he might find.

'Come on, do! Do you want to hold her? You can, you know. She won't bite,' Mrs Weller said.

'No, it's all right, I'll just look at her.' But there was an expression of awe and love and wonder on his face.

'You all right, Carrie?' he asked roughly.

'I'm fine. Mrs Weller was just asking if we'd thought of a name. I told her we hadn't really made up our minds, though I like Jennifer. Or Gillian.'

'Gillian,' Frank said at once.

'Yes, she looks like a Gillian,' Mrs Weller said.

So Gillian it was. A week or so later Frank managed to get himself to the register office on the bus to register her birth — one hell of a job for him on his crutches, but he was determined to be the one to do it.

'Gillian Augusta,' he said when he came back, exhausted.

'Augusta!' I repeated, shocked. 'You've called her *Augusta?*'

'They wanted to know if we wanted a second name, and I couldn't think of anything else.'

'*Augusta!*'

'It's all right, isn't it?' Frank said defensively. Then: 'It was my mother's name. I thought . . .'

I bit back my initial horror. 'Yes, of course it's all right,' I said. 'It's a nice thought, Frank, calling her after your mother.'

From the first, Frank doted on Gillian. When she woke at night he'd jiggle her up and down in his arms. When I pushed her pram out onto the bricks for her to get some fresh air he'd sit beside it, looking in at her, and swinging the blue fluffy ball we'd managed to get and which we'd attached to the hood of the pram where she could see it. Later on, when she took her first faltering step, it was to Frank, and he was responsible for her getting her first proper dress. He'd managed to get himself a job, as an electrician's mate at the engineering works, and one of the women in the canteen there did a bit of sewing on the side. Frank got hold of some parachute silk and the woman – Florrie Hill, her name was – made it into a dress and worked some blue smocking on the bodice so that the skirt fell in full gathers down to Gillian's chubby little legs. The first time I got her hair cut he took a curl, wrapped it in a bit of tissue paper, and put it in his wallet. He never said anything about it, but he kept it there right up until he died. I know because I found it after I came out of prison and went through his things that Mother had packed up and left in the cottage.

Yes, Frank doted on Gillian, not a doubt of it, and she doted on him. It pleased me, made me feel less guilty that I didn't love him myself.

But it was another trap, of course. If Frank hadn't loved Gillian so, he might be alive today. But I didn't know that then, couldn't see into the future, and a good thing too, considering what the future held. As it was, we bruggled on from day to day, trying to do our best in a bleak world. Wondering when the war would end, and how. Caught up in queuing for a bit of meat and counting clothing coupons. Watching the skies and listening for the sound of enemy aircraft. Patching and mending and reading the names of boys we knew, killed in action, in the local newspaper. It was hard then to imagine ever getting back to normality, just as when it's cold and pouring with rain it's hard to imagine the sun will ever warm your skin again. The war had become the way things were, and we just got on with it.

There were bright spots, of course, and chief of those for me was Gillian. She was a constant joy to me, watching her grow from a baby into a beautiful little girl who played happily out on the bricks, pushing a little wooden cart Father had made her, sorting bits of old china she found in the garden, collecting stones that she lined up under the wall and called her 'children'. The love I felt for her never failed to amaze me; the warm glow that suffused me when she climbed up onto my lap and wound her chubby arms around my neck, the contentment of kneeling beside her cot when she slept, singing softly to her until she fell asleep – 'The White Cliffs of Dover', 'Lilli Marlene', 'Good Night, Sweetheart' – then smoothing her hair away from her flushed face before creeping away; the pleasure in the funny little things she said. She was my baby, and the love I felt for her was so fierce it frightened me sometimes. If she grazed her knee the pain was mine; when she caught whooping cough, I felt the tearing of her lungs in my own chest and wished with all my heart that I could bear it for her. I would endure anything if I could save her from it; I'd die before I'd see her hurt, my precious baby.

Another bright spot was the friendship I'd forged with Mary Hutchins, as she is now. I think I'd have gone crazy with loneliness if it hadn't been for Mary.

'You'll meet her,' I tell Kathryn. 'She lives on the farm next door to the Hall, and always has. In those days she was the farmer's daughter, now she's the farmer's wife. Geoff, her husband, took over the farm when Mary's father retired. And their two younger sons went into farming too . . .'

But we're getting off the subject.

'Your mother loved going up to the farm,' I say. 'That's how I came to get friendly with Mary. I used to take Gillian up to see the cows, and Mary asked if she'd like to come in and feed the hens.'

I smile, remembering Gillian, her face alight, pointing with chubby fingers at the herd of Friesians looking at us over the hedge. I got her out of her pushchair and lifted her up so she could pat their noses, and Mary happened to come by and see us there. She stopped to chat, and it all started from there.

I took to calling in at the farm almost every day when I took Gillian out for her daily constitutional, and sometimes Mary would send me home with a pat of butter or half a dozen eggs – a great luxury in those days of rationing. Gillian would potter round while Mary and I gossiped and set the world to rights.

'You ought to try and get a job in the hospital,' Mary said one day when I was bemoaning the fact that I was finding it hard to make ends meet on Frank's meagre wage. 'They're always looking for people to help out, and with your experience . . .'

'I think I would,' I said, 'if it weren't for Gillian.'

'Wouldn't your mother look after her?'

'I wouldn't like to ask. I feel I'm putting on them enough already. Mother's not getting any younger, and her legs aren't too good.'

I didn't add that Mother and I always seemed to be falling out these days. It seemed I could do nothing right. I'd made peg marks on the washing, I'd killed her maidenhair fern by overwatering, I'd put too much salt in the potatoes. Sometimes I felt like hiding away in the cottage as Frank did. Except that being with Frank was as bad as being with Mother – worse. He'd been getting a lot of what I called his 'black moods' again lately, even losing patience with Gillian, and with me he was impossible, argumentative and contrary. I swear if I said something was black, he'd say it was white, and vice versa. He didn't enjoy his job, his stump was paining him, and he was really low, not being able to do the things he used to. I tried to make allowances for him but it was driving me crazy.

'Well,' Mary said, 'if you wanted to do a few hours a week, Gillian could always come to me.'

'But surely she'd hinder you,' I said doubtfully.

'Oh, she's no trouble. I like having her about the place. So if you want to go for a job at the hospital and earn a bit extra, you can. And I'll look after Gillian.'

'Well, if you're sure . . .'

'Course I am. We'll be all right, won't we, Gill? But not if you keep chasing those poor birds.' She laughed, scooping Gillian up and allowing a beleaguered hen to escape, squawking.

I was really grateful and looked into it straight away. The hospital was only too glad to have me, and I arranged to do a few hours, four days a week, which I thought was ideal. But Frank was furious.

'You know I don't want you working, Carrie,' he fumed. 'I don't want people thinking I can't keep my own wife and child. And I certainly don't want you leaving Gillian with a stranger.'

'Mary's not a stranger,' I said. 'Gillian loves her.'

'Gillian needs her mother.'

'For goodness' sake, Frank, it's only a few hours a week.'

His face darkened. 'What do you want to work in a hospital for, anyway? There's not something behind this, is there? That bloody doctor hasn't moved up here, has he?'

'Of course not!' But his immediate reaction confirmed my suspicion that Frank was far from forgetting what had happened.

I don't tell Kathryn any of this, of course, but she's fascinated by my account of the time I spent working up at the Hall when it was a hospital, though it's far less dramatic than my experiences as an ambulance attendant in Bristol.

'I never did much beyond cleaning and helping out with general orderly duties,' I tell her. 'Everyone's dogsbody, that was me. It wasn't even a proper hospital, more a convalescent home for officers. I met some great characters, though. There was one, scarcely more than a boy, who'd been told he'd never walk again, but refused to accept it. Every time our backs were turned he'd be levering himself up out of his wheelchair, trying to make his legs work. I can't tell you how many times I had to call for help to pick him up off the floor. And there was an old colonel – well, he seemed old to me at the time; he was a regular who'd seen service in the First War – who took quite a shine to me. He'd lost his right arm and the other one wasn't much use, it shook so much. He had to be shaved and helped with his meals. If he tried to feed himself it all ended up down his front. But he wouldn't have anybody but me do it. "Bugger off!" he'd shout at the other nurses. "I don't want you spoon-feeding me like a blasted baby! Where's Carrie? I want Carrie!"'

Kathryn laughs. 'I expect you were quite the glamour girl.'

'Oh, I shouldn't think so! But I did treat him like a normal human being. A lot of the others talked to him as if he'd lost his wits rather than his arm.'

'And you were there until the end of the war?' Kathryn asks.

'Until the hospital closed down. That was getting on for a year after VE Day.'

'And all that time Mom went up to the farm while you were working?'

'Yes. It was very convenient. I could drop her off with Mary, walk next door, and be there. Gillian loved it, and it was good for her too, all that fresh air. And the animals . . . she adored them. I swear her first word was "Moo-cow".'

I smile, picturing Gillian, rosy-cheeked, in a little pair of Wellington boots I'd managed to get for her and blue dungarees that had come in a parcel of hand-me-downs from a neighbour along the lane. The dungarees had belonged to her little boy, and Frank hated Gillian wearing them.

'She ought to be in a pretty dress,' he complained. But I retorted that beggars couldn't be choosers and, in any case, the dungarees were very practical for her up at the farm.

'When she was big enough, Mary started teaching her to ride,' I tell Kathryn. 'Well, maybe "teaching her to ride" is a bit of an exaggeration. She used to put her up on the pony and walk her round the field.'

'So there were horses there even then.'

'Well, of course there were!' I laugh. 'Farming wasn't all mechanical in those days. Horses were used for everything. They didn't have such things as combine harvesters, for instance. It was all threshing machines, horse-drawn, and a lot of back-breaking work. And a horse pulled the milk cart and the baker's cart, and the parcel delivery van.'

I pause, thinking of what a different world it was. Drawing our water from the village pump, wind-up gramophones, a cold-slab in the larder instead of a fridge, no vacuum cleaners or washing machines, no telephone in your own house, certainly no mobile, a wireless that ran off a battery that was recharged on an accumulator, no television . . .

Footsteps on the bricks. The back door opens. It's Andrea.

'Good lord!' she says. 'Are you two drinking already?'

She tosses her riding gloves down on the table, goes to the sink and washes her hands.

I'm a bit shocked to see her. 'Surely it's not lunchtime?'

'By my reckoning, it is.'

'Where's the morning gone?' But I am feeling hungry too. 'I'd better see about getting you something to eat, I suppose.' I push back my chair.

'Stay there. I'll see to it.'

'You will not! Sit down, have a glass of wine, and tell Kathryn about the horses they used to have up at the farm.'

I've enjoyed Kathryn's company, but it's tiring, too, being careful about what I say. I could do with a few minutes' respite.

'Talking about the farm, I saw Tom today.' Andrea gathers a handful of knives and forks from the cutlery drawer, stands for a moment holding them between both hands. She's turned a little pink. It might be the fresh air, I suppose, but I can't help wondering . . .

'Tom is Mary's eldest son,' I explain to Kathryn, though of course I don't mention that once upon a time I had great hopes he and Andrea might end up together, and so did Mary. We used to joke about how lovely it would be if we ended up related. And at one time it had looked hopeful. They spent a lot of time together, mostly around the horses, and I was fairly sure Andrea was sweet on Tom. But nothing ever came of it. Perhaps growing up together as youngsters had been a damper on a romantic attachment.

He's been off the scene for a long time now. Unlike his brothers, who both went into farming, he left to work for a big multinational company. He did well too, climbed a long way up the management ladder, but it's meant he's spent most of his life overseas. I'm surprised to hear he's in Timberley; Mary complains that she hardly ever gets to see him. But he lost his wife a couple of years ago, so maybe he's feeling the pull of home. And I can't help feeling a little spring of hope – that he and Andrea . . .

'How is he?' I ask.

'I didn't see him to speak to. He just passed us in his car in the lane when we were coming back from our ride.' Andrea moves her riding gloves, sets the places, looks at Kathryn. 'I've got a couple of hours free this afternoon. I was thinking I could show you round the district. If you'd like to, and you're not too tired. Marlow is quite a pretty little town . . .'

She's changing the subject, I know. Perhaps there are things she doesn't want to talk about. Perhaps, like me, she has her secrets. Oh, I do wish things would work out for Andrea. I really would like to see her with someone. And Tom would be ideal . . .

I pull myself up short. I mustn't be such a sentimental old fool, and I mustn't interfere. We have to let our children sort out their own lives.

And certainly I'm hardly the one to give advice, considering the mess I managed to make of my own!

NINETEEN

I can't blame Andrea for being evasive about Tom, if indeed, there is anything to be evasive about. She gets that from me. There are plenty of things I don't talk about, never have, except to Grace and to Mary; never will. But that doesn't mean I don't think about them in the dark hours of the night.

What happened at the end of the war, for instance. I'm thinking about that now.

The house is silent, except for Andrea's gentle snoring, reverberating across the landing, and the occasional creak, like a ghostly footfall, of a timber settling. But I'm not at all sleepy. I had a good nap this afternoon when Andrea took Kathryn to Marlow, with a detour past the engineering works where Frank was an electrician's mate, or so I understand. I do enjoy an afternoon nap — there's a feeling of luxuriousness about it — but I dare say I'd sleep better at night if I didn't have it.

Now, in the darkness, the memories are so clear I feel I could almost reach out and touch them. And the regret for what might have been if things had been different is a sadness settled around my heart. Not a sadness for the woman I am now – I'm content enough, or would be if only I could have Gillian back for just a day – but for the girl I once was. And the love that was never meant to be.

I push back the sheet and bedspread – Andrea has never been able to persuade me to change to a duvet – and get out of bed. I cross to the window, draw back the curtains and moonlight streams in, bright as day. Good thing we're not still at war; this is just the sort of night for one hell of a bombing raid.

I go to my dressing table. It's big, heavy, old-fashioned, with two long drawers, two half-drawers above and two more small ones, set in the frame that supports the mirror. I open one of these and take out my handkerchief sachet. No one uses proper handkerchiefs any more, of course, even me – why make washing when you can use a tissue and throw it away? But I've kept a couple, lace-edged and with a little flower worked in a corner, and it's not a handkerchief I'm after, anyway. It's the letters, folded carefully beneath. Dev's letters, written in the early days when he first joined the RAF and before I wrote to tell him I couldn't leave Frank and it would be best if we ended it. Did he keep mine? I wonder. Men don't usually hoard such things, but he did have a bit of a sentimental streak. The romantic Celt in him, I suppose.

I take them out, unfold them, and it seems to me they are still faintly scented with lavender, though I expect that's just my imagination. I pad back to the bedside table, fetch my glasses and return to the window and the moonlight.

It's years now since I looked at them, but all this talking

about the past has started a yearning in me to read them, and as I do there's a warm place inside me as if it were sunshine, not the cold light of the moon, streaming in at the window. Even though the letters ceased after I told him they must, I know now that he had never stopped loving me.

There's another letter amongst them, on blue Basildon Bond. From Grace, of course. I'd forgotten I'd kept that one. I didn't keep any of her other letters. But the minute I look at it I'm transported back in time. To 1945. The end of the war. Peace at last, the peace we'd thought would never come. And an invitation to a get-together that would turn out to be not at all what I was expecting.

It came with the second post. I'd run across the road to the little shop for a loaf of bread, and I met Clarence Cross, the postman, at the gate.

'Letter for you, Carrie,' he said, handing it to me.

I recognised Grace's handwriting at once, though I didn't often hear from her any more. She'd married her young man and our lives, once so closely intertwined, had moved in quite different directions. I slipped the letter into the pocket of my apron and took the loaf of bread into the kitchen, where Gillian was happily scribbling with coloured pencils on yesterday's News Chronicle. The minute she saw me, Mother commandeered me to help her fold the sheets that she'd just taken in from the washing line and it was a good half-hour before I found a minute to sit down and open the letter. Grace had written:

Sorry not to have been in touch for so long, but hopefully we can have a good catch-up soon. I've got a few of the old gang coming over for a get-together on Saturday week to celebrate the end of the war, Bonnie and Phyl to name but two. Do hope you'll be able to make it. Can you let me know?

Lots of love . . .

'Frank,' I said that evening, 'Grace has invited me to a girls' get-together on Saturday week. I'd really like to go. Is that all right?'

We were in the cottage. Frank still went out there every night when he'd finished his tea, just as he'd used to in the old days, and sat there reading his newspaper or listening to the wireless, and smoking a cigarette, which Mother frowned on in the house.

'A girls' get-together?' He sounded doubtful.

'The Red Cross girls. Oh, please, Frank, I haven't seen Grace for ages. I could get the train, and Gillian will be in bed and asleep. She'd be no trouble.'

'You've got it all worked out, haven't you?' Frank said. 'Well, if it's just the girls I don't suppose there's any harm.' He had a quarter-bottle of whisky open beside him, I noticed. He often did, these days, and though if he drank too much of it he became morose or even bad-tempered, early in the evening, when he'd had just a nip, it made him far more amenable.

I didn't give him the chance to have second thoughts. 'Oh, bless you, Frank!' I said.

'Just make sure,' Frank said, 'that you don't miss the last train home.'

* * *

By the Saturday of the party I was in a great state of excitement. It was so long since I'd been out for an evening, or, in fact, done anything but be a housewife, a hospital orderly, or a mother. I put on my best dress, wishing I could have got something new to wear. This one had seen so much service the fuchsia-coloured flowers had faded to pale pink on their white background. I managed to scrape enough lipstick out of an old tube to redden my lips a little, and rubbed a bit of boot polish into my eyelashes. There was still a drop of Evening in Paris perfume in the bottle on my dressing table; I dabbed a few precious spots behind my ears and onto my wrists. The scent was a haunting reminder of a long-ago past. Mother had got Gillian ready for bed, and when I went downstairs she was sitting at the kitchen table with a cup of warm milk. I kissed her and went in search of Frank.

I found him in the garden, mowing the lawn with the unsteady gait I'd grown used to.

'I'm off then, Frank.'

He looked me up and down. 'You look nice, Carrie.'

'Thank you. I feel nice!'

'Come here.' He let go the handles of the mower and caught my hand, pulling me towards him.

'Frank, what are you doing! Father's just down on the bricks . . .'

'He can't see us. The hedge is in the way.'

He was sweating a bit from his exertions with the lawn mower and he smelled faintly of the grease he'd used on the blades to make them run more smoothly. It was all over his hands, I felt sure.

I wriggled away, anxious that he shouldn't get any on my dress, and, as always, preferring to avoid physical contact with him. It didn't happen too often these days, with Mother and Father always on the scene, and knowing they were just the other side of our bedroom wall was almost as good as a dose of bromide. But when it did, I was as reluctant as ever, though I tried not to show it. Now, when Frank sighed and limped back to the mower, I followed him. I was happy and excited and I didn't want to leave him feeling hurt and disgruntled.

'Thank you, Frank.'

'What for?'

'For letting me go to the party, of course.' I planted a kiss on his cheek.

'Just you go careful.'

'I will.' The gluey lipstick had left a scarlet cupid's bow on his cheek; I reached in his pocket for his handkerchief, a square of khaki-coloured cotton left over from his days on the railway, and wiped it off. 'Don't wait up for me.'

'We'll see,' he said.

I walked the mile or so to Gatsford Halt. It wasn't a manned station, but the train would stop when the driver saw me waiting. By the time I got there my feet were throbbing and my calf muscles tight – I wasn't used to high-heeled shoes these days. But too bad, I had no intention of looking like a country bumpkin in front of my old friends.

I had another long walk ahead of me when I got to Bristol, and there were no trams nowadays. The tram depot had been decimated in the bombing and it would be a long time, if ever, before they were running again. But I was lucky enough to find a bus that would drop me off at the top of Park Street, and from there I walked to Canynge Square, where Grace now lived with her new husband.

The square, too, had suffered some bomb damage, but the lovely old house where Grace and Arnie, her husband, lived was untouched. When I rang the bell, Grace came down to let me in and we hugged on the doorstep.

'Oh, Carrie, it's so good to see you! Come on in. Several of the others are here already . . .' She looked, and smelled, as good as ever – nothing faded or worn about her dress – but then, she'd always had an extensive wardrobe to choose from and had no need to keep wearing, and washing, the same things.

Beyond the front door was an impressive hall with stained glass in the windows, and the evening sun shining through them made sparkling patterns on the tiled floor. Grace led the way up two flights of stairs and into a spacious flat. We passed the kitchen, where I caught a glimpse of plates of food set out on the table and covered with a cloth, and went into an elegant drawing room, which overlooked the square and the private garden that sat, island-like, in the centre.

Bonnie and Phyl were both there. They put down their glasses to hug me as Grace had done.

And a voice from behind me said, with an unmistakably Irish accent: 'Hello, Caroletta.'

I spun round, disbelieving.

'Dev!'

My first impression was that he was thinner, the lines between nose and mouth more deeply etched. There were a few streaks of grey in his hair, and it seemed to have receded a little, so that his forehead appeared higher. But the smile was the same, that wicked grin that made his eyes narrow. And they still sparkled with mischief, that deep, dark blue.

'Oh, Dev!' Tears were pricking at my own eyes; I remembered the boot polish and blinked them away. 'It's so wonderful to see you!'

'And you, my darlin'.'

'What would you like to drink, Carrie?' Grace was asking.

There was a certain smugness about her that told me she must have known all along that Dev would be here, yet hadn't mentioned it in her letter. Had they planned it together, she and Dev?

'What have you got?'

'Gin, whisky – not a very nice one, I'm afraid, but the best Arnie could get hold of. He's made himself scarce, by the way. Said if this was going to be a get-together of the old crowd he didn't want to be the odd one out. A good excuse for a night out with his own chums, if you ask me . . .'

'Caroletta will have whisky,' Dev said wickedly. 'She likes her drop of whisky, isn't that right, Caroletta?'

I certainly needed it! My head was spinning and my heart thudding so hard I thought it would burst.

'Whisky, then? With dry ginger? Or peppermint?'

I'd never had whisky with anything but a drop of water.

'I'll try the peppermint.'

'One whisky and pep coming up.' She went to get it for me.

'So how is the world treating you then?' Dev asked, but before I could answer, Bonnie was there at my shoulder.

'I hope you're going to be a bit more respectful to this man than you were in the old days. He's a squadron leader now, you know.'

'A squadron leader!' I repeated, astonished.

'Grand, isn't it? And there's me a humble garage mechanic – or training to be one, anyway.' Bonnie laughed. 'But you know me – I was always more interested in what went on under the bonnet of the ambulance than what you attendants were doing with the patients inside. And I was lucky enough to find a one-man garage proprietor willing to take me on when the war finished. A lot of the girls are out of work.'

'Not me,' Phyl chimed in. 'I'm going to be a proper nurse. I start my first year of probation next month.'

Grace was back with my drink; I sipped it cautiously and quite liked it. The other girls moved off.

'How come you're a squadron leader?' I asked Dev.

'Well, the fact is I've signed on as a regular,' he said.

'But why?'

He shrugged. 'It seemed like a good idea at the time,' he said breezily. 'The life suits me, and I'd no civilian job to come back to. And what about you? Are you still with that husband of yours?'

'Yes, worse luck.'

Before I could elaborate, more of the old crowd arrived, buzzing excitedly round Dev and making intimate conversation between us impossible. I wasn't sorry. It was enough that I could hear his voice and feast my eyes on him; I didn't want to spoil it by the inevitable questions he would ask me when we were alone, and for which I really had no answers.

Until that happened, it was as if my decision to stay with Frank and the estrangement between me and Dev as a result of it had never been. The past years had melted away, all the old magic was there between us and nothing else mattered. Dev was here and I was here, I loved him just as I'd loved him then, before everything had gone horribly wrong.

Though we were separated by a press of laughing, chattering old colleagues, I knew he was still as aware of me as I was of him. Whenever our eyes met there was a flare of electricity between us, and more often than could be down to pure chance I found him by my elbow.

'You planned this!' I whispered to Grace as she refilled my glass yet again.

She grinned at me impishly. 'Maybe . . .'

'You should have warned me!'

'I didn't want to spoil the surprise.'

'You thought I might not come if I knew, more like!'

'And would you?'

I couldn't answer that. Oh, the temptation to see Dev would have been pretty well irresistible, but I wasn't at all sure that it was a good idea. I'd more or less accepted my lot. Now the floodgates were open again and all my old emotions a raging whirlpool. It would be harder than ever to go back to the life I'd imposed upon myself.

'The way I see it, Carrie, is that you deserve some happiness,' Grace said.

Phyl was hovering, trying to overhear our conversation. Grace turned to her, all innocence. 'Phyl, there's something I have to ask you. Now the war's over and you don't have any more sea-boot socks to knit, how on earth do you fill your spare moments?'

The evening was flying by. I looked at the anniversary clock on Grace's mantelpiece and realised I was going to have to leave soon if I wasn't to miss my train. Dev was in the centre of a small group. I joined them.

'So you're still standing, Caroletta,' he said mischievously. 'The whisky hasn't hit you yet?'

'No thanks to you! I saw you trying to nudge Grace's arm when she was pouring my drink.'

'Now would I do a thing like that?'

'You certainly would! But it hasn't worked. I'm as sober as a judge.'

It wasn't quite true. I wobbled a little on my high heels even as I said it, and he gave me a sideways glance.

'Are you sure?'

I ignored that. 'I'm going to have to go. I've got to get down to Temple Meads in time for my train.'

'And how are you going to get all the way to Temple Meads?' Dev asked.

'By bus and shanks's pony, the same way as I got here, in reverse.'

'Carrie, you can't! Not at this time of night!' Hilda Barnes, one of the former drivers, sounded horrified. 'The pubs will be turning out.'

'So?'

'It's not safe, honestly. Bristol's changed at night since the war. There's a lot of lads about with nothing better to do than look for mischief, and worse. No jobs, no home to go back to, some of them, a cheap demob suit, a bit of money in their pocket, and the old Adam still in them from the service they saw . . . There's been a fair bit of trouble lately. I wouldn't care to be walking the streets on my own after dark.'

Coming from a girl who had driven an ambulance through the horrors of the blitz it was a pretty sobering admission.

'I'll take you, Caroletta. No, no arguments, now. If anything happened to you I'd never forgive myself.' Dev fished in his pocket for his car keys. 'Come on now, say your good nights. I wouldn't want you to miss that train.'

What could I do? To refuse would have aroused more comment among the girls than accepting. And I wanted to, of course I did. But I was dreadfully afraid, too. My heart was pounding; a million butterflies fluttered in my stomach. I was fast approaching a crossroads in my life, and I honestly didn't know which road I was going to take.

TWENTY

His car, the same Humber, was parked in the square. He unlocked the door and helped me into the front passenger seat, got in beside me.

'Alone at last,' he said. But there was a steeliness now beneath the banter, the only outward sign of how much I had hurt him.

'It looks like it.' I tried to make my tone light, but I could hear the tremble in my voice.

He hadn't started the engine; he had swivelled in his seat so he was looking directly at me.

'So you stayed with your husband, then.' Same hard tone.

'You know I did. I wrote to you.'

'Ah, yes. Not a letter I was glad to receive, though it came as no great surprise. I knew all along it was hoping for too much that you'd get up the courage to leave him.'

'It wasn't a question of courage,' I said, bristling a little. 'I couldn't leave him. He was in a terrible state, threatening suicide, even. I couldn't have that on my conscience.'

'He'd never have done it. People who talk about it never do. He was just trying it on, Caroletta.'

'He'd lost his leg. He'd lost his job. If he'd lost me too . . . I couldn't take the risk, Dev. I couldn't have lived with myself if he'd done away with himself because of me.'

'Still wearing the hair shirt, eh?' I was silent. 'Oh, Caroletta, it's you that should be the Catholic, not me.'

'Shouldn't we get going?' I suggested.

'Well, perhaps we should.' The frostiness of his tone made me want to weep. He started the engine, pulled out of the square onto Canynge Road, heading in the direction of Clifton village.

'So how have things been?' he asked.

'Oh . . . you know . . .'

'No, I don't. That's why I'm asking you.'

'Well, you know I have a little girl now. Gillian. She's just beautiful. Did you see her picture?'

I'd been proudly showing around a snapshot of Gillian, taken on Frank's Brownie Box camera.

'I did indeed. And I'd say she takes after her mother.'

'I don't know about that, but she's my pride and joy.'

'I'm sure she is, but it was Frank I was asking about. How is he now?'

'Well, a lot better than he was. But . . .' I really didn't want to talk about Frank.

'And are you happy with him?'

I chuckled mirthlessly. 'What do you think?'

'I think you're wishing you'd left him for me.'

'I wish I'd been *able* to. You know that. You know how much you meant to me.'

262

'Meant? Past tense?'

'Mean,' I said softly. 'I've always loved you, and I always will.'

We had been driving through the quiet streets, past bomb sites that carved great chasms in the symmetry of the rows of Georgian buildings, whole areas that were fenced off or boarded up. At The Horsefair, Dev turned left.

'Temple Meads is straight on,' I said, frowning.

'Is it?'

'You know it is! Where are you going?'

'This is the Gloucester Road, isn't it? Now I've got you in the car and comfortable, I might just as well drive you home.'

'Dev – you can't!' I was panicking, imagining what would happen if his car drew up outside our house. 'Turn the car round. Take me to the station!'

'Not a chance. I think it's time you and I had a serious talk, don't you?'

The butterflies were going crazy in my stomach again, my mind was whirling. I felt as if I were caught in some crazy dream.

'Yes. Perhaps.'

'No perhaps about it.' But for the time being he said no more, and for all the emotions churning inside me, there was a comfortable rightness in the silence.

We passed the turning to Brenton Stoke, and the aeroplane works. The suburbs of Bristol thinned and we were in open countryside interspersed with villages. Dev's left hand found mine and held it, using his right hand to change gear, and the point of contact became a focus to me, as if all my yearning was concentrated in those few inches of skin. I could feel my resolve weakening, the longing gaining in strength. He was in every beat of my heart, every breath I breathed; the physical need drew my flesh towards him like a magnet, the aching longing to be with him always, simply in his presence, filled every corner of my soul.

We had almost reached Timberley; the signpost on the road, clear in the light of the headlamps, read '4 miles'. Dev slowed the car to little more than walking pace; I could see him looking from side to side rather than straight down the road ahead. After a few hundred yards we came upon a gap in the hedge, a farm track, gateless, with thick trees on one side. Dev stopped, reversed, drove into it.

Then he pulled in beneath the trees, out of sight of the road, and turned off the engine and headlights.

'So – what are we going to do? Are you going to leave that husband of yours at last and come with me, or are you going to send me away again disappointed?'

'Oh, Dev . . . you know what I want, more than anything in the world. But it's not that simple.'

'What's not simple? You complicate everything, Caroletta. Let's just look at the basics. Do you love me?'

'Of course. You know I do.'

'And what about Frank? Do you love him?'

'No. I've never loved him. Not in that way.'

'So leave him. You say he's better now, not threatening suicide any more?'

'No, but it could set him back again.'

'It's not your responsibility, Caroletta. You can't live your life to protect others, no matter how much you feel you should.

And in any case, if he's any sort of a man, he wouldn't want you on those terms. How do you think he feels, knowing his wife is only staying with him out of pity? It's humiliation, so it is. I'd chop my right hand off before I'd let any woman make such a fool out of me.'

'But you're not Frank.'

'Ah, give him a little credit!'

'There's Gillian to think of, too.'

'I know that.' He was silent for a moment, thinking, I knew, about the enormity of what it was he was suggesting. 'It's a big thing, I know, taking a child from her father. But if we want to be together, then it's something we're going to have to face up to. She'll have you, and one thing I can promise you is that I'll love her as my own. I'll see she wants for nothing.'

'I know you would. Frank dotes on her, though. He's going to be in such a way about it.'

For a long moment, Dev said nothing, and I wondered if he was hurt that yet again I was considering Frank's feelings and not his. Conflicting loyalties seemed to be wrenching me apart, and suddenly I wanted to cry. I looked at Dev, his face craggy and set, all planes and shadows in the soft moonlight, and wanted him more than I had ever wanted anything in my life.

'We're losing the point again, Caroletta,' he said, breaking the silence, and his voice was as hard as the set of his jaw. 'The main question is – do we want to be together? If we do, then surely we'll find a way to overcome whatever obstacles are in our path. We'll work something out. I've waited for you too long to walk away now. The only question is, do you feel the same way?'

'You know I do.'

'Then let's do it.'

He put his arm round me, pulling me close, and the need of him was a surge of white heat, drowning me. He kissed me and I pressed closer, wanting his hands, his body, aching to be as close as two people could be. And he wanted it too; I could feel the power of our mutual desire sparking between us, charging the very air so that it felt as if the whole of the universe was crammed into a bubble and we were at the centre of it. Beyond it nothing existed. Not the guilt of the past and present, not the impossibility of the decision I had to take, not the problems we still faced. I loved Dev and he loved me. The here and now, and being together, was all that mattered. I abandoned myself to it, as drunk on desire as I was on whisky and pep.

Then, quite suddenly, Dev drew back.

'Ah, you'll drive me mad, so you will.'

'I want you, Dev,' I whispered urgently.

'And I want you. But not here, not like this. When I make love to you, Caroletta, it's going to be special, not a quick fumble in a farm gateway. Besides, we still have things to discuss, and we don't have much time to do it. I've got to get back to my base the day after tomorrow, and what I'd like is to take you with me. I know of a nice little place we could rent – a cottage not more than ten minutes down the lane—'

'Hang on, hang on! What are you talking about?'

'I've been thinking, Caroletta, ever since I knew there was a chance I'd get to see you at Grace's party, making a few plans in my head. Riding for a fall, maybe, but if the chance came, I wanted to be sure you didn't slip through my fingers again.

266

The cottage is ours, if we want it. I've only to pick up the key and we could be in and settled before I'm due back on duty.'

'Oh my God . . .' My voice was breathy with nervous disbelief. Excitement was beating like a pulse under my heart. 'This can't be happening! It feels like a dream!'

'No dream, darling. Just something we've both wanted for a very long time.'

A nerve was jumping in my throat. 'The day after tomorrow, you say?'

'Monday, yes. I'll come and collect you and the little one on my way back to base. No need to bring anything but the barest essentials — we'll sort out everything you need when we get there. A whole fresh start. And no more putting it off, Caroletta. I'm coming to fetch you, and that's that.'

His decisiveness was a rock to cling to. We could do this. Together. But . . .

'You mustn't come to the house.'

'Sure I will. I told you a long time ago I was done with creeping about like a thief in the night.'

'No, no, you mustn't. Frank won't be at home, but Mother and Father will be, and it would cause the most dreadful to-do. The last thing I want is for Gillian to be upset.' I hesitated, thinking. 'There's a pub at the end of the lane, the King's Head. It's right on the main road. It would be better if I met you there.'

'OK, if that's what you want. I'll be there at three.' He gave me a long hard look. 'Are you sure, now, Caroletta, that you aren't going to change your mind and I'll be waiting there in vain?'

A flash of reality again, digging at my euphoria with sharp cold fingers that felt like icicles in the pit of my stomach, and I was shaking all over.

'This is all happening so fast! You're sure we shouldn't take a bit longer to—'

'If we put it off again, Caroletta, it's never going to happen,' Dev said. 'I'll be waiting for you the day after tomorrow. If you don't come, well, let's just say I'll have to accept that it wasn't meant to be. It's all up to you, and how much you want this.'

'Oh, I want it!'

He kissed me again, his lips lingering. 'And if you knew how much I've wanted you. From the first moment I saw you, with that water swirling round your ankles.'

'Will you never let me forget that?'

'Probably not.' He sighed. 'And now I suppose I'd better get you home.'

He started the engine, pulled out onto the road. I sat beside him in a haze of unreality.

Almost before I knew it we were on the outskirts of Timberley.

'Drop me outside the pub,' I said. 'I don't want to get into a confrontation tonight by having you stop outside the house.'

He pulled up onto the cobbled forecourt.

'This is where I'll be then. Three o'clock, the day after tomorrow.'

I nodded, unable to speak.

We kissed again, briefly, then I got out of the car and began walking down the lane. I turned once, looked back. The Humber was still there. I could see its sidelights, twin eyes in the night, watching until I was out of sight.

* * *

Bush Villa was in darkness. I went in through the old stable on the side. As I emerged onto the bricks I saw a faint glow of light at the kitchen window, shining through, I guessed, from the living room. My heart sank. It wouldn't be Mother or Father – they were always in bed soon after nine. It must be Frank, waiting up for me.

I stopped, teetering on my high heels as I checked my hair and the buttons of my dress, licked my finger and ran it round my mouth to erase any smudges of lipstick. I didn't want a showdown tonight.

The back door was not locked; out here in the country we never bothered with such things. I went in, kicked off my shoes – a great relief – and padded across the kitchen and down the steps to the living room.

At first I thought the room was empty. Then I saw them, hidden, at first glance, by the high back of the easy chair.

Frank and Gillian, both fast asleep. Frank's head was tucked to one side in the wing of the chair, Gillian was snuggled into him, her face buried in his chest, her hair fanned out across the Fair Isle knit of his pullover. Her feet, bare beneath her nightdress and dressing gown, dangled over his good leg.

'Frank?' I said it softly, and repeated it a little louder. 'Frank.'

He came to with a little jolt, his head snapping upright, blinking to clear the sleep from his eyes.

'Carrie. You're home.'

'Why isn't Gillian in bed?'

Frank freed one hand, gesticulating at me warningly. 'Ssh! Don't wake her!' Cautiously, he shifted himself to the front of the chair. 'Can you take her?'

I leaned over and we carefully transferred her from his arms to mine. Over her head I was still questioning him with my eyes.

'She had a bilious attack,' he mouthed, levering himself up.

'Oh, no!' But the faintest odour of vomit, still clinging to her, confirmed it.

'I've changed her nightie and the sheets on her cot, but I kept her up in case she was sick again,' he said softly. 'I think she's all right now, though.'

'Oh, the poor little love! Being ill, and me not here . . .'

'We were all right,' Frank said, sounding a little annoyed. He bent over, tucking a strand of hair behind her ear, letting his fingers rest for a moment on her cheek. 'We were all right, weren't we, my babs?' he said more gently.

'I'll get her to bed then.' It was up to me to carry her up; Frank still had difficulty managing the stairs. He followed us, though, pulling himself up slowly and painfully by hanging onto the wall.

The drop-side of the cot was down – we didn't put it up any longer, since she was big enough to climb over it now anyway – and as I laid her down the fresh smell of the clean sheets wafted up. They weren't as neatly tucked in as they might have been, but at least Frank had made the effort. I tucked her in, kissed her, and Frank did the same.

'I'll stay up here now,' he said. 'No sense doing the stairs again. Are you coming to bed?'

'I think I'll have a cup of tea first.'

'Did you have a nice time?'

'Yes. I enjoyed it.' Sudden guilt, choking me.

'Good. But I'm glad you're home. Don't stay down there too long, now, or you'll be good for nothing in the morning.'

'I won't. Thanks, Frank.'

'What for?'

'For looking after Gillian.'

'Well, you don't have to thank me for that! What sort of a father would I be if I couldn't look after my own daughter?' He sounded huffy again.

'I know, but with her being sick . . .'

'It was nice, looking after her. You don't often give me the chance. Oh, I put the sheets to soak, by the way.'

I went back downstairs, set the kettle to boil. I was stone-cold sober now, and the euphoria had dissipated as if it had never been. All I could see was the scene that had greeted me when I came in – Frank asleep in the chair with Gillian curled in his lap, his whispered recital of how he'd cared for her, the tender way he'd tucked her hair behind her ear and gentled her cheek. And the knowledge that I was planning to walk out on him and take his beloved daughter with me was a weight around my heart.

I made the tea, poured a cup, and sat down with it at the kitchen table. But when I sipped it, hot and sweet, it tasted bitter in my mouth and raked my stomach.

If I took Gillian away it would finish Frank. He might get over losing me. He would never get over losing her. And Gillian . . . How could I deprive her of her father? Dev would be good to her, I knew. He'd let her want for nothing. But he wasn't her father. It could never be the same for her, no matter how much love he gave her. I wished with all my heart that I had left Frank before she was born, but I hadn't, and now I was being torn apart all over again, caught in a trap between duty and longing.

I sat at the kitchen table, my head in my hands, whilst the clock ticked away the minutes in the otherwise silent house, each one sounding to me like the hammer blows of nails being driven into the coffin of my hopes and dreams.

I honestly did not know what I was going to do.

The cold hard light of day did nothing to lighten the terrible turmoil I was going through. Everything I had ever wanted was there, almost within my grasp, yet as elusive as ever. What had seemed possible last night, with Dev beside me, now felt like a crazy dream, so far removed from reality that mountains, oceans and deserts stood between me and its realisation.

I thought of how it had been when I had told Frank before that I was leaving him, and the terrible consequences. The guilt of believing I was responsible for his accident had never left me, and I trembled inwardly with dread that something similar might happen again. I thought of Gillian, torn from her father, her family, her home. I thought of Mother and Father, who had always stood by me, and how hurt and upset they were going to be. How could I do this to all of them?

But equally, how could I let Dev down again?

Gillian was young, she'd adapt. She'd have a wonderful life, travelling, maybe, with opportunities that living in Timberley could never offer her. Mother and Father would come to understand in time, and come to terms with my decision. Gillian could visit them, for long holidays. They'd never liked

Frank, and I could not see how they could fail to like Dev. A few years down the line, when all the upset was over, all this would seem like a distant bad dream.

Around and around in my head went the arguments, tossing me first one way and then the other, and even though I was still not sure I could do it, I began making preparations.

There was no way I could tell Frank what I was planning; it would be like setting a match to an incendiary bomb. So I wrote him a letter, which I intended to leave where he would be sure to find it. In it, I told him how sorry I was, and promised to be in touch so that we could work something out regarding his access to Gillian. I wrote another to Mother and Father, saying much the same, as well as thanking them for all they'd done for me over the years, but explaining that I had never been happy with Frank. Then, for the time being, I hid both letters in the dressing-table drawer.

I packed my small case with the essentials Gillian and I would need and put it back under the bed where it always lived.

And acknowledged for the first time that I really was going to do this. Because for all the doubts and guilt, I simply couldn't bear the thought of a future without Dev.

Monday. 'D-Day', as I'd mentally dubbed it. Departure Day. But I was still in turmoil. My heart never seemed to stop racing, my stomach felt like a badly set jelly, and my nerves were jangling. Time took on a strange character, stretching and contracting, so that sometimes the hours were speeding by and sometimes the hands of the clock seemed to move so slowly I thought it must have stopped.

As I helped Mother prepare lunch — or 'dinner', as we called the midday meal — it was on the tip of my tongue to tell her what I was planning, but I couldn't bring myself to do it. Coward that I was, I couldn't face the terrible row I knew would ensue. In my emotional state it was just too much to contemplate, and I only hoped that one day she would forgive me.

When we'd eaten and cleared away, Mother went into the front room for her customary nap and I went upstairs. I put a few last things into my little case, along with Gillian's teddy bear, and, hating myself for the deception, managed to sneak the case out and hide it under the peony bush by the front gate from where I could retrieve it when we left. I went back upstairs, got out the two letters from their hiding place and read through them once more, adding a few words here and there to say again how sorry I was and that I'd be in touch very soon.

I heard the Westminster-chime clock strike quarter to the hour and the nerves knotted in my throat again. Almost time to go. But it would take only five minutes to walk up the lane, and I didn't want to be waiting for too long outside the pub with my suitcase. I had to time this just right.

I went back downstairs. After dinner, Gillian had gone out to play on the bricks, and I expected her to be there still. But when I looked out, she was nowhere to be seen.

'Gillian!' I called. 'Gillian! Where are you?'

No reply. My nerves, already taut, ratcheted up a notch. I crossed the bricks, looked in the garage — it was empty. I hurried up the path, looking behind the bean sticks, in the little greenhouse, on the lawn, anywhere she might be hiding.

'Gillian! Come here, there's a good girl! Mummy hasn't got time to play silly games!'

Still no reply and no sign of her. Beginning to panic, I ran back into the house, still calling her name, and ran straight into Mother, who had emerged from the front room.

'Have you seen Gillian?' My voice was rising. 'I can't find her anywhere.'

'No, you won't,' Mother said. Her face was set into an expression that was somehow almost triumphant, but also brimming with anger. 'Your father has taken her out for a walk.'

'What?' It wasn't unheard of for Father to take her for a stroll down the lane, but he never did it without telling me. That he should do so today was beyond belief.

'I asked him to.' Mother's voice was taut. 'I think you and I should have a bit of a talk, Carrie, and I wanted her out of the way. No sense upsetting the child with what I've got to say.'

'What are you talking about, Mother?'

But there were rivers of ice in my blood. I think I already knew.

'You've been a silly girl, haven't you?' Mother said sternly, for all the world as if I were fifteen years old again. 'I don't know who this man is, Carrie, or what you've been up to with him. But it's got to stop here and now, before you do something you'll regret.'

I stared at her in astonishment and horror, gaping like a goldfish.

'Don't try to deny it,' Mother said tightly. 'You're planning to run away with him. I've seen the letters you meant to leave for us. Letters, Carrie! Letters! How could you do that to us?'

'You've been poking about in my things!' I accused, outraged.

'And a good thing too. Though I wasn't "poking about", as you call it. I was putting away some of your clothes that had been airing. When I saw those letters . . . well, it's a wonder I didn't have a heart attack on the spot. I can't believe a daughter of mine would even think of such a thing – carry on behind her husband's back with another man, run off without so much as a word to us, after all we've done for you. What in the world are you thinking of? I should think you've gone funny . . .'

'Mother, I should have told you, I know, and I'm sorry. But—'

'You certainly should. And then I could have talked some sense into you. You can't do this, Carrie! You're a married woman, whether you like it or not, with responsibilities. And just think of the talk you'll cause . . .'

Suddenly I was very angry.

'That's all you care about, isn't it? People talking!'

'If you go running off, you're not the one who'll have to put up with it.'

'What other people think is far more important to you than whether or not I'm happy.'

Mother snorted. 'Happy? What sort of silly talk is that? Moonshine, that's what it is. Happy is having enough food on the table and a bed to sleep in nights. Happy is being respected by your friends and neighbours. Not making an exhibition of yourself with some . . . *man*.' She spat the word, as if it offended her.

'It might be your idea of happiness, Mother; it's not mine.' I could hear the Westminster-chime clock gearing up to strike the hour. 'Look, I'm really sorry you had to find out this way. I should have told you, I know. But I really can't stop to have this conversation now. I have to find Gillian. I'm due to meet Dev right now. He'll be waiting for me.'

'Waiting for you? Where? When? You can't mean you're planning to go now, today?'

'Yes, Mother.'

'Well, it's a blooming good job I found those letters when I did, then, isn't it?' Mother sounded outraged. 'I never thought you were going to do it so soon, just like that . . .'

'Well I am,' I said defensively. 'Now please will you tell me where Father has taken Gillian.'

'Oh, no, Carrie.' Mother shook her head. She planted herself firmly between me and the door. She wasn't a big woman, but she was solid, and very determined. 'You're not taking our Gillian.'

'Mother—'

'If you want to go racketing off goodness knows where with your fancy man, I don't suppose I can stop you. But you're not taking our Gillian.'

'Of course I'm taking Gillian!' My voice was rising again. 'You don't think I'd go without her?'

'We'll see about that, my lady. She's not here, is she? And won't be, for a good hour or more. And don't think you can send for her later, because I'll see to it she stays here, where she belongs.'

I was trembling now.

'You can't do that!'

'Just you watch me!'

'She's my daughter!'

'And Frank's. And our grandchild. This is her home, and this is where she's staying, if I have anything to do with it. And I will, I promise you, Carrie. You're not taking her out of this house today, and when Frank gets to hear what's going on he'll make sure you don't take her any other time either.'

'You'd take his part — against me? You don't even like him!'

'Liking's got nothing to do with it. There's right and there's wrong. He's her father.'

'And I'm her mother!'

'And a pretty poor one, if you ask me. Going off to live in sin and taking an innocent little girl with you . . . you've got me beat, Carrie. But I'll make sure she stays here with us where she belongs if it's the last thing I do.'

'Mother, please . . .' This was every bit as bad as I'd antici-pated; worse. I hadn't for one moment imagined that Mother would take Frank's part against me when it came to custody of Gillian.

Mother stood aside, suddenly, pointing to the back door.

'Go on then, go if you want to. I'm not stopping you.'

Tears of frustration and sheer panic were pricking at my eyes and thickening my throat.

'You know I can't go without Gillian!'

Mother shrugged.

'I can't believe you're doing this,' I cried in anguish.

The doorbell rang, cutting through the charged atmosphere like a knife. I froze, startled. Practically no one ever came ringing at the front door. The same thought must have occurred to Mother.

'Come calling for you, has he?' she asked archly.

'He promised he wouldn't . . .'

But it would be Dev all over to do just that when I didn't turn up outside the pub where he was waiting. *No more creeping about like a thief in the night* . . .

'You'd better answer it,' Mother said coldly.

Trembling, torn apart by my conflicting emotions, shaken to the core by Mother's attack on me, I went to the door, pulled back the bolts and opened it. Mother had followed me; she stood in the living-room doorway, her eyes boring into my back.

Dev was there, on the doorstep. The Humber was pulled up in the road outside.

'Caroletta? Are you not coming?'

'Oh, Dev . . . I can't . . . Gillian . . .'

'What about Gillian?'

'I'll tell you what about Gillian.' Mother stepped forward. 'She's not leaving this house, I shall make sure of that. I don't know what kind of a man you are, enticing a married woman away, but I'll tell you the same as I've told her. She can go with you, if that's what she wants – she's a grown woman and I can't stop her. But Gillian stays here. And if it comes to that, any court in the land will back us up.'

Dev's eyes narrowed dangerously.

'We'll see about that. Where is she?'

'She's not here. Father's taken her for a walk.'

'Then we'll go and look for her.'

My head was spinning, tears of panic gathering again. Images of what would happen if we did as Dev was suggesting crowded into my mind. We couldn't do it like this, dragging a startled

Gillian away from her grandfather, into a strange car. It would frighten the life out of her. And that would be only the beginning. Frank, backed by Mother, would pursue us, no doubt of that. Through the courts, if necessary. And Mother was right about one thing: I might be Gillian's mother, but I couldn't see any judge giving custody to a woman 'living in sin', as Mother called it, over a stable family background with her natural father.

'No, Dev, I can't . . .'

His eyes narrowed again, his jaw setting to give his whole face a hard, shut-in look.

'You're not coming then.'

'I can't! You must see—'

'Oh, yes, Caroletta, I see. In fact I knew, when you weren't there waiting for me, that you were doing it again. I just hoped I was wrong.'

'Please, Dev . . . I was coming, I really was. Look, here's my suitcase.' I jerked it out from its hiding place under the peony bush.

'Ah, Caroletta . . .' He shook his head. 'But you won't be needing it now.'

'No, she will not,' Mother said. 'And now will you kindly get off my doorstep?'

For a long moment his eyes held mine. 'Is that it then, Caroletta?'

My eyes were swimming with tears. 'I can't come with you, Dev. I can't leave Gillian behind, and I can't risk losing her.'

He sighed. 'All right, if that's what you want.'

'It's not what I want!'

'No, so you say. 'Bye, then, Caroletta.'

He turned and walked away down the path. I wanted to run

after him, but what was the point? I simply stood in the doorway, watching him go through a haze of scalding tears.

'Well, that's that, then,' Mother said from behind me. And reached over and closed the door.

Part Three

TWENTY-ONE

Kathryn is pushing the stroller alongside the lake, talking all the while to Ben.

'Look at that beautiful boat, Ben! The wind's in the sail – it's making it go really fast . . . And there's another one! Do you think they're racing? I think they might be . . .'

She stops, crouches down beside the stroller, pointing. Ben follows her finger, wide-eyed. He's clutching his favourite toy, Maurice Mouse. The long, soft grey tail trails down over his blue cotton shorts onto one chubby knee. There's a sticky ring around his mouth, the remains of an ice cream Kathryn shared with him just now. She finds a tissue in her pocket, wipes the mess away, then touches her finger to the dimple in his cheek. He chuckles, a soft, infectious gurgle.

'Shall we look for more boats?'

Ben bounces eagerly against the restraints of the stroller, anxious to be free. He's learning to walk, pulling himself up on the furniture, but Kathryn knows he can only manage a few steps yet before he tumbles over and reverts to a rapid, crab-like crawl.

'No, you can't get out here,' she says. 'You'll fall over and hurt yourself.'

Ben bounces some more, and Maurice Mouse slides off his knee onto the cobbles.

'Hey, you're going to lose Maurice!' Kathryn lets go of the stroller, bends down to rescue the mouse. 'Here, hold on to him tightly now . . .'

She turns back. The stroller – and Ben – are no longer there.

'Ben?' she says, bewildered, and then, as the panic begins, her voice rises with it. 'Ben! Ben – where are you?'

She twists and turns, looking around, but she can't see him anywhere. There are crowds of people milling about – where did they all come from? A minute ago it was just her and Ben. She battles her way through the crowd, calling Ben's name, but she's not getting anywhere. Her feet seem to be anchored in soft sand, and it's growing rapidly dark.

'Ben! Where are you?' She's frantic now, and rolling over her like a cloud of sea mist is the dreadful certainty that she is being propelled towards something so terrible it defies description and there is nothing, absolutely nothing, she can do about it.

A chuckle. That infectious chuckle she knows so well. Relief floods through her, her knees go weak with it. 'Ben, you naughty boy! Don't ever hide from Mummy again.' She whirls round. The quay is deserted, the crowds all gone. And still no Ben. She's crying, sweating, desperate. She can still hear that chuckle, but somehow it's beyond her reach.

Kathryn's eyes fly wide open, the choking aura of the nightmare pressing in on her. And in the quiet of her hotel bedroom she can still hear that chuckle, leading her on like a will-o'-the-wisp. She shoots bolt upright in bed, a moment's wild hope constricting her chest. And reality dawns.

A dream. It was just a dream. But so real, oh, so real! The wonder that was Ben, with her once more. The joy in showing him the boats, holding an ice cream for him to lick, cleaning his face afterwards with a tissue. And the agony of losing him all over again . . .

Kathryn covers her face with her hands; it is wet with tears. She gets out of bed, goes to the en suite to use the loo, comes back and goes to the window, looking out at the unfamiliar landscape, trying to escape the spell. But still the aura envelops her. And still in the quiet of the night she can hear the heart-rending chuckle of a little boy lost.

She can still feel it, fainter, but pervasive, when she wakes next morning. She hadn't expected to go back to sleep at all, but presumably she must have done since it's no longer dark, but broad daylight, and she has no recollection of seeing the pearly hue of dawn. She showers, dresses, and goes down for breakfast. Apart from a man in a button-down-collared shirt and tie, who has draped a suit jacket over the back of his chair, she's the only one in the dining room. A waitress brings her a pot of coffee and invites her to help herself to the breakfast buffet laid out along one wall.

Kathryn peeks into the chafing dishes, but is not tempted by the grilled bacon, tomatoes or mushrooms. She makes a piece of toast in the rolling toaster, marvelling at the speed with which a slice of bread fed in at one end emerges crisp and golden brown at the other, and tops it with a spoonful of scrambled egg. She pours a glass of orange juice and takes the whole lot back to her table. She's really not hungry, but thinks she should eat something – she's going over to the stables later and might even go for a ride. Andrea's suggestion, and Kathryn's not sure about it. She's never been on a horse in her life. Andrea said that was no problem – she has a mare who is gentle as a baby, all Kathryn has to do is sit in the saddle and Lady will do the rest. And she has spare hard hats and boots Kathryn can borrow. She made it sound so pleasant and easy, Kathryn had thought that perhaps she should take advantage of the opportunity. Now, however, she's feeling nervous at the prospect.

But perhaps she's just on edge after that dream.

She manages to eat most of her scrambled egg and pours herself another coffee. The man puts on his jacket, retrieves a laptop from under the table, and leaves. Kathryn's now quite alone. Even the waitress is nowhere to be seen.

Mindful of the difference in time zones, Kathryn had turned off her mobile when she went to bed last night, not wanting to be woken by a call or a message coming through. Now she gets it out of her bag, depresses the 'on' button and lays it on the table beside her plate. The minute it connects, it beeps at her. She checks it. Three messages.

The first is from Gillian. 'Just wondering how things are. Keep in touch. Love, Mom.' Each word is spelled out in full; Gillian never uses text speak; words abbreviated to phonics offend her.

In contrast, the second message – from Rob – is full of them. 'How r u? Mis u.' Not even a signature, just 'xx'. Short and to the point. But it shows that he is thinking of her. Kathryn, still raw from last night's dream, feels tears prick her eyes and there is an ache, not unlike homesickness, deep inside her. Suddenly she wants Rob fiercely, not the stranger he has become, but the man she married. Wants to be able to tell him about the dream, cry into his shoulder, have him understand and comfort her. Except that he wouldn't. He'd tell her she was being morbid again, that she had to move on. Kathryn hardens her heart and views the third message.

Gillian again. 'Don't forget to go and see Lizzie and Walter. They'd be very hurt if you didn't visit. Mom. x.'

Kathryn's heart sinks. Gillian is right, of course. She really should go to Somerset, but she doesn't want to at all. Lizzie and Walter have an effect on her that is almost claustrophobic.

Well, the best remedy for claustrophobia could be a dose of fresh air. She'll certainly get that if she takes up Andrea's offer of a ride on a horse. Kathryn puts her mobile back in her bag, finishes her coffee and leaves the dining room.

The stable block is at the rear of Timberley Hall. Kathryn, wearing denim jeans and a T-shirt, with a fleece knotted by the arms around her waist, walks around the building to reach it. Andrea's Saab is parked in the yard and Andrea herself is just coming out of the main stable entrance carrying an aluminium bucket.

'Hi, Kathryn!' she calls. 'Won't be a minute. Just watering the horses.'

Kathryn approaches the stables and peeks inside. A row of loose boxes runs the length of the block; equipment dangles from hooks on the wall of the narrow passage that fronts them. Heads that look huge to her, poke over the stable doors, a black, a grey. One nudges Andrea as she passes.

'I wouldn't come in if I were you,' Andrea calls over her shoulder. 'It's a bit mucky underfoot.'

Kathryn can believe it though it's too dim to be able to see properly; the smell of horses is overpowering. Andrea disappears into a loose box at the far end of the stable, re-emerges and bolts it behind her.

'All done.' She comes back down the passageway, wiping her hands on the seat of her jodhpurs. 'How are you today? Did you sleep well?'

'Yes, fine.' Kathryn doesn't want to talk about her disturbed night.

'Ready for a cup of tea? I know I am.'

'Not for me, thanks. I just got through a whole pot of coffee.'

'Well, I'm having one.'

There's a small and very old caravan parked up in a corner of the stable yard. She heads for it, and Kathryn follows. She sits on the step while Andrea ducks inside and lights a Calor gas ring under the kettle; truth to tell she doesn't fancy the caravan much more than she fancied the stable block. Grubby-looking curtains drape drunkenly at the windows and the bunks are piled high with what look like horse blankets. Andrea shifts some of them, making space.

'Are you coming in?'

'Oh, it's so nice out here in the sunshine . . .'

'I suppose it is. I've been too busy to notice. OK, I'll bring my tea out. There's a bench under the wall.'

'I see you brought your car today,' Kathryn says as they make for the bench, Andrea carrying a chipped mug of tea and a packet of HobNob biscuits.

'I've got to run into Marlow for a few things later on.'

'Right.' Maybe she's going to escape having to get on a horse, Kathryn thinks. But no.

'All ready for your ride then?' Andrea asks, breaking open the packet of HobNobs.

'I guess. I wore jeans and sneakers. Is that OK?'

'The jeans are fine, but definitely not the shoes. You need a heel. You could have a nasty accident if your foot slipped through the stirrup. I'll lend you some boots. I should think mine would fit you. You've never ridden before, you say?'

'Never. To be honest, I'm not sure—'

'You'll love it,' Andrea says confidently. 'You might get a bit stiff and sore at first, but you'll be back for more, I guarantee it.'

Kathryn, doubtful, hopes Andrea is right.

Half an hour later they're ready to go. Andrea has tacked up her own horse, Jason, a bay gelding, and Lady, a dainty piebald. She has also put a leading rein on a fat pony called Mickey who, she says, needs the exercise. Kathryn wishes she could ride the pony, but Andrea won't hear of it. He's strictly for children only.

Kathryn, all kitted out, now feels self-conscious as well as nervous. The hat feels tight, though Andrea assures her it's a perfect fit, and the boots feel huge. Andrea's also loaned her a crop, and Kathryn practises holding it while she waits for Andrea to lock up the caravan.

'OK, let's get you aboard.'

Andrea gives her a leg up, and she's in the saddle. The ground looks an awfully long way away. Andrea shows Kathryn how to hold the reins, then mounts the bay in one fluid leap that reminds Kathryn of an Olympic high jumper clearing the bar. She touches the bay's flanks and moves off, calling to Lady over her shoulder, 'Walk on!'

Lady takes a couple of steps. Kathryn clutches her neck, terrified that either she is going to fall off, or Lady is going to run away with her, or both. But as they cross the yard and head down the drive she begins to get used to the rolling gait and feels a little more confident. But ahead is the road. She's tensing up again.

'What if a car comes?' she calls to Andrea.

'Just keep her in the side. She's quite used to traffic. And don't let her nibble the hedge.'

Oh my God, so much to think about!

They walk sedately along the roadside, Indian-style, cross the road, go a short way down the lane that leads to Bush Villa, and turn into a narrow track, sloping steeply upwards, bordered by high banks and hedges of hawthorn. Here and there they overhang the track, forming a canopy. Unbelievably, Kathryn is beginning to enjoy herself.

'Where are we going?' she calls to Andrea.

'Up on the hill. You'll be able to have a trot there if you like. Or even a canter.'

'No way!'

Lady turns her head to a clump of thick fern, obviously fancying a snack. Kathryn tugs on the reins, tugs harder, and Lady reluctantly relinquishes the treat. Kathryn feels inordinately pleased with herself.

The track ends quite suddenly. One minute they are in a green tunnel, the next they emerge into bright sunlight. Ahead is an expanse of coarse undulating turf. Andrea turns left, tracking a small copse, then stops and points.

'There's our house – see?'

Far below, in a fold of the hill, is Bush Villa. From here it's almost a bird's-eye view of the garden, a square of hedged lawn, and the sun glinting on the glass roof panels of the greenhouse. A figure is out on the bricks – Carrie, bending over to pull a weed from the border. Then she straightens and goes inside the house, out of sight. Andrea turns the horses.

'We'll go the other way. I just wanted to show you.'

They head back, across the plateau that Andrea calls 'the hill'. Kathryn's beginning to get the hang of this now, though every time she begins to relax she gets worried again, about the way she's holding the reins, or the position of her feet in the stirrups. They trek for maybe twenty minutes across the open ground, and along the outskirts of another small wood. Then Andrea reins in on the edge of an escarpment.

'How's that for a view then?' Her voice is full of pride. 'The Severn Vale.'

Kathryn stops alongside her. Beneath them, spread out as far as the eye can see, are miles of open countryside, broken only by the occasional copse or farmhouse. Away in the distance the sun sparkles on the blue ribbon that is the River Severn.

'Awesome!' Kathryn is struck, suddenly, by the thought that this is the land of her forebears, a land she has never before seen.

After a few minutes, with the horses becoming a little restless, Andrea clicks her heels to Jason's flanks and motions Kathryn to do the same. Kathryn tries; Lady stands stubbornly, cropping a juicy patch of grass. But the moment Andrea moves off, calling 'Walk on!' over her shoulder, Lady obediently follows.

Kathryn sighs. 'I'll never make a horsewoman.'

'It's just practice. You're doing well for a first time.' The horses fall into step, side by side now.

'You've no idea what it means to Mum, you being here,' Andrea says. 'I only wish Gillian could have brought herself to come too.'

'So do I. But you never know. Maybe now that I've broken the ice . . .'

'Oh, I do hope so. Mum's had a hard life. It would mean the world to her to see Gillian again. There's no recapturing the lost years, but at least—' She glances at Kathryn from beneath the brim of her riding hat, and, with her hair obscured and her eyes in deep shadow, the similarity between her and Gillian strikes Kathryn suddenly. The shape of the jaw, the wide mouth . . . Though superficially they are very different, yet there's no mistaking that they are sisters.

'Have you been in touch with her since you arrived?' Andrea asks.

'We've texted one another briefly.' Kathryn hesitates, reminded of her mother's admonition. Perhaps this is as good a time as any to mention the other relatives she really should visit whilst she is in England, but she's unsure how to broach the delicate subject.

'Andrea, I know the main reason for me being here is to meet you and Grandma, and I know you haven't got much time for them, but I really think I ought to go to Hillsbridge and see Lizzie and Walter.'

Andrea's reply surprises her. 'Yes, of course you must.'

'You don't think it will upset Grandma?'

'I'm sure she'll understand that you want to see them,' Andrea says shortly.

'I don't actually *want* to,' Kathryn admits. 'They're nothing to me and I don't actually like them very much. I just think I ought to, that's all.'

'The girl's got taste,' Andrea says drily. 'But of course it's only right you should visit while you're in England. They did bring Gillian up, and though I think what they did — turning her against Mum — was despicable, I suppose it was understandable. Frank was Lizzie's brother, after all. The great pity is that they were allowed to take Gillian at all. The problem, as I understand it, was that what happened broke my grandparents. Mum's father had a stroke and died, and on top of being unexpectedly widowed, her mother was very Victorian in outlook, and obsessed with respectability and appearances. She never got over the shame of it all, and though Gillian had never known any other home, my grandmother said she couldn't cope with looking after her, traumatised as she was. And Lizzie and Walter came and took her away. Just like that. Mum had no say in it

295

at all, and of course, it wasn't as if she had any brothers or sisters to speak up for her. Lizzie and Walter were the closest family Gillian had, apart from her grandmother, who didn't want to know. And to give them their due, I think they treated her very well.'

'I think they did. Mom is very fond of them. To her, they replaced her parents. It's just a pity that going to them meant you and she were separated. If they were so determined to take Gillian, how come they didn't take you as well?'

Andrea considers. 'I've sometimes wondered that. Perhaps they thought coping with Gillian was enough for them. A child of eight is one thing, a young baby something else entirely. I was born in prison, remember. Not many people can say that.' She grins. 'Mum was only allowed to keep me for a little while, then a home had to be found for me, or I'd have been placed in care, as they call it these days. Lizzie and Walter didn't come forward, so Mary and Geoff stepped in.'

Kathryn is silent, appreciating the full dreadfulness of the situation, perhaps for the first time, and marvelling at Andrea's calm acceptance of it, so different from her mother's bitterness. Much of that must be because of the way Mary and Geoff had handled things, she thinks, although the differences in temperament between the two sisters probably had something to do with it as well.

'I'm really looking forward to meeting them,' she says.

'And they're looking forward to meeting you.' Andrea smiles. 'You'll like them. Mary has always been a very good friend to Mum. Still is, come to that. And believe me, she has needed her friends. Especially when she first came out of prison.'

'It must have been awful for her,' Kathryn says. 'Especially in a small village like this, where everybody knew her. I'm surprised she came back here.'

'She really had nowhere else to go. And in any case, it's not in Mum's nature to run away. She believes in facing up to things.'

They are almost back to the point where the leafy green tunnel meets the open ground.

'Look, Kathryn, if you want to go to Hillsbridge, you can borrow my car,' Andrea says.

'Oh, I couldn't do that!'

'Why not? You've got a driving licence, haven't you? It would be a lot easier for you than having to use public transport. It's only about thirty miles. You could drive it in an hour, no trouble, but going by bus would take ages by the time you'd coped with all the connections. I'd take you myself, but I really can't spare the time, and in any case, I have no wish to see those people. I'd probably end up giving them a piece of my mind.'

'Well, thank you, that's very kind,' Kathryn says.

They go back into Indian file to negotiate the track, and all Kathryn's concentration is required not to tumble over Lady's neck as she trips daintily down the steep path of dried mud and loose stones. On the way up, Kathryn hadn't noticed just how steep it is.

But she's feeling more comfortable now. Much more at ease. And in a way she can't quite understand, she feels as if she's come home.

TWENTY-TWO

Andrea wants to go round to the farm and sort out a convenient time for Mary to meet Kathryn, but she's strangely reluctant. Seeing Tom yesterday was quite a shock, and now she's worried that if he is staying at the farm she might run into him. Stupid, of course. What in the world difference does it make? They're both adults – good grief, they're middle-aged! But the habits of a lifetime are hard to break. She's barely seen him since she was a teenager, shy, awkward, desperately in love. Now, thirty years on, the thought of meeting him makes her a teenager again.

Not that she's in love with him now, of course. She put all that nonsense behind her years ago. It's the fact that she humiliated herself, so crazy about him was she in those days, that still has the power to make her cringe. Tom may well have forgotten. Probably has. But Andrea hasn't. The shame of it haunts her still. Though she rarely thinks about it now, it lurks in her subconscious, and comes bubbling to the surface at the very thought of coming face to face with him.

She'd have got over it long ago, of course, if he'd been around. They might even have become good friends. But he hasn't been around. He'd left Timberley soon after she'd made such a fool of herself, and his job with a multinational company took him all over the world so that he was rarely at home. When he was she avoided him. His life moved on: he'd climbed the ladder of success to ever-more senior appointments in ever-more exotic locations, married, had two children. But somehow hers never had.

She experimented with other relationships, but none of them worked out. Her fault, she knows. She was just too wrapped up in her horses. But in a way it was as if she had simply moved into a parallel world and the old one was still there, untouched by time, beyond the thinnest of veils.

There the young Andrea lives on, the little girl who had first hero-worshipped Tom and then developed the most enormous crush. But there are two Toms. There is the boy who was as close to her as a brother, who taught her to ride a bicycle, running around the farmyard behind her, holding onto the saddle until at last she'd shouted: 'I can do it! I can do it!' and soared a full twenty-five yards before wobbling and crashing into a grassy bank; the same Tom who got into a fight on her behalf when the school bully jeered at her that her mother was a murderer. She can see them now, rolling over and over on the concreted school playground, gouging, grabbing, punching when they could, until they were pulled apart by a teacher. Tom was given three strokes of the cane across the palm of his hand for that, and it seemed to her that he was the knight on the white charger, riding to the aid of the damsel in distress.

And then there is the older Tom, her first love. She looked at him one day and felt her tummy tip; there was a magic about him and about the way she felt about him that was like nothing she'd experienced before or since. There was a magic too about the time they spent together, mostly with the horses, practising the gymnastic events for the Pony Club point-to-points, or racing, shoulder to shoulder across the hill. She thought about him constantly, wove dreams and fantasies about him, spent every spare moment up at the farm.

All might have been well, and the infatuation died a natural death, if it wasn't for the Young Farmers' Ball, the first one she was allowed to attend. She was excited about it for weeks, planning what she would wear – her new dress, pale blue, empire-line, with an overlay of creamy lace on the bodice and a pair of strappy white sling-back shoes with heels higher than she'd ever worn before. She had her hair done at the hairdresser's in Marlow; it was backcombed into a stiff beehive that could only be tidied by digging the long metal tail of a special comb into the midst of the arrangement and lifting it. And Carrie loaned her a mohair stole, which made her feel more grown up than ever.

Tom, three years older than her, had a car, and he was to take her and bring her safely home. But of course, Andrea saw it as far more than simply escort duty arranged between their respective mothers. When he collected her, Tom looked incredibly handsome in a black dinner suit with silky lapels and a black bow tie, and his hair was quiffed up at the front with a touch of Brilliantine. Andrea thought she would die with excitement.

But things went horribly wrong. At the village hall he left her in the company of a group of friends of her own age and as the evening wore on Andrea felt more and more depressed and desperate as she had to watch him dancing with other girls and even taking one of them into supper – a girl in a strapless gown that Andrea thought was quite shameless. An hour or so before the end of the ball he disappeared for a very long time and when she saw him again, he was sneaking back in through the main doors with the same girl, who looked muzzy-haired and starry-eyed. Andrea felt her heart was breaking in two. She'd already drunk more cider than was wise, and now she had another, to drown her sorrows. It was to prove her undoing.

She didn't have the slightest intention of letting Tom know how she felt about him and how much he'd hurt her – she'd have died first. But somehow it happened anyway. She was very quiet, trying not to cry, in the car on the way home, and when Tom asked her what was wrong, and put his arm round her, it all came pouring out. And to her horror, even as she said it, she was telling him she loved him, and begging him to forget the shameless girl in the strapless gown and take her out instead.

Tom was pretty shaken, and embarrassed too. He wasn't unkind, but he did make it quite clear that what she wanted wasn't going to happen; that he was really fond of her, but she was just like a little sister to him. But Andrea, desperately trying to make things come right, just wouldn't let it go. She'd begged and pleaded with him to give her a chance, somehow quite unable to stop herself. And it made no difference at all.

It was only when she'd cried herself dry that the shame began to creep in, and when it did it completely overwhelmed her. She desperately wanted to talk to him and tell him she hadn't meant a single word of it, she'd just had too much cider, but she was terrified she'd lose control all over again. So she avoided him, and quite understandably, he avoided her. The gulf grew, and became a habit. When they did meet Andrea raised the defensive barricades she should have retreated behind in the first place, but the old ease between them was gone for ever. And then he'd left for university, and to work for the multinational, and somehow they never did find the opportunity to put things right between them. Which is why now, after all these years, she still feels horribly awkward at the thought of meeting him.

What makes it worse is that he's a widower now – he lost his wife to cancer a couple of years ago – and Andrea can't rid herself of the awful feeling that he will think she is after him if she turns up on the doorstep.

She goes to the wall that separates the farm from the Hall and peeks over, trying to see if his car is parked in the farmyard. She can't see it, but that doesn't necessarily mean it's not there.

'Oh, don't be so damned stupid!' Andrea says to herself, and sets off to walk round to the farm.

The top half of the stable-type door is open; Andrea leans in, calling through.

'Anybody home?'

For all that she knows she's behaving like the teenager she once was, she can feel her heart beating an irregular tattoo. But it's Mary who answers.

302

'Is that you, Andrea? Come on in.'

Andrea opens the bottom half of the door, goes into the big, dim kitchen. Mary is sorting eggs at the table. She's alone. Andrea breathes again.

'Hi. How goes it?'

'Busy. As usual.' Mary is a big, comfortable woman. Her hair, iron grey now, is pulled back into an untidy bun, her face weather-beaten and rosy. She wears a baggy jumper, shapeless brown cords and Wellington boots. 'What about you? How are you getting on with Gillian's girl?'

'Kathryn. She's lovely. Actually, that's why I'm here. She'd like to meet you and I know you'd like to meet her.'

'I certainly would.'

'So I wondered if we could fix something up.'

Mary nods, filling the last tray with eggs, some brown, some speckled.

'Why don't you all come up for lunch on Sunday? I'm roasting a nice piece of beef. Tom's home, you know, and he does like his roast beef.'

Instantly, Andrea is uncomfortable. 'I'm not sure. I'll have to check with Mum.'

'Or bring her round any time. I'm here pretty well all the time except for Wednesdays – Farmers' Market, you know? But it would be nice if you could make Sunday. I haven't seen Carrie lately. And like I say, Tom's here.'

'On holiday, is he?' Andrea realises that to avoid the subject would be more telling than to address it.

'I suppose you could call it that. He's in England for a couple of weeks to suss out his options for when he retires.'

'That's a long way off, surely.'

'Huh!' Mary snorts. 'Not so long as you'd think. Just a few months, or so he informs me. Would you believe it, my son is taking early retirement while I've still got my nose to the grindstone. Very nice too, if you ask me. Call it a day, pick up a nice lump sum and a pension, and still be young enough to do whatever you fancy or not, as the case may be . . .'

'Tom – retiring! I can't believe it.' Andrea shakes her head. Where have the years gone?

'No, you're like me, Andrea. We'll go on working till we drop.' Mary brushes a strand of grey hair that has come loose from her bun behind her ear. 'Truth to tell, he's had enough of foreign parts, if you ask me. Where he hasn't been these last thirty years is nobody's business. Saudi Arabia, Hong Kong, Singapore . . . you name it, he's lived there. But the gilt's gone off the gingerbread since he lost Deirdre. He wants to come back to England.'

'But to retire . . . Surely work's an anchor for him just now. Is he going to take another job, or just . . . play golf or something?'

'I think he's got a few plans that may or may not work out, and until we know I'm not really at liberty to say. The trouble is, his family is so scattered – Adam in London, Josh in Manchester – with their parents moving about abroad and them going to boarding school here, they've put down their own roots where their caravans landed. And Tom . . . oh, I don't know, we'll have to see.'

Andrea checks her watch. 'I'm going to have to go. I'll check with Mum about Sunday lunch and let you know.'

But she's already made up her mind. Carrie and Kathryn can do what they like; there is no way, absolutely no way, she is going to sit through a three-course meal with a recently widowed Tom.

Carrie, of course, has other ideas. When Andrea relays the invitation, and the news, a glint comes into Carrie's eye.

'That would be really nice, Andrea. I'm sure Tom would love to see you.'

'I'm sure he wouldn't! In any case, Sunday is my busiest day, as you well know, and so does Mary. It's probably why she suggested Sunday.'

'Don't be so silly! She just wasn't thinking, that's all. You and Tom used to be such good friends, it would be a crying shame to miss him.'

'Mother, I cannot spare the time to sit over one of Mary's roasts on a Sunday, so please don't go on about it. Now, can we talk about something else? I've offered Kathryn the use of my car so she can go and see Lizzie and Walter.' She sees Carrie stiffen. 'It's only right she should visit them while she's over. But she's a bit worried it might upset you. I told her you'd understand. Which is why I'm telling you now, to warn you. I don't want you letting her see that you mind.'

Carrie sniffs. 'Of course I won't let her see I mind. What do you think I am?' She bangs a pot on the stove. 'Just as long as they don't try to turn her against me the way they did Gillian.'

'I don't think it would work, even if they tried. She's a grown woman, not a traumatised little girl, who's lost her memory. And she doesn't actually like them very much. She just thinks she should go, that's all, and so do I.'

'Oh, I expect you're right,' Carrie says.

But it lies heavily on her stomach, all the same. She's just found Kathryn and, selfishly, she doesn't want to share her with anyone. Especially not the couple who robbed her of her daughter.

She's worried, too, about what Lizzie might say to Kathryn. She had, after all, sat through the trial. She can still see Lizzie's weasel face amongst a row of others in the public gallery, glaring down at her, Carrie, in the dock. Every day Lizzie had been there, listening, glowering, her eyes never, for one instant, leaving Carrie's face. 'Shooting daggers,' her mother would have called it. As if she had thought she could murder Carrie with her eyes just as she'd thought Carrie had murdered Frank. There were things that came out at the trial Carrie would far rather Kathryn didn't know about, unless, of course, she knew them already. But Carrie doesn't think she does know.

She shakes her head, trying to dispel the feeling of foreboding.

Oh, it's wonderful to have Kathryn here. But all this raking up of the past is very disturbing. It would be wonderful to have Gillian back, too, just to see her again. But that's not going to happen. And Carrie doesn't think she could bear to lose her all over again.

Part Four

Carrie

TWENTY-THREE

It was the hardest thing I ever had to do, letting Gillian go. But really I had no choice. She wasn't a little girl any more, she was almost a grown woman. Thirteen years old, with a mind of her own. And she hated me.

Throughout those five long years in prison, it was the thought of my family that had kept me going, though in the beginning it was being parted from them that was the most unbearable thing of all. I can't bring myself to think about those early days. The raw agony of the separation from Gillian was so overwhelming I've closed my mind to it. And when Andrea was born, and they took her away from me . . . Dear God, I can't. Even now, I simply cannot talk about it. The emptiness, the despair, the physical pain . . . it is beyond description. I wanted to die. But I had to survive, for them, if not for myself. And I did.

My girls were the ones I clung to in the long hours of darkness when the door of my cell had clanged shut for the night.

I would lie on the hard, narrow bunk under my hard, scratchy blanket and think of them. The knowing that they were growing up without me was a weeping wound that would never heal, but I tried not to think about it. That way lay madness. Instead, I pictured how it would be when we were all together again. I listened to the rattle of the warders' footfalls on the iron stairs and walkways outside my cell and heard only my children's laughter. I wrapped my arms around myself and pretended I was holding two firm little bodies to my heart. I counted away the long minutes and longer hours in making plans.

It wouldn't be easy; I was under no illusion about that. I would have to get to know them again, and they would have to get to know me. But I truly believed my love for them was strong enough for all of us.

I wondered too, in those long and lonely hours, about the wisdom of going back to Timberley. Whether I could bear to go back to the house where it had happened. But for the immediate future I had nowhere else to go, and Bush Villa was there, waiting for me; Father had died a couple of days after Frank, and Mother during the last year of my sentence. And, most importantly, Andrea would be close to Mary, who had been a surrogate mother to her.

I would have to face the talk in the village, of course, and the stares, and the conversations that ended abruptly when I passed within earshot. But I was the local girl whilst Frank was the outsider, and given the things that had come out at the trial, Mary had told me, there was a certain amount of sympathy with me, though there were those who, like Lizzie, thought I'd brought it all on myself. I'd put up with being a nine-days' wonder before, and I'd do it again. Hold my head high, rise above the whispers and the sideways looks, and wait for people to begin to forget, or at least to treat me as they always had, and not as if I were some kind of freak.

I did, I must admit, worry about Gillian. She was of an age when she would be very conscious of any attention that was directed towards us and, unlike Andrea, who had never lived anywhere else, her return was bound to attract interest on her own account, never mind mine. Added to that, terrible things had happened to her in Timberley. She had, or so I had been told, no memory of the night Frank died, or any of the things that led up to it. But that didn't mean she wouldn't have bad feelings about the house. There was even the possibility that going back would act as a trigger to her remembering part, or all, of it.

I was going to have to tread very carefully with Gillian, I knew.

But I never, even in my darkest moments, imagined that I would lose her altogether. If I had, I think it would have broken me.

It's the one thing in the whole terrible affair I have never got over. And yet I still cannot regret what I did. Given that I could go back and have my time over, I would still do it all again.

For all the plans I'd made, for all the days I'd crossed off on the calendar, counting them down one by one to the moment I would be with my daughters again, I experienced nothing but total disorientation when I stepped outside the gates of the prison, a free woman, wearing the black skirt and yellow shirt blouse I'd worn when the armoured van took me from the court to the prison. The glare of the sun on the wet road hurt my eyes — everything, in fact, looked garishly bright — and the vast emptiness around me was daunting. I stood there on the pavement, clutching my bag to my chest, and felt the panic constricting my chest, cutting off breath.

And then Mary was there, dear Mary, putting her arm around my waist, and urging me towards the car, which she'd parked a little way down the road.

Has anyone ever had such a good friend as Mary? Throughout it all, she had stood by me, though Geoff was far from happy about that. Mary, of course, knew the truth; Geoff did not. But even so, what she did went far beyond what anyone has the right to expect of a friend. The debt of gratitude I owe her for giving Andrea a happy home and raising her alongside her three boys is one I can never repay. She'd written and visited me regularly, though it must have been hard to find the time in her busy life, and sometimes she had brought Andrea with her, which had been both a delight and a torment, but for which I was eternally grateful. And now here she was, easing me back on the long road to the rest of my life.

Andrea was with her now, sitting in the back seat of the car. She was wearing a pink dress with frills, ribbons in her hair, pink to match her dress. Her eyes, wide and anxious, searched my face; her bottom lip was caught between her front teeth, and I saw that one of them was missing. My throat constricted again, this time with tears. I wanted to sweep her into my arms and never let her go, but I knew it would be too much, too soon.

'Look who it is, Andrea!' Mary said. 'It's your mummy! We're going to take her home.'

'Hello, Andrea,' I said, my voice catching on the words.

''Lo . . .'

'Can I sit with you?'

She didn't answer, but she moved along the seat, making room for me. I slid in beside her. She was very quiet for a long while, casting sidelong glances at me and pleating the hem of her skirt between her fingers, and I was equally tongue-tied. It was left to Mary to fill the silence. Then, as we turned in through the farm gate, Andrea suddenly tapped me on the knee.

'This is where I live,' she offered. 'Are you coming to live with us too?'

'Well . . . yes, in a way.' I didn't want to go into too many details. We had decided, Mary and I, that I would stay at the farm for a while so that Andrea could get used to me in familiar surroundings. In any case, I had to get things together at Bush Villa. Mary, who had a key, had been in, opened the windows and lit fires in all the rooms, and – she had told me with disgust – cleaned up the mouse droppings that were all over the kitchen floor, and set traps. But there was a good deal to be done to turn the house back into a home for myself and my children.

'That would be good,' Andrea said solemnly. And for the first time since I had been sitting beside her she smiled at me, that same, gap-toothed smile that somehow made her look all the more cute.

My heart fell away; tears were misting my eyes. Through them, I smiled back. It was early days yet, and I was still a stranger to her, but the hope and joy in my heart were telling me that, given time, Andrea and I were going to be perfectly fine together.

I was, of course, bursting with eagerness to see Gillian, but Mary persuaded me to be patient for a few days, to give myself a chance to adjust to life outside prison walls and concentrate on bonding with Andrea. One step at a time, she counselled, and I accepted, reluctantly, that she was most likely right. I did write to Lizzie, though, telling her I'd been released and saying I'd like to come down to Somerset when she'd had a chance to prepare Gillian. I told her I hoped Gillian would come home with me for good eventually, but that I realised it was going to mean another upheaval in her life and I didn't want to rush things; that perhaps it would be best if she were to come to stay for a weekend or two to begin with, and the best time for her permanent move would be at the beginning of the school summer holidays. I thanked her for looking after Gillian, but said I was sure she would understand that I now wanted to have my family back together again.

I went over and over every line of that letter, changing a word here, a phrase there, and got Mary to read it over before I wrote out the fair copy. I had to tread carefully with Lizzie; she was no friend to me and never had been, even before Frank's death. I was grateful to her for giving Gillian a home when I could not, but there had been something in the way she'd done it, the haste, the tight-lipped determination, that had disturbed me. I would have preferred Gillian to go to Mary, but Lizzie had been adamant: Gillian's place was with her own flesh and blood. I had been in no position to argue and I had thought that if I did, Lizzie would apply for custody through the courts. It would mean more trauma and uncertainty for Gillian, and in the end, Lizzie would probably win the day. So I raised no formal objection.

When Andrea was taken from me, I'd expected Lizzie to give her a home too, in fact, I hoped she would, so that the sisters could be together. But when she was approached she flatly refused. At the time I thought it was because she doubted Andrea was Frank's child, now I think it was more than that. She had the child she wanted so badly – she and Walter had no children of their own – and she was determined to keep her. Isolating her from the rest of her family made that easier.

I didn't know that, of course, when I wrote that first letter. And there were plenty of other things I didn't know, either – how she'd never passed on a single letter I'd written to Gillian whilst I was in prison, for instance. I didn't know, and though I was well aware that things might not be easy, it never crossed my mind that Lizzie would go so far as to steal my daughter from me.

The first inkling I had came in her reply to my letter.

I think I should make it plain I am very much against uprooting Gillian. She's doing well at the Grammar School. I can tell you too that she would not want to be away from us and her friends for a whole weekend. In the circumstances, I do not think you coming to see her would serve any purpose. Kindly respect my wishes in this matter.

Yours Faithfully, Mrs Elizabeth Yarlett

Naturally, I was very upset, and Mary furious.

'How dare she! Who does she think she is?' she fumed.

'What am I going to do, Mary?' I was still institutionalised; in five years, I'd almost lost the ability to think for myself.

'Well, you're not going to roll over and let her call the tune!' Mary said angrily.

'You think I should write again?'

Mary tossed the letter down dismissively on the kitchen table.

'Fat lot of good that would do! No, you need to talk to Gillian. And with that woman out of the way, too. Where is it she goes to school?'

'It says here she's at the Grammar School.' Pride swelled in my chest. Gillian had passed her eleven-plus and nobody had bothered to tell me!

'Well, find out where it is, and we'll go down one afternoon and meet her out.'

My breath was coming so fast I was practically hyperventilating. 'Could we?'

'I'm up for it if you are. Geoff will keep an eye on Andrea while we're gone.'

'But how am I going to find out . . . ?'

'Oh, for goodness' sake!' Mary said impatiently. 'There's a telephone in the hall. If you want to see your daughter again, I suggest you get on and use it!'

*   *   *

316

In the end it was Mary who did the telephoning. I sat on the stairs, my nerves jangling, while she rang County Hall and made her enquiries as to the location of the school, her voice tight and brisk because she was still seething at Lizzie's letter.

'That's it then,' she said, replacing the receiver and turning to look at me. 'I've got the address, now all we have to do is find it. When do you want to go?'

I was trembling. It didn't take much to make me tremble in those first weeks of freedom. I, who had always prided myself on my ability to cope with whatever life threw at me, could be undone by the smallest thing, or even a wash of emotion. So it was no wonder that my stomach was a churning nest of ants and I had to knot my hands together on my knees to keep them still as Mary and I sat in her car outside Gillian's school on a warm afternoon in late May.

It was a square building of red brick set behind a narrow playground on a hill overlooking South Moulton, Hillsbridge's twin town. To one side a meadow sloped away; on the level ground at the top of the rise I could see the wire netting of what I presumed to be tennis courts. As we sat there waiting, a teacher emerged from an entrance on the side of the building, walked round to one of the three or four cars that were parked at the front, got something out, and went inside again. She was quite small, grey-haired, and walked with a determined stalk, black gown flying out behind her so that she looked like a fluttering rook. A chill hand closed over my heart. The uniform might be different, but it was still that of a figure of authority. My instinctive reaction was to imagine that she possessed the same cruel streak as some of the warders I'd known, those who delighted in wielding power over those in no position to fight back. She certainly looked haughty and somehow ruthless. I hoped that if she taught Gillian, she was kind to her.

Mary glanced at her watch. 'Can't be long now.'

A moment later the bell began jangling, the sound of it carrying clearly out through the open windows. Again I was reminded of prison, of the bell that echoed through the halls and walkways, or rang out from the wall of the exercise yard, bringing conversations to an abrupt end as we fell into line and trudged back to evil-smelling, claustrophobic confinement. A shudder ran through me and I wondered how I had borne it. Then the first children emerged, boys from the left of the building, girls from the right, not erupting as they did from the village junior school but in orderly fashion. I craned forward, jaw set against the nerves that were making me tremble again.

'Let's go and stand by the gate,' Mary said. 'We don't want to miss her.'

Some of the children were collecting bicycles from a shed at the rear of the yard, others were forming a queue at a bus stop just a few yards from the main gate. There were also two coaches lined up and waiting. My nerves tightened another notch. It hadn't occurred to me that I wouldn't know Gillian – such a thing was inconceivable. Now, as the trickle of emerging children became a flood, I wasn't sure that I would. The little girl I'd left behind was thirteen now, a young woman almost. I didn't know how tall she'd grown, or how she wore her hair, and it seemed to me, suddenly, that she could be any one of these girls, all identically dressed in checked cotton dresses, navy-blue blazers and berets and white socks.

The same thing must have occurred to Mary. Practical as ever, she approached a girl who looked to be about Gillian's age.

'We're looking for Gillian Chapman. Do you know her?'

'Gillian? Yes. She's in Three B.'

'You couldn't point her out to us, could you?'

The girl frowned, looking around. Two more girls of similar age were heading our way. I scanned their faces, rejected the idea that they were Gillian, twisted and turned, searching, searching.

'Have you seen Gillian Chapman?' the girl Mary had approached asked the other two.

One shook her head, the other squinted from behind the pink plastic frames of National Health spectacles. 'She was in the cloakroom. Talking to Veronica Hillier.'

'I don't suppose,' Mary said, 'that you'd fetch her for us?'

In this day and age, I imagine such a request would elicit suspicion, maybe even outright hostility. But this was the 'fifties, when there was still an innocence about children, and respect for their elders.

'I'll tell her.' The girl in National Health spectacles assumed an air of importance. She dumped her satchel on the low wall and scurried back to what I supposed was the girls' entrance.

I could feel my heart beating so hard that the deep, almost painful, pounding echoed in my ears. I wanted to follow the girl into the cloakroom, so anxious was I to see Gillian, but of course I did not. I stood, hanging on to the railings that topped the low wall, and the sleeves of my blouse felt clammy cold against my burning skin where the perspiration pouring from me had soaked them through.

Two girls emerged from the door at the right of the building. The one in National Health spectacles. And Gillian.

How could I have doubted for even a moment that I would know her? She was taller, of course, maybe a full foot taller. Her hair was pulled back into a ponytail, her regulation beret sat, flat as a pancake, on her head, resting between it and a thick, full fringe. She had lost her baby roundness, her legs were long and slim beneath the knee-length skirt, her breasts small developing mounds under her blazer. But the way she moved was unmistakable, that air of poise she'd had even as a little girl. She walked like a ballerina. And as she came closer I could see that her features were simply an older version of the eight-year-old Gillian.

She was frowning, her brows puckered in exactly the same way they had puckered when she pored over a new jigsaw or a long word she'd never encountered before in a book. Not a worried frown, but puzzled. She didn't know who I was.

My hands were clenching and unclenching in the folds of my skirt. I'd waited so long for this moment, now I was literally dumbstruck, and paralysed too. I simply stood, staring at her, tears gathering in my eyes.

'Gillian,' Mary said, 'could we go somewhere a bit private, love? We want to talk to you.'

'But . . . who are you? I don't know you.' She didn't recognise Mary either, I realised.

'You've forgotten us, that's all.' Mary's tone was gently

320

reassuring, but I saw the first gleam of something like panic flicker across Gillian's face.

'How do you know me?' she demanded. 'Who *are* you?'

'I'm Mary. Mary Hutchins. I used to look after you when you were a little girl. And this . . .' she put a hand on my arm '. . . this is your mother.'

For a long moment Gillian stared at me, wide-eyed, shocked and disbelieving. Then the panic flared again, full blown this time.

'I don't have a mother.' She said it defiantly, but the words came trembling from her lips.

'She's been away, my love.' Mary gave my arm a little shake, urging me out of my trance. *Say something*, that shake said. *Don't leave this all to me!*

'I've been away,' I parroted. 'But I'm back now. And, Gillian, oh, sweetheart, I know this is a shock for you, but—'

'No!' Gillian's voice rose hysterically. 'No! It's not true!' She backed away, her eyes still riveted to my face.

'It is true, darling. I am your mother. And I just want to talk to you.' I was holding out my arms, beseeching. 'Please, Gillian, please don't . . .'

'No! I don't want to talk to you!' She was still backing away, tears welling in her eyes. Then, abruptly, she turned and began to run, her hands pressed to her mouth, her satchel bumping against her hip.

I hadn't noticed a bus pull up at the stop, nor the queue of children dwindling as they boarded. Now I saw Gillian dart towards it.

'Gillian!' I started after her, blind to anything but her fleeing figure, collided with a drop-handlebar bicycle being wheeled by a tall, fair-haired boy. 'Oh – I'm sorry . . .' I disentangled myself, skirted the cluster of children. Gillian was on the step of the bus now, looking fearfully over her shoulder. As I reached the bus it began to move off.

'Wait . . . wait!' I was running alongside, desperate not to lose her. But either the conductor didn't hear me or chose to ignore me. The bus pulled away from me, leaving me standing. For a moment I stood staring after it, then I ran back to Mary.

'She's gone on the bus! Follow it, Mary! If we're quick we can overtake it and be at the stop when she gets off.'

'It wouldn't do any good, Carrie. Not today. She's in shock. You've got to give her time to think about it.'

'Mary, please!' I was beside myself, beyond reason.

'All right, get in the car.' I did, shaking with urgency. 'Do you know which stop she'll get off at?'

'No, not really. I think the bus must go more or less past Lizzie's street, though. They live just off the main road.'

'All right.' Mary paused in the act of turning the car, indicating the glove compartment. 'There should be a pen and some paper in there. Write down your address and telephone number.'

'But I haven't got—'

'You're staying with me, aren't you? My address and telephone number.'

I found a couple of sheets of folded-up notepaper in the glove compartment and, at the back, behind a tin of boiled sweets and a dried-out chamois leather, a stub of pencil. I wrote down my name with 'Mum' in brackets after it, and the address of the farm, but Mary's telephone number eluded me. She dictated it to me and I wrote that down too. I hoped it was legible – writing while the car was in motion wasn't easy.

I only vaguely remembered the geography of Hillsbridge from that long-ago Christmas when Frank and I had visited, and coming at it from the opposite direction made everything look different. But when we reached them, I thought I recognised the ranks of houses that lined the main road, and sure enough when the bus pulled up at a stop outside a small general store, Gillian got off.

I had the car door half-open before Mary stopped me. 'Whoa, Carrie. You stay here. I'll give it to her.'

'But—'

'Better for you to keep out of the way today. She's upset enough already.' She got out of the car. As she approached Gillian, I saw my daughter shrink away and I shrank inwardly myself. I was terribly afraid Gillian would turn and run again. Mary spoke to her, held out the scrap of paper, and after a moment, Gillian took it, thrusting it into the pocket of her blazer. Then, head down, she walked away without so much as a backward glance, crossing the road and heading towards a gap in the rank of houses.

'What did she say?' I asked when Mary came back to the car.

'Nothing.' Mary squeezed my hand briefly. 'I think, Carrie, that you are going to have to be patient for a bit longer.'

TWENTY-FOUR

Patient! I didn't want to be patient. I'd been patient for five long years. Now, to be so near my beloved daughter and yet so far from her was torture.

'At least you know she's all right,' Mary said, and that much was true. But it wasn't enough. Not nearly enough.

'Lizzie's turned her against me,' I said, flat with disappointment, the pain of rejection a leaden weight around my heart.

'You don't know that.'

'I didn't want her to have Gillian, but I didn't have any say in it. And she never brought her to see me, not once. You brought Andrea. Why didn't she bring Gillian? What's she told her about me, Mary?'

'She's told her you killed her father,' Mary said bluntly. 'Which is the truth, as she sees it.'

'But how could she turn her against me so completely she won't even talk to me?' I was distraught. 'I'm her mother! When all's said and done, I'm still her mother! What am I going to do, Mary?'

'You've just got to give it time. Write to Lizzie again.'

'And what good will that do? You saw her letter . . .'

'Write to Gillian, then.'

'I've been writing to her, all the time I was in prison.'

'Tell her the truth.'

Fierce metal jaws clamped around my heart like the wire of one of Mary's mousetraps on a small furry neck.

'I can't do that.'

'It may be the only way. She's old enough now to understand.'

'I couldn't. Not in a letter.'

Mary sighed. 'Well, it's your decision.'

'Yes,' I said, 'yes, it is.'

'Look, Carrie, let's be sensible about this. Honestly, what did you expect? That she was going to run into your arms? That we'd be taking her home with us? It was never going to happen. She doesn't remember you. She lost her memory, you know that.'

'I know she lost her memory. But I thought she'd remember me.'

'Well, she doesn't. But maybe seeing you will start to bring it back. You were a wonderful mother to her, Carrie. All that has got to be still there, buried beneath the surface. It'll come to her eventually, you'll see.'

Tears of desperation were filling my eyes.

'I have to be there for her, Mary.'

'And you will be. But you can't rush it.'

'I suppose you're right. I was expecting too much.'

'Write to her. Tell her how you feel. And next time it'll be different.'

'Oh, I hope so! I'm scared, Mary. I'm really scared that I've lost her.'

'Of course you haven't,' Mary said briskly.

But she was wrong.

As Mary had suggested, I wrote both to Lizzie and to Gillian, and got no reply from either of them. I wrote again. And again. Still no response. Or at least, not the kind I was expecting.

A few weeks after we'd visited the school, the phone rang one morning as we were clearing away the breakfast things, Mary up to her elbows in soapsuds at the sink, me drying the stack of crockery that the men left behind after they'd come in for bacon, eggs and 'fatty bread', as Mary called fried bread.

'I'll get it,' I said.

I picked up the phone, heard the clank of coins dropping as the person on the other end – in a call box, obviously – pressed Button A, followed by a moment's silence. Then: 'I want to speak to Carrie.'

I went very still. Even though it was distorted by the telephone line, I recognised that voice.

'This is Carrie,' I said.

'Right. And you know who this is, don't you? Well, I'm ringing to warn you. If you don't leave Gillian alone, I'll have the law on you.'

'What?' I was stunned, totally winded by the suddenness and the viciousness of the attack.

'You heard me. You can stop writing to me, and you can stop writing to Gillian, or I'll have you up for harassment.'

Totally shocked, I actually laughed.

'You can't have me up for contacting my own daughter, you silly woman.'

'We'll see about that. If you know what's good for you, you'll leave her alone. She doesn't want anything to do with you, do you understand? She doesn't want anything to do with the bitch who murdered her father.'

And with that the phone went down.

I was, of course, furious as well as upset. If Lizzie thought she could frighten me off with threatening phone calls, she was quite wrong.

Mary and I held another council of war and came to the conclusion the only answer was to go to Hillsbridge again and confront Lizzie face to face. I'd tell her in no uncertain terms that Gillian was my daughter and I wanted her back, and if she, Lizzie, didn't stop trying to come between us, I was the one who would be taking legal advice.

We went a couple of days later, when I'd taken Andrea to school. She, at least, was beginning to accept me and the greatest happiness in my life was having her run across the playground to me each afternoon, fitting her plump little hand into mine and chattering all the way home about her day. We hoped to be back in time for me to meet her. If not, Mary's boys would bring her home.

I was, I confess, all geared up for a fight. Normally, confrontation is not in my nature, but this was different. This was about getting Gillian back, and I'd have walked into the jaws of hell for that. Though I told Mary to wait in the car, she refused.

'I'm going to give that woman a piece of my mind,' she said.

'Just be careful what you say,' I warned her.

'It's time she knew the truth.'

'No, Mary, I don't want that,' I said emphatically.

She raised her eyebrows, shook her head. 'All right. Have it your way.'

We found Lizzie in the long back garden, which was separated from the rank of houses by an alleyway of cobbles. She was pegging out washing. When she saw us she stopped, a vest of Walter's dangling between her hands like a white flag of surrender.

'What are you doing here?'

'It's time we talked, Lizzie.'

'I've got nothing to say to you.' She was blustering, bristling. She dropped the vest into the laundry basket, pushed past us, back down the path in the direction of the house.

I followed her. 'Well, I've got plenty to say to you. I'm very grateful to you for looking after Gillian while I was in prison . . .'

'For murdering my brother!'

'. . . but I've served my time now. I'm out. I want to see my daughter, and you're doing everything you can to stop me. Well, I won't have it. I want her home with me, where she belongs.'

'She belongs here! This is her home now! Why don't you just go back to wherever it is you've come from and leave us alone!'

'You can't really think I'll go away and leave my daughter with you.'

'She doesn't want to know you,' Lizzie grated. 'Is that any surprise after what you did? You're a wicked woman, Carrie.'

'You can think what you like, Lizzie. I'm not going to discuss it with you,' I said, with a warning glance at Mary, who was on the point of flying to my defence. 'Anything I have to say, I'll say to my daughter. I just want to talk to her.'

'And I don't want you upsetting her.'

'I don't want to upset her either! That's the last thing I want. But I have to see her . . .' I was beginning to lose my cool, and our raised voices were attracting attention. Doors were opening up and down the terrace, net curtains stirring at windows. 'I have to talk to her,' I said. 'I won't stop until I do.'

'All right!' Lizzie was quivering. 'Talk to her then. She's home from school today, studying – or supposed to be. They've got exams tomorrow. She can tell you herself. The same as I've told you. She doesn't want anything to do with you.'

'Gillian's *here*?' I'd begun to tremble myself.

'Give me a minute.' Lizzie went to her back door, which stood ajar. 'Let me prepare her.' She disappeared inside the house.

Mary touched my arm. 'Take it easy, Carrie.'

I scarcely heard her. The blood was roaring in my ears.

'Come in then.' Lizzie appeared, standing ramrod straight in the doorway.

I followed her through the scullery into the little living room beyond. Gillian was there, standing awkwardly at the foot of the narrow staircase, one hand pressed against the wall, one foot on the bottom stair, as if poised for flight. Lizzie went to her, put an arm around her.

'Go on then, say what you have to say, and go.' And to Gillian, she added: 'Don't be frightened, my love. I won't let her hurt you.'

My jaw dropped at the outrageousness of it. At that moment I would certainly have liked to do serious harm to Lizzie. But to react to her goading would be to play into her hands.

'There's no reason to be afraid, Gillian,' I said. 'I want to talk to you, that's all. Just you and me. Couldn't we . . . ?'

Lizzie's arm tightened round my daughter's shoulders. 'Whatever you have to say, you can say it in front of me.'

It wasn't what I wanted, but I could see I had no choice. There was no way Lizzie was going to let me be alone with Gillian.

'Darling, I love you so much . . .' I faltered, began again. 'You must believe me, Gillian, it wasn't the way you think, and everything I did, I did for you.'

Lizzie snorted. 'You killed her father. And not content with that, you tried to blacken his name. The things you accused him of, Carrie, when he was no longer there to defend himself! A decent man like our Frank.'

'I was only telling the truth,' I said quietly.

'The truth? Huh!' Lizzie snorted again. 'Our Frank would never have done the things you said. Never!'

'Not the old Frank, maybe. Not the Frank you knew. But he changed, Lizzie. Losing his leg changed him.' My eyes went to Gillian's face. She was very pale, and she looked as if she might be going to cry. My heart bled for her, that she should be put through this. 'Oh, darling, he wasn't a bad man, don't think that. But he was ill, and he did bad things. He couldn't help himself, I realise that now. But I had to protect you. I couldn't take the risk . . .'

'That's your story,' Lizzie said harshly. She was clearly determined to harangue me every step of the way. 'You wanted to run off with your fancy man, and Frank was standing in your way. That's the truth of it. If our Frank wasn't himself, it was because he knew you were carrying on behind his back. You didn't tell them *that* at the trial, did you? You didn't tell them you were planning to run off with him and take Frank's daughter with you. You didn't tell them *that*.'

This was all going horribly wrong. Gillian shouldn't be subjected to this.

'Lizzie, please . . .' I begged.

But there was no stopping her. 'You were even having that dirty bugger's baby.'

I gasped. '*What? What* did you say?'

'Oh, don't think I don't know who fathered your other kid. Why do you think I wouldn't take her in like I did Gillian? I wasn't going to have that bugger's bastard here.'

'You've got this all wrong . . .' But it wasn't the time to go into all that. Gillian was my only concern.

'Gillian, Andrea is your sister, I promise you,' I said. 'And she wants to see you as much as I do.' I fumbled in my bag, pulled out a snapshot, held it out to her. 'This is her. This is Andrea. Won't you at least come to Timberley and meet her? Think how lovely it would be to have a sister!'

Gillian's jaw wobbled. For a moment hope flared in me that

I had at last struck a chord with her. Then her face crumpled, her eyes filling with tears.

'I don't want a sister. Oh, why can't you just leave me alone?' She twisted suddenly, pushing Lizzie away, and ran up the stairs.

'Now see what you've done!' Lizzie sounded more triumphant than concerned for Gillian. I pushed past her, running up the stairs after Gillian, ignoring Lizzie's indignant: 'Where do you think you're going?'

Gillian had flown into one of the bedrooms. As I followed her, she turned on me.

'Leave me alone, can't you? I hate you! I hate you!'

'Gillian . . .' There was some kind of kerfuffle going on downstairs – Mary preventing Lizzie from coming after us, I found out later – but I scarcely noticed. 'Gillian . . .' I stopped, across the room from her, holding out my hands to her. 'Lizzie is mistaken, really. It wasn't like she's told you. And I really, really want us to be a family again. But I won't take you away from here if this is where you want to be. Your happiness is the most important thing. Just come and see us, get to know us. Give us a chance, please!'

Gillian was cowering, arms wrapped around herself.

'You killed my father. You said awful things about him. Things that weren't true, just to excuse what you did.'

'It wasn't like that, Gillian.'

'It was! Auntie Lizzie's told me.'

'Auntie Lizzie doesn't know the full story. She's angry with me, she blames me, but she's got it all wrong.'

'I don't believe you.'

I bowed my head, overcome with desperation. Lizzie had

332

done a thorough job of turning her against me. My only chance was to tell her the truth, and I couldn't bring myself to do that. Gillian had been through so much, I couldn't burden her with anything else. She was already fragile; the truth would destroy her.

I raised my head again, looking directly at her.

'All I ask is that you give me a chance. And one day, perhaps, you'll understand.'

Gillian's lower lip jutted. 'I won't. I'll never understand. Just leave me alone, can't you? I just want you to go away and leave me alone!'

For a long painful moment I looked at her, my little girl, who had been taught to hate me. And knew that, for her good, I had to let her go, for now at least.

'Very well,' I said, my voice breaking. 'If that's what you want. But please remember, I'm always there for you. Whenever you're ready. You know where to find me. And I'll be waiting, however long it takes.'

I went to the door, turned back, seeing her through a haze of tears. I pressed my fingers to my lips, blew her a lingering kiss. She glowered at me, eyes full of hate in her crumpled face.

'I love you, Gillian,' I said softly.

And walked away from the daughter I'd have given my life for.

Part Five

TWENTY-FIVE

Edmondsville, Ontario

The telephone is ringing. Gillian waits, hoping Don will answer it, then calls: 'Don? Are you there?'

No reply. He's probably gone out to the garage to program the radio on his newly acquired Subaru. He was complaining earlier, on their way back from Gillian's check-up appointment at the hospital, that he couldn't find the station he usually listened to amongst the mêlée of ready-tuned channels. Gillian levers herself up, reaches for her crutches, and swings across the room to answer it. In the back of her mind she's thinking – hoping – that it might be Kathryn. Strangely, since she has never been a possessive mother, she is really missing her daughter. It's unusual for them to see one another more often than once a week, but now, with Kathryn on the other side of the world, Gillian feels as if she's lost a limb.

It's not Kathryn, though. It's Rob.

'Hi, Gillian. How are you doing?'

'Oh, improving, I think. At least, that's the received wisdom from my doctor. Sorry it took me so long to answer. I thought the phone would stop before I got to it.'

'I allowed you plenty of time. I know your crutches slow you down.'

'Actually I'm getting quite good on them. You should see how well I can swing along! It's my hands that are suffering most.' She glances ruefully at the red blistered ridge across her palm, evidence of skin protesting against the unaccustomed pressure upon it. 'But hey, the doctor says another month and I can go to partial weight-bearing, as long as the X-rays are positive.'

'That's good news.'

'Yep. And I'll have muscles like a weightlifter by then, too.' Gillian likes Rob. She has an easy relationship, denied to many mothers-in-law, with him. 'You didn't ring to talk about my hip, though,' she says.

'Actually, I was wondering if you've heard anything from Kathryn.'

'Not really. Just a couple of texts, that's all. I did wonder when the phone rang if it might be her.'

'Sorry to disappoint you.'

'Oh, don't be silly. You haven't heard anything either, I take it.'

'No more than you. Just a text.'

'She's busy, I expect. And the time difference . . .'

'I wish I'd gone with her,' Rob says.

'I wish you had too. Apart from anything else, it would have given you some time together. A chance, maybe, to resolve your differences.'

'Yes, well, it's too late for that now.' Rob is shutting down, retreating into his private cave. Gillian wishes she hadn't said it. She mustn't interfere. And she wonders, too, whether he meant it was too late to accompany Kathryn to England, or too late for resolving their differences. But she's not going to ask. She knows when it's time to leave well alone.

'I'll let you know if I hear anything,' she says.

'Thanks. I'll do the same. Take care, Gillian.'

'Don't worry, I will!'

She puts the phone down, swings back across the room to her chair, then decides against it. She's fed up with sitting, fed up with reading, even though under normal circumstances she would consider it a luxury to be able to get through a whole book at more or less one sitting without feeling guilty, fed up with watching television, fed up with being confined to the house, alone. A friend took her to the supermarket yesterday, the first time since her accident that she didn't do her weekly grocery shop online, and it felt like the most incredible treat. A trip to the supermarket, a treat! How sad is that?

Gillian decides she'll go out to the garage, see how Don is getting on with his radio programming. Anything rather than plopping down in the chair again. But she takes the telephone with her, just in case Kathryn should call.

As she thought, Don is in his new car, sitting in the passenger seat, head leaning back onto the headrest, eyes closed. From the stereo speakers, Don McLean is belting out 'American Pie'.

'You fixed the radio, then?'

His eyes flare open, but she thinks he was probably asleep. 'What are you doing out here?'

'Aren't I allowed?' She goes round to the driver's door, opens it and manoeuvres herself into the driving seat. 'I'm tired of looking at four walls.'

'I expect you are. Never mind, you'll soon be back to normal.'

They sit without saying anything for a minute or two, listening to the haunting anthem, not the music of their youth, exactly, but certainly of the days when they were a good deal younger, when Kathryn was small, when they used to get a baby-sitter and go out dancing. They had been very special, those stolen evenings, when they could luxuriate in a few hours' freedom and rekindle romance, yet be comfortable with one another at the same time.

Don is singing along with the refrain; Gillian remembers him singing it into her hair on the dance floor and feels the tug of bittersweet nostalgia. Where have the years gone?

When the song finishes she returns reluctantly to the present.

'Rob rang. He wanted to know if I'd heard from Kathryn. I told him we hadn't. Not really.'

'You didn't expect to, surely?' Don says, pragmatic as ever. 'She's got better things to do than phoning home.'

'I suppose. It would be nice to hear her voice, though. And Rob obviously feels the same. Oh, I wish they'd sort things out! Rob is such a nice fellow and they were so happy before—' She breaks off, staring into space. Ben's death had hit her hard too. 'I'm worried about her, Don,' she says after a moment.

'I know, but there's nothing you can do. You've just got to let her come to terms with it in her own time.'

'You think she will?'

'I certainly hope so.' No empty words of optimistic comfort from Don. That isn't his way.

Eric Clapton is on now: 'Tears in Heaven'.

'Can't we have something a bit more cheerful?' Gillian says.

Don reaches over and switches the radio off.

'I don't know what we're doing sitting in the car anyway.'

'You started it. I just joined in.'

'It's a nice car, isn't it? I'm pleased with it.' Don has the manual open on his lap and he starts flicking through it. Gillian couldn't care less about the special all-singing, all-dancing features. As far as she's concerned, if a car gets her from A to B that's all she wants.

'I'm worried about her being in England too,' she says.

'What?' Don is scanning the section covering the built-in sat-nav.

'Kathryn. I don't like it, her being in England.'

'You can't do anything about that either. You worry too much, Gill.'

'I've just got this awful feeling . . . suppose she doesn't come home?'

Don doesn't even look up from the manual. 'Now you really are being silly.'

'She's been so unhappy since we lost Ben. If she gets on well with Andrea and my mother, she might decide she's got nothing to come home for. That she'll make a fresh start, right away from anything that reminds her.'

'She's not going to do that.'

'How do you know?'

'I just do.'

'But how can you be so sure?' Gillian is beginning to work herself up. 'She was really angry with me for keeping my family a secret from her. Oh, she didn't actually say so in as many words, but I could tell. She might feel she wants to make up for lost time. Oh, Don, if she stayed in England, I couldn't bear it. I know it sounds stupid. After all, it's only eight or nine hours on a plane, not weeks away like it used to be. But all the same, I'd hate it if she were so far away. I miss her. I really do.'

'She's been gone less than a week,' Don says reasonably.

'I know. And I know I'm being silly. But there you are, it's how I feel. She is my daughter, after all.'

For a moment Don is silent, then he closes the car manual and clicks the snap fastener on the leather tab shut.

'Don't you suppose that your mother might feel like that?'

His words come as quite a shock to Gillian. Don gave up expressing an opinion on her estrangement from her family a long time ago. Even when they'd talked about Kathryn going to meet them he'd merely said he thought it was a good thing, and left it at that.

'It's quite different!' Gillian retaliates hotly.

'Why?'

'Well, of course it is! I would have thought that was obvious.'

'You're Kathryn's mother. She's yours. She carried you for nine months, gave birth to you, raised you for eight years. I really can't see why you would think she'd feel any differently about it than you do.'

For no reason that she can explain, Gillian feels wrong-footed. She shifts her weight awkwardly.

'My hip's hurting. I'm going indoors.'

'That's it. Run away.'

'I'm not running away. I've got a fractured pelvis and I want to take a painkiller.'

'Any excuse. I try not to be judgemental, Gillian, but it's more than your hip that's hurting, if you ask me. And you'd be a lot better off if you'd face up to it.'

'Well, thanks for the sympathy.' Gillian is being unreasonable, and she knows it. Don has really been very good in his typically masculine way. But she always snaps when she finds herself on the defensive.

She struggles to get her legs out of the car without putting any weight on her hip.

'Do you need help?' Don is already getting out of the car, coming round to her side. He retrieves a crutch that's fallen on the floor out of Gillian's reach, hoists her out of the car, and steadies her whilst she gets the crutches into position. 'All right now?'

'I can manage, if that's what you mean.' She begins to hop around the car.

'I'll be in in a minute.'

'OK.' She doubts it. He's too enamoured of his new car.

'Gill – think about it, love, please. For all our sakes.'

She knows what he means, but she doesn't answer. She heads back into the house. But the truth of the matter is she can't think of anything else.

Has she been wrong all these years to shut Carrie out of her life? Never to give her the chance to explain, perhaps rebut some of Lizzie's accusations? In her youth, Gillian had accepted

343

them absolutely, but she knows now there are two sides to every story. So why has she stuck to her guns so stubbornly?

The problem is that the only memories she has of her mother are bad ones – the times when she suddenly appeared on the scene like the wicked witch in a pantomime, trying to take Gillian away from the only home she knew. Carrie was a bad woman, Lizzie said; a liar, an adulteress, a murderer. And the young Gillian believed her – of course she had. Lizzie was her anchor, her surrogate mother. 'You don't want anything to do with her,' Lizzie said, and the warning became inextricably linked with the dark memories that were locked away inside her, inaccessible, yet still potent, tainting her with the aura that came from something too awful to face.

Gillian remembers her confusion when she came out of school one afternoon to be confronted by two strange women, one claiming to be the mother she had been taught to despise and fear. She remembers the day Carrie and the same woman came to the house, remembers Carrie and Lizzie shouting at one another, remembers the blind terror that engulfed her. Remembers running upstairs to her room and Carrie following, virtually trapping her in the very place where she'd thought she'd be safe. Carrie didn't do or say anything dreadful, but she didn't need to. Her presence was enough. Just by being there she posed a threat. So overwhelming were the emotions that assailed her then that even now, fifty years on, they still have the power to make her cringe inwardly, catapult her back through time to the confused, frightened child she once was.

But she is not a child any more, and increasingly over the years between, her emotional reaction has become more and more complex. Don is absolutely right, there is an inner conflict going on that will never quite let her be at peace with herself. Most of the time she chooses to push it to the back of her mind, because to face it is just too disturbing. Yet still it seethes away beneath the surface. There are pangs of something that might be regret, a kind of emptiness at the very heart of her, a sense of loss, of deprivation, even. She is aware of a primeval need to connect with her natural mother. The umbilical cord still tugs at her deepest instincts. And sometimes she is unsettled by an emotional glimpse of a past she has forgotten. A certain scent might trigger it, or a snatch of a melody, and for a few brief seconds she feels that her lost past is almost within her grasp, before, frustratingly, it slides away again, leaving nothing but a haunting shadow.

Oddly, there is nothing threatening in those glimpses – or most of them, anyway. She doesn't like the smell of whisky – that makes her stomach contract – and for a long time, as a young girl, she was frightened by the cracks and bangs of fireworks, though she got over that a long time ago. But these other unexpected emotional responses are, on the whole, pleasurable and they make her realise that not everything about the lost years can be bad.

Gillian is then tormented by a feeling of guilt, and a sense that she may be perpetrating an injustice. But the flip side of this is that she knows it would hurt Lizzie dreadfully if she thought that Gillian was seeking contact with Carrie; she would see it as nothing less than betrayal. After the years of love and care Lizzie lavished on her, Gillian feels she owes her absolute loyalty. It's one of the things that has held her back from making contact with Carrie.

Now, however, she wonders if that is just an excuse that she's been hiding behind. Ever since Kathryn expressed her intention of going to England, Gillian has been unable to shake off a nagging suspicion that she is guilty of cowardice. That it is time she confronted her own past before it is too late. And a desire to see her mother once more has been gaining strength until it is almost equal to the compulsion to shut her out that has stultified Gillian all these years.

Long ago, Don urged her to visit a therapist and try to unlock the vault of her memory, but she shied away from it. She must have been there, she thinks, when her mother shot her father – it's really the only thing horrific enough to cause her to blank out that night, and everything that went before, so completely. It's that memory she cannot face, and she's terrified of reliving the traumatic event through the eyes of an eight year old. Cowardice again! But she's beginning to think that she must. For there to be any hope of a reconciliation, she has to be able to understand what drove Carrie to do such a terrible thing, and she has to be able to remember her early life, with Carrie and Frank. The good things as well as the bad.

She hears the door open and close. Don is coming in from the garage.

'Why are you sitting here in the dark?' he asks.

Gillian comes back from a long way off. She hadn't even noticed it was getting dark. Don switches on the light; she screws up her eyes. Sudden brightness in a world she didn't realise was all grey shadows. Will it be the same if she visits a hypnotherapist? Or will remembering illuminate things she doesn't want to see?

'Are you all right?' Don asks. He sounds concerned.

'Yes. Just thinking.'

He doesn't ask what she's thinking about. If it was the other way around and she found him sitting in the dark and staring into space, she'd have to dig away, trying to get to the bottom of it. But Don, like most men, is singularly incurious. Or perhaps he already knows, given their earlier conversation.

For a moment or two Gillian stays in the silence, turning it all over in her head, wondering if she dare take this enormous step from which she has always shrunk. Then she says: 'Do you really think I ought to be regressed?'

Don is scanning through the newspaper she left on the table. He looks up, surprised. 'You know I do. Why – are you coming around to the idea?'

'I'm wondering if maybe I should. But I'm scared, Don.'

'I'm sure there's no need to be. It's the fear you're afraid of.'

That's pretty profound for Don, she thinks. He probably read it somewhere. But it makes sense.

'Look, Gillian, whatever it is that frightens you so, it's all in the past. It can't hurt you now. I'm sure if you were to face up to it, you'd find it's nowhere near as bad as you think. And if it is . . . well, you've got me, and you've got Kathryn.'

'No, I haven't got Kathryn. That's what sparked all this off.'

'Well, you've got me. I'm right behind you, sweetheart, and I'm not going anywhere.'

Another silence. Then Gillian says: 'Would you fix it up for me?'

Now he really is surprised. Gillian is usually totally independent and self-sufficient.

'You want me to sort out a hypnotherapist and book you an appointment?' She nods. 'Well, if you're sure . . . ?'

'I'm not sure at all.' She's shaking already at the prospect. 'I just think I should. But if it's left to me, I'll probably go on putting it off. If you make an appointment, I'll have to go, won't I?'

'You don't *have* to do anything.'

'I think I do. I think I need to sort this once and for all, or try to. At least then I'll know whether or not I've been right all these years. And if I'm wrong . . . Oh, Don . . .' Her voice tails away into something like panic.

'Come here.' He goes to pull her towards him; she yelps.

'Mind my hip!'

'Sorry.' His arms go round her more gently, she leans into him, face buried in his shoulder, one hand braced against the solid wall of his chest.

He's right. Whatever she has to face from the past, however upsetting, this is her world now. The past cannot touch her, not really. If it does, she can retreat to the castle of her marriage and pull up the drawbridge.

'I'm glad you've decided to face up to it,' Don says against her hair. 'I'll make some enquiries tomorrow. When do you want to do the deed?'

Gillian lifts her face, and her voice is much more normal.

'As soon as possible,' she says.

TWENTY-SIX

When she gets back from her ride, and after she's showered and changed, Kathryn goes down to the hotel bar for a drink and a snack. Eager though she is to spend as much time as possible with her grandmother, she doesn't want to impose at every meal time.

The bar is all but empty. Kathryn takes a stool at the curved oak bar and orders a lemonade-and-lime and a ham baguette.

'You're very quiet today,' she says to the bartender, a young man who looks as if he might be a moonlighting student.

'Mid-week lunchtime, always quiet.' He sets the drink in front of her. 'Weekends!' He pulls a face. 'You can't move in here then. Especially if we've got a wedding.'

'It's well used, then.'

'Certainly is. It's the place round here. My girlfriend has her eye on it for when we get married next year, but I've told her, we can't afford their prices. And that's with my staff discount, mind you.'

'Right.'

'It's a little gold mine, this place.' The boy seems glad of the opportunity to chat and break the monotony of polishing glasses and realigning bottles. 'I don't know why they want to sell. I'd buy it like a shot if I had the readies.'

'It's being sold?'

'So the rumour goes. We haven't been told anything officially, but then, why would they tell us? We just work here.'

'That must be a bit unsettling for you.'

'Not really. Whoever buys the place, they'll still want staff, and they're not that easily come by round here. In any case, I won't be here much longer. Once I've passed my exams I shall be looking for something with a bit more responsibility and better pay. I've already got a couple of interviews lined up.'

'Good for you.'

But she's wondering whether Andrea knows about the proposed sale, and how it will affect her when the place is under new ownership. These people are obviously happy to let her rent the stables; new management might have different ideas.

The baguette arrives, crusty and bursting with what smells like home-cooked ham.

'Will you charge it to my room, please?' Kathryn says, and takes both it and her drink to a corner table.

When she's finished eating Kathryn decides she'll go for a walk before going down to Bush Villa. It's a nice day, and she'd like to explore a bit.

350

As she emerges from the drive onto the road, a big old car is pulling out of the entrance to the farm, driven by a woman. It crosses the road and passes her, then reverses back and pulls up, and a voice calls to her: 'Excuse me!'

She half-turns. The driver's window is down and a head is poking out.

'Excuse me!' the woman calls again. 'Are you Kathryn?'

'Yes.' Kathryn retraces her steps. She's already guessed who the woman is. Since the car has driven out of the farm, it wouldn't take a genius to work it out, and even sitting in her car, with the width of the road between them, she looks every inch a farmer's wife, weather-beaten and homely. Besides which, she knows Kathryn's name, and there can't be many people in Timberley who do, even if gossip does spread like wild fire.

Kathryn crosses the road.

'You must be Mary.'

'I am that. Well, Kathryn!'

A white Transit van comes haring along the road; Kathryn presses in tight against the Renault as it whooshes past, horn blaring.

'Oh, the way they come along here!' Mary grumbles. 'Take no notice of the speed limit. Somebody's going to get killed one of these days.'

'It is quite narrow.' Kathryn looks around anxiously. 'I think I'd better get out of the road.'

'Are you in a hurry? Why don't you come in and have a cup of tea? I've been dying to meet you.'

'But . . . you were on your way out . . .'

'Oh, it can wait. That's where I live — just there.' She nods in the direction of the farm entrance. 'You go on in.'

Kathryn is not entirely sure about this. She's wanted to meet Mary, it's true, but she thought she'd have Andrea or Carrie to introduce her. Mary, however, has left her no choice.

By the time she's reached the farmyard, Mary is pulling in too, parking untidily and pulling on the handbrake with an audible jolt. Kathryn is reminded of Andrea's atrocious driving. Is it the norm among English countrywomen? Perhaps they're more used to driving tractors!

'Come on in.' Mary opens the door and leads the way in to what Kathryn imagines is a typical farmhouse kitchen. 'This is a real treat. I can't believe it — Gillian's daughter! Do you know, your mother used to come up here when she was just a little girl. She loved it, Gillian did. Loved the animals. Is she still the same?'

'She's got a dog.'

'A collie? We've got collies. They're out with Geoff today, or they'd have been barking fit to raise the dead when you walked in.'

'Mom's dog is a golden retriever.'

'Oh, they're nice dogs too. But your mother loved our collie. Ben, his name was.'

Ben. Just to hear the name spoken brings a lump to Kathryn's throat.

'Yes, lovely dog he was. Course, he's long since dead and gone.'

The lump in Kathryn's throat is growing. Mary's Ben might have been a dog, not a child, but it's all a little too close to home for comfort.

Mary is bustling about, putting the kettle on to boil, warming a brown earthenware teapot that looks big enough to slake the thirst of a whole army of farm workers, setting a jug of creamy milk on the table.

'This is from our own cows,' she says proudly. 'Nothing like that rubbish you get in plastic containers at the supermarket.'

'I'm sure.'

'I can't tell you, Kathryn, how glad I am you're here. Though till you wrote, Carrie didn't even know she had a granddaughter. All I hope is, you can make your mother see sense.'

'I honestly don't know whether—'

'Carrie didn't deserve that,' Mary says roundly. 'And if there's any justice in this world, one of these days Gillian will come back to her. It broke Carrie's heart, losing her like that on top of everything else. She worshipped that girl.' She looks sharply at a rather disconcerted Kathryn. 'She's never got her memory back, I suppose.'

'No. Everything before she went to Lizzie is a blank.'

'I thought so. Wicked woman. Turned Gillian right against her. But I'd have thought when she got old enough to think for herself she'd have realised—'

Kathryn feels obliged to defend her mother.

'She's never been able to forgive Carrie for killing her father. And saying things to blacken his name.'

'All of which were true.' Mary sniffs, bangs a couple of pottery mugs down on the table. 'She didn't do it, you know. Though you'll never get her to admit it.'

Kathryn sits forward, intent. 'But why?'

'Hmm.' The kettle has boiled; Mary pours water into the teapot. 'She had her reasons.'

353

'But what?'

'It's not for me to say. I've kept quiet because that's the way she wanted it. But you can tell Gillian from me, her mother wasn't the one that did it.'

'Hello-o!'

A man has come into the kitchen from outside: a tall, well-built man of perhaps fifty. His hair, close-cropped and receding from a high forehead, is dark, flecked through with silver, and although he is casually dressed in stone-coloured denims and a zipped fleece over a checked shirt, open at the neck, he exudes a sophistication that is oddly out of place in the farmhouse kitchen.

'Tom.' Mary is beaming suddenly. 'You're back.' She gestures towards Kathryn. 'You'll never guess who this is!'

'So enlighten me.'

'This is Gillian's daughter, Kathryn. She's come over from Canada to meet her grandmother.'

'Nice to meet you, Kathryn.'

'And you.'

'Tom is my eldest son,' Mary says with obvious pride. 'We don't see much of him. He has a very good job but it means he's been working abroad—'

'All right, Mother,' Tom interrupts her. 'Is there a cup of tea for me, or have you drunk it all?'

'I've only just made it,' Mary says, affronted. 'Do you want one?'

'I certainly do! One of the best things about coming home is being able to get a decent cup of tea.' He takes off his fleece, hangs it over the back of a chair, and sits down. 'So you're Andrea's niece. How is she?'

354

'Tom and Andrea grew up together,' Mary says, pouring the tea. 'And I told you, Tom, Andrea is fine. I saw her this morning. Invited her and Carrie and Kathryn to lunch on Sunday. Not that Andrea will come, of course. Says it's her busiest day at the stables.'

'I expect it is. You should know that, Mother.'

'All she thinks about is her horses, that girl.' Mary stirs two spoonfuls of sugar into Tom's tea before passing it to him, ever the mother, even if he is a middle-aged man who has spent his adult life away from the fold.

'No change there then,' Tom says drily.

They continue chatting, but Kathryn feels frustrated that the conversation she and Mary had been having has been cut short. But what Mary did say has given her plenty to think about. Mary seems adamant that Carrie was not responsible for Frank's death and this gives Kathryn a shard of hope. If only she could get to the bottom of what really happened, perhaps there is still hope for a reconciliation. But she's puzzled by all the secrecy, and cannot imagine why on earth Carrie would confess to a murder she did not commit.

'I must go.' She pushes back her chair. 'It's been lovely meeting you both.'

Tom gets up too, the perfect gentleman. He really is rather nice, Kathryn thinks.

Mary accompanies her to the door.

'You be sure to tell your mother what I said,' she says quietly. Her mouth is a tight line, her tone conspiratorial.

'I will,' Kathryn says.

*   *   *

Rob is sitting at his computer in the niche under the stairs. It's a small, cramped space with just room for an MDF desk unit and swivel chair, and he has to be careful, when he moves about, not to crash into the shelves he put up on the one straight wall. Once upon a time he used the small bedroom as an office, but that had been before Ben. He was quite happy to move to the space under the stairs and convert the bedroom to a nursery when Kathryn was pregnant. He happily painted the walls a sunshine yellow, erected the cot (which took the best part of an evening by the time they sorted out which bit went where) and hung new curtains and mobiles under Kathryn's instruction. And he never uttered a word of complaint about the dark niche that was really the only place to which he could relocate. He was far too delighted at the prospect of becoming a father.

Now, however, with the nursery empty and no prospect of it being needed again any time soon, he wishes he could move his things back to light and space. It makes no sense, leaving the room as a shrine to a little boy who no longer needs it. In fact Rob thinks it is distinctly unhealthy, a door closed on an empty room where soft toys are still piled against the bars of the cot and tiny pink and blue mice dance on their marionette strings above it when a draught catches them. But when he said as much, Kathryn became terribly upset, accusing him of trying to airbrush Ben out of their lives, so he's said no more. She'd simply take it as yet further evidence of his lack of feeling.

In fact, nothing could be further from the truth. Rob idolised his son and was devastated by his loss. There was a huge well of pain deep inside him, a void where once there had been hopes and dreams and love. It gutted him that he would never see Ben grow up, teach him to play ball, swim, skate. Stand on the touchline, cheering himself hoarse. Help him with his math homework, fly a model aeroplane, buy him his first car. The future he envisaged died with Ben and he never knew it was possible to feel such despair, such raw grief. He's had to move on or go crazy with it; he can't be doing with morbid sentimentality, and he thinks it time Kathryn stopped wallowing in it. But she can't let go, and she blames him for trying to.

Blames him, too, for not spotting just how ill Ben was that night. But she can't blame him more than he blames himself. He can't get away from the feeling that if Kathryn had been there she would have known instinctively that something was very wrong. If he had been given prompt medical attention, perhaps they wouldn't have lost him.

But if Ben had survived, they were told, there was a possibility he would be severely disabled, and that, Rob thinks, would have been even worse than losing him altogether. To see their perfectly beautiful healthy boy reduced to a shadow of his former self. But he hasn't dared say this to Kathryn. She'd have devoted her life to caring for Ben, if that was what it took; made any pact with the devil if it meant she could keep him with her.

Oh, Kathryn . . . Wretchedness claws at Rob's heart. With Ben's death he lost not only his son but his wife too.

The keyboard shelf has slid back beneath the desk unit; Rob pulls it back out and in the confined cubbyhole it jabs him in the stomach. He's supposed to be working on accounts for a client. But he's finding it impossible to concentrate. He clicks on Google and enters 'Timberley, Gloucestershire, England' into the search engine. He picks one of the sites and stares, mesmerised, when it unfolds onto the screen, a village with quite a history going back to Roman times, but with modern amenities, and all set against the backdrop of the rolling Cotswolds.

He checks his watch, works out the time difference, wonders what Kathryn is doing now. He misses her like hell, and he wonders if she misses him. But even if she is, he can't see that it will do much good. The gulf that's opened up between them seems unbridgeable. Rob sighs heavily, pushes his personal thoughts to the back of his mind – something he's really rather good at – and with a couple of clicks of the mouse replaces the apparently idyllic Timberley on the computer screen with the much more mundane Office suite.

On her way to Bush Villa, Kathryn sees a figure she recognises as Carrie walking down the lane ahead of her. She quickens her step, but makes precious little headway in catching up with her grandmother. When she is within hailing distance, she calls: 'Grandma!'

Carrie doesn't appear to hear her. She's almost reached the gate. Kathryn tries again. This time Carrie cocks her head, then turns, her smile expressing her pleasure.

'Kathryn! I wasn't expecting you just yet. I thought you'd be out enjoying the sunshine.'

Kathryn smiles. 'It's glorious, isn't it? But these two weeks are going to fly by, and I don't want to waste a minute of them.'

'Well, I'm not going to complain.' Carrie turns in at the gate, walks up the narrow path, Kathryn following. At the door she turns, handing Kathryn a wicker trug she was carrying over her arm. 'Hold on to this for me, would you?'

Kathryn takes it, noticing with surprise that it contains a trowel, secateurs and a pair of gardening gloves. Carrie bends down to retrieve the front door key, which is concealed beneath a flowerpot to the side of the doorstep.

As she straightens Kathryn asks: 'What's all this in aid of?'

'What?'

'The gardening gear.'

'Oh, that. I've been up to the churchyard, seeing to the graves. They get so overgrown at this time of year. You should see some of them! Grass and nettles so high you can't even see where they are, let alone who they belong to.'

She has the door open now and Kathryn follows her into the house.

'You look after the churchyard?' Kathryn asks, startled.

'Oh my goodness, no! Only our graves. Mother and Father's, my granny and granddad's, and Frank's. And the ones right next to them, where the weeds are encroaching on ours.'

Frank's grave. Carrie is supposed to have killed him, but she cares for his grave. The very thought of it is touching somehow.

'I take a few flowers up too, when I've got something suitable in the garden,' Carrie says. 'I like to keep them looking nice.'

'I'd rather like to see the graves,' Kathryn says. 'They're my family too, after all. Will you take me up sometime? Show me where they're buried?'

'Of course I will. I shall go tomorrow or the next day anyway, if we don't have any rain. The chrysanths and Michaelmas daisies last pretty well, but they won't if the water in the pots dries up.' She unbuttons her jacket. 'And now I'm ready for a cup of tea. How about you?'

Kathryn feels that by the time she goes home she'll have drunk enough tea to sink a battleship.

'Actually I've not long had one. With your friend Mary. She saw me coming out of the hotel, recognised me, and asked me in for a chat.'

'Well, well. That's Mary for you. She never was backward in coming forward. But I'll tell you this much: she's the best friend anyone could wish for.'

In the light of what Mary said, Kathryn doesn't doubt it. She's made up her mind to mention it to Carrie and see if she can get her to talk about what happened, and this opening would make the ideal opportunity. But for some reason she doesn't feel quite ready to broach the subject yet. It's going to be awkward, and she wants to be better prepared. Instead, she steers right away from the delicate subject.

'The barman up at the Hall was telling me the owners are putting it on the market,' she says.

Carrie's lips tighten. 'So I understand. They had a word with Andrea. Well, it will affect her, you see. Or could do. Between you and me, she's rather worried about it.'

'They wouldn't turn her out, would they?' Kathryn says, horrified.

360

Carrie pulls a face that says 'Who knows?'

'Depends what plans they've got for it. The Parkers have always been very good to Andrea, keeping her rent low, never making any trouble for her. Except the once, when a frisky filly kicked out the stable door and ran amok in the grounds.' She smiles wryly. 'That was a to-do and no mistake. But they understood. Well, they're local, been around horses all their lives. It could be a very different story if townies buy the place. They could have big ideas, turning it into another Babington House, something like that.'

'Babington House?' It means nothing to Kathryn.

'A place down in Somerset, big old house and estate. Very trendy. All the stars go down there – well, television people and the sort that get their photos in glossy magazines and gossip columns. If something like that was in the plan, I don't suppose they'd want a stables in the grounds.' She shakes her head. 'But you don't want to talk about our problems. And neither do I.'

'But what on earth would Andrea do?' Kathryn can't dismiss it so lightly.

'Have to find somewhere else, I suppose. She couldn't get rid of her horses, that's for sure. It would break her heart. But a stables like that, in the right place, at the right price . . . Oh, well, it's no good worrying about what might never happen. I learned that a long time ago. Now, there is something I want to talk to you about. When I've got my cup of tea.'

She's bustling about the kitchen, to all intents and purposes the same Carrie, amazing for her age, and very matter-of-fact, but Kathryn is suddenly aware of a tension that wasn't there before. Carrie is a little flushed too.

She pours her tea. 'Sure you don't want one?'

'Quite sure, thank you.'

Carrie sits down, the cup held between both hands. To Kathryn, they don't look quite steady.

'Andrea tells me you're going down to Somerset to see Lizzie,' Carrie says, and Kathryn can hear the tremor, however well disguised, in her voice.

'I really think I ought to,' Kathryn says apologetically.

'Yes, well, I suppose it's only right. But there're things I think I should tell you before you do.'

'I know there's bad blood between you,' Kathryn says. 'And really, Grandma, the last thing I want to do is upset you, but—'

'I know, I know,' Carrie interrupts. 'You don't have to explain. It's just that there are things I expect she'll tell you, and I'd rather you heard them from me. I've told you about when I was in Bristol in the war. How I was an ambulance attendant.'

'Yes.'

'But I didn't tell you the whole story.' Carrie is knotting and unknotting her hands on the table top, clearly nervous. 'There was a man. A doctor at the hospital. We fell in love—' She breaks off.

'Oh, Grandma.' Kathryn, far from being shocked, melts inside. 'That's OK; I wouldn't hold something like that against you. The things you were living through – the blitz and everything – I'm sure there must have been loads of people who had wartime affairs.'

'I expect there were,' Carrie says ruefully. 'Except that this wasn't just an affair. The truth of it is, Dev was the love of my life. I was going to leave Frank to be with him. If things had worked out, I'd probably be in Ireland now – Dev is short for Devlin, which is Irish, as you can probably guess.'

Her face softens as she says his name, the lines of age seeming to melt, so that for a moment Kathryn gets a glimpse of how she must have looked then, in the days when she was young and in love. Then the moment passes, and with it the illusion.

'But everything went terribly wrong,' Carrie says, and once again, her face is the face of a woman approaching her eighth decade. 'Instead of going to Ireland, I went to prison.'

Kathryn nods, not really knowing what to say, but wondering if Carrie is about to tell her the truth of what happened that night in 1950. Her fingers are still working, knotting and unknotting, and as if she has suddenly become aware of it, she clasps one hand firmly over the other to still it.

'Lizzie will very likely tell you that's the reason I shot Frank,' she goes on. 'That I wanted him dead so that I'd be free to go off with Dev. And she'll tell you I made up the stories about what Frank was like, and how he was treating me and Gillian, too, to excuse what I did. I'm not going to go into details. I didn't want to talk about it then – though of course when it came to trial I had no choice – and I don't want to talk about it now. It wasn't Frank who did what he did. After he lost his leg he "went funny", as we used to say. And I'm not pretending I wasn't partly to blame for that. But the fact of the matter is that he turned violent and . . .' She pauses, checks herself. 'Anyway, Lizzie couldn't accept that her brother was capable of such things. She reckoned I was making it up so I could claim I'd acted in self-defence. And she's never forgiven me, either, for shooting her brother, or for, as she thinks, blackening his good name.'

She raises her bowed head.

'That's about it, Kathryn. I just wanted to tell you my side of it before Lizzie does.'

So Carrie is sticking to her story. Kathryn feels a sense of disappointment. But if she has never told Andrea what really happened, how likely is it that she would suddenly unburden herself to a granddaughter she met only a few days ago? Perhaps it is the truth. Perhaps Mary is wrong: either Carrie misled her so as to keep at least one friend and ally, or perhaps she's just fooled herself. Kathryn has entertained such high hopes of being able to tell Gillian that Carrie is innocent of anything other than concealing the truth; now, dispirited, she wonders if there is anything more to it than the facts as they were told in court.

She believes Carrie, though, when she says that Frank behaved badly towards her. The very fact that she doesn't want to elaborate somehow makes it ring truer than if she had regaled Kathryn with a lot of detail. And she can understand too that Lizzie refused to accept a word of it. It's only natural she would spring to her brother's defence when he was no longer there to defend himself. Between grief and righteous indignation it is hardly surprising she had condemned Carrie as a liar as well as a murderer.

Perhaps that much alone will be enough to persuade her mother to give Carrie a hearing, and if Frank also behaved violently towards Gillian, then the case would be even stronger. Gillian's recollections of anything to do with that have been lost with her memory, of course, and what Kathryn needs is more detail. She's reluctant to press Carrie just now, so soon after she'd expressly said she didn't want to talk about it. Perhaps Andrea could help, or, failing that, perhaps she could get hold of a transcript of the court proceedings. She'd really rather like to read them in any case. They must be available, surely – though she hasn't the first idea of how to go about getting access to them.

Rob would know. Or if he didn't, he'd find out. Rob was very good at that sort of thing . . .

'I looked out some snaps of your mother when she was a little girl,' Carrie is saying. 'Would you like to see them?'

'Oh, yes!'

Carrie fetches them, not in an album, but in the manila wallets they came in from the chemist's where she had them developed. The wallets are dog-eared now, the photographs grainy black and white. But they show a little girl who looks remarkably like Kathryn herself in her early photographs, a little girl in white ankle socks, with ribbons in her hair, or, in one, a poke bonnet and double-breasted coat. They show her looking serious but untroubled, they show her smiling, with her arms around a collie dog and astride a fat little pony. There's one of her at the seaside, wearing a knitted swimming costume and sunhat, a bucket in one hand, a spade in the other.

Kathryn is enchanted. She's never before seen a picture of her mother before the age of eight or nine. And Gillian won't have seen them either, or if she has, she won't remember them.

'Do you think I could borrow some of these and take them home to show Mom?' she asks.

For a moment Carrie's fingers linger on them, the only things she has left of her elder daughter. Then she slides them back into the folder and pushes it across the table towards Kathryn.

'Of course you can. I would like them back, though.'

'I'll take really good care of them,' Kathryn promises. 'And you never know – they might just help.'

'Let's hope so,' Carrie sighs. 'Oh, Kathryn, you don't know what it would mean to me.'

'I do. Believe me, I do.'

'Yes.' Carrie leans across, pats Kathryn's hand. 'You've been through the mill too, haven't you?'

Kathryn nods, and tears fill her eyes. And the tears now are for all of them. For Carrie, who lost her child, for Gillian, deprived of her parents, as well as for herself and for Ben.

'Do you want to tell me about him?' Carrie asks gently.

The unanswered questions slip to the back of Kathryn's mind as she opens up to the grandmother she never knew she had. But later they will still be there and she will wonder again. What happened that long-ago night? Did Carrie shoot an abusive husband? Or is she still covering up for someone? And if so – who – and why?

TWENTY-SEVEN

It comes to her in the dead of night, and Kathryn wonders why she hasn't seen it before. She is sure, quite sure, that she is right — it's the only thing that makes sense — and the sudden realisation brings her wide awake.

If Carrie was covering up for someone it could be only one person — the man she called 'the love of my life' — the man she planned to leave Frank for. He would know that Frank was ill-treating her and Gillian, and was going to take them away from him. But when crunch time came, somehow it all went wrong. Perhaps there was a terrible scene and things turned violent. But however it happened, Dev killed Frank, and, in order to protect him, Carrie claimed she did it. She knew that if she pleaded not guilty to murder, but admitted to manslaughter in self-defence she would get a reasonably short sentence. Knew, too, that it would be very different for Dev. Back in the 1950s the death penalty was still in force, Kathryn feels sure, and he might well have hanged.

So, Carrie loved him enough to take the rap herself. Perhaps they planned it together, with the intention of her joining him in Ireland when she'd served her sentence. But if that were the case, why didn't it happen? Or could it be that he went on the run after killing Frank, and the cover-up was all Carrie's idea? Whichever, for some reason he abandoned her, and perhaps found someone else by the time she came out of prison.

Or was it Carrie who didn't want, after all, to live her life with a man who could kill in cold blood and allow her to take the blame? If that were the case, why was she still prepared to carry on with the deception?

There are still so many unanswered questions, so many loose ends, but the essence of it remains the same. A crime of passion, the French call it, but in this case the passion led to the wrong person being convicted and serving a sentence that has, in effect, lasted a lifetime. Kathryn is certain of it, and she's determined to put things right. How on earth she's going to manage that she doesn't know. But for the sake of the unity of her long-divided family, she has to find a way.

Next morning the sun is in hiding. It's grey and overcast, and according to the forecast in the *Daily Mail*, which Kathryn leafs through while she's having breakfast, rain is expected later.

The weather forecast, the headlines and the horoscopes are about the limit of her concentration, though. Her thoughts are still churning around the revelation that came to her in the wee small hours. She wondered if in the cold light of day the whole thing would seem preposterous, but even after a full English breakfast and a pot of coffee it still seems feasible, though she acknowledges it might be wishful thinking. The possibility still remains that Carrie has been telling the truth all along and she, like Mary, is snatching at an alternative because neither of them wants to believe Carrie guilty. But Kathryn is not going to let it go. If Carrie was covering up for Dev, then Kathryn has to try to make her see that to come clean now is the only chance she has of ever being reconciled with Gillian; persuade her that it can make no difference to him now, but all the difference in the world to her daughter.

She wants to try to elicit the truth before she goes to Hillsbridge to see Lizzie, too. Kathryn cannot help but anticipate the grim satisfaction of being able to tell Lizzie that she had been wrong all along.

She finishes her coffee, goes up to her room to collect her jacket. Coming back down the stairs, she sees a man she recognises as Tom Hutchins, Mary's son, crossing the lobby with a man in a dark suit. They are deep in conversation, and by the time she reaches the foot of the stairs they've disappeared through one of the doors leading off the lobby. She's surprised Tom should be staying here at the hotel, but perhaps he likes to be independent after a lifetime of living and working all over the world. Anyway, the domestic arrangements of the Hutchins family are no concern of hers. She thinks no more about it. She's too busy planning what she's going to say to Carrie; how she can steer the conversation to give herself the best chance of finding out the truth.

Andrea is mucking out the stables when a voice from behind says her name.

'Morning, Andrea.'

She swings round. 'Tom!'

He's standing in the doorway, in deep shadow, but her eyes are sufficiently used to the dim light for her to be able to see he's looking effortlessly elegant, a dark jacket over an open-necked shirt, the epitome of businessman meets country casual. Instantly she's acutely aware of her own dishevelled appearance – well-worn jodhpurs and mud-caked boots, hair flattened to her head because she hasn't combed it since exercising the horses earlier. And in practically the same instant, berates herself for a fool. What the hell does it matter what she looks like? Tom's not likely even to notice, and if he does, it won't make the slightest difference to him one way or the other. But all the same, she wishes that at least she was clean and tidy, meeting him for the first time in years.

'I thought I'd look in and say hello since I was passing.'

She doesn't even wonder what he means by that, she's too flustered.

'OK, I'll be with you in a minute. Just let me finish here.'

'Want a hand?'

'Good Lord, no!' Alarmed at the thought of him shovelling shit in his smart clothes, Andrea leans her spade against the wall and walks towards him, wiping her hands on the seat of her jodhpurs.

'I wouldn't mind,' he says. 'It would be quite like old times really.'

'Maybe. But you weren't wearing highly polished brogues then.'

'True. How are you doing, anyway, Andrea?'

'OK. Worried about the Hall going on the market, but otherwise fine. And you?'

'Mustn't grumble. Looking at taking early retirement actually.'

'Yes, your mother said.'

He chuckles. 'I might have known. What else did she tell you?'

'Just that really.' Andrea doesn't want to repeat everything Mary said; she doesn't want him to think she and his mother were discussing his personal business. And though she really doesn't want to mention his wife either, she feels she should.

'I was very sorry to hear about Deirdre,' she says.

'Thank you.' It seems he doesn't want to talk about it either.

'We've got a visitor from Canada,' she says as they move out of the stables and into the yard. 'Gillian's daughter, Kathryn.'

'Yes, I met her yesterday. My mother had her in for a cup of tea. She seems a very nice young woman.'

'She is. She and Mum seem to be getting along famously.' Andrea is beginning to feel more comfortable, the residual echoes of her adolescent self receding.

They chat for a few more minutes, then Tom says: 'Actually I have an ulterior motive for calling in. I was wondering if you had a horse I could take out for an hour.'

'Oh, of course.' So he hasn't come to see her. Why would he? But she's aware of the edge of disappointment anyway. Nothing changes, she thinks wryly.

'I don't want anything too mettlesome,' Tom says. 'I haven't ridden much in years.'

'I don't do mettlesome,' Andrea says. 'When you're catering for the inexperienced, or people who claim they can ride but actually haven't a clue, it's really not advisable. But neither of those applies to you. Even if you are out of practice. You can take my horse if you like. You'd be bored to tears on either of the others that are big enough for you to ride. They're real plodders.'

Tom grins. 'I'll leave that up to you.'

'When do you want to go?'

'Well, the rest of the day's my own.'

'No problem.'

'Give me half an hour to go home and get changed then. How do you want paying, cheque or cash?'

Andrea raises her eyebrows. 'I don't want paying at all.'

'Come on, I insist. You're running a business here, Andrea. Probably on a very tight budget.'

'And I absolutely refuse. I'm not into charging my friends.'

'Well, we'll argue about that later,' Tom says. 'But if you won't take money, I shall find some other way of repaying you. See you in a bit, then.'

'OK, I'll get Jason saddled up.'

Tom has begun to walk away; he turns back. 'Why don't you come too?'

'Oh, I've got a lot to do here . . .'

'I can help you out once I'm dressed for the part. Come on, Andrea. It would be like old times.'

Too much like old times, Andrea thinks. But the memory of galloping shoulder to shoulder across the open ground up on the hill is sweet.

She runs a hand, which smells of horse manure, through her hair; unbeknown to her the cuff of her shirt deposits a smudge on her cheek.

'Oh . . . we'll see . . .'

Carrie is in the garden, cutting a cabbage, when Kathryn arrives. She's put on her gabardine coat over her overall because she doesn't feel too well this morning and she's feeling the cold. It's all the excitement taking its toll, she supposes, and she's been a little apprehensive as to what Kathryn's reaction to her revelations will be when she's had the chance to think about them. Now, she's mightily relieved to see her granddaughter – a relief that is short-lived when she senses a slight unease in Kathryn's manner.

'You said you wanted to see the graves,' she says. 'We could go now, if you like, while I've got my coat on.'

'I'd like to see them, yes,' Kathryn confirms.

'I'll take some water for the vases.' Carrie fills a bottle at the sink and stoppers it. Kathryn offers to carry it for her and they set off up the lane.

The cemetery lies just off the main road, in the shadow of the church but accessed by a separate gate. The first rows of graves, relatively recent, judging by the new stones and vases of flowers, are well kept, but as they go deeper into the cemetery Kathryn can see that much of it is indeed overgrown, tall grass and nettles waving between partially obscured kerbs and encroaching onto dirty gravel. A couple of tombstones lie flat on the grass: they've been taken down because they were deemed to be unsafe, Carrie tells Kathryn. 'Very sad, but they can't risk getting sued if youngsters come in, playing the fool, and hurt themselves. Everybody's compensation crazy these days.'

Ahead is a small oasis, clear of any weeds, where two graves with identical grey granite headstones and surrounds lie head to foot, and another, to the side, is in a dark speckled stone. The fresh Michaelmas daisies and chrysanths Carrie brought yesterday are bright splashes of mauve, purple and yellow.

'Here we are then,' Carrie says. She points to the two grey-stoned graves. 'The top one is my mother and father, the other my grandparents. They bought the plots at the same time, when my grandfather died, so they could all be together. And that one . . .' she nods towards the other grave, 'that's Frank's. The room was there, so we took it.' She smiles, a wry smile. 'I don't know what my father would think if he knew he was lying next to Frank. He never liked him. But I think Mother felt we owed it to him to keep him with the family. When I go, I expect they'll put me in there too. My ashes, anyway. I'll be cremated, I hope. Or I might be scattered, up on the hill. I think I'd rather that.'

'Don't even think about it, Grandma!'

But there's something very moving, that these generations of her family are all resting together in this peaceful spot. Kathryn studies the names and the dates.

'So your father died just a week after Frank,' she says.

'Yes, he had a stroke the night Frank died, and he never regained consciousness. It was a blessing really. He'd have been in a terrible way if he'd known about me going to prison. To be truthful, I don't think Mother ever got over it either. She was gone by the time I was released.'

Carrie stands staring at the headstone, as if in silent communication with her mother. Then she sniffs, drawing the back of her hand across her face and becoming her usual self. 'Let's top up the water, then.'

'I'll do it.' Kathryn feels she would like to. She kneels down in the shorn grass, wet still with dew, and leans across the gravel to pour water from the bottle into the vase. She repeats the exercise with the other two graves, making her own silent communication with the forebears she never knew.

'That's it, then. Let's go home and have a cup of tea.'

The eternal tea! Kathryn would have to smile if it were not for the nervousness knotting her stomach. She's going to have to make her move soon; no excuse to put it off any longer.

As they walk back down the lane, Carrie seems to be going more slowly than usual.

'Are you all right, Grandma?' Kathryn asks.

'Yes, it's just that I feel my age some days more than others.'

Kathryn links her arm through Carrie's. 'There's no hurry.'

'Don't worry about me. I'm just kecking for that cup of tea.'

And certainly she does seem to perk up once it's made and in front of her.

'I know what you're thinking,' she says with a smile. 'You think it's a wonder I haven't turned the colour of the inside of the pot. I've always loved my cup of tea. It's one of the things I missed most when I was inside. Dishwater, they served up there.' She clucks with disgust. 'Dishwater!'

'Was it dreadful?' Kathryn asks. 'Prison, I mean?'

She thinks she's on to a way of getting around to what she wants to say, then realises how crass it sounds. 'Well, of course it was dreadful. The loss of your liberty, if nothing else.'

'It was certainly no picnic,' Carrie says flatly. 'Being separated from my girls was the worst part, of course. But you don't want to talk about prison, and neither do I. I've tried to put it behind me.'

'Yes, but—'

'And it did have its compensations. Working in the garden – I might never have found out I had green fingers if it hadn't been for that. And time to study. I did all my nursing theory while I was inside, even got to help out in the infirmary. It stood me in good stead for later. And the matron put in a good word for me, got me into Berkeley Hospital.'

'Even so. Five years of your life . . .' *For something you didn't do* . . . But she can't quite bring herself to say it.

'What's done is done. There's no going back now.'

'There's one thing we can try to change.' Kathryn leans forward on her elbows on the table. 'We can try to get Mom to make things up with you.'

'Oh, my dear . . .' Carrie sounds hopeless, resigned.

'Listen, Grandma, I've been thinking about what you told me yesterday.'

Carrie sighs. 'I was rather afraid you might.'

'And everybody I talk to is convinced that you were innocent of killing Frank.'

'Everybody?' Carrie is bristling suddenly. 'What do you mean, everybody?'

'Andrea. Mary. It was Andrea who told me she was sure Mary didn't believe you did it.'

'She had no business doing that.'

'Well, she did. And I have to say, now I've met you, I can't see you killing anyone, either.'

'I didn't mean to. It was self-defence. I told you. I told *them* . . .'

'It wasn't the truth, though, was it?' Kathryn has gone this far, she can't stop now. 'Grandma, it wasn't you who shot Grandpa, was it?'

Carrie goes very still. She doesn't actually look very well, Kathryn thinks. Perhaps she shouldn't pursue this just now.

'Are you all right?' she asks anxiously.

'Oh, I'm fine,' Carrie says impatiently. 'It's just a touch of indigestion.'

'Are you sure? I'm really sorry, I shouldn't be asking you all these questions. But I really want to see you and Mom reconciled. And I think she's had the wrong end of the stick all these years. I think you were covering up for someone. Trying to protect them.'

'Oh, Kathryn, Kathryn . . .' Carrie is becoming distressed. 'I can't talk about it. It's all so long ago. I did what I had to do. It's too late now to turn back the clock and I wouldn't if I could. I just wish . . .' Her voice tails away; there are tears in her eyes.

'Did he mean so much to you?' Kathryn asks gently.

Carrie's expression turns puzzled. 'What?'

'The man you were in love with. The one you were going to leave Grandpa for. What was his name?'

377

'Dev. But what—'

'I think I know what happened,' Kathryn says. 'It was him, wasn't it? There was a terrible row, and somehow it ended with Grandpa being shot. And you thought Dev would hang for it. After all, murder was still a capital offence in those days. So you took the blame, said it was self-defence. That's what I meant about him meaning so much to you. That you were prepared to lose everything for his sake.' She pauses, shaking her head. 'I can't think how he could have let you do it. He can't have been much of a man. But . . . oh, Grandma, you've got to tell the truth now. You've got to explain to Mom that it wasn't what she thinks. That you loved him so much . . .'

'Kathryn,' Carrie says. She still sounds puzzled. 'I don't know where you got all this from.'

'I put two and two together. You said yourself, it's all so long ago. And it need not come out publicly. But Mom needs to know that you were innocent. It's the only way you're ever going to get her back now.'

Carrie is silent, remembering that long-ago day when she had the opportunity to tell Gillian the truth and couldn't bring herself to do it, even though it had meant losing her. There's a supreme irony in this, that now Gillian's daughter is here, begging her to do just that.

But she's got it wrong. All wrong.

'My dear—' She stops.

She has kept her secret for so long it's locked deep inside her. Perhaps the time to reveal what really happened that night has come and gone. She's endured a lifetime of estrangement from Gillian because of her determination to shield her daughter from the truth. Much as she longs to see her again, is it worth the trauma that the truth would inflict on those she loves the most?

The pain is there in her chest, creeping up into her throat.

And the night of Frank's death is as clear in her memory as if it happened only yesterday.

Part Six

Carrie

TWENTY-EIGHT

Life with Frank had become a living nightmare. In the years since I so nearly ran away with Dev, I had tried my best to make our marriage work. But things had gone from bad to worse in every possible way.

I suppose these days there would be a medical name and treatment for Frank's increasingly worrying behaviour. Post-traumatic stress, or clinical depression, at the very least. But things were very different back then, when being mentally ill was referred to as 'going funny', and people were whisked off to an asylum and subjected sometimes to electric shock treatment, which had all kinds of awful effects on them.

I don't think we even realised that Frank *was* ill. We just thought he was being awkward, and put it down to him losing his leg. He became more and more objectionable, more and more unpredictable, more and more morose, and we just put up with it. I did worry, as I had done in the early days, that he might try to do himself some harm.

Father had been in the army in the Great War, and had brought home a service revolver and ammunition as a trophy. He shouldn't have had it, of course, and it had been out of sight for years, but Frank must have found it, because one evening I went into the cottage to find him sitting in his chair with it in his hands, just staring at it. I went cold, reminded of my fears about the rat poison when we'd lived in Bristol. I managed to get it off him, took it in to Father, and told him it was time he got rid of the thing. He didn't, but he did lock it away in a cupboard and I never saw Frank with it again. But I was only too well aware there were plenty of ways Frank could take his own life, if he had a mind to.

He had begun to behave violently towards me too, but I managed to keep that to myself, pretending I'd fallen downstairs, or walked into a door, to explain my bruises. It was, in a way, my fault, I felt. I'd driven him to it by cheating on him and he couldn't forgive or forget. Perhaps if he had been the whole man he'd once been it would have been different. But he wasn't. He hated the menial job he was reduced to, he thought of himself as a cripple, and he dwelled on past wrongs, feeding them day by day while they grew like a cancer, destroying everything about him that had been decent and good.

Mother and Father came to detest him and the atmosphere in the house ranged between the frosty and the explosive. Fortunately, there was the cottage, and he spent most of his time there, out of their way. The one person who escaped his vicious temper in those early years was Gillian. She was the light of his life.

But Gillian was growing up fast. Though she was still very

384

much a daddy's girl, she was discovering a world outside the walls of Bush Villa, and Frank couldn't bear it. He sulked and snarled whenever she chose to do something other than spend time with him, and I wondered if in a way that was my fault. Perhaps it was because I'd slipped away from him that he now feared Gillian doing the same. Whatever the reason, his love for her seemed to be turning into insane possessiveness.

One evening in early June, the summer when Gillian was six, something happened that really started me worrying.

From the time she was a little girl, Gillian had always waited in the front garden for her father to come home from work. From there she could see the bus he travelled on pass by the end of the lane. Once Frank came into sight, she was allowed to go out of the gate and run up to meet him. He'd let her carry his canvas tuck-bag, slung around her chest, or, if his leg wasn't hurting too much, he'd give her a piggyback.

That evening, however, Gillian had gone to play with a school friend, Molly Shergold, in the village. She'd gone by herself – in those days there was scarcely any traffic, and you weren't worried about anyone doing your child harm as parents are today. It was only a few hundred yards. I'd told her to go straight there and come straight home when the church clock struck seven, and she'd promised she would.

Frank got home, as usual, at half-past six. He looked tired, and in one of his moods, and his first words when he came in were: 'Where's Gillian?'

I told him and saw his face harden.

'She's not down there on her own? At this time of night? You had no right, letting her go down there!'

I was at the stove, getting his dinner, which we plated up when we had ours in the middle of the day and I warmed up for him over a saucepan of boiling water.

'Whatever are you talking about?' I lifted the covering plate, holding it with a tea towel, and banged it down on the draining board, annoyed by Frank's censorious tone.

'I don't like those Shergolds,' he said bad-temperedly.

'Maybe they don't like you,' I snapped. 'That's no reason why Gillian shouldn't play with Molly. She needs friends her own age.'

'What for?' I didn't answer; it was too silly a question to warrant a reply. 'I'm talking to you!' Frank raged. 'Answer me when I speak to you, you ignorant bitch.'

'Oh, for goodness' sake!' I was just about to remove the plate of dinner from the pan of boiling water when Frank lunged at me. Out of the corner of my eye I saw the flat of his hand coming at me, and I dodged away. The tea towel caught on the handle of the saucepan; the saucepan toppled over. The plate smashed as it landed on the flagged floor, and scalding water cascaded down, splashing my feet and legs.

'My dinner!' Frank expostulated, outraged at the sight of pota-toes, cabbage and a pork sausage sitting on the floor amidst fragments of broken china and a pool of gravy.

'Damn your dinner! I've scalded myself!' My legs and feet felt as if they were on fire, but Frank showed no remorse or concern for me.

'Your own fault, you clumsy mare.'

Mother, who had heard the commotion, came running in.

'Whatever is going on? Oh, my Lord!'

Frank disappeared out of the back door. By the time things were more or less back to normal, he was back with a disgruntled Gillian in tow. When she saw me, sitting with my feet in a bowl of cold water, she broke free from him and rushed to me.

'Mummy! Why is Daddy cross with me? You said I could go to Molly's! Tell Daddy you said—'

'Leave your mother alone!' Frank caught her roughly by the arm, jerking her away, and I noticed a red mark across the back of her thighs, roughly the size and shape of his hand.

'Frank, you didn't *smack* her?' I was standing up, one foot still in the bowl of water.

'She's got to be made to know she can't just do as she likes.' He gave Gillian a little push. 'Go on, upstairs to your room. It's bedtime.' Gillian's lip wobbled. 'Go on, do as you're told.'

He turned to me. 'What are you going to do about my dinner? I've had a hard day, and I want my dinner.'

'I'll fry you an egg and bacon,' I said, though I felt like telling him to go hungry.

'Just make sure you don't break the egg.' He limped off across the kitchen and a minute later I heard him struggling upstairs.

I threw away the bowl of water and dried my foot, which was still stinging. I peeled a potato and cut it into flat chips, heated some lard in the frying pan and cooked them on both sides. I put them in the oven to keep warm while I fried a couple of rashers of bacon and cracked an egg into a teacup. Then I went to the bottom of the stairs and called up. 'Frank, I'm putting your egg in the pan now.'

He didn't reply. I went back to the kitchen and fried the egg, then went to the bottom of the stairs and called again, knowing that if the egg had gone hard by the time he came to eat it that would upset him all over again.

Still there was no sound of movement from upstairs, but I thought I could hear Frank singing softly. I decided to go up and find him.

Gillian's bedroom was the one that opened directly off the broad landing, the one through which we had to pass to reach our own. I looked round the door. Frank was sitting on Gillian's bed; she was nestled in his arms, almost asleep. As I watched, he smoothed her hair away from her face and eased her head from his shoulder onto the pillow. He was still crooning softly – a Donald Peers song, 'By a Babbling Brook'.

As the song ended he leaned over, kissing her cheek and straightening the covers under her chin, once more the doting father. But somehow it failed to reassure me. Frank had been so incensed that his beloved daughter had been out playing with her friends instead of waiting at the gate for him that he had smacked her hard enough to leave marks on her legs. And it made me fearful for the future.

There was no way Frank could keep Gillian his little girl for ever, and nor should he. But if he reacted so badly to her innocently going out to play with friends of her own age, if he threw a tantrum because she'd been up at the farm, riding a pony, or helping Mary bottle-feed an orphaned lamb, what was going to happen when boys came calling? It was, of course, a long way off yet, but the prospect of his possessive fury shivered down the years ahead.

* * *

Frank had always wanted a motorbike, but with his false leg it had seemed like just another lost dream. In the year that Gillian was seven, however, one of his workmates was getting rid of his old motorcycle and sidecar, and after having a test run to see if he could handle it, Frank decided to buy it off him. Though as these things go it was quite a bargain, it was still money we could ill-afford, but I went along with it. The sidecar gave him stability, he said, and he was so enthusiastic I hoped that perhaps having his own transport would lift him out of his black depressions.

And certainly for a little while after he got the bike he was almost back to his old self. He spent hours out in the old stable, stripping it down and cleaning and oiling every working part. I was really nervous the first time he took it out on the road, clambering awkwardly astride the saddle, but he looked steady enough as he pottered off down the lane, and he came back quite safely an hour or so later. He took to going out for a ride most evenings, and even Mother remarked on how cheerful he seemed.

It didn't last, though. When the novelty wore off and he realised the limitations of riding with the cumbersome sidecar, his mood darkened again. In some ways, I think, it actually made him worse. He'd had a taste of what motorcycling could be like, and had to face the fact that the real thrills of speed and skilful handling would always be out of his reach.

When he first asked Gillian if she would like to go for a ride in the sidecar, I was horrified. But Frank said she'd be fine, and Gillian herself was eager and excited.

'Hold on tight, Gillian!' I yelled as they pulled away – quite an unnecessary warning, given that Gillian was safely tucked into the well of the sidecar, with only her head and shoulders visible.

I fretted the whole time they were gone, but when they returned, Gillian's cheeks were whipped rosy by the wind, her eyes sparkling, her hair tangled and her ribbon gone, and she was so full of her trip it was a long while before she calmed down enough to go to sleep.

After that, a ride in the sidecar at weekends became a regular treat.

One Saturday, however, Gillian came home visibly upset. When I questioned her, her small face clamped mutinously shut and she stomped off up to her room.

I went out to the garage where Frank was messing about with the motorbike.

'What's wrong with Gillian?' I asked him bluntly.

'Oh, nothing. She's in a funny mood. You try to please them, and they just throw it all back in your face.'

'What are you talking about?'

'I took her down to the Forest of Dean to see the ponies, and all she wanted to do was run off and chase butterflies with a couple of boys. I don't know what gets into her. You'd think she'd be satisfied – I don't suppose there are many girls her age who get to go for a nice ride in a sidecar. But it's never enough, is it?'

'Perhaps the novelty's wearing off. And she sees plenty of ponies up at the farm. Catching butterflies with a couple of lads was probably more interesting.'

'Probably was. Yes,' Frank said bitterly.

Half an hour went by and Gillian was still upstairs. I went in search of her and found her sitting on her bed, cuddling Rosie, her rag doll.

'Come on, Gillian,' I said. 'It's a lovely day. You don't want to be skulking away indoors.'

Gillian began pulling at a strand of Rosie's wool hair.

'I don't want to come down. I don't want to see Daddy.'

'Why ever not?' I was a bit shocked. 'He's just taken you for a nice ride . . .'

'It wasn't a nice ride,' Gillian muttered. 'Daddy was cross with me.'

'Oh, Gillian, he was just disappointed because you weren't interested in the ponies. Come on now, don't be silly. Come downstairs.'

She said nothing, just went on tugging at the length of brown wool, which was now hanging loose.

'Rosie's going to end up bald if you keep doing that,' I warned.

Gillian only shrugged as if to say she didn't care.

'Come on downstairs, there's a good girl,' I said. 'I think I might just be able to find a new dolly-dressmaking book for you . . .'

Dolly-dressmaking, as it was called, was one of Gillian's favourite occupations. The dolls were printed on the front and back cover and stood up on little cardboard stands when they had been pressed out. Then the paper dresses had to be cut out too and affixed to the dolls with fold-over tabs. I usually kept a new one in the cupboard, along with a couple of colouring books, so there would be something to keep her occupied on a rainy day.

Gillian brightened at this, but she still seemed worried about Frank.

'Promise me Daddy won't be cross with me again.'

'Of course he won't,' I said, and eventually she got up from the bed and followed me downstairs.

But the extreme reaction to him simply 'being cross' was bothering me. I questioned her gently, anxious not to put such an idea in her head, should I be wide of the mark, whether Frank had punished her physically. I could get nothing out of her, but there was something in her very silence that made me uneasy. It was as if she was ashamed, or thought she would be in yet more trouble if she told me the truth.

Still worried, I went upstairs that night with her when she went to get ready for bed so I could look out for any marks on her body. But somehow she managed to whip off her dress and be into her nightie before I could get a proper look, again almost as if she was determined not to let on what had happened – if anything had. Short of insisting that I examine her there wasn't really anything I could do, and I didn't want to do that. But I made up my mind to be extra vigilant in future, whilst still trying to tell myself it was all in my imagination.

The trouble was, I had first-hand experience of the cruel but sly streak that had come out in Frank. Though once it would have been beyond belief that he would ever hurt Gillian, except for the odd slap on the legs, now I was not so sure. His violence towards me was getting worse, but he was becoming ever more adept at making sure no one else was aware of it. I was very afraid that as Gillian grew up her burgeoning independence would try his patience too far and he might mete out to her the same punishment as he did to me; he might go further than to give her the slap on the legs that was his custom. And one day, in the early summer of 1950, it happened.

Gillian was late back from playing with her friends along the lane. It was almost dark when she got home and, though I didn't realise it, Frank was lying in wait for her. I was in the kitchen, doing some ironing, when I heard her scream. I ran out and into the cottage, where the commotion was coming from. Frank had her across his knee and he was beating her across her bare bottom with the belt from his trousers.

I flew at him, grabbing the belt and hitting out at him. Frank let go of Gillian, who scrambled free and cowered in a corner.

'In the house, Gillian!' I shouted at her.

Frank, beside himself with rage, tried to follow. I kicked out at his good leg and he went sprawling on the hard flagged floor.

'How could you do that, you horrible beast?' I screamed at him.

Frank was pulling himself up by the arm of the chair, yelling obscenities. I knew I was next in line as the target for his anger, but I was past caring.

'I'm leaving you, Frank, and taking Gillian with me!' I yelled.

The flat of his hand caught me full in the face. I staggered, my legs giving way beneath me, and Frank caught me by my hair, jerking me to my knees.

'Just you try, you bitch.'

'I will,' I grated through chattering teeth. 'I should have done it long ago!'

'You just try and I'll kill you.' He let go of my hair, pushing me backwards, then, as I rolled myself into a ball to try to protect myself, he kicked me hard in the kidneys with the toe of his boot and towered over me, his face contorted with fury.

'I mean it, Carrie, I'll kill you and Gillian too before I'll let any other bugger have you.'

And he limped out of the cottage, leaving me dazed, hurt and terrified.

That night he raped me.

TWENTY-NINE

It couldn't go on. I couldn't go on. If the situation was unbearable now, it could only get worse.

I'd thought I'd have an ally in Mother; she'd never liked him, after all, and though she'd supported him before when I'd been on the point of leaving him, I thought that now, when she saw the state of me and Gillian, and I told her what had been going on under her nose for a very long time, she'd tell Frank to pack his bags and go. But I'd reckoned without her horror of scandal, her need to keep up appearances at all costs. Even with my bruised face as evidence, I'm not sure she believed me when I told her just how bad things were. Or perhaps she didn't want to believe it because if she did, something would have to be done about it, and inevitably that would mean 'our dirty linen being washed in public', as she would have termed it.

Father was no use either. He had become rather peculiar lately, vague and forgetful, sometimes talking of going to look for his own mother and father, though they had been dead for years. And he was always hiding things and talking to himself. Besides, even when he had been young and strong, he had always allowed Mother to call the tune for the sake of peace. No, though in his more lucid moments I saw him looking at Frank with loathing, I couldn't see that Father was going to be of any help.

With Mother categorically refusing to throw Frank out, I knew I had to take matters into my own hands, take Gillian away and make a new life for us, somewhere Frank couldn't find us. But where? My first thought was Bristol. I thought I could probably get a job at the hospital, and though I'd scarcely seen my old friends since the war, I thought one of them would take us in until I could find accommodation for myself and Gillian.

But Bristol was too close to home, and it was the first place Frank would come looking for us. I thought of London – wasn't that where most people went when they wanted to disappear? But the prospect of fetching up in a strange city with an eight-year-old child was a daunting one. If it had been just me, I could have slept on park benches or railway platforms until I found my feet, but with Gillian to think of, that was out of the question. And I thought of Dev.

It was five years now since the day I had sent him away for fear of losing custody of Gillian. Five long years, but they had done nothing to change the way I felt about him. If anything I wanted him more now than I ever had, a longing that ached in me with all the poignancy of a love lost, and more. Lonely, afraid, worried out of my mind, I yearned for Dev, not just as a lover but as a friend. Someone to comfort me, make me laugh, hold me. But for all I knew he was married, with a family, and had forgotten all about me.

I said as much to Mary one afternoon as we sat in her kitchen over a cup of tea. I'd told Mary everything – without her, I think I'd have gone quite crazy.

'Why don't you try to get in touch with him?' she said.

'Oh, Mary, I haven't a clue where he is. And in any case he'll have moved on, have someone else by now.'

'He might not. And even if he has, that doesn't necessarily mean he wouldn't want to help you out if he knew the predicament you're in. If he's got family in Ireland, they might be able to help you find a job and somewhere to live. Frank would never think of looking for you there.'

'I couldn't do that.' My fierce pride was kicking in.

'Well, I think that's a pity. I really don't know what else to suggest.' Mary sipped her tea, then, like a dog worrying a bone, she insisted: 'Haven't you any idea where he might be?'

'No. Still in the RAF, I presume – he signed on for ten years. Which means he could be anywhere in the world. The last time I saw him he was going to Germany.'

'BFPO.'

'What?'

'*Two-Way Family Favourites*. Cliff Michelmore and Jean Metcalfe.'

'Oh, right.' The Sunday lunchtime Forces' request programme. I didn't often get the chance to listen to it; Mother didn't like the wireless on, unless it was for the news or the weather forecast.

'They might be able to find him. You ought to write in. Ask them to play something for him, and ask him to get in touch.'

'I don't think so!'

'I don't suppose the RAF would give you any information.'

'I don't suppose they would.'

'Your friend in Bristol might be able to find out his where-abouts. She had connections, didn't she? What was her name?'

'Grace Moxey. Well, Grace Fielding, now. But, Mary, I am not going to ask her. I can't go chasing after Dev now. I'm not going to.'

'Well, you have to do something.'

'I know. The question is — what?'

'Exactly,' Mary said.

A couple of weeks went by and I was no closer to finding a solution. Things had calmed down a bit at home, as if that night of violence had purged Frank for a little while at least, and I was going out of my way to make sure Gillian didn't do anything to set him off again.

It wouldn't help anyone to do anything in too much haste, I'd decided. I had to be sure I wasn't jumping out of the frying pan into the fire. The most important thing was to find a job that would bring in enough money to support both me and Gillian, and I wrote off to a couple of the big London hospitals, giving my address as the farm, as I couldn't risk any reply coming to Bush Villa, where Frank or Mother might see it. So when, one afternoon, Billy Carter, one of the farm labourers, called in on his way home and told me Mary wanted to see me, I assumed that there was mail there waiting for me.

I couldn't go right away. Mother had gone over to Dursley to visit her cousin, and I was in the middle of making a meat-and-potato pie for Frank's dinner. Besides, I wanted to see Gillian safely to bed before I went out.

It was half past eight before I judged I could safely go out for half an hour. Gillian had at last fallen asleep – the light nights kept her awake much longer than usual. Frank was in the cottage, listening to the wireless, and Father, who was in one of his better spells, was pottering and muttering to himself. Mother was due home from Dursley on the ten o'clock bus.

'Will you be all right if I pop up to see Mary, Father?' I asked.

'Course I'll be all right. I'm not a babby.'

I went to the bottom of the stairs once more and listened. All was quiet. I went out by way of the front door. I didn't want to pass by the open door to the cottage and draw Frank's attention to the fact that I was out.

The light was beginning to soften towards dusk but the air was still warm from the heat of the day. A blackbird fluttered into hasty flight as I closed the door after me, swooping up from the narrow patch of front garden and disappearing into the hedge. The sound of a threshing machine carried on the still air; somewhere in the valley a farmer was working late getting in the hay. Otherwise nothing stirred and I saw no one as I walked up the lane, apart from a young couple leaning against a gate.

The door of the farmhouse was ajar. I knocked and called out, and Mary's voice answered, 'Carrie? Come on in.'

She was at the big old stone sink, rinsing a bucket of nappies.

'Hang on, let me just finish this. I'm running late. It took for ever to get Tom to go to sleep tonight, and David will need feeding again soon. I never seem to get two minutes to catch up with myself.'

'I know the feeling.' But I envied her. Two little boys on top of all her duties as a farmer's wife might make for an exhausting round, but they were a normal, happy family. I'd have given anything to be able to say the same of mine.

'Do you fancy a drink?' Mary was drying her hands. 'I've got a jug of cider in the larder.'

I wasn't overly keen on cider, but I was thirsty.

'All right. Go on then.'

Mary filled two glasses with amber liquid and set them down on the kitchen table.

'Cheers.'

'Cheers.'

We clinked glasses.

'My, that's good. Better than the stout they reckon I should have to keep my milk going.' She was still breast-feeding.

'Billy Carter said you wanted to see me,' I said. 'Does that mean there's a letter for me?'

'Not exactly,' Mary said enigmatically. 'But we're going to book an international phone call in a minute.'

'An international phone call? What are you talking about?'

Mary smirked. 'To Malta. To someone who's expecting to hear from you.'

A flash of white light seared my senses.

'Mary – you haven't!'

'Yes, I have. I've found Dev for you – or Grace has, to be more precise. Now, don't look like that, Carrie. I was very worried about you, and so was Grace when I told her what's been going on.'

'You've talked to Grace?'

'I had to do something. You conveniently gave me her married name, and I got her phone number through directory enquiries. I took the bull by the horns and rang her up. Told her I was worried to death about you, and asked if she knew Dev's whereabouts. She didn't, but she said she'd make it her business to find out. And she did. I don't know how she managed it, but she's a force to be reckoned with, that one. As I say, he's in Malta, and she got in touch with him there. Told him what I told her. That things have got really bad between you and Frank and you're desperate to leave him, but you've nowhere to go.'

'Oh my Lord!' My heart was beating like a drum. 'What did he say?'

'Just what I knew he would. That he wanted to speak to you. So if we can get an international line, we'll give him a ring. He'll be waiting for your call.'

'Oh, Mary!' I was so stunned I didn't know what to say. Emotion was making my head spin and my stomach churn. Disbelief, shame, delight. Most of all, delight. Dev! Just his name could twist my heart; the thought of speaking to him again was overwhelming.

A sharp pang of reality. 'He's not married?'

'I don't know,' Mary said. 'Grace didn't say. But that doesn't matter for the moment. What matters is that he's going to help you. If he can arrange for you to go to Ireland, you and Gillian can make a fresh start. Anything else is a bonus.'

'Yes, you're right, of course.' But oh dear God, I didn't want him to be married! I wanted us to be together, as we had been. As we should be.

'So there you are. I've done my bit, now it's up to you. Are you going to book that call, or am I?'

'Oh, Mary, would you?' I really wasn't that used to telephones, especially when it meant talking to the operator.

She clucked her teeth at me, but she was smiling. I was shaking from head to foot as I waited, hardly able to believe that in a few minutes I might be speaking to Dev, and wondering what on earth I would say to him. But I was to be disappointed. The international lines were all busy; the best Mary could do was book a call for the following day.

We went back to the kitchen and Mary's hand hovered over the jug of cider.

'Do you want another one?'

'Better not.' I felt quite drunk already, on bubbling excitement.

'Oh well, I expect it will be Guinness where you're going. I shall miss you, Carrie.'

'And I'll miss you. If I go . . .'

A thin wail came from the big coach-built pram in the corner. Mary always kept David downstairs until bedtime.

'I'm going to have to feed that little one.' She got up, lifting David, who immediately snuggled into her, bird-mouth seeking her breast.

'I'd better go, Mary,' I said.

'Stay if you like.'

'No, Gillian's alone in the house with Father and Frank. Mother won't be home till the ten o'clock bus.' I went to the door. 'I don't know how to thank you, Mary.'

'Oh, it was Grace who did it all . . .'

'And you who contacted Grace. You two are the best friends any girl could wish for. I'll see you tomorrow, then.'

I walked back down the lane in a daze. I was almost afraid to hope things were going to work out with Dev. I'd had too many knocks to take anything for granted. And yet the excitement was singing in my veins. It was beginning to look as if Gillian and I would soon be free to begin a new life. Anything else, as Mary had said, would be a bonus.

I began to skip like a child, euphoria building. I paused by the gate, collecting myself. I pushed open the front door and went into the house.

The first thing I saw when I went into the living room was Father lying at the bottom of the three little stairs that led up to the kitchen. I gasped, freezing for a moment, then running to him.

'Oh my God, Father! Are you all right?'

An idiotic question. Clearly he was not. His eyes were open, though one drooped heavily, and he was trying to say something, but his words were guttural and slurred and I could make no sense of them. He was struggling to get up and falling back again.

Even without my smattering of medical experience, I think I could have guessed what had happened. There really is no mistaking the signs of a stroke.

Father wasn't a big man, but I knew that I would never be able to lift and support him on my own.

'Don't try to move, Father.' I managed to drag his legs from under him and fetched a cushion from the sofa to put beneath his head. 'I'm going to get Frank.'

Again Father struggled to get up, forcing frantic grunts and gurgles from his twisted mouth and clawing at my skirt with his good hand when I stepped over him.

'Stay still, Father. We'll get the doctor to you, and then we'll get you to bed.'

The indistinguishable sounds that passed for words followed me up the steps to the back door, which was ajar. That didn't surprise me. We rarely locked a door, and on a warm evening like this one there was nothing unusual about it standing open.

The cottage door, too, was open.

'Frank!' I called. 'Frank, can you come here?'

His wireless was blaring; through the open door I could hear what sounded like the commentary of a boxing match. Frank loved his boxing, he wouldn't be best pleased to miss the action, and I thought I might end up paying later for interrupting him. Too bad.

I crossed the bricks. Went into the cottage. And into my nemesis.

I stop talking. I really don't feel well. I can feel the tightness in my chest again, making it hard to breathe, and there's a sensation of being a very long way off, of looking down on myself and Kathryn from a great height. I feel a bit sick too, but that's probably just the stress of wondering if I should tell Kathryn the truth, or stick with the story I concocted all those years ago.

She's looking intently at me, her expression compelling. I struggle to find the words. Cannot. My silence has lasted too long, it is a part of who I am. And to speak out now will have such far-reaching consequences . . .

'Grandma?' Kathryn leans forward, reaching out so that her hands almost touch mine across the table. 'What happened? When you went into the cottage? Did Frank attack you?'

'No . . . no . . .'

'What, then?'

Kathryn has become a blur to me; I can't really see her properly at all. But there are some things I can see all too clearly. Frank. The blood, pooling on the flagged floor. Gillian . . .

'She shouldn't have been there . . .' I say.

'Who?' Puzzled, Kathryn leans closer. 'Who shouldn't have been there?'

'She should have been in bed and asleep. When I went out, I thought she was in bed and asleep . . .'

'Mom?' Kathryn's voice is no more than a whisper, but urgent, wondering. 'Mom was in the cottage?'

I close my eyes, but there's no way I can shut out the images.

I hadn't noticed Gillian at first, still as a statue in the deep shadow.

I drop to my knees beside Frank, my medical training kicking in automatically, feeling for a pulse even though I already know I won't find one.

He's still warm, but there are no signs of life. How could there be, with all that blood? My hands are sticky with it. I cringe away. Half rise. And see her.

'Gillian!' For a moment utter shock freezes me into a state of paralysis. Then I run to Gillian, falling to my knees in front of her. 'Oh my God, Gillian!'

But Gillian makes no move nor sound. She simply stands there, staring down at the body of her father.

Part Seven

THIRTY

The previous day, Edmondsville, Ontario

The hypnotherapist is a dapper little man wearing a pink and white striped shirt, matching pink tie, and tailored trousers with a sharp crease right down to his highly polished black laced shoes. His hair, iron grey, has receded to a tuft that springs from the crown of his head; rimless spectacles are perched on a snub nose. The spectacles make his eyes look so large Gillian finds them daunting. As if she weren't nervous enough already! The brass plaque beside the door names him as Christopher John Staunton, and there's a string of letters following, but when he greets her in the reception area of his consulting rooms he insists she call him John.

'And may I call you Gillian?'

'Uh . . . yes, of course,' Gillian says, wishing that Don had come in with her, rather than waiting in the car outside. This man is, after all, soon going to have her in his power. He could suggest anything and she'd be helpless to do otherwise, if what she's heard about hypnotism is true.

'Shall we go through?' His voice is soft and silky. She wishes she dare tell him she's changed her mind; she really does not want to do this. But Don will be very annoyed with her if she chickens out now, especially since she's already paid the session fee on her credit card. In any case, she feels compelled now to finish what she has begun.

The inner sanctum is quite a small room, dimly lit, with a dark blue blind covering the window. There is an oak desk and a couple of swivel chairs with high backs, but Gillian is both relieved and puzzled to see that the couch looks more like a reclining chair than a bed. John indicates that she should sit in it. He fetches a pad and pen and sits himself in the swivel chair on her side of the desk.

'Let's have a chat then,' he says in that silky voice, obviously cultivated to put her at her ease.

The 'chat' consists of a series of questions about herself and her reasons for seeking hypnotherapy, the answers to which he notes down on his pad. Then: 'Shall we begin, Gillian?' he says.

Gillian can't answer. Her voice has been lost in a knot of nervousness in her throat. John fetches a contraption from his desk and attaches it to her left hand, explaining that it will monitor her impulses electronically, a little like a lie detector. At least, she thinks that's what he said; she doesn't understand, and doesn't like to ask. He dims the lights and depresses a button on a tape machine stationed on his desk. Then he sits in the swivel chair facing her, but with a good six feet between them, which she finds comforting. She'd

410

expected him to dangle a pendulum in front of her face and swing it to and fro, but no.

'I'm going to relax you, Gillian,' he says, 'and then I'm going to count down from ten to one. By that time you should be in an altered level of consciousness. We'll conduct the therapy, and when we're finished, I'll count you back up again. That's all there is to it. If at any time during the session you become too distressed, I shall end it immediately. That's what the monitor is for. So there is absolutely nothing to worry about.'

'OK,' Gillian manages, though it comes out as a croak.

'Right then. Now, breathe deeply, think about the top of your head, think calm, think relaxed. Moving down, your forehead, your eyes, all the tiny muscles around your eyes, smoothing out, feeling good as the tension drains out, drains away . . .'

He continues to talk the process of relaxation down the whole length of her body, and she does indeed seem to be sinking down into the chair. He's reached her thighs when she suddenly gets an itch on the side of her nose, and wonders if she's allowed to scratch it. Her hands are supposed to be relaxed already; using them again can't be in the plan. But the itch is becoming ever more persistent, and she decides it's better to scratch it than continue to be distracted. As she does so, John's voice never falters, and he reaches the tips of her toes.

'And now I want you to imagine you are standing at the top of a beautiful staircase of just ten stairs, covered with a soft, deep carpet in a colour of your own choosing. Your own favourite colour . . .'

Green, Gillian thinks. Moss green. Then changes her mind. She wants it to be a natural oatmeal colour.

'. . . and you are going down that staircase. Step one, relaxing, feeling good, feeling calm . . .' His soothing voice continues, taking her down a step at a time until: 'And step ten. All the way down. You are in a beautiful place, maybe a meadow, or your own room at home, somewhere you always feel safe and happy . . .'

Gillian does, indeed, feel very good, but her thought processes are quite clear and logical. She doesn't believe she's been hypnotised at all. She must be one of those people who are resistant to it. She doesn't know whether to be disappointed or relieved, but it doesn't really matter much either way.

'And now we are going back in time. You're seventeen years old. It's your birthday. Where are you?'

Gillian smiles. 'I'm having a party. We've hired the Church Hut. All my friends are coming. I've got a lovely dress. It's turquoise, with broderie anglaise trimming and a circular skirt.' She giggles. 'I've got a new paper nylon petticoat, with about six layers of net. I'm so excited! Don is coming. I've got to look good for Don.'

'Go on.'

'I'm doing the food myself. Well, Jenny is helping me. She's my best friend. We're doing jacket potatoes and egg rolls and anchovies on little wooden sticks – I love anchovies! Jenny said I've got to stop eating them or there won't be any left for the party. Oh, no! I've dropped one and made a greasy mark on my skirt! Oh, no!'

'I'm sure it was fine. You had a good party, then?'

412

'Oh yes, wonderful! Don's here. He brought me a present – an amazing record – Shirley Bassey, "As I Love You". And he kissed me!' She giggles again. 'I really do like Don. I have got the biggest crush on him ever. I think he might ask me out.'

'Let's go back a bit further.' John's soft voice interrupts her. 'Another birthday. This time you're ten years old. Where are you now?'

'Well, at Aunt Lizzie's, of course.' Gillian frowns, realising she hadn't described the house in Hillsbridge as 'home'. But what does it matter? She's not hypnotised at all, just relating things she remembers in order to make John think it's working. But she's puzzled to discover that instead of feeling elated as she did a moment ago, she's feeling sad, though for the life of her she doesn't know why. The table in the little living room is laden with a bowl of jelly, plates of sandwiches and little fairy cakes topped with buttercream and hundreds and thousands, and there is a birthday cake in the centre with ten candles. Aunt Lizzie is pouring orange squash from a glass jug for half a dozen other little girls who sit around the table, all eager smiling faces, dressed in their party best with ribbons in their hair But she feels terribly, terribly sad. In fact, she thinks she might cry, but she doesn't want to show herself up in front of the others.

'Why do you feel sad?' John asks.

'I don't know.' Gillian's face puckers, her lips tremble. 'I can't remember.'

'We'll go back further still then. It's still your birthday, but you're five.'

Five. But she can't remember being five. Five is three years before it happened.

'I can't—' She breaks off. The sadness has lifted as if by magic and she's happy again, really happy, the way only a child can be with no fear for the future. Totally secure. Surrounded by love.

'Where are you?'

'Timberley.' Of course, she knows that, she's just repeating what she's been told. But her voice sounds very odd, not at all like her own voice. She's got a little lisp. Why is she lisping? She runs her tongue over her front teeth and finds the top two in the middle are missing.

She can see grainy images. A table, covered with a yellow cloth. An earthenware teapot, a big pottery jug of milk, a basin of sugar, a plate of bread and butter. And a pot in the shape of a cottage, which contains blackberry and apple jelly. She loves that 'cottage' pot, loves to lift off the roof and dig her spoon into the jam. It's chipped in one corner, though, white pottery showing through the brick-coloured glaze, and she feels guilty when she looks at it. She did that, dropped it when she was helping to wipe up. Her lip puckers momentarily. It would have been so awful if she'd smashed her cottage to smithereens! But it was all right, Mummy said, they'd stick the bit of glaze back on. Except that they never had.

'What's happening?' John's voice, perfectly clear, though coming from a long way off. Gillian smiles again.

'They're singing "Happy Birthday".'

'Who is singing?'

'Mummy and Daddy. And Granny and Grampy.' She giggles. 'Can I blow out my candles now?'

'Tell me what your family look like, Gillian.'

414

She considers. 'Well, just like them. Granny and Grampy are quite old. Granny's got a flowered overall and fat legs. And she makes awful smells sometimes.' She wrinkles her nose. 'Mummy says it's rude, but I'm not allowed to say so, because that would be rude too. Grampy gives me rides on his shoulders. He pretends to be a horsey. Sometimes Daddy does too, but not often. He's got a bad leg. In fact, he hasn't got a leg at all. It's not real. It's made of . . .' She hesitates, screwing up her face in concentration. 'Cork!' she says triumphantly.

'And your mummy?'

'My mummy is really pretty. She's got long dark hair. She lets me comb it sometimes. She's called Carrie. Everyone calls her Carrie. But her real name is Caroletta. I think that's pretty too.'

'All right, Gillian, we're going to go further forward in time now, and I want you to be really brave,' John says. 'Just remember, everything that happened, happened a very long time ago, so there's nothing to be afraid of. And we can stop any time you want to. Now, let's move on a year at a time. You're six . . . seven . . . eight. You've had your eighth birthday, and we're nearly at the time that upset you so much you've tried to forget it. But you were just a little girl then. Now you're a grown woman, and whatever it was that happened, you're going to see it through the eyes of a grown woman. It's a summer evening, isn't it? Who put you to bed?'

Gillian hesitates. Her breathing is becoming a little uneven. 'Mummy.'

'Mummy put you to bed. Are you asleep?'

Gillian shakes her head. 'No. Mummy thinks I am, because

I pretend. But I'm not really. I don't want to go to sleep! It isn't really dark. I want to go out and play. But Daddy gets cross if I'm not in by seven. The others stay out even when it's getting dark. I wish I could too, but I don't want Daddy to get cross. He frightens me when he's cross. He beats me . . .' She falters.

John's eyes narrow, but he lets it go. 'So you're in bed, but you're not asleep. What happens then?'

'I get up and get a book. Enid Blyton. I love Enid Blyton! There are always lots of children, having adventures. And they've got brothers and sisters and friends and dogs . . .' Her voice goes wistful. 'I wish I had a dog! Like Ben at the farm. But Mummy says Granny wouldn't let me. She says dogs make a mess.'

'So you are reading?' John urges her gently back into the narrative.

'Yes. And the front door closes. I go to the window. It's Mummy, going out. She's looking back at the house and I have to duck behind the curtains really quickly so she doesn't see me. Oh! My friends are coming down the lane! They're playing "What's the time, Mr Wolf?". Freddie Walton's "it". They're all creeping up on him. He'll have them in a minute.' She giggles. 'Oh, I want to go out to play too! I'm pushing up the window, leaning out, calling to them. "Watch out! Freddie will have you!"' A pause. 'I'm coming down! Mummy and Granny are out, and Daddy's in the cottage. He'll never know if I creep out of the front door. Oh, I'll be in real trouble if he catches me, but . . .' She giggles again.

'I'm being really naughty. I'm going down the path in my nightdress. "What's the time, Mr Wolf?" "Supper time!"' She screams in mock terror. 'You can't catch me! You can't catch me, Freddie Walton!'

Another pause, then a gasp. 'Oh, no!'

'What is it?' John asks.

'It's Daddy! He's seen me. Oh, Daddy, I'm sorry, I'm sorry . . .' She falters, her breathing becoming rapid again and when her voice comes again, it is rising, tearful, frightened.

'I only came out for a minute! I wanted to play with the others . . .'

'Your father is cross with you?'

Gillian ignores the hypnotherapist. She's completely, utterly lost in the past.

'Don't take me to the cottage! Daddy, don't hurt me, please!' She's sobbing now, practically hysterical. 'No, Daddy, no, no, no!'

John is totally alert now, one anxious eye on Gillian, the other on the electronic monitor. She's becoming dangerously distressed. But they are close, so close . . .

'What's happening, Gillian?' he asks urgently. She's silent, her eyes, wide open, full of terror. 'Gillian!'

'No! No!'

John dare not leave her any longer. 'It's time to leave the past behind now, Gillian.' For all his concern, his voice is as soft and soothing as before. 'You are going back up that beautiful staircase. Step ten, beginning to come back up. Nine . . . a little further. Eight . . .' he drones on . . . 'and one!' He snaps his fingers. 'All the way up, back to full consciousness.'

He looks at her, only his narrowed eyes betraying the fact that he is at all worried. Gillian is sitting motionless, tears rolling down her cheeks.

'How are you feeling?' he asks.

'Awful! Oh my God – awful!'

'And do you remember now what happened?'

'No!' Her face contorts with frustration. 'Not really. Not the end of it.'

'Your father was going to beat you?'

'Yes, but it's more than that . . . All I know is that something terrible was going to happen.' She begins to sob. 'Something really terrible. But I don't know what. You stopped me . . .'

'I had to,' John says. 'Your reading was off the scale.'

'But I still don't know.' She finds a tissue, blows her nose. 'I have to know what happened. I can't leave it there. Not now.'

'We can arrange another appointment. Next time you may well be able to reach the vital moment without such trauma. You've been through quite a lot of it, and your conscious mind will begin to deal with it. You may even get further flashes without being regressed again. Now the door has been unlocked, it may begin to come back all by itself.'

Gillian shakes her head. She still feels oddly detached.

'I can't believe it. I didn't think I had been hypnotised. I was thinking . . . well, quite normally. I thought if you were hypnotised, you didn't know what was happening.'

'A common misconception. You were hypnotised, I assure you. Very much so. I've rarely had a better subject. Now, do you want to talk some more?'

'Not right now. I want to go home.'

'Your husband is waiting for you, you said?'

'Yes. He's right outside.'

'I'll see you to the car. Now, don't be alarmed by any flashes of memory. Remember you are now seeing what happened to you as a child through the eyes of an adult. It's all over, Gillian. But if you become disturbed in any way, you have my number. Call me at any time, or have your husband call me. And we'll make another appointment for next week.'

'Next *week?*' Suddenly Gillian is impatient, but at the same time not sure she can face another session so soon.

'It will give you time to recover some equilibrium, and perhaps for some of the memories to develop. Are you all right now?'

'Yes.' She feels stunned, shaky, but she's fighting to become her usual competent, confident self.

'Well?' Don says as she slides into the car beside him and props her crutches on the back seat. 'How was it? Did it work?'

'I'm almost there, Don. I almost remembered. And it scared the hell out of me.'

'What then? You were there when it happened?'

'Yes, I was there. But I don't want to talk about it at the moment.'

Don starts the engine. 'Come on, then, let's get you home.'

Gillian feels tired, drained, and she keeps slipping back into the past, reliving it, or the little she'd recalled, and she knows the rest is there, in the shadows, waiting to be drawn out into the light of day. She's afraid, but also strangely excited, as if she has been liberated after a long incarceration.

She sits in the easy chair in her living room with her eyes closed, trying to put that awful last scene and her terror out of her mind and concentrate instead on that other memory, the birthday party when she was five years old.

'My mummy is really pretty,' she had said in that little child's voice.

She sees her again as she had seen her then, and a feeling of warmth and safety envelops her.

When Don looks in on her, he sees there is a smile on Gillian's lips.

THIRTY-ONE

All the colour has drained from Carrie's face and her eyes have gone opaque. Kathryn has the impression her grandmother is no longer aware that she is there. She is lost, utterly and completely, in the past. Alarmed, Kathryn speaks her name, but Carrie does not respond. She's back in the cottage with Frank dead on the floor in a sea of his own blood.

And Gillian, her grandfather's old service revolver clutched to her chest, is cowering against the wall.

Carrie's thoughts are racing and whirling now like a flock of terrified birds just as they did that terrible night.

How the hell has this happened? How did Gillian come to have her grandfather's gun? Had he left it lying about again? How did she know how to use it? The only question that Carrie does not need to ask herself is – why? She's convinced Frank had threatened Gillian again and she was defending herself, perhaps unaware of the consequences. All the blood seems to drain from Carrie's

421

body and she thinks for a moment she is going to faint. And then, quite suddenly, she is icy calm.

Frank is dead and Gillian has killed him. That is what she has to deal with.

She goes to Gillian, who appears to be in a catatonic trance.

'It's all right, my love. Everything is going to be all right.' Gently she eases the gun out of Gillian's hands. Her fingers are clasped tightly around it; Carrie has to peel them back one by one. Then she lifts Gillian's stiff, unyielding body into her arms, holding her close for a moment, still murmuring words of comfort while she works out what to do.

The first, most important thing, is to get Gillian away from this horror. With Gillian's face turned into her chest, Carrie backs away from Frank's body, out onto the bricks, into the house. Her father struggles into a sitting position as she goes down the steps into the living room. It occurs to her that his stroke is connected with what has happened; he must have discovered the same scene, and the shock has been too much for him.

'Stay there, Father. Don't try to move,' she warns him.

She carries Gillian upstairs, washes the unresisting hands and cold bare feet, takes off her blood-spattered nightgown and slips a clean one over her head. It seems bizarre that she should be bothering with such trifles at a time like this, but she's acting on autopilot, doing the things she would do if Gillian had merely been sick over herself, not shot her father.

The covers on Gillian's bed are all turned back, or, rather, thrown aside. Carrie lays Gillian down and pulls a single sheet over her.

422

'Don't be frightened, sweetheart. You had a bad dream, that's all. Go to sleep now, and forget all about it.'

Still no response from Gillian. Then, quite suddenly, her arms go round Carrie's neck, limpet-like, and a tremor runs the full length of her body.

'Shush, my darling, shush! You didn't know what you were doing. You didn't mean it. But it's all right. Mummy is going to make everything all right.' Her voice is calm, though inwardly she's churning. She frees herself from Gillian's clinging arms, settles her back on the pillows. Retrieves the blood-stained nightdress from the floor where she had let it fall, takes it into her own room and stuffs it into a battered attaché case that she keeps under the bed.

The sound of the front door opening and closing. Mother. Mother is home! Carrie goes back to Gillian, kneels beside her for a moment. Gillian is back in her catatonic state; Carrie smooths the hair back from her clammy cold face.

'Stay here, my darling. Mummy will be back soon . . .'

She hears a cry of alarm from downstairs; her mother has discovered her father lying on the living-room floor.

'I have to go, Gillian. Forget all about it and go to sleep now, there's a good girl.'

Downstairs, her mother is beside herself. And as yet she has no idea of the extent of it, Carrie thinks, the black panic threatening to overwhelm her again.

'Your father! What's the matter with him! Oh my Lord, Carrie, we've got to get a doctor! He's had a stroke, hasn't he? How long has he been like this?'

Her hysteria, oddly, has a calming effect on Carrie.

'I'll go and phone now. You stay with him. And Mother . . . don't go out to the cottage.'

'The cottage? Why would I go out to the cottage? Oh, hurry up, do, Carrie! We've got to get the doctor to him! Do you know the number?'

'Try to calm down, Mother.'

'But do you? It's in my address book.'

'It's all right, Mother. I'll deal with it.'

She doesn't need the doctor's number; she already knows what she's going to do, and it's not running to the telephone box.

No, she's going to the police station. She's going to kill two birds with one stone. It has to be done, sooner rather than later. But she's not going to mention Gillian's part in this. The child is traumatised enough already. Gillian must be protected at all costs.

She goes out the front door, back up the lane where just a little while ago, in another life, she had skipped for joy. Her feet feel leaden now, but she forces them to move at a brisk pace. She must be quick. She must get back to Gillian.

The police house is on the outskirts of the village, square, stone-built, with a blue lamp alight over the front door. Carrie knows the policeman well – everyone in Timberley does. They're used to seeing him cycling about sedately on his bicycle, stopping to cuff a misbehaving youth, or herd a stray cow off the road, or see a drunk home from the pub. Nothing much happens in Timberley.

Until now.

Carrie opens the gate, walks up the neat path, rings the bell.

PC Whatley answers, still more or less in uniform, though he has taken off his tie and is wearing carpet slippers.

'Carrie!' He sounds surprised. 'What can I do for you?'

'I need the doctor for my father, if you could phone him please. He's had a stroke.'

'That's not really my job, you know—'

'But there's more. I'm really sorry to bother you at this time of night, but you're going to have to come down to Bush Villa.'

'For your father's stroke? Carrie—'

'No. The cause of it.' Carrie takes a deep breath, knowing that what she is about to say will change her life for ever. 'You need to come, PC Whatley, because I have just shot my husband.'

Carrie is almost unaware that she has been recounting aloud her memories of that terrible night. Now she realises Kathryn is staring at her in horror, unwilling for the moment to comprehend what she thinks her grandmother is telling her.

'What are you saying, Grandma? That it was Mom? Mom shot her father?'

Carrie's eyes are squeezed tight shut, one hand pressed over her mouth. Then she shudders, and opens them.

'I had to protect her,' she says, her voice very distant. 'I couldn't put her through what she'd have gone through. Can you imagine it? And she was in no fit state. If you'd seen her that night . . . She wouldn't speak, even to me. What would she have been like if it had been the police asking her questions, trying to get to the bottom of it? And to be told she had killed her father, when her poor mind was trying to block it out . . . It would have pushed her right over the edge. I couldn't let them do that to her.'

Kathryn is silent, fighting her way through the shock waves that are overwhelming her.

'She could have ended up in an industrial school or a mental institution,' Carrie goes on. 'At least, that's what I thought then. So I did what I thought was best. That's all there is to it, really.'

'Oh, Grandma . . .' Kathryn can scarcely believe what she is hearing. And yet, somehow, it all makes sense. Carrie had sacrificed herself to save her child and she can understand that. Wouldn't she have done the same for Ben? But to keep silent all these years . . . that was something else.

'Grandma, Mom has to know the truth,' Kathryn says gently. 'She's not a little girl now. She's a grown woman and has been for a very long time. You should have told her years ago.'

Carrie shakes her head. 'I couldn't. It wouldn't just be that she shot her father, would it? It would be that I served five years in prison for her. And to tell her that he had taken a strap to her, God alone knows how many times – the father she worshipped – I couldn't do it. In any case, I'm not sure whether telling her would have served any purpose. If she'd got her memory back it would have been different. But she hasn't, and Lizzie did a very good job of conditioning her, turning her against me. I doubt she'd have believed me. She'd have thought I was coming up with some made-up tale to excuse myself.'

'Well, I think the time has come to take that risk,' Kathryn says. 'If you ever want to see her again, that is. I shall certainly tell her when I go home, but I think it would be better coming from you.' She breaks off. 'Grandma! Are you all right?'

Carrie's eyes have half-closed, she's swaying, and she doesn't answer.

'Grandma!'

Kathryn is on her feet, but before she can reach her, Carrie has slumped down on the table.

It's been a fabulous ride. Andrea doesn't know when she last enjoyed herself so much. She'd let Tom have Jason, her gelding, and she'd ridden Bella, a frisky little filly who needed no urging to keep pace, and race with Jason. They'd gone across the hill, cantering at first, then working up to a full gallop, and when they slowed once more to a trot, they were breathless, laughing with exhilaration, ready to take things easy for a bit and talk.

Up here on the hill, on horseback, Andrea was in her element and much more relaxed. She was happy to answer Tom's questions about her life – not that there was much to tell – and he, in turn, talked about some of the places he'd lived and worked, and about losing Deirdre.

'There's nothing worse than watching someone you love suffer so,' he said. 'Except perhaps losing them. But to be honest, in the end it was almost a relief. You can't wish for anything but that they should be released from their pain. But that doesn't mean you don't miss them like hell and wish things could have been different.'

'I'm so sorry, Tom.' There's no denying, Tom loved his wife very much, but it has no power to hurt Andrea now, she discovers. She left her vulnerable young self behind a very long time ago.

'Your mum said you're planning on retiring and coming home to England to live,' she says.

'That's the general idea.'

'So what are you going to do? I can't imagine you're ready to do nothing but twiddle your thumbs all day.'

'Not really, no. I'm considering my options.'

She waits, but he doesn't elaborate. Same old Tom, keeping his cards close to his chest.

The horses are becoming restless again. Andrea glances at her watch.

'I'd better be getting back.'

'Pity.'

'You go on, if you want to.'

'No, I'll come with you. But let's do it again when you've got an hour to spare.'

She squints at him from beneath the brim of her hard hat.

'How long are you here for?'

'I'm not sure. The next week or so, at least.' He turns, touching his heels to the gelding's flanks. 'Come on then. And I'll bet I can beat you back to the cut.'

The phone in the stables is ringing as they get back to the yard, the tinny sound of the amplified bell bouncing off the brickwork and reverberating in the air.

'I hope that's not somebody ringing to cancel,' Andrea says grimly, dismounting.

'Think positive. It's somebody wanting to make a booking.'

'Let's hope so.' The summer rush is over; with winter approaching she'll be running on very tight margins. 'Hang on to Bella, will you?' She tosses Tom the reins, ready to sprint across the yard, but the phone stops. In the sudden silence, almost as deafening in its way as the penetrating jangle, Andrea swears.

428

'Don't you just hate it when that happens?' She takes the reins back from Tom, leads Bella to the hitching post and drapes them over.

'They'll ring again.' He dismounts with the fluid grace of the natural horseman, smooths out the wrinkled knees of his jeans. 'I must get myself some new jodhpurs. I thought I might get into my old ones, but no chance.'

'You don't look any different to me.'

'Well, thanks for that. But I reckon I'm a good stone heavier than I used to be.'

The phone bell begins to shrill again. 'There you are, I told you so.'

Andrea sprints across the yard and into the stables. The phone is just inside, on a rather rickety wall mounting. She grabs it up.

'Hello. Timberley Riding—' Before she can finish, she's interrupted.

'Andrea? Oh, thank goodness I've got you at last.'

Sharp alarm twists in Andrea's stomach.

'Kathryn? What's wrong?'

'It's Carrie. She's been taken ill. She's had a heart attack.'

Really, the ambulance seemed to take for ever to arrive. Heaven knows, out here in the country, it had some way to come. And it didn't help that she dialled 911 to start with instead of 999.

She told herself fiercely then to calm down. Panicking would help no one.

'Have you got any aspirin?' she asked Carrie – remembering that she'd read somewhere that aspirin was a good first aid in the case of a heart attack, and a heart attack was what she was fairly certain Carrie was having.

She was obviously in pain, and breathing with difficulty, but she managed to indicate the kitchen cabinet. Kathryn flew to it, pulling out flour and salt, baking powder, custard powder, a tin of black treacle, dumping them haphazardly on the work top. No aspirin.

'The drawer,' Carrie managed from behind her. 'Try the drawer.'

Wooden spoons, clean teacloths, and – thank God! – a packet of soluble aspirin. Kathryn popped a couple out of their foils.

'Take these. Chew them. I'll get you a drink.'

She found a tumbler, filled it at the sink. When Carrie indicated that the tablets had gone, she put it to her grandmother's lips. Careful as she was, some dribbled down Carrie's chin, and she took the glass herself, drinking in shuddering gulps.

'Oh, Kathryn, I'm sorry to be such a nuisance . . .'

'Don't be silly, Grandma.'

She didn't think she should move Carrie too much, so she fetched some cushions from the living room to make her more comfortable, and a jacket of Andrea's that was hanging on a peg to put around her shoulders, but Carrie pushed it away.

'Don't fuss. I'm all right.'

But she didn't look all right. She looked ill and old and in pain.

'I'm going to ring Andrea. What's the number?'

Carrie told her, and she called it on her mobile. No reply. And then, really, there was nothing left to do but wait anxiously and pray. And continue, every few minutes, to try to get hold of Andrea.

A paramedic on a motorbike was the first to arrive. Kathryn let him in and stood by while he assessed Carrie, administered some sort of treatment, and fixed her up with oxygen. Then he called in on his mobile, confirming an ambulance was required.

It arrived, maybe ten minutes later, and a cheerful crew got Carrie into a chair and carried her out. A couple of women were standing on the pavement outside the shop opposite, staring.

Carrie removed her oxygen mask.

'I used to do this, you know.'

'Did you, love? Well, just you leave it to us and be quiet,' one of the attendants said soothingly, replacing the mask. But her input was encouraging, Kathryn thought. She got in the ambulance and sat down opposite Carrie. Tried, yet again, to get hold of Andrea, with no result. And then they were off, siren wailing, blue lights flashing, heading for Gloucester.

Once there, everything happened very fast. Carrie was whisked into a cubicle and Kathryn stood anxiously by as a doctor examined her.

'You've had a heart attack, Carrie,' he said. He was young, good-looking, Asian.

'I know that. And it's Mrs Chapman to you,' Carrie said, affronted. In her day no one would have thought of addressing an elderly lady by her Christian name.

'That's OK, Mrs Chapman.' The doctor appeared unfazed.

A tiny smile quirked her lips. 'But you can call me Caroletta, if you like.'

'Well, you seem to be doing OK now, Caroletta,' he said, and then, to Kathryn: 'We'll be admitting her, of course. We need to get her stabilised and run some tests to find out exactly what's going on.'

'Right.' Kathryn reached into her bag for her cellphone to try, yet again, to contact Andrea.

The doctor raised an eyebrow. 'I'm afraid you can't use that in here.'

'Sorry . . .' She stood uncertainly, still clutching the phone.

'Step outside if there's someone you need to call.'

'I won't be a minute, Grandma.'

She went outside, hitting the redial button as soon as the automatic doors slid open. The phone rang and rang. Kathryn was beginning to get desperate. *Where the hell are you, Andrea?* She walked the length of the building and back again. It was beginning to rain, a fine mist blown onto her face by a rising wind.

I'll try just once more before I go back in, Kathryn decided. She hit the redial button without much hope. But this time, after just a few rings, Andrea answered.

'Hello. Timberley Riding—'

'Andrea! Oh, thank God I've got you at last!'

'Kathryn?' She could hear the alarm in Andrea's voice. 'What's wrong?'

And at last she could share the burden.

'It's Carrie. She's been taken ill. She's had a heart attack.'

Andrea gasped in shock. 'Oh my God! Is she all right?'

'She's stable, I think. Luckily I was there when it happened and I could call for help right away. They've been very good . . .'

'Where are you now? Where's Mum?'

'We're at the hospital. Gloucester. They're going to admit her.'

'I'll be right there. Tell Mum I'm on my way. And give her my love.'

'Andrea . . .' An already vulnerable Kathryn couldn't help but remember her aunt's erratic driving, even when she was in no particular hurry. 'Drive carefully, won't you?'

But Andrea had already hung up.

THIRTY-TWO

Kathryn sits beside her grandmother's bed, looking at her anxiously. She's sleeping now, but she looks terribly frail and vulnerable, the flesh of her cheeks sinking into hollows and pouches, blue veins visible on her closed eyelids. She's aged ten years in the space of a few hours and it opens up a deep well of sadness in Kathryn.

This is so not fair! Kathryn can't bear the thought of having found her, only to lose her. And she can't bear the thought that Carrie might not live to see the injustice of Gillian's rejection put right.

Kathryn closes her own eyes briefly as the enormity of what Carrie told her hits her all over again. This is really the first chance she's had to think about it – for the past few hours there has been room for nothing but concern about Carrie's condition. Now it's all there, bubbling to the surface in a confused stream. But the theme is constant. Carrie was innocent, and she lied in order to protect the person who was actually responsible for

Frank's death. Not Dev, as Kathryn had thought, but Gillian. And for that Carrie paid the most terrible price. Not simply the gaol sentence, as if that were not bad enough, but the loss of her daughter, the very one for whom she sacrificed everything.

It's beyond belief, and yet it makes perfect sense. As Carrie herself said, who else would she be prepared to lie for? And who else would allow her to do so? An eight-year-old girl, so traumatised by what she'd done that she'd blanked all memory of it fitted the bill perfectly. After all these years, Carrie has finally told the truth and Kathryn believes her.

Gillian has to be told. She can't be allowed to continue to shun all contact with the mother who had, almost literally, laid down her life for her. She has to be given the chance for reconciliation, to make her peace, to thank Carrie for what she did. But Kathryn quails inwardly at the thought of it. How on earth do you go about telling someone something like that? What repercussions are there likely to be? Gillian is going to be devastated and guilt-ridden, not only for killing her father, but for her mother serving what turned out to be, in essence, a life sentence for something she didn't do. Kathryn feels she needs time to think it all through, decide how, and when, she hits Gillian with the truth. The trouble is, with Carrie being taken ill, she's not sure how much time she has. Carrie is in good hands now, but nothing is certain. If she should have another, more serious, attack, she could die. Gillian would never forgive herself if she learned the truth too late. But Gillian is on the other side of the Atlantic and this isn't something Kathryn feels she can do by telephone. It has to be approached with sensitivity and care, face to face.

Would Gillian come to England if Kathryn simply tells her Carrie is in hospital? Somehow she doubts it.

She could ring her father, Kathryn thinks, and get him to break it to Gillian. They are a strong unit, Gillian and Don. But it seems like the most awful cop-out. It's another week before she's due to go home, and though she supposes she could get an earlier flight, she doesn't want to leave Carrie until she's sure her grandmother is out of the woods. And she certainly doesn't want Carrie put under the additional stress of knowing she's gone home to break the news to Gillian. It was being forced to tell the truth after all these years that brought on the heart attack, Kathryn is fairly certain, and that makes her feel dreadfully guilty. If she hadn't confronted her grandmother with her half-baked theory, Carrie might not be lying here now in a hospital bed. She has discovered the truth, but at what cost?

Kathryn is so deep in thought she's pretty oblivious to the comings and goings in the ward. At this time of day the nursing staff aren't much in evidence; they've congregated in the nursing station doing whatever nurses do when they are not handing out medication or taking temperatures, perhaps grabbing a cup of tea or coffee. But there are quite a few visitors arriving, greeting their loved ones with false cheeriness or hushed voices, dumping bunches of grapes or bottles of lemon barley water on bedside lockers. Kathryn is sitting with her back towards the swing doors that are the main entrance to the ward, and she doesn't see Andrea until she speaks.

'How is she now?'

When Kathryn finally got hold of her this morning, Andrea rushed up the motorway, and she and Kathryn sat with Carrie in the A & E Majors cubicle, waiting whilst she was wheeled away for tests. They talked to the doctor together, and then, when Carrie was pronounced stable, and there was nothing more to be done than wait for a bed in the cardiac unit to become available, Andrea asked Kathryn if she'd be OK for a couple of hours while she went home to see to the horses.

'Of course, you go,' Kathryn said. 'I'll stay with Grandma.'

Now she's back, her pleasant, weather-beaten face furrowed with anxiety.

'She seems fairly settled,' Kathryn says. 'She was very tired, though. Hopefully a sleep will do her good.'

'I heard that.' Carrie opens her eyes, but the weight of the lids seems too much for her, and she closes them again. 'Are you still here, Kathryn?'

'I've been here all the time, Grandma.'

'But you won't have had your dinner!'

'That's the least of my worries.'

'And I've come prepared,' Andrea says. She delves into a plastic supermarket bag and pulls out two packs of sandwiches sealed in plastic. 'I don't know what they'll be like, but I expect they're better than hospital food. There's egg and cress, and chicken tikka. And I got a box of apple pies and a couple of Kit Kats too.' She thrusts the bag at Kathryn, looks around for a chair. 'I'm going to find something I can sit on. Or, alternatively, you could go and get yourself a cup of coffee, have a bit of a break, and I'll have your chair and sit with Mum.'

Carrie opens her eyes a fraction again, squinting at them from beneath those drowsy lids.

'There's no need for either of you to stay. I'm not going anywhere.' But her protest is a parody of her usual confident independence, and again Kathryn is aghast at the change in her.

'I suppose they'll be kicking us out soon anyway,' Andrea says, and sits down on the edge of the bed, well aware that this will very likely precipitate a reprimand from a figure of authority, and really not giving a damn.

'Oh, I am so sorry, causing all this trouble . . .' Carrie says.

'And so you should be!' Andrea says. 'Giving us a scare like that.'

And: 'Don't be silly, Grandma,' Kathryn says. 'You can't help being ill.'

'Kathryn . . .' Carrie hesitates, then works her mouth and smacks her lips. 'My mouth's like the inside of a parrot's cage. You wouldn't get me a drink, would you, Andrea?'

'There's a jug of water on your locker. Shall I pour you some?'

'What I really want is a cup of tea.'

'I'll go and see if you're allowed.' Kathryn starts to rise, but Carrie's fingers fasten around her wrist.

'Andrea will do it. You stay here.'

'But Andrea's only just arrived.'

'She hates hospitals,' Carrie says. 'She doesn't want to be sitting there looking at sick old women. She'd rather be up and doing, wouldn't you, Andrea?'

'I'd rather you weren't here,' Andrea says equably. 'But since you are . . . yes, Mum, I'll go and see if I can get you a cup of tea.'

'And get one for Kathryn while you're about it.'

'I can see you're feeling better, Mum,' Andrea grumbles, but she raises her eyebrows at Kathryn and smiles, a look that conveys her relief, before heading off down the ward.

The minute she's out of earshot, Carrie tugs at Kathryn's hand, indicating that she should come closer.

'I had to get rid of her for a minute. You haven't said anything to her yet, have you?'

Kathryn is in no doubt what she means.

'No, of course not. We've been far too worried about you.'

'Don't say anything. She'll have to know, of course. But I don't want you telling her. I ought to do it myself.'

Kathryn's anxiety level rises. The last thing she wants is Carrie upsetting herself again.

'Grandma, forget about it. Just concentrate on getting well.'

'I can't forget it if I think you're going to . . .' Her fingers tighten around Kathryn's. 'She'll be back in a minute. Promise me, please, that you won't say anything.'

What can she do? 'I promise.'

'Good girl. Here she is. Mum's the word.'

Andrea is indeed back.

'They say they'll be round with the hot drinks trolley as soon as visiting is over. So until then I'm afraid you are going to have to make do with water.'

'Oh, well, water it is,' Carrie says with resignation. But as Andrea pours her some into a plastic beaker her eyes meet Kathryn's conspiratorially.

Kathryn manages a wintry smile. She had hoped to be able to talk this over with Andrea. Now she realises that unless she breaks her promise to Carrie that is out of the question. For the moment she must bear Carrie's secret alone. And decide, alone, what she is going to do about it.

At 11.05 p.m., Kathryn is in her hotel room. It has been an exhausting day, both emotionally and physically, but she's far too wound up to sleep. She's raided the mini-bar in her room for a gin and tonic, but instead of helping, it's making her morose.

The enormity of what Carrie told her is going round and round in her head, and she's in an agony of indecision as to what she should do about it. She hates it, too, that Andrea is still in the dark. It seems wrong that she should be the last to know, when she is the one who has always been there for Carrie.

One thing at least is certain: she must let Gillian know that Carrie has been taken ill, give her the chance to come to England to make her peace with her mother, and if she should decide to do that without knowing the truth, so much the better. If she doesn't, then Kathryn thinks it would be best to enlist the help of her father. But even that is not without its problems. There's a fifty/fifty chance that if she rings it will be Gillian who answers the telephone. She could, of course, call him on his cellphone, but if he was at home when the call came through, Gillian would think it very peculiar. Kathryn checks her watch and does a quick calculation of the time difference. It'll be early evening now in Canada. Chances are they'll be having a pre-dinner drink. She'll have to wait until tomorrow if she wants to catch Don in his office, and she really doesn't think she should delay until then.

No, best to do it now and play it by ear. Fortifying herself with another gin miniature from the mini-bar, Kathryn scrolls to her mother's home number in the menu on her cellphone, punches the 'select' button and tries to formulate the words as she waits for it to connect.

It's ringing. Kathryn takes a couple of deep, steadying breaths. And the answering machine kicks in.

'Sorry, we are unable to take your call right now, but if you leave your name and number . . .'

Shit.

'Hi, Mom, Daddy. It's me, Kathryn.' To her own ears, her voice sounds false. 'I really need to speak to you . . .' She hesitates. Then: 'The thing is, Grandma has been taken ill. She had a heart attack this morning. Don't worry, she's stable now, but they're keeping her in hospital, and I really thought I should let you know. It's quite late here, and I'll be going to bed in a minute, but I'll be in touch again tomorrow. Love you.'

She ends the call, goes to slide her phone shut, but her hands are shaking and she sits staring at the display. Then, quite suddenly, she pulls up the directory again, scrolls to her own home number, and presses the connect button.

For all the anger and resentment she's been harbouring against him these last months, there's really only one person she wants to talk to right now. The one person who was always there for her before grief tore them apart. Rob. Her whole being is aching for him – not the stranger he's become, but the rock he used to be.

The phone is picked up. Across the continents she hears his

voice, low, steady, safe. Breath catches in her throat and becomes a sob.

'Rob. It's me.'

'Kathryn!' He sounds surprised, but pleased. 'Hey, is everything all right? You sound—'

'Not really, no. Oh, Rob, it's so good to hear your voice.'

'And yours. But, Kathryn, what is it? What's wrong?'

And of course, she tells him.

Just as John, the hypnotherapist, had said, Gillian is getting flashes of the past. Though flashes is not quite the right word, perhaps, to describe what is happening to her. It's more like seeing an old photograph taking shape when the negative is immersed in developing fluid. Blurry shapes gradually materialising, taking on a certain amount of detail, but not enough. Never enough. Deep in the recesses of her mind, memories are stirring, a potpourri of trivia, unrelated, indistinct, teasing her then slipping away once more. Mostly there's nothing threatening about them, these snippets, far from it. Their aura is benign, imbuing her with a pleasant warmth, and the desire to know more. But at the same time she's apprehensive. Beyond the veil lies something darker, something so horrible that her mind shut down and blocked it out. This morning, on the verge of uncovering it, she was overcome with terror; even now, hours later, she can feel the panic fluttering in her chest like a trapped bird. Whatever it was she was on the point of remembering upset her so much she went, in John's words, 'off the scale'.

The very thought of undergoing more hypnosis and confronting it again makes Gillian shrink inwardly and brings tears of sheer panic to her eyes. But something is frightening her even more – that unwelcome memories will come back to her when she's alone, no Don to put his arms round her, no psychotherapist John to talk her through it in soothing tones. She's afraid it's going to blow her mind and her emotions wide open, and she won't be able to cope or control herself.

She's already practically made up her mind that no way is she going to wait a week before going back to John for another session, when she picks up Kathryn's message, and that is the deciding factor.

If her mother is ill, perhaps dying, the time left is at a premium. Having avoided facing the past for nearly fifty years, Gillian is suddenly tingling with urgency. Now that she's begun this, she has to go on. It's imperative she finds out, once and for all, whether she has been right to cut Carrie out of her life, or whether she has been perpetrating the most terrible injustice.

'Don,' she says. 'Would you be able to take me back to the hypnotherapist tomorrow if I can get an appointment?'

He looks at her over the rim of his spectacles, perched on the end of his nose.

'Do you think that's wise?'

'I don't know. But I do think it's what I should do.'

'It's your decision, Gill.'

'Yes,' she says. 'I'm going to ring now. He may still be there, doing late appointments.'

It's John's answering machine. Gillian leaves a message asking to see him, tomorrow, if possible. And for all her apprehension, feels she's taken a step in the right direction.

* * *

There is, of course, someone Kathryn can talk to, someone not a million miles away, and who also knows Carrie's secret. It comes to her in a flash of inspiration in the middle of her conversation with Rob, when he says: 'It's beyond belief, your grandmother keeping something like that to herself all these years.'

'Mary!' she says.

'Mary?'

'Grandma's friend at the farm. I'm pretty sure she knows the truth. I think I might go and see her tomorrow.'

'How can she help?' The typical man's reply, the kind of logic that might have irritated her a week ago. Now she finds comfort in familiarity.

'Well, obviously she can't, as far as telling Mom goes. That's got to be down to me. It would just be nice to chat it over with somebody who knows all about it. I wouldn't feel quite so isolated.'

'Well, fine, just as long as you're sure she does know. And won't go spilling the beans to Andrea.'

'I don't think there's any chance of that, since she's never betrayed Grandma's confidence in all this time.'

'Fair enough.' He pauses, the silence made longer by the transatlantic connection. 'Do you want *me* to have a word with your father?'

Kathryn considers. 'It might be an idea. But let's wait and see, first, what happens when Mom picks up my message. I'm hoping it might make her think. If she'd come over just on the basis of that, it would be by far the best.'

'OK, I'll hold fire.' Another pause. 'Do you want *me* to come, Kathryn?'

Yes! Oh yes! But: 'You can't just drop everything and hop on a plane,' she says. 'Besides, I may need you to have a word with Dad.'

'Well, ring me again, sweetheart. Keep me in the loop.'

'I will.'

'I hope your grandmother goes on all right. And take care of yourself, do you hear?'

'I will. And thanks, Rob.'

'What for?'

'For being there. For listening. For everything.'

'No problem.'

And then he's gone and Kathryn is alone again. Except that she doesn't feel so alone. There's a warmth in her solar plexus like the warmth that comes from hugging a hot-water bottle on a cold winter night. And though every one of her dilemmas is still there, unsolved, they weigh on her less heavily.

She gets ready for bed, slides between the sheets, and thinks about Carrie and what a remarkable woman she is. And says a prayer that she, Kathryn, will be able to do something to bring Carrie and Gillian together once more before it is too late.

Next morning, as soon as she's had breakfast, Kathryn goes round to the stables to see if Andrea has rung the hospital to check how Carrie is.

Kathryn practically had to sit on her hands not to phone herself, but she didn't suppose the nurses would be very pleased to have multiple enquiries and, as Carrie's daughter, Andrea really should be the one to do it.

She finds Andrea in the caravan, drinking coffee and eating

a sandwich that consists of two very thick, and very unevenly cut, slices of bread, that are oozing strawberry jam onto the palm of her hand.

'Breakfast,' she says.

'Right.' Kathryn takes a guess that she made the sandwich herself. 'Have you phoned the hospital yet?'

'Mm.' Andrea catches the spill of jam with her tongue.

'And?'

'The usual crap. "She had a comfortable night." That's more or less all they were prepared to say. We need to see her for ourselves to get any real satisfaction.'

'Is visiting more or less any time? If you've got things to do here this morning perhaps I could get a bus.'

'They're not keen on visitors in the morning,' Andrea says through another mouthful of jam sandwich. 'That's when the consultants do their rounds, apparently. Leave it till lunchtime and we'll go together.'

'I was thinking,' Kathryn says, 'we ought to let Mary know.'

'She does. I went in to see her just now.'

'Ah.' There's her excuse to go and see Mary blown out of the water. But perhaps that's not such a bad thing. In the cold light of day, talking with anyone about this even if she did know the truth somehow seems a betrayal of Andrea. Speaking to Rob last night fulfilled her need to share the burden, and no harm done.

Kathryn decides she'll spend a quiet morning until it's time to go to the hospital with Andrea.

THIRTY-THREE

Christopher John Staunton, who likes to be called John, is looking very concerned. He's wearing a yellow striped shirt today and a yellow tie; he fingers it as he greets Gillian, smoothing it down with soft white fingers topped by perfectly manicured nails.

When he picked up Gillian's message last evening, he called her back and booked her into the slot he keeps for emergencies. She's been on his mind in any case, given her violent reaction to the regression, but it's a counselling session he has in mind, not another voyage into the past.

'It really is a little too soon,' he says earnestly. 'Much better to wait a few days at least, assimilate what you recalled yesterday, and become more comfortable with it.'

'I'm not sure I have the time to wait,' Gillian says, and explains. 'I have to know what happened that night,' she finishes.

Eventually, reluctantly, he agrees — provided she is prepared to take full responsibility for any consequences of the regression.

He takes Gillian's crutches, settles her in the reclining chair, and they begin.

The preparatory routine is the same as before, but this time as Gillian sinks into the state of altered consciousness she accepts that she really is hypnotised and the answers to his questions are not just something she's doing to please him. He's leading her very gently today, repeating at regular intervals that she has nothing to fear. That whatever she remembers is in the past, when she was just a child. That she is now an adult, and can see it for what it is, something that happened a long time ago and is no threat to her any more.

They reach the point where she is playing 'What's the Time, Mr Wolf?' with the other children in the road outside Bush Villa and Frank comes out, furious to find her there in her nightdress in the twilight. Her pulse rate has increased, her breathing is fast and shallow. She's speaking in a childish voice, her phraseology that of an eight year old.

'No, Daddy! Don't take me to the cottage! Daddy, don't hurt me – please! Don't . . .'

'Step away, Gillian,' John says, his silky voice hiding the anxiety he's feeling. 'This isn't happening to you now. You are just watching. It can't hurt you. Step outside yourself and tell me what you see.'

'I can't! I can't . . .'

'Yes, Gillian, you can. It's just like watching a film, that's all.' Her stress levels are worrying him.

'He's making me go to the cottage. He's dragging me across the bricks . . .' She's sobbing.

'*Her*, Gillian. Not you.'

448

'Don't, Daddy! Please don't!'

The calming measures aren't working. There is something so deeply traumatic here that it is rendering his platitudes impotent. He has to end this quickly one way or another. Either bring her back to the conscious present, or . . .

'We're going to move on, Gillian,' he says. 'When I clap my hands, you are going to remember what it is that's frightening you so.'

It's a calculated risk, and he knows it. He just hopes she's strong enough to face whatever it is that her conscious mind has rejected.

'Where are you?'

'The cottage. I'm in the cottage. With Daddy. Oh, no – he's taking off his belt and . . . I don't know! I don't know!'

'Don't be afraid. You can leave all this behind just as soon as I have clapped my hands, and you have remembered. Are you ready?'

He pauses for just a moment. And claps his hands.

Gillian's body goes rigid, her mouth opens in a silent scream. And then:

'He's dead! He's dead! I don't want him to be dead!'

'It's all right, Gillian. We're at the foot of the staircase now. We are going to come back to the real world. Ten . . . beginning to return to consciousness . . . nine . . .' He can feel the palms of his hands moist with sweat, but he keeps his tone soothing as ever as he counts back to one. He clicks his fingers again. 'Eyes open, wide awake and feeling good . . .'

To his enormous relief, Gillian's eyes snap open. But they are full of horror.

'Oh my God!' she whispers, and again, her voice trembling with shock: 'Oh my God!'

'You remember what happened?' John asks.

She nods, biting down hard on her lower lip. Tears are streaming down her face.

'You want to tell me about it?'

She shakes her head, and then she's trying to rise from the reclining chair, scrabbling to reach her crutches.

'Gillian, I think you should rest for a minute . . .' But there's a sense of urgency about her, dulled only by the torpor that is the legacy of having been deeply hypnotised.

'I want Don!' she says. 'I have to talk to my husband!'

When Kathryn and Andrea get to the hospital, they are very relieved to find Carrie sitting up in bed and looking much better. In fact, she's so much more like herself that she scolds them for having brought a bunch of chrysanths, which Andrea cut from the garden.

'They're supposed to be for the front-room window, and the living room.'

'I'll take them home again, then, if you don't want them.'

'Oh, now you've cut them I might as well get the benefit of them, I suppose,' Carrie grumbles, and Kathryn hides a smile at the ease between them, even when they're sparring, and goes off to find a vase.

When she comes back, Andrea is asking Carrie if she has any idea when they're going to discharge her.

'I've got to stay another couple of days, by the sound of it,'

Carrie says. 'They're sorting out my medication, and they have to be sure they've got it right before they turn me loose.'

'You'll be lucky!' A shrill voice from the next bed. Kathryn looks round and sees a birdlike woman, wearing a pink frilled bed jacket, and with a fluffy scarf wound around her neck. She's obviously been listening in to their conversation.

'I beg your pardon?' Andrea says.

'I said, she'll be lucky. Nobody much gets out of here alive. They make sure of that.'

'Oh, ignore her,' Carrie snorts. 'She's a bit . . .' She makes a screwing motion with one finger against her temple.

'Mum, ssh! She'll hear you!'

'I hope she does. She's driving me crackers. If I don't get out of here soon I'll be as daft as she is.' Carrie lowers her voice. 'Look at her, wearing that scarf. Just look at her! It's stifling in here, but every time they open a window she kicks up a hell of a fuss. Says it's only by the grace of God she hasn't caught her death of cold. She's got religion, too. One of those evangelical lots. They come in to visit her and do the "Alleluia! God be praised!" bit when they find her still alive. Crackers, I tell you. Isn't that right, Gladys?' she says to the woman in the bed on her other side.

'What's that?' Gladys, a big woman with a mane of grey hair tumbling loose, cocks her head and screws up her face.

'Oh, never mind,' Carrie says, and to Andrea and Kathryn: 'And she's deaf as a post. Oh, I shall be glad to see the back of this place, I can tell you.'

'Don't work yourself up, Mum,' Andrea says.

'It's enough to try the patience of a saint, I can tell you,' Carrie snorts, and the snort turns into a laugh. 'Ah well, you know what they say. Nurses make the worst patients, and I dare say there's something in that. Well, what news have you got? What's happening in the outside world?'

'Nothing, really. You've only been in here a day, after all.'

'Seems a lot longer than that. So you've heard no more about the Hall, then?'

Andrea shakes her head. 'These things take time, don't they? Selling a place like that isn't like selling a pound of sausages.'

'It'll be a relief when you know something, though.'

'I don't really want to talk about it,' Andrea says.

They stay for another hour, making the kind of awkward small talk that passes for conversation on hospital visits. But at least they have the satisfaction of knowing Carrie is much more herself.

The journey home is as hair-raising as always when Andrea is driving. She shoots out onto roundabouts when there's traffic she should give way to, her lane discipline on the motorway is lamentable, her speed through the villages definitely illegal. But they make it back to Timberley without incident, and Kathryn breathes a sigh of relief.

'What do you say we have something to eat up at the pub?' Andrea suggests. 'I don't know what food we've got in, and I don't feel like cooking anyway.'

Remembering the doorstep jam sandwich she'd made this morning, Kathryn doesn't think she fancies Andrea's cooking either.

'There's always the restaurant at the hotel,' she ventures.

'They charge through the nose for a few tarted up bits and pieces that wouldn't feed a fly,' Andrea snorts. So the King's Head it is – Kathryn's first visit to a real English pub.

They find a table in the bar, order steak pies and chips, Andrea has a lager and Kathryn a generous-sized glass of wine. Most of the customers seem to know Andrea and ask after Carrie. Word has spread that she was taken off by ambulance yesterday. Andrea introduces Kathryn to some of them, which causes a certain amount of interest. Kathryn can see heads going together, discreet glances directed at her over shoulders. But nothing can detract from the steak pies when they arrive in individual pottery dishes with thick puff pastry crusts that release the most mouth-watering aroma when cut into. Kathryn had not realised until now just how hungry she is; she'd been too distracted to eat much breakfast, and has had only a sandwich since then. They linger over their drinks, chatting, though Kathryn is once again aware of the awkwardness that comes from knowing something Andrea does not.

They're just thinking about leaving when Kathryn's cellphone rings. She answers it, but the signal in the bar is not very strong, and the background chatter of the customers distracting. She goes outside to take the call, standing on the forecourt in the soft, dark, slightly damp air.

It's Gillian.

'How is Mum?' she asks.

'Doing OK, I think. Though they're keeping her in for a couple more days to sort out her medication and monitor her.'

'Thank goodness!'

Kathryn is surprised at the relief in Gillian's voice. Such a short time ago she'd given the distinct impression of not caring much about Carrie one way or the other.

Then: 'Kathryn,' Gillian says. 'I'm coming over.'

Kathryn's heart leaps, but at the same time her stomach seems to fall away.

'You are?'

'As soon as I can organise a flight.'

'Oh, I am so glad.' But she's also nervous at the thought of what she has to break to Gillian. 'Is Dad coming with you?'

'I'm not sure. It all depends if he can take time off work at such short notice.'

'Oh, I hope he can.' She needs her father to help share the load when Gillian learns the truth. 'You shouldn't be travelling alone with your hip,' she adds lamely.

'I'm sure the airline will take good care of me. Though there's always the possibility . . .' she hesitates. 'How would you feel about Rob coming with me?'

'Yes, fine by me.' Wasn't she thinking only last night how she'd like to see him? But . . . 'I still think Dad should come with you if he can manage it.'

'We'll sort something out at this end and I'll let you know.'

'Would you like us to meet you at the airport?'

'Again, I'll let you know. If Rob or your father is with me, I should think we'll hire a car. But if I'm on my own . . .' She hesitates. 'You'll tell Mum I'm coming?'

'Of course.'

'And . . . that I have something to tell her?'

Kathryn frowns. 'You have something to tell her?'

'Yes. I can't talk about it now, Kathryn. But I've got a lot of apologising to do.'

Kathryn's frown deepens. She really doesn't understand. Has Rob broken her confidence? Told Gillian what she, Kathryn, had told him? If so, Gillian really is taking it very calmly.

'Mom—'

'I'll call you tomorrow when we've fixed the flights. I'd better go now.'

'OK. Good night, Mom.'

'Good night, Kathryn.' And she's gone.

Kathryn stands, staring into the darkness, seeing nothing.

'Ready to go then?' Andrea. She's emerged from the pub, slipping her wallet into her bag, zipping it up. 'It's OK, I've paid.'

'Oh, Andrea, you shouldn't have. Let me . . .' Kathryn is fumbling in her purse. Andrea lays a hand on her arm.

'You can do the honours next time.'

'Well, as long as you be sure to let me. Andrea, that was Mom. You'll never believe this. She's coming over.'

Andrea's breath comes out on a startled whistle. 'No! You don't say!'

'Yes. She's arranging a flight tomorrow.'

'Well!' Andrea says. 'All I can say is: thank God for that! Or,' she chuckles, 'as Mum's neighbour in the next bed would say . . . Alleluia!'

Gillian phones again the following afternoon as Kathryn and Andrea are once again on their way to Gloucester to visit Carrie. She has booked a flight, Rob is coming with her. Don, as she

455

had thought, had been unable to take time off work at such short notice. Kathryn's heart sinks at this news – she really does wish her father had been able to accompany them – but at least Rob is already in the picture and will be able to help her deal with the fallout when Gillian learns the truth. If he hasn't already told her. It is really the only explanation Kathryn can think of for Gillian's sudden change of heart. Gillian says they should be arriving at Heathrow at about ten tomorrow morning, and will hire a car to drive down to Gloucestershire. And then: 'I must go. I've got to do all my packing, and everything takes me that much longer on crutches.'

Kathryn's itching to ring Rob, ask him if he has told Gillian what she told him, but she can't do that with Andrea sitting next to her. When they reach the hospital she tells Andrea to go on in while she finds a parking space, and then she sits on a wall outside the hospital and keys in her home number. It rings and rings – obviously Rob is not there – and the answering machine fails to kick in either. She tries his cellphone and he answers almost immediately.

'Rob, it's me. Mom just called. I hear you're coming over tomorrow.'

'That's the plan, yes. We arrive at Heathrow at ten.'

'So Mom said. Rob, have you told her?'

'No, of course not. You asked me not to.' He sounds a little put out.

'I just can't understand why she should change her mind like that after all these years.'

'Because your grandmother's time might be limited, I suppose. I don't know, Kathryn. The way your mother's mind works has always been a mystery to me. Look, I can't talk now, I'm driving. I'll see you tomorrow.'

'OK.' But when the line goes dead, she feels a sense of loss. She hopes the rapport they enjoyed yesterday wasn't just a blip. She doesn't want to lose him again in the wilderness of mis-understanding.

She goes into the hospital, finds her way through the maze of corridors to the cardiac unit. Carrie is sitting up in bed, looking much better. From the way her face is wreathed in smiles, Kathryn knows that Andrea has already broken the news to her.

'Oh, Kathryn, isn't it wonderful?' she says before Kathryn can even find a chair and sit down. 'Really, I can't believe it! I'm going to see Gillian again after all these years! My little girl!'

'She's not a little girl now,' Kathryn says, thinking that it might be quite a shock for Carrie, coming face to face with a middle-aged woman. She's shown her photographs, of course, but even so, the reality will be something quite different.

'Well, no, I know that,' Carrie says tartly. 'Andrea's not a little girl either, and she's eight years younger than your mother.'

'True.'

'And the best of it is they're letting me out tomorrow morning, if Andrea can come and fetch me. So I shall be at home when Gillian arrives. Oh, my goodness, where is she going to stay? Have they got room at the hotel? If they haven't, perhaps you could come down to us and let your mother have your room.'

'We'll sort all that out, Mum,' Andrea says briskly. 'Just stop worrying.'

But another thought has occurred to Kathryn. Given the terrible thing that happened there, would Gillian want to go to Bush Villa at all? Even if she didn't remember it, she might have really bad vibes about the place.

Oh God, this is all so complicated!

'I'm going to see my daughter tomorrow!' Carrie says happily.

'You'll be lucky.' It's the woman in the next bed, listening in again. 'They'll never let you out of here alive. Unless you turn to Jesus, they'll never let you out of here.'

'Oh, don't talk such rubbish!' Carrie scoffs. 'And you want to look out. That scarf's slipping down. And the draughts are everywhere.'

But she's smiling again. Smiling so hard her face aches. Smiling as if she'll never stop smiling again.

THIRTY-FOUR

Gillian feels disembodied, as if she's unreal. She's all too well aware of the physical, that she's crammed into the front seat of a hired car and that her hip is aching, but her head, and the essence of her, is somewhere else entirely. The long flight is partly to blame, of course, the wretched, fitful dozing, the persistent throb of the jet engines, which still vibrate through her body, the disorientation that comes with crossing time zones. But it's also the way she seems to be lurching between past and present, with old emotions resurfacing and forgotten vignettes first knocking on the periphery of her consciousness, then coming gradually into focus. It's been happening ever since her regression, this filling in of the lost years like pieces of a jigsaw puzzle, more vivid, perhaps than the usual memories of early life.

Now, as they drive towards Gloucestershire, the once-familiar sweep of countryside unlocks yet another strata of awareness, a kind of bittersweet nostalgia that brings her to the verge of tears, though she doubts they are tears of sadness or regret, simply her reaction to emotional overload. She can not only see the rolling hills, she can smell them, taste them. And the experience overwhelms her. She actually feels like a child again, with all a child's innocent wonder. In spite of everything, being here feels somehow very right.

'Are you OK?' Rob asks. It's the first thing he's said in a long while. Rob isn't one for idle chat. In that respect he's very like Don. If she doesn't instigate a conversation, they'll drive for miles in silence. But that's all right by her today. She doesn't feel like talking.

'Yes, I'm fine.'

'Your hip's not playing up?'

'Well, a bit,' she admits.

'Do you want to stop, get out and stretch?'

'No, let's just get there. It can't be too much further now.'

He checks the sat-nav. 'About another thirty miles.'

Nervousness jumps in her throat. She bites down on it, taking slow deep breaths, the way she was taught in a yoga class she attended briefly a few years ago. But the apprehension is really kicking in; much as she wants to see her mother and put right some of the terrible wrongs she has perpetrated, the years of estrangement are an arid wasteland between them. And the overwhelming sense of guilt doesn't help, either.

She leans her head back against the headrest and closes her eyes, seeing again one of the scenes that has surfaced since she left John's consulting rooms, and which is still gradually becoming clearer and clearer, small details fleshing out the bare bones.

She's in her old bedroom at Bush Villa. It's almost dark, the thick grey that falls when the sun has sunk below the horizon but still reflects in the lowering sky. She's frozen like a statue, not just her limbs, but her mind, her emotions. Her eyes are wide and staring. They feel dry, but she doesn't even blink.

Carrie is sponging her hands and face with water from the jug and basin on the wash-stand. The water has a tepid feel to it because it's been standing for hours in the heat of the day. Carrie lifts her unresponsive arms, pulling her nightdress over her head, eases her into a clean one. She sits Gillian on the edge of the bed, lifts up her legs, pulls the sheet over her.

'Don't be frightened, sweetheart. You had a bad dream, that's all.'

The silent sobs that have been shaking Gillian come harder, so that her whole body begins to convulse.

'Darling – hush. My darling, hush . . .' Carrie is bending over, smoothing Gillian's hair. Quite suddenly Gillian throws her arms around Carrie's neck, holding on for dear life to the one anchor in this nightmare that has enveloped her. And Carrie is rocking her, crooning softly against her hair.

'You didn't know what you were doing. You didn't mean it. But it's going to be all right. Mummy is going to make everything all right . . .'

That puzzles her, because she really doesn't know what is wrong. Doesn't know why she is so upset. But it also comforts her. Whatever it is, Mummy will make it go away. She always does.

Tears fill Gillian's eyes. She understands now, and the enormity

461

of the injustice is too great to bear. And Carrie is not the only loser. Gillian has missed out too.

Once again she's that traumatised little girl who wants nothing but to bury her head in her mother's chest and have her make things right. Except that she knows now that Carrie doesn't have the mystical powers the young Gillian bestowed on her. She can't wave a magic wand; she never could. She could only do what she thought best. And even then it wasn't enough.

Carrie is feeling dreadfully nervous too. Of meeting Gillian again after so long. Of suffering another heart attack. 'Avoid stressful situations,' the doctor had warned her, and what is this if not stressful? Even now she can feel her chest tightening.

She can see her own anxiety reflected in Kathryn's eyes. Kathryn knows this is going to be difficult. Kathryn is a good girl. As Andrea is. And, very likely, Gillian too. None of this is her fault. It's Lizzie's, for turning her against her mother, and Carrie's own, for keeping her secret.

Carrie, sitting in state in the big wing chair, watches Kathryn and Andrea bustling about, making things look nice, laying the table and setting out food they went into Staunton earlier to buy – ham, a cold cooked chicken, salad in bags (salad in bags – whatever next!) and hopes very much that things will work out for both of them. In fact, it's her dearest wish, more important to her even than seeing Gillian again. Oh, she wants that desperately, but she's old, she hasn't got much longer, however she tries to deny it. In just a few years' time, what happens or doesn't happen between her and Gillian won't make much difference to her one way or the other. But they still have their lives before them. It would be terrible for Andrea if she were to lose the stables – Carrie prays that whoever buys the hotel, they'll let her stay on. And Kathryn . . . her heart contracts as she thinks of what Kathryn has gone through. Carrie, too, has lost a child – not only Gillian, but the baby she miscarried – and though the circumstances were quite different it helps her to empathise. She remembers too how Frank's lack of understanding of her feelings when she lost her unborn baby soured her towards him. She never really loved him, but she might have grown to love him if she hadn't lost the baby and found him so unsympathetic, so uncaring. She hopes with all her heart that Kathryn's marriage is not beyond saving.

But Rob is coming with Gillian, and that has to be a good sign. Just as long as Kathryn gives him a chance. It would be so nice if they were to get back together, rebuild their life together, and their love. Have more children. Kathryn needs that.

'Oh my God, they're here!' Andrea has seen the hire car cruising, pulling in onto the slope that leads to the garage.

'I'll go,' Kathryn says, heading for the door.

'Kathryn . . . bring them in the front way,' Carrie says.

'Oh Mother!' Andrea scoffs, assuming that Carrie is treating them like visitors. But it's not that at all. Carrie feels instinctively it's better that Gillian doesn't have to pass the cottage.

She goes to get up; Andrea stops her.

'You stay there, Mum. And try to keep calm.'

'Oh, do stop fussing, Andrea!' Carrie says.

But she does as she's told, sitting there with her hands tying knots in themselves in her lap, and waiting for the daughter she hasn't seen in over forty years.

Rob is helping Gillian out of the car. Her hip has stiffened up, making movement both difficult and painful, but she's glad of the distraction. While she's thinking about where to put her foot, she's not thinking about being back in Timberley. And when Kathryn rounds the corner, she's glad of that too. Her daughter, her ally. Independent-minded Gillian has never felt more in need of moral support.

'You're here!' Kathryn kisses her, mouths: 'Thank you for coming' to Rob, who is reaching into the rear seat for Gillian's crutches.

'How has it been?' she asks her mother.

'Rob has looked after me very well,' Gillian says.

'Oh, I haven't done anything. But the airport staff certainly treated her like a celebrity. Wheelchairs and priority boarding all the way.'

Gillian looks around, at the hedges bordering the narrow front garden, at the shop on the other side of the road, at the house itself. The feeling of familiarity and strangeness, both at the same time, is peculiar. Since her memory began to return, she's pictured it, but the reality is different somehow, as if the proportions have subtly changed. And the apprehension is gnawing at her stomach again, apprehension that comes from knowing she is back in the place where the terrible thing happened, and somehow she has to confront it.

'How is Mum?' she asks, apprehensive about that too.

'Quite well really, considering. She is so looking forward to seeing you, Mom. I am really glad you decided to come over. But she's supposed to be taking things quietly, so . . .'

'Don't worry, I won't do anything to upset her.'

'Shall I bring the luggage, or leave it in the boot for the time being?' Rob asks.

'Oh, leave it in the boot. We've managed to book you into the same hotel that I'm staying in, just up the road,' Kathryn says. 'Are you all right now, Mom? Shall we go in?'

Gillian's throat tightens and her heart is racing. Suddenly she's not at all sure she can do this. But she has to, of course. She follows Kathryn along the side of the road under the hedge, her crutches skittering on the loose gravel. The view up the lane plucks a chord deep inside her. She used to wait out here by the gate for Daddy. When she saw the bus go down the main road she'd know he was home. She can see him now, heaving into view, walking with that funny lurch that Mummy called 'dot and carry one'. She hadn't been afraid of him then. That had come later. In those days he had been her hero, the first man she had ever loved.

She turns in through the gateway, up the short path. The front door is painted green. It didn't used to be green, it used to be brown. Granny was superstitious, she remembers, convinced that green was unlucky. Well, brown didn't bring them much luck either! Her throat tightens again, a knot of nerves.

There's something familiar about the smell of the house as she steps inside. Lavender polish, chrysanthemums and cooking, blended into the unmistakable potpourri of home.

Home! It really is beyond belief! Such a confusing tangle

465

of memories, some good, some terrible. That night . . . *Don't think about it now. Not yet . . .*

Into the living room. A large-boned woman in cord trousers and a sweatshirt is standing in front of the hearth. Andrea, her sister, she presumes. But for the moment she has eyes only for the diminutive figure in the wing chair. A figure who is determinedly rising to her feet. Whose face is playing out a gamut of emotions from wonder through to tearful joy, with all stops in between.

Gillian has wondered exactly how she will react when she sees her mother. How she should react. Carrie has wondered the same thing. In the event instinct takes over. Without even thinking about it, they speak one another's names, almost simultaneously. And then they are in one another's arms, hugging as if they will never let the other go. They are laughing and crying both at the same time.

For the first time in almost fifty years, they are truly reunited.

Andrea stands by the hearth, embarrassed by the overt display of emotion and unsure as to whether something similar is expected of her. She sincerely hopes not. This smartly dressed – chic, even – woman might be her sister, but she is also a stranger. A stranger to whom she has written on several occasions and not even had the courtesy of a reply. She's glad, for Carrie's sake, that she's here now, but she finds it impossible to forgive her for leaving it so late in the day.

Perhaps she thinks if Mum is going to die, there might be something in it for her, Andrea thinks, rather uncharitably. What other explanation can there be for this sudden change of heart?

Gillian doesn't look as if she's in need. Her hair is styled in a sharp cut that looks expensive, and though there's not a single thread of grey to be seen, it's not obviously coloured either. No home dye off the supermarket shelf for Gillian. And her linen jacket has class about it, even if it is a bit crumpled from the flight. Or maybe it's meant to look that way – Andrea doesn't know, she's never taken the slightest interest in fashion. Whatever, Gillian certainly doesn't appear to be short of a penny or two. But that doesn't mean she isn't after her share of whatever Carrie may leave. The more people have, the more they want, in Andrea's experience.

Well, if she thinks she's walking back into an inheritance, she's going to be disappointed, Andrea thinks with a certain muted satisfaction. Apart from the house, which Carrie made over to her a good ten years ago, there's nothing but a couple of thousand pounds in National Savings. Her share would barely cover her flight from Canada.

Andrea is surprised, though, that she's having such spiteful thoughts. She's not normally a spiteful person. And then, as Carrie and Gillian draw apart, looking at one another as if they are quite oblivious to anyone else, then go into another hug, she realises.

She's jealous! How petty is that? For her entire life, it's been just her and Carrie. Now Gillian is here. The prodigal has returned. And the fatted calf will certainly be rolled out in her honour. And she, who has been here all the time, will have to take a back seat.

It shouldn't matter. It doesn't matter, and she's rather ashamed of herself that she should entertain such an unworthy emotion for even a moment. She's glad for Carrie, really glad, of course she is.

But she still feels very awkward, very shut out.

'I really should go up to the stables and check on the horses,' she says softly to Kathryn. 'I'll catch up with your mother later.'

'OK, I'll explain when she's up to listening,' Kathryn says.

'Save me a chicken leg if you can.'

Unnoticed by Carrie or Gillian, she slips away.

Kathryn, touched by the reunion, can feel tears pricking at her eyes, but she too feels like an outsider, and though, of course, that doesn't matter in the least to her, she doesn't like the feeling of intruding on what should be a private moment. She sidles over to Rob, who is standing in the bay window looking out, though there is practically nothing to be seen but the high privet hedge.

'Would you like something to drink?'

'What's on offer?'

'I got some beer in. I couldn't get your brand, but the girl in the off-licence said this one is pretty popular.'

'I'm sure it will be fine.'

'Why don't you come out to the kitchen with me to get it? Leave those two on their own.'

She heads off and he follows her. She'd put a six-pack of Stella Artois in the fridge; she hands him one, he pulls the tab and takes a long swig straight from the can.

'Oh, that hits the spot!' He jerks his chin in the direction of the living room. 'The reunion seems to be going well.'

'Thank goodness! Just as long as Grandma doesn't overdo it. She only came out of hospital this morning.'

'She seems OK.'

As if you'd notice if she wasn't. The thought is there, unbidden, unwelcome. *You didn't even notice your own son had meningitis.*

Aloud, she says tartly: 'Well, she's not. She's been very ill and I'm worried about her.'

'OK!' Rob raises a hand like a policeman stopping traffic, and his tone is stroppy. Of course he knows exactly what she meant; it was a repeat of a theme he's heard many times before in the past year. 'I'm only saying she looks all right to me, but I'm sure you know best.'

Kathryn wants to weep. She hoped so much that things could be back to where they used to be between them, but they've been in one another's company less than ten minutes and already they are sniping at each other.

'I think I'll have one of those beers,' she says in a light tone that somehow still manages to sound strained. She cracks open the can and drinks from it, emulating Rob in an effort to establish some sort of rapport. 'How was your journey?'

'You know what flying's like. It's only a week since you did it yourself.'

She tries to bite back her irritation.

'I didn't mean the flight. I meant the drive down.'

'OK. Luckily the car is fitted with a sat-nav. Your mother didn't have the first idea about how to get here.'

'Well, she wouldn't,' Kathryn objects. 'When she lived here I don't suppose she ever went far beyond the village, let alone London.'

'She's been over to Somerset a few times, though, hasn't she?

I'd have thought she might at least have known how to get onto the motorway.'

'Well, I wouldn't,' Kathryn snaps. 'When you're a passenger, you don't take notice of those things.'

'OK, OK, I'm just saying . . .'

Kathryn checks herself again, scarcely able to believe they're arguing over nothing. It doesn't bode well.

'So you found it easily enough, thanks to the sat-nav.'

'Yeah. It didn't send us into the middle of a ploughed field or over a cliff.'

Kathryn laughs. 'I don't think there are any cliffs in Gloucestershire.' She cocks her head for a minute, listening. She can hear the rise and fall of Carrie and Gillian's voices now, and wonders what they're saying to one another.

'Did Mom say anything to you as to what made her change her mind?'

Rob takes a long pull of his lager. 'Actually, yes. She said she'd been to see a hypnotherapist.'

'Oh my God!' Kathryn claps a hand over her mouth. 'You mean she *knows*?'

'Well, I'm assuming so. She didn't say, and of course, I couldn't let on I knew anything. But it was a bit odd really.'

'Odd how?'

'She seemed very matter-of-fact about it. I'd have thought if you'd just found out you'd killed your own father, you'd be in a bit of a state. But she . . . oh, I don't know. All she said was she'd come to see things in a different light.'

'Strange.' Like Rob, Kathryn expected Gillian to be devastated and guilt-ridden when she discovered the truth. Perhaps she simply didn't want to talk to Rob about it and has successfully hidden the inner turmoil she is feeling. But: 'She went to see a hypnotherapist! I can hardly believe it! She's resisted it so strongly in the past. I wonder what happened?' She narrows her eyes, thinking. 'Perhaps she *doesn't* know. He just made her "see things in a different light", as she put it.'

'That could be it. Yes, actually it makes more sense.'

'And so the bombshell is still to come. Oh, Rob, I'm really worried as to what's going to happen. I wish Dad was here.'

'She's got you.'

The weight of responsibility weighs heavy on Kathryn's shoulders. 'I know, but . . . I'm scared, Rob.'

He squeezes her hand, the first time he's touched her since he arrived. 'You'll be fine. You're really close, you and your mom.'

There's a moment of the old tenderness, when Kathryn wants to burrow into him, lay all her worries on his broad chest. Then he says: 'You managed to book us into the hotel, then?'

'Yes. It's not their busiest time of the year. We've got two rooms for you on the same floor as mine.'

And the moment is gone. She feels his withdrawal, and knows the reason for it. Separate rooms is a statement that nothing has changed. She'd wondered about it when she made the booking and hadn't wanted to presume. It was so long since they had shared a bed.

'Good. That's OK then,' Rob says off-handedly.

Before she can say anything to make it better, Carrie calls from the foot of the steps.

'Are you there? I think we ought to have something to eat so Gillian can get off and have a rest. She's tired out.'

'We're coming.' Kathryn thinks that whatever the emotional issues, Carrie's maternal instincts are kicking in. There's going to be a respite, then, before they get down to the nitty-gritties, which is just as well. Carrie probably needs a rest herself.

'Where's Andrea?' Carrie asks, puzzled, as Kathryn and Rob go down into the living room.

'She's gone up to the stables to check on the horses. She said to save her a chicken leg.'

'She didn't say anything to me!' Carrie sounds vaguely affronted.

'Your attention was elsewhere,' Kathryn says lightly.

'Oh, well, as long as she doesn't think we're going to wait for her . . . Come on, Gillian. You sit here, and help yourself.' She begins moving the platters on the table around.

'Sit down, Grandma,' Kathryn says firmly. 'You've only just come out of hospital, and you mustn't overdo things.'

'Oh, I'm fine,' Carrie says breezily. But she does as she's told, and Kathryn thinks she looks very tired.

She sincerely hopes all this is not going to be too much for her.

Andrea sits on the steps of the caravan, head bent, arms hanging loosely between her trousered knees. She feels as though she has the weight of the world on her shoulders, unusual for her. It's her nature to be prosaic, worrying about things only when they can no longer be avoided, and then only one at a time. But when depression does hit her she falls into a bottomless black pit, which is all the more daunting for being a place with which she is not familiar, and her usual pragmatism is replaced by pessimism.

The shock of Carrie's heart attack, the awful fear that she had lost her, the stress of having to juggle the things she has to do at the stables with driving up and down to Gloucester, the continuing anxiety that Carrie might suffer a relapse, all have taken their toll on Andrea. Gillian's arrival – another emotional jolt to the system. All that, and on top of everything else, her concern as to what is going to happen to her when the hotel is sold. The stable is her life, the horses her children. The thought that she might have to let it all go if she's given her marching orders is just too dreadful to contemplate. But she has to. She should be looking around for alternative premises, just in case, she knows. That, presumably, is why the owners of the hotel – her landlords – had warned her they were putting the place on the market. But there are never enough hours in the day, and anyway, she doesn't actually want to look for somewhere else. This is where she belongs.

'Penny for them.'

She looks up, startled. 'Tom! What are you doing here?'

'I thought maybe you could do with a hand. Gillian's arrived, hasn't she?'

'How do you know that?'

'Not much goes unobserved in this village. A strange car parked outside your house is a pretty good giveaway.'

'You can't see our house from here,' she objects.

'I drove past just now, on my way back from Staunton.'

'Yes, Gillian and Rob – that's Kathryn's husband – got here an hour or so ago. Mum, as you can imagine, is over the moon.'

'But you're not.'

'I feel like a spare prick at a wedding.'

Tom laughs. 'That's not a very ladylike expression!'

'When have I ever been ladylike?'

'True. So you don't want me to take over so you can go back and see her?'

'I suppose I should. Are you really offering?'

'That's the general idea.' He looks at her. 'You're very glum today. Your mum is OK, is she?'

'I think so. I am still worried about her, though. It's really knocked the stuffing out of her. And though it's not top of my list of priorities just now, I'm worried about this place. I've got the sale of the Hall hanging over my head like the Sword of Damocles. If the new owners kick me out, I don't know if I can uproot, start all over again, even if I can find suitable premises.'

He grins. 'Andrea, if I know you, you're the last person to give in without a fight.'

His words touch a nerve and she wonders if he's remembering her dogged persistence as a teenager, trying to get him to give her a chance at love.

'Well, I wouldn't worry about it. Not yet. The new owners might well let you stay on.' He says it almost as if he knows something. For a moment hope sparks, then she tells herself she's imagining it.

'I suppose they might.'

'Come on, cheer up, Andrea. Things will work out, I guarantee it.'

'Mm. So you're going to mind the shop for me for a couple of hours, are you?'

'Just give me a list of what needs to be done, and leave it to me. I'm a bit out of practice, but it'll do me good to do a bit of mucking out again.'

He's grinning at her in a way that should have lifted her spirits. But the depression is still there, a darkness inside her head, an undigested meal in her stomach. Andrea is very afraid of what the future holds on every imaginable front.

By the time she gets back to Bush Villa they've virtually finished lunch and Rob is preparing to take Gillian to the hotel so they can both have a bit of a nap. But they've left her a chicken leg. Andrea picks it up, chewing on it, as she goes out to the door to see them off, and Kathryn with them.

Carrie is looking very tired, though also very happy. Andrea ushers her into the front room, where she's made up a bed for her on the Put-u-up so that she doesn't have to do the stairs, and sets about tucking into the remains of the lunch, and clearing away.

THIRTY-FIVE

'Kathryn, I really need some time alone with your grandmother,' Gillian says. 'We have a lot to talk about.'

It's next morning, they're having breakfast in the hotel dining room, Rob making short work of a full English, while Kathryn and Gillian go for the lighter, Continental option.

Kathryn's heart comes into her mouth. This is when Gillian gets to learn the truth. If she doesn't already know it – and Kathryn can't believe she could be so calm, so normal, if she did. Should she try to prepare her in some way? But maybe, now that she's here, Carrie will decide there's no need to tell her after all. In which case, if Kathryn says anything she will be putting her foot in it.

She throws a pleading glance at Rob; Gillian notices it.

'I expect you and Rob would like some time to yourselves too,' she says. 'If you'll just drive me down to the house, Rob, you and Kathryn can spend a couple of hours doing whatever you fancy.'

Rob is mopping up the last of his egg with a piece of toast. 'I'll take you as soon as I've finished this.'

'No rush.'

But Kathryn can tell she's anxious to be gone and her anxiety ratchets up another notch.

Be careful of what you wish for. You might just get it . . .

She wanted her mother to come to England, but she is now very concerned as to what the consequences will be.

Carrie is sitting in the big wing chair feeling very frustrated. She hates this enforced inactivity, but supposes she has to be sensible. She doesn't want to bring on another attack. She's also worrying about whether it's necessary to tell Gillian the truth. She's here, that's the main thing. Is there really any point in burdening her with all that guilt? The trouble is, Kathryn knows now. She'll keep quiet about it, no doubt, if Carrie asks her to. But it seems wrong that she should know the truth when her mother does not.

The doorbell rings, the door is opened and closed, and Gillian comes in. That's it, then. No more time for wondering. 'Come on in, Gillian,' Carrie calls.

And tells herself to simply enjoy having her daughter here again after the long years of separation.

'I was just thinking,' Kathryn says when Rob comes back from ferrying Gillian to Bush Villa, 'about this Dev that Grandma was in love with. I wonder what happened to him.'

Rob pulls a face. 'Goodness only knows. They lost touch, I suppose, when she was in prison.'

'Exactly.' She chews her lip. 'I was wondering if we might be able to find him. Grandma's had such a hard life, and she really deserves something nice to happen.'

'I thought your mom coming over was something nice.'

'Yes, but wouldn't it be a lovely surprise for her if we could trace him?'

Rob shakes his head. 'Oh, I don't think so. He's probably dead by now. And even if he's not . . . You're talking about an affair that happened over fifty years ago. He'll have a wife, children, grandchildren.'

'So? It's not as if Grandma would be a threat. They're not going to run off together now, are they? I'm just thinking it would be nice for her to be in touch with him. Or even just know what happened to him. When they get older, people do want to contact friends from the past.'

'But not lovers. It's not a good idea, Kathryn.'

'You're probably right.' She sighs, resigned, then brightens. 'It's a lovely day. Why don't we go for a walk? I'll take you up to the hill where Andrea took me. You can see for miles.'

'Sounds good to me,' Rob says.

'I expect you're wondering why I didn't bring Kathryn with me,' Gillian says.

'Not really.' Carrie smiles. 'It's good for us to have some time on our own. There's so much to say.'

'But only one thing that really matters.' Gillian eases forward on the sofa, trying to get more comfortable. The sofa is low, not the best thing for her hip, but that is the least of her worries. 'I just want to say how really sorry I am. For cutting you out of my life all these years.'

Carrie smiles wanly. 'I can't find it in my heart to blame you. I can't imagine many children would want to acknowledge a mother who was in prison for killing their father. You're here now, that's all that matters.'

'No, Mum, it isn't.' Gillian swallows hard at a sudden lump in her throat. 'It's all right. You don't have to pretend any more. I've got my memory back. Well, quite a lot of it. I know it wasn't you who shot Daddy.'

A ripple of shock runs through Carrie. She goes rigid, her hands claw on the arms of her chair, and the colour drains from her face.

'Oh, Gillian!'

'Mum, don't. Don't upset yourself, please. I just want to know why you did it. Why you took the blame, went to prison, lived all these years with the stigma . . .' *Allowed me to believe you guilty . . .* But she doesn't say that.

Carrie is silent for a moment, only her face working as if to bite back tears.

'What else could I do? You'd do the same for Kathryn.'

'Perhaps.' Gillian is not at all sure she could be so selfless.

'You would. I know you would. It's a mother's instinct to protect her child.'

'Except,' Gillian says quietly, 'that I didn't need protecting. Or not in the way that you thought, anyway.' A note of bitterness creeps into her voice, bitterness for lost years, for a family torn apart.

'You may not think so now,' Carrie says, bristling a little, 'but you were just a little girl, Gillian. You were in such a state! I couldn't put you through it.'

You didn't know what you were doing. You didn't mean it. But it's going to be all right. Mummy will make everything all right . . .

When she remembered what Carrie had said to her that terrible night, remembered how she had washed her, gentled her, comforted her, Gillian realised there could be only one explanation, little as she wanted to believe it.

'So I'm right,' Gillian says. 'You thought it was me. You were so sure, weren't you, that I was the one who shot Daddy?' The hard edge is still there in her voice. Touched though she is that Carrie should make such an enormous sacrifice for her sake, it only makes her own guilt at having cut Carrie out of her life much worse, so that she actually feels quite angry that her mother had made the assumption. 'Oh, Mummy, how could you think that?'

Carrie closes her eyes. She is very pale.

'Oh, Gillian, are you really going to make me say it? You were there, darling. You were covered with blood. And you were still holding the gun.'

'I know,' Gillian says. 'But that doesn't make me any more guilty than you.'

'But—'

'I've remembered what happened, you see. And it wasn't the way you thought.'

Carrie stares at her, uncomprehending. 'What are you talking about?' she asks, bewildered.

And Gillian tells her.

* * *

Kathryn and Rob have actually spent a couple of hours together without arguing.

They've gone for a walk up the track where Andrea took Kathryn on her ride, to the top of the hill. It's a beautiful day to be out, the sun shining low through the branches of the overhanging trees, where the remaining leaves are a cloud of red, ochre and gold, and those that have fallen form a thick-pile carpet underfoot.

Up on the hill the sweep of turf, lush from the recent rain, spreads like infinity to the canopy of sky, the deep azure that comes as a last defiant fling before turning pale or lowering grey for winter. Kathryn and Rob are used to glorious falls back home, but this has a quality that is subtly different and it is balm for the soul.

They walk to the point from which it is possible to look down on Bush Villa. Nothing stirs.

'How do you think they're getting on?' Kathryn asks anxiously.

Rob thrusts his hands into the pockets of his fleece.

'That's between them now. There's nothing more you can do.'

'Except pick up the pieces.'

'Yup.'

'Oh, I do hope it's going to be all right . . . To do what Grandma did . . . it's incredible, really.'

'You'd have done the same,' Rob says, unconsciously echoing Carrie's words to Gillian.

'Oh, I don't know. What a dreadful situation to be in! I suppose she thought what she was doing was for the best, but I wonder if she'd still have done it if she knew how it was going to turn out? Losing the very one she'd sacrificed herself for. Her child . . .' Suddenly her eyes are full of tears. Rob reaches for her hand, squeezing it.

'And we know all about that, don't we?'

She nods wordlessly. The valley below them is a blur now, the ache in her heart, raw as ever, rising into her throat. Then the tears spill over, running down her cheeks and drying almost instantly in the stiff breeze.

'Oh, Rob, I miss him so!' It comes out on a sob.

Rob pulls her towards him so that her face is buried in his fleece.

'So do I, you know.'

She raises her head, looking up at him, and sees that he is crying too.

'He should be here with us.' His voice is rough; he raises a hand and dashes it across his eyes.

'He'd love it, wouldn't he? All this space to run about in? And the animals . . . perhaps he could have had a ride on a pony . . . Can't you just see him?' She breaks off, a fresh wash of tears welling, but she's smiling through them as she pictures it.

'Yeah. I see him all the time. I know you think I don't, but I do.' His voice is raw. 'And I blame myself. That I didn't realise how ill he was. If you'd been there . . .'

'It might not have made any difference.' Compassion softens Kathryn, melting some of the ice around her heart.

'You'd have known. You're much more alert to that sort of thing than I am. I see only the obvious. Always have.' He snorts with derision at his own shortcomings.

'But it might still have been too late. And suppose . . . suppose they had saved him, but he'd been left terribly damaged? Oh, we'd have been grateful we still had him at all, of course, coped with . . . whatever . . . and loved him even more, maybe. But . . . well, if he'd been born that way it would have been him. But to see our perfect little boy diminished, suffering . . . our Ben, and yet not our Ben—' She breaks off. It's something she's never said aloud before; even to think it makes her ashamed. But she *has* thought of it, in the dead of night. 'That would have been terrible. I couldn't have borne it.'

'Well, we'll never know now, will we?' Rob says harshly. 'We lost him.'

For the first time she can truly feel his pain, as real as her own. How could she ever have thought he didn't care? Of course he did! Ben was his son too. Like her, his hopes and dreams, vested in the child he adored, were shattered. Like her he bleeds for the loss of his son. It's just that he doesn't find it so easy to show his feelings. He has locked them away inside, afraid that to put them on display would make him less of a man. Only now, for the first time in months, is he letting her into his private hell.

'Oh, Rob,' she says with a sigh. And then: 'At least we still have one another.'

'Have we?' He sounds uncertain.

'I'd like to try again, if you would.' He nods without speaking. 'I do love you,' she says softly. 'It's just that I've been in a very dark place. But I do love you.'

He wraps her in his arms, muttering against her hair. But she's fairly sure that what he's saying is: 'I love you too.'

He's never going to be demonstrative. Never going to woo

her with effusive words and flowery sentiment. It isn't his way. But would she really want that? It just wouldn't be Rob, the man she fell in love with and married, the father of her dead child. Kathryn acknowledges that she loves, and wants, Rob, just the way he is.

Tom finds Andrea cleaning tack. When she sees him, she goes a little pink with surprise and pleasure.

'What are you doing here?'

'Looking for you.'

There's no answer to that.

'The thing is, I think it's time to come clean. I've not said anything before in case it didn't work out, though I was sorely tempted when I was here yesterday. But now the Is are dotted and the Ts crossed, there's no reason why I shouldn't tell you.'

Andrea looks up at him, shielding her eyes from the low glare of the sun with a rather grubby hand.

'What are you talking about?'

'The hotel sale. Your tenancy here. I thought you'd like to know you're quite safe. You'll be able to go on renting the stables as long as you want to.'

Andrea whistles through her teeth. 'That would be a big relief. But how can you know that?'

'Because,' Tom says with a grin, 'I'm the new owner.'

'What! You've bought the hotel?'

'Well, not just me. I'm just one of a consortium. But it was my idea in the first place. As you know, I'm taking early retirement, but I'm not ready to be put out to grass just yet. I wanted a new project, something to keep me out of mischief.

The hotel was on the market and I reckon it's got a lot of potential. So I put it to a few people I know, suggested they might like to invest, and I heard this morning that our offer has been accepted.'

'I don't believe this!'

'Believe it.'

'Oh, Tom!' She's laughing now with sheer relief. 'And you're really saying I can stay?'

'Can you really see me turning you out? You wouldn't be likely to lend me a horse if I did, would you? Truth to tell, it has crossed my mind to ask if you've got the room to stable another one if I should decide to get one of my own.'

'Do you even need to ask?' She's beaming happily.

This is a far better outcome than she had dared hope for. She wants to hug him, but she's aware she's filthy, and in any case, shows of affection are not her way.

'This is just brilliant, Tom,' she says.

Carrie and Gillian are still sitting in the living room when Kathryn and Rob arrive. They look flushed and relaxed.

'We've been up on the hill,' Kathryn says, but she's looking surreptitiously at her mother, worried as to what Carrie has told her, and how she has taken it. 'Is everything all right?'

'Yes.' Gillian reaches for Carrie's hand, squeezes it. 'Fine. But we really do need to talk to you. There's been an awful lot of misunderstanding.'

'Misunderstanding?'

Carrie stirs. 'Andrea needs to hear this too. And Gillian's not going to want to keep going over it.' She looks at the clock.

'It's nearly lunchtime. Why don't you give her a ring, see if she could come home now?'

Kathryn is puzzled. Gillian doesn't seem as upset as she would have expected her to be, but there is definitely something.

'Mom, are you *sure* you're all right?'

'I'm fine. Worry about your grandma. She's the one who's had a dreadful shock.'

'What?'

'No!' Carrie interjects sharply. 'Wait until Andrea gets here, please. I want Andrea.' She's becoming agitated.

'OK, Grandma, we'll wait for Andrea.' She glances at Rob. 'Give her a ring, Rob. Her number is programmed into the phone.'

'I got it all wrong,' Carrie is muttering. 'How could I have got it so wrong?'

'Grandma, don't upset yourself,' Kathryn says. 'Andrea will be here soon.'

'No reply,' Rob says.

'Maybe she's already on her way home,' Carrie says.

And, as if on cue, the back door opens and Andrea calls: 'I'm home!' She sounds extremely cheerful. 'You'll never guess what's happened . . .'

She appears at the top of the steps, bursting with her news, then checks as she sees the tableau in the living room. 'What's going on? You all look as though you're going to a funeral.'

'Andrea,' Carrie says, clearly relieved that the daughter she's shared her life with is here. 'It's all right, don't worry. But Gillian and I have something to tell you. I made a terrible mistake the night Frank died, and we've been paying the price for it ever since.'

'What in the world are you talking about, Mother?'

Carrie looks at Gillian. 'Are you going to tell her, or am I?'

Gillian smiles wanly. 'You tell your story, I'll tell mine.'

But she's not looking forward to going over it again. Bad enough the first time. Already she's reliving it once more, the nightmare that changed her life, just as she did when she was with John, the hypnotherapist.

She's out in the road, in her nightdress, playing 'What's the time, Mr Wolf?' with her friends. And suddenly Daddy's there. He must have looked out of the cottage window and seen her! She's quaking with fear.

'I only came out for a minute, Daddy! I wanted to play with the others . . . I'm sorry, Daddy. I'm sorry!'

But Daddy has hold of her by the shoulder, pushing her up the slope, through the old stable, across the bricks. He is angry, so angry. 'I'll teach you, my girl, to go off outside when you're supposed to be in bed. Get in there – now!'

The cottage door is open; he's propelling her towards it. She knows what that means. 'No, Daddy, no! Don't beat me, please don't beat me . . .' She's screaming.

'You've got to learn, Gillian. I won't let you turn out like your mother.' He's snarling. She's screaming, kicking, fighting him. He holds her fast, tucked under one arm while with the other he removes his belt.

'No, Daddy, please . . . please . . .' Sobbing. Hysterical. 'I won't do it again. I won't . . .'

'It's too late for that, my girl.'

'No! No! No!'

487

A shadow in the doorway, cutting off daylight.

'Grampy!' Gillian screams. 'Grampy, don't let him! Please don't let him.'

'Get away from that child!'

Frank checks, shocked. Then he recovers himself. 'Mind your own business, you old fool. She's got to be made to know.'

'Not like that. You lay a finger on her and I'll—'

'Oh, yes? What?'

'I'll kill you, Frank.'

'You and whose army?' He's pulling up Gillian's nightdress, exposing her bare bottom ready for his belt. Emboldened by the presence of her grandfather, Gillian manages to wriggle out of his grasp, cowers back against the wall. Daddy is coming for her again.

'I mean it, Frank.' Grampy comes into the cottage and she sees the gun in his hands. He's pointing it, rather unsteadily, at Daddy. Daddy laughs.

'You bloody old fool! That thing doesn't even work any more.' He takes a step towards her.

And the world comes to an end. The report is so loud in the confined space that it hurts her ears. Daddy is on the ground. He's making a terrible noise. He doesn't sound like her daddy. He sounds like a wounded animal. And the blood! Oh, the blood!

'Daddy!' she screams.

His hand shoots out and fastens round her ankle. She can feel his fingers gripping so hard it hurts, pulling her down beside him. She doesn't want him to. She doesn't want to touch all that blood. She tries to shake free, and he grabs her nightgown.

There is another sharp crack and he releases her, slumping back onto the slab floor. She darts for the door, to Grampy, but Grampy doesn't seem to see her. He's shaking much more than usual and staggering. The gun falls from his hands. Gillian picks it up. She doesn't know why; she's not thinking at all. Grampy is making a strange keening noise now; he lurches towards the door and goes out. Gillian wants to follow, but somehow her legs just won't work. She backs up against the wall and slides down it into a crouch. Her eyes are wide and staring. She's drowning. Drowning in terror and darkness. She is not even aware the gun is still in her hands.

She is still there when Carrie finds her.

'Oh, Grandma! Oh, Mom!' Kathryn is almost beyond words. 'It's terrible. Just awful. What a waste . . .'

'She did it for me.' Gillian is close to tears. 'She did it for me, and look at how I've repaid her.'

'You weren't to know,' Carrie says. She's still visibly upset too, but after protecting Gillian for the whole of her life, she's not going to let her take the blame now. 'No, it's my fault for assuming the worst. But what else was I to think? You were there, covered with blood, the gun in your hands, and Father . . . well, you know Father went into a coma that same night and never came out of it. I thought it was the shock of seeing what I saw that brought on his stroke, but I was wrong. And he couldn't tell me different, and neither could Gillian. But I should have known . . .'

'You were in shock too, Mum,' Andrea says. 'You wouldn't have been thinking straight.'

'That night, maybe,' Carrie concedes. 'But afterwards . . . I should have thought afterwards. A little eight year old? What would she have been doing with Father's gun? Even if he'd left it lying about again, it would never have entered her head to take it out there, let alone use it. I should have known! But I couldn't think beyond keeping her safe. She was in no fit state to face up to all the questions they'd have asked her. And what if they'd taken her away? Put her in an approved school? Or even an asylum? That was what I was most afraid of.'

'Surely they wouldn't have done that,' Andrea says, shocked.

'They might have. Things were different in those days. You could get committed to an asylum for all sorts of reasons, and once you were in there, that was your lot. You might never get out. I couldn't risk that happening to Gillian.' She wipes her mouth and chin with a tissue that's crumpled in her hand. 'That's why I did it. And maybe it was the right thing, even if she didn't do it. The police might very well have thought the same as I did. All the evidence pointed to her, and neither she nor Father could say any different.'

'Oh, Mum, how can I ever make it up to you?' Gillian asks brokenly.

Carrie wipes her mouth again with the screwed-up tissue, reaches with her other hand for Gillian's.

'What's done can't be undone. You're here, my love. That's all that matters to me now.' She smiles sadly. 'Let's try and put it behind us. Start afresh. That's the only thing I want now.' She glances around at her assembled family. 'And for you all to be happy.'

* * *

Carrie has been having a much-needed rest in the front room that Andrea has turned into a bedroom while the rest of the family, still shocked by the revelations, continued to talk over the implications. Andrea, feeling guilty now about the unkind thoughts she has been having about her sister, is putting out feelers of friendship. Gillian has suffered too, dreadfully, she realises; she can't be blamed for any of this. And, when all is said and done, she is her sister. It will be a long time before they can build a close relationship. At present they are still strangers, but at least they can make a start on trying.

It's now the middle of the afternoon; Andrea makes a pot of tea before going back to the stables, and Kathryn takes a cup in to Carrie.

'Are you awake, Grandma?' she asks softly.

'Yes, I think so. Though I must say this is all a bit like a dream.' Carrie pulls herself up into a sitting position. 'Tea. How in the world can anyone get by without a nice cup of tea?'

Kathryn draws back the curtains, letting in the daylight.

'Well,' Carrie says. 'You'll certainly have something to tell Lizzie now, when you go to see her.'

With everything that has been going on, Kathryn hasn't given another thought to visiting Lizzie, and to be honest, now that Gillian is in England, that – and telling Lizzie the truth about what happened – is down to her.

'Let's not talk about Lizzie,' she says.

'No, let's not.'

Carrie is sipping her tea with obvious relish. Kathryn sits down in the chair beside her.

'I can't imagine how you must feel, Grandma. To do what

you did – sacrifice everything – and then . . . well, to lose Mom like that. And Dev . . . do you still think about Dev? You must, mustn't you?'

Carrie smiles sadly. 'Oh yes, I think about Dev.'

'I don't suppose . . . well, I was wondering . . . Would you like us to try and find out what happened to him? With the internet and everything there's a good chance we might be able to.'

Carrie smiles again, but it's still a sad smile. 'Oh, my dear, what a good girl you are. So thoughtful. But there's no need for that. I know, you see, what happened to Dev.'

'You do?' Kathryn says, surprised.

'Oh, yes.' Carrie sets down her tea; the cup rattles slightly in the saucer as if her hand is trembling, and her eyes have gone opaque and very far away. 'We were together for a little while after I came out of prison. But it wasn't meant to be. It was in our stars, I think. It was never meant to be.'

'Grandma . . . ?' Kathryn says, gently questioning.

But Carrie has gone away into a world of her own and Kathryn knows she will have to wait for another day for the answers to her questions.

THIRTY-SIX

CARRIE

It cannot be.

Those words have haunted me down the years. Events always conspired, or so it seemed, to keep Dev and me apart. And yet, for a time, during my dark years in prison and for a little while afterwards, I dared to hope that at last we had broken the jinx and when I was free, in every sense, we would at last be able to be together.

It had, of course, been far from easy. When I was charged with Frank's murder, Mary had got in touch with Dev and told him what had happened, and he had immediately arranged some compassionate leave and come back to England to see me. At that time, Mary had not known that I had admitted to the shooting to protect Gillian, and Dev naturally assumed that Frank had been ill-treating me again and I had acted in self-defence. I don't think I ever saw him as shocked as he was when I told him the truth, and he was totally opposed to me taking the blame.

'She's just a child, Carrie! They'll take that into account,' he said, and when I told him my fears of what might happen to Gillian if the truth came out he became very impatient and angry. I suppose that over the years he had grown tired of me making a martyr of myself, as he saw it, and who could blame him? Dev saw things very much in black and white; he couldn't understand that for me they were always so much more complex. But it hurt me a lot, all the same, that he seemed to think that once again I was just finding excuses to avoid commitment to him. So upset was I that I actually told him to go back to Malta and forget about me. Right up until the trial he was still trying to persuade me to tell the truth, and when I refused I was petrified he might do so himself, although I made it clear that if he did, I'd deny it.

By the time I stood trial, Dev was back in England. He was an air commodore now, and offered at the very least to speak for me as a character witness. But I was still afraid he might take the opportunity to tell the court I was not guilty of anything but lying, and in any case my lawyer didn't think it would be helpful to my case to parade my lover in front of the jury.

But he was there, in the public gallery, when I was found not guilty of murder, but guilty of manslaughter, and the last thing I remember seeing before I was led down between two grim-faced wardresses was his face. For just a moment our eyes met and the anguish I saw in his made me shrink and shrivel inside the calm façade I had maintained throughout the trial like a magic firework from a cracker, burned in a saucer at a festive tea-party. It was all I could see as I was driven away in the prison van to begin my incarceration. That, and my darling

494

Gillian, covered in her father's blood. Later, when I had all the time in the world to reflect, it seemed to me that whilst all the decisions I had made in my life had sprung from a genuine desire to do what was the right thing, somehow all I had achieved was to hurt those I loved most. The road to hell, they say, is paved with good intentions. Mine certainly was.

Dev was stationed abroad again, in Cyprus, by the time I came out of prison – released on parole earlier than I had expected, so we had no firm plans in place. Not that we'd been able to do much planning, in any case. With a bare table between us and a warder looking over my shoulder and listening to every word that passed between us it had been difficult to discuss such things in detail on the occasions Dev visited me. Our correspondence came under scrutiny too, and I was very conscious that association with a convicted prisoner might reflect adversely on Dev, who had a responsible position to maintain. So really there was nothing for it but for me to return to Timberley, which, I told myself, was probably the best plan, in any case. Much as I longed to be with Dev, my first priority must be the children. Andrea knew no other home than the farm, no other mother but Mary, and to uproot her without proper preparation would be very wrong; Gillian would need a lot of love and attention. She had still not regained her memory of the events of that dreadful night – thank God! – but I could well imagine that she would be in a state of emotional turmoil when I brought her home.

Of course, then I had no idea of the extent of it. In quiet moments I dreamed of the four of us together – me, my precious daughters, and Dev, the love of my life. A proper family, doing all the ordinary, everyday things a family does. Perhaps we would have other children too, little ones the girls would love to mother. These dreams kept me going as I struggled to rebuild my life.

I'd been a free woman for about four months before Dev managed to get back to England to see me. When I received the letter, telling me he'd engineered a few days' leave, I was as excited as a child on Christmas Eve, wanting to skip and sing and laugh out loud, and joy pulsed in my veins in time with the frenzied beating of my heart.

We decided we would meet in London, and for once I did not feel in the least guilty about putting my own needs and desires first. Andrea would be absolutely fine with Mary, and Dev and I would be able to concentrate on one another without anything to distract us. That we were going to be together properly — at last! — was like a dream come true, and every time I thought of it, I melted inside, my physical response every bit as ecstatic as the emotional one.

I travelled to London on a Friday afternoon. It was a pleasant summer's day, and as the train sped through the countryside I struggled to control my nervous excitement, staring out at the sunshine and shadow, cows gathered in knots beneath stands of trees, farmers hay-making. For the first time in weeks I was not worrying about how I was going to get Gillian back, but rather feeling wildly optimistic. In my state of euphoria, anything seemed possible. And still the nerve of desire and excitement twisted and leaped deep inside each time I thought of Dev kissing me, holding me, making love to me.

Countryside began to give way to crowded sidings and smoke-blackened buildings, and then we were beneath the great glass canopy of Paddington Station. The platforms were crowded, people milling everywhere, and for a panicky moment I wondered how on earth I would ever find Dev.

And then I saw him. All the knots of nervous excitement exploded in my throat. I wanted to run to him, but somehow I contained myself – running, in any case, would have been pretty difficult whilst lugging my little case. He had seen me too. We headed for one another, our faces wreathed in smiles.

'Well, Caroletta,' he said, taking my suitcase.

And then I was in his arms.

A wonderful stolen weekend. That is how I always think of it now. There were other times, warm, loving and wonderful, but none of them can match the magic of those two days and nights. In the joy of our reunion all the shadows seemed to melt away and our love was reborn, fresh and new. We had been through so much together and yet somehow, miraculously, it was as if we had returned to the very beginning. The sound of his voice, the scent of him – pipe tobacco and soap – the way his eyes crinkled when he smiled, the touch of his hand on mine, made the blood sing in my veins and imbued me with a sense of wondering awe that one man could make me feel this way, and that that man loved me.

And of course in a way it was a beginning. We had never before been together as close as two people can be; finally consummating our love was even more wonderful than I had dared imagine it would be.

In the hotel room he had booked for us, we clung together with all the urgency of years of need, every inch of my flesh was being drawn to his as if to a powerful magnet, and the longing for him was a physical pain deep inside me. His mouth was hard and deep on mine, one hand pressing me to him, the other cupping my breast. I slid my hand beneath his shirt, loving the feel of taut muscle and warm skin, wanting nothing more than to have him inside me now – now! When he drew back I wanted to cry out in protest, ghosts of the last night we had been alone together flittering through my mind, fear of denial panicking me suddenly.

His eyes were on my face, deep pools of intense concentration.

'What?' I asked, and my voice was husky with desire.

'I want to remember you the way you look today. For ever.'

'Oh, Dev . . .' I thought it was the most beautiful thing anyone had ever said to me.

And then there was no more time for looking, or for talking. With Dev I climbed to heights I'd never before dreamed of, let alone experienced. With Dev I discovered just how wonderful making love can be. How you can soar in a universe of delight; how afterwards the stars come down to touch the earth.

For me that weekend will always be special. Besides the love-making there was the talking, holding hands as we made plans, talking as if we had never talked before. There were the walks through the streets of the capital, when I wondered at the well-known landmarks I'd seen in pictures but never before in reality: Buckingham Palace, the guardsmen in their tall black bearskins standing like statues in their sentry boxes, the Beefeaters at the

Tower, the boats on the Thames. There were the meals in dimly lit little restaurants, exotic food I'd never tasted before – spaghetti Bolognese, chicken Madras. And there were the nights when I could enjoy the luxury of sleeping all night in Dev's arms and waking to see his head next to mine on the pillow.

'You're mine, Caroletta,' he said. 'Nothing is going to keep us apart again.'

And I so wanted to believe him I ignored the persistent little voice in my head telling me: It cannot be.

Dev had been posted back to England, to Yorkshire. We managed to meet up a few times, and he came down to Gloucester-shire to meet Andrea. He had already written to her, letters on airmail paper adorned with little drawings of birds and animals in brightly coloured ink, and sent her a lace hand-kerchief hand-embroidered with flowers of Cyprus, which she treasured as a special gift from 'Mummy's friend'.

When he arrived she was a little shy at first, but she soon came round, showing him her favourite toys and even climbing onto his knee; by the time he left, I could tell that she was very taken with him and I couldn't see that there would be any problems with them bonding.

It would have been a different story if Gillian had been living with me, I expected, but for the moment I'd had to abandon any thoughts of bringing Gillian home. I was still reluctant, though, to be too far away from her; if she did have a change of heart I wanted to be accessible, and I wasn't sure how she would react to finding someone else in her daddy's place.

We'd have to cross that bridge when we came to it, though,

I decided. I couldn't let yet more barriers come between me and Dev.

We were making plans to be married, and – apart from the dreadful hole in my heart that was my estrangement from Gillian – I was happier than I'd ever been. And then, once again, the fates conspired and once again my world fell apart.

Dev was coming down to Gloucestershire again for the weekend; he was due to arrive late on the Friday night. I'd prepared happily for his arrival, shopping for his favourite food, cleaning the house from top to bottom, and baking pies and a fruit cake. Andrea wanted to stay up to greet him; I insisted she went to bed at her usual time. She'd be able to see him in the morning. Then I put a stack of records on the gramophone I'd acquired and settled down to wait for him.

He never came. By morning I was frantic with worry and, not knowing what to do, I went up to the farm, telephoned his base. And that was how I learned the news. On his way down to Gloucestershire, Dev had been involved in a road accident.

He was dead. My wonderful Dev, the love of my life, had been killed instantly. After all we'd been through in the war he had died in a road accident. The little time we'd had together was all we would ever have.

Once again, I was on my own.

'Grandma, that is terrible,' Kathryn says. 'How could you bear it? After all you'd been through?'

I sigh. 'It wasn't easy, I must admit. But what else can you do but get on with it? I had to be strong for Andrea. She had to be my priority. And what a wonderful daughter she has turned out to be! I don't think I could have gone on without her – she's been my companion and friend as well as my child.'

'All the same . . . you've been so unlucky!'

'Well, it hasn't been an easy ride, that's for sure. But unlucky? Who's to say? In many ways I have been very blessed.'

'It's incredible you can look at it like that.'

'As I say, I have Andrea, and now, thank goodness, I have your mother back. Two lovely daughters. I had a rewarding job in nursing. I have my own home and my garden. And I know what it is like to love and be loved in return. Some people are never lucky enough to experience the sort of love I did. And now I have a wonderful granddaughter, too.'

I smile at Kathryn, who's sitting there with tears in her eyes.

'Treasure what you have, Kathryn,' I say. 'It's more precious than you know.'

Kathryn nods. 'I will, Grandma.'

With all my heart I hope she does.

EPILOGUE

1 January 2001 — Timberley, Gloucestershire

It's happened again!

I must have dozed off in my chair and, just like that other time, Dev was here with me.

It's not surprising I dozed off. We had a very late night last night. We stayed up to see the start of the new millennium.

It was quite a party, up at the Hall, which of course Tom and his consortium now own. We had a big table in the restaurant — Mary and Geoff, Tom, Andrea, me — of course! — and Gillian and Don, her husband, and Kathryn and Rob all came over from Canada to be with us for the great occasion. I couldn't imagine it happening; Kathryn and Rob have a baby now, the dearest little soul named William, and I couldn't believe they'd want to bring him on such a long flight while he's so young. But Kathryn was determined she wanted me to see him, and by all accounts he was as good as gold on the plane. I'm overwhelmed by the thought that I am a great-grandmother! It makes me sound so old! But what an achievement. I am very proud and happy. He slept through the millennium celebrations, of course, but when he woke up to be fed I managed to get a cuddle. I'm so pleased for Kathryn. Nothing can ever replace the little boy she lost, of course, but at least she now has another baby to go some way to filling the terrible void in her heart.

I'm happy for Andrea, too. Tom buying the Hall meant an end to her worries about losing her stables, and I have to say it looks as though she and Tom are getting on very well. They are spending a lot of time together, and I'm keeping my fingers crossed.

Anyway, by the time we'd toasted the new millennium and watched the firework display it was very late, so this afternoon, after lunch, I thought I really should have a nap. My heart seems to be behaving fairly well as long as I take my medication, but I do get tired very easily, and I know I've got to be sensible and listen to what my body is telling me.

So I dozed off in the chair. And there was Dev.

This time it seemed to me that we were in that hotel in London where we stayed for a weekend soon after I came out of prison, and the magic aura was all around me again, just as it was then. The joy of being with him after so long, the electricity between us, the warmth, the love, the hope for the future.

'You're mine, Caroletta,' he said. 'Nothing is going to keep us apart again.'

I buried my face in his chest, closed my eyes and clung to him, wanting to believe it, but the voice was there again in my head. It *cannot be.* And the sweet sadness tore at my heart.

But I smiled at him. Kissed him. And looked down at my hands. Just as in the previous dream.

This time they were my hands as they are now. Veined and blemished with age spots. But now they were clean. No blood. Finally, after all these years, my hands are washed clean.